# KILL THE GRACKLES!

First in the Thomas Martin Series

Edmund T. Calvin

**Golden Publishing**

The characters and events portrayed in this book are fictitious. Any similarity to real persons, living or dead, is coincidental and not intended by the author.



ISBN: 978-1-7363915-1-8

Cover by: Darren Garlock of Viggen Design

Printed in the United States of America

*To Ellen, my loving wife for 34 years and counting. An incredibly avid reader who was gracious enough to be the first to read it as initially written, tactful enough in providing good counsel, and was unflinchingly supportive as always.*

*To all of those who've been part of my story and especially those who've helped make this one possible.*

*"It is easier to find men who will volunteer to die, than to find those who are willing to endure pain with patience."*

JULIUS CEASAR

# CONTENTS


Title Page 1
Copyright 2
Dedication 3
Epigraph 4
Chapter I 7
Chapter II 15
Chapter III 18
Chapter IV 25
Chapter V 30
Chapter VI 55
Chapter VII 63
Chapter VIII 75
Chapter IX 84
Chapter X 114
Chapter XI 127
Chapter XII 180
Chapter XIII 194
Chapter XIV 249
Chapter XV 253

Chapter XVI 268
Chapter XVII 297
Chapter XVIII 334
Chapter XIX 355
Chapter XX 373
Acknowledgement 379
About The Author 381

# CHAPTER I

## *The Client*

Glass and steel – Hong Kong oozes it. Shipping magnate Ho Lee's empire was built on steel: steel ships, steel containers, and steel nerves. But his office was all glass. His all glass desk rose from a point in the floor and spread a dozen feet wide like an inverted curved pyramid. His quick temper rose even quicker, and no English-speaking employee who wished to remain so employed would ever refer to him as "holy," or any of the various otherwise comical quips about his name. His temper was quick as ever this last month as no less than six of his ships were attacked by pirates.

There could have been more; those were only the six that made the news. Some ransoms were paid out without any public knowledge. It wasn't just the ransoms that bothered him, though. It wasn't even the couple of dead employees or the damage to the ships. Attacking him was inviolate, and that's what really stung. He grew the business his father bestowed to him because he was a shark in business, and to be attacked by lowly pirates, it was personal. Plus, although clients don't blame shippers for attacks, they do stop shipping with them eventually.

Pirates. The word for pirate in Chinese is Hai dao,

pronounced "high dial." He disliked even calling them pirates, as the word aggravated him given the English sounding translation. They weren't pirates – they were terrorists of the high seas provoking a response. But the translation of "high dial" made him think. By attacking *his* ships so often, these pirates were "dialing things up" as they say, so his response would do the same.

The rounded penthouse office had exterior glass from floor to ceiling that was cleaned daily. Of course, it had to be cleaned before he arrived, as having workmen banging around outside while he occupied the room would not do. There were few days off from this routine, as he was not one to travel. He'd invite clients to entertain them in Hong Kong. He preferred the home-court advantage in business dealings, and even the luxury of a private plane didn't make travel enjoyable. It upset his routine, and he was all about routine.

But today, in a way, he was venturing way out of the routine. He reached out to various security companies whose only solution involved more guards, more cameras, more water cannons, more delays, more money, and none of which offered any real long term solutions. After venting with a rival days ago, who was in the same boat, so to speak, hoping to find out a common solution, his rival offered the name of a security consultant. Mr. Lee recalled the conversation, especially the way Mr. Chu hesitated before offering. "His name is Thomas. I used him years ago in a complex personal matter. He is a man of ideas. He foresees the future, and makes it happen."

Mr. Lee smirked. "I'm not looking for a fortune teller, I'm looking for men of force to solve a problem."

Mr. Chu shook his head. "That he is. This man solves the problem, whether by force or guile."

"Well, then why haven't you used him to solve this one?" Lee exclaimed. Lee remembered the way his rival looked at him, so vulnerable. He was not afraid but definitely unnerved.

"Because once he's started, there's no stopping. And his help for you may only be part of his plan from the beginning. I was glad for his help, paid him handsomely, and he provided exactly what he said he would. But there was more that I will not talk about."

"So why should you refer him to me?" Lee asked, noticing the obvious contradiction.

"To be fair, I regret to point out that my losses in the area have not fared nearly as badly as your own. Had I suffered as you have, I would have surely contacted him." Chu said somewhat ashamedly at what he believed to be his own weakness.

Lee nodded, acknowledging the difference. The degree of vengeance in the business world is still an analysis of risk and reward.

Chu continued. "How much risk are you willing to take? How much can you live with?"

Chu's words hung with Lee as he waited for Thomas' arrival. Lee sipped his Earl Grey as he reviewed the report of Thomas Martin. He served in the Marine Corps, graduated from the University of Connecticut on the GI bill, then returned to the service as an officer. They were eager to get him back apparently. His MOS was straight 300 infantry, which made little sense according to his own security chief. The military occupational specialty number specifies the job you're qualified for within the service, or compelled to remain in as they see fit. 300 is a grunt, doing grunt work. Lee expected more.

In fact, there was little that could be found about his service. There were no pictures of him in uniform with his service ribbons, which would have told a story. Nothing other than, "he was in, he was out." The one picture in the file couldn't provide a more general description: six feet tall, average build, brown hair. He briefly worked for a D.C. consulting company that mainly lobbied defense contractors, but there was little news of him joining, and even less of his departure. Of course, a couple of years isn't brief anymore. Nobody is loyal to the company the way they used to be. Interesting, but nothing outlandish. This man was no ghost.

Lee continued to thumb through the bland report. Thomas then partnered with several others and started their own security consulting company. Rumors were they were just spun off by their previous employer, the kind of thing a company does to have more than just a subsidiary - the business version of plausible deniability and retaining profits.

But there was no reason given for why. They did well financially, but there was no indication that they were flush with cash. No lavish parties, or examples of a big lifestyle. They didn't even attend many of the D.C. parties, he was boring by most accounts. What was more revealing was the fact that Thomas Martin traveled, doing much of the work personally, and Lee knew that the boss doesn't travel if he doesn't have to.

Mr. Lee would often have the person he was scheduled to meet brought into his office first in his absence. Let them sit there. They'd peruse the opulence, see the shipping awards, the framed magazine articles, the history of Lee Shipping on display. The visitor would be reminded of his position in the order of things, get them to long to be lucky enough to work for him, and they'd be far more likely to bend to Lee's will. Lee opted to do the same with Thomas, so he stood and walked into the adjacent room, an office within the office. He told his aid Jiang to seat Thomas upon his arrival. Thomas arrived for the 1:00 pm appointment with time to spare, and Jiang seated him promptly. Mr. Lee watched on the camera as Thomas sat in front of the desk. Lee was unimpressed, though more muscular in person than the gala photo suggested. He appeared to look straight ahead out the window and did nothing more than take in the view. Perhaps this Thomas didn't even have the sense to use the time to learn about his host. *And he foresees things?* Lee thought. He's not even looking at what surrounds him.

Mr. Lee exited the side room to the hall to enter from the main doorway with his aide, who was carrying part of the day's work. Thomas didn't even turn but waited for Mr. Lee to round the chair to stand with his hand extended. "Good afternoon Mr. Lee."

A quick shake later and Lee returned the pleasantry. "Good afternoon Mr. Martin. One moment please. I'll be right with you." Jiang handed Mr. Lee several items that needed his approval, signature, or comment. All items were actually necessary, but in this case, all part of the show. This demonstrated the decisiveness and control

Mr. Lee exuded and all who bore witness were to get with his program. Thomas continued to appreciate the view. While only a minute passed, it seemed like an eternity of wasted time to Thomas. *He just doesn't get it yet,* he thought to himself wryly and smiled.

"Well Mr. Thomas," Lee started as he waived Jiang away, who acted so appreciative to be a subjugated minion, "I'm told that you may be able to provide a security service that we may be able to find useful."

"No Mr. Lee, you were told that I can solve your problem, where others can't. And it's just Thomas."

"Well, just Thomas, forgive me if I'm a bit suspect. You're not even fully aware of the problem itself, the severity of the problem, or the feasibility of any solution. This sounds more like bluster than consulting."

Mr. Lee smiled as if he was going to get something for nothing. Push a consultant to prove his worth, and you often get the advice for free. This was not to be.

"Mr. Lee, your problem is pirates. Your problem isn't just the cost of the losses, the ransoms, the extra security, but the missed deliveries, unhappy customers that don't return tomorrow, bad press, and the loss of prestige that goes along with it. If a pirate can steal from you, it emboldens others. Not just other pirates of the sea, but the business pirates who smell blood in the water. It delays invoices getting paid, it emboldens shippers looking to lowball on price to try to take advantage of the situation. Prestige is," Thomas paused "like all the little trophies you have around the room." Thomas now bent his neck ever so slightly to the display Mr. Lee was obviously so proud of.

Mr. Lee felt that sting as if the display of accomplishments was something to be ashamed of. "Mr. Thomas, Thomas. What is your solution?"

"Hiring me is the total solution of course. Here, in this blue folder, is an outline of what needs to be done, and how I would make it happen." Mr. Lee reached for the blue folder, only to be left hanging. "The blue folder, Mr. Lee, will cost $250,000. If you choose to continue with having me execute the plan, you'll see a breakdown of costs in the folder." If you choose to have someone else execute the plan, you are certainly free to do so. However, while I guarantee my work, if you farm it out to others, I can give no such guarantee."

Lee suspected a big investment but didn't expect something close to extortion. Paying $250,000 for a binder of info wasn't his usual M.O. He stewed on being dictated to, and considered a tirade.

But before the moment got away, Thomas went on. "Mr. Lee. Here's what the plan will accomplish: First, it will stop the current type of pirate attacks on your ships in the long term, not just the short term. Second, you will receive notable recognition for your generosity to the starving in Africa, and as such become the go-to company that other similar charitable organizations will seek to reward with handling their shipping, which is an ever-growing market. Third, the expansion of handling the charities of billionaires, governments, and the United Nations will provide contacts that help, shall we say, in a more varied way, given your need. This will be another "accomplishment" for your shelves. Moreover, it won't cost you anything beyond what you must invest now. But after completion....then it will be incredibly profitable, for both of us." The hook, Thomas thought.

"Laughable." Mr. Lee heard braggadocio before, but this was overwhelming. "Thomas, you lost me at profitable. How..."

"Write a check, Mr. Lee. If you want to know how this operation will not only surely recover your entire cost but will produce a profit many times over, write a check for the $250,000, and I'll sit here while you read. I'll not run off" Thomas said with a confident smile. "You're paying for an idea, and ideas have value."

# CHAPTER II

## *The Pitch*

Lee wrote the check. Well, he had it written. A few minutes passed with nary a movement from Mr. Lee, nary a breath. His eyes moved but with purpose, never gazing up to acknowledge Thomas. The man was stoic, always mentally aware of giving away any tell to an opponent. While no doubt Mr. Lee had Thomas there to help, during negotiations, everyone was an opponent. Thomas saw it, Lee's expression changed. There it was, on page two and Lee's eyes flared. Taken aback, Lee looked up at Thomas briefly before returning to the proposal. Mr. Lee got to the part about using the stick. It never reads well. Everyone may think about what should happen to evil men doing evil things, but say "just kill them" to a friend who knows you mean it and watch how they look at you differently. Then put it to paper with detail, grizzly and seemingly heartless detail, and you're a manifesto title short of Ted Kaczynski. There's an inherent human revulsion to it, even if it's what you're hoping for, and even if the outcome is what you expected. To the reader, they always wonder if you enjoy the violence, and sadly, most hope you do. They confuse the level of violence with clarity of purpose.

Mr. Lee got to page four: ah, the profit. Thomas saw Lee's head tilt to the side, again, the quintessential "what?" move of human emotion, no matter the race or culture. There are no less than eight different meanings of the Indian "head bob" depending on the region, but the "what the hell?" face is universal. His eyes raised going back to earlier in the page, and then again. Three reads and it was like the Carnegie epiphany of saving millions by reducing the number of welds required on an oil drum from 40 to 39. Carnegie began his entire path to fortune on that simple idea. It was so simple, yet never done. The choice to do what's never been done has value.

Mr. Lee smiled, put the blue binder in front of him, and patted it like a baby. He looked to the shelf of accomplishments and realized he'd need more shelving. Where Mr. Lee enjoyed wielding the power from his position of strength, it was all laid bare to an idea. Just an idea.

"Thomas," he said, but then took an unnecessarily long pause. "I believe we have more than a deal in this matter, but perhaps a long term partnership."

"Mr. Lee, the deal applies to this matter, which I'll faithfully and personally fulfill as stated, but I can not commit to a long term arrangement. You're our client, that's enough for now."

"But why?" Lee, who moments before was about to toss Thomas out on his ear for daring to be so bold, was now annoyed at being rebuffed. "You could always use my backing to make this work. You will need...."

"Mr. Lee," Thomas said calmly, "remember why I'm here. You have dead employees, you have escalated shipping costs, you have a problem. First things first. Take the solution to solve the problem."

Mr. Lee took a deep breath and stared at Thomas for a minute, annoyed. He could farm it out and try to do more, but "can't guarantee the work" mattered here. He wanted to find a flaw, but there was none. He finally surrendered and thought: *take the deal, solve the problem, make a big profit....and then do another deal later.*

"Very well Mr. Thomas – ah, I will call you Mr. Thomas – you have a deal."

Thomas smiled. *If calling me "Mr. Thomas" is the win he needs to make this deal,* he thought, *it's a deal.* Plus, Thomas had to hide why he needed the deal so badly. It wasn't the money, but it was definitely in the right place at the right time and with all the right resources for his purpose. "Excellent. I'd prefer to work with clients directly, but given your stature and the nature of the work, if you have a truly loyal aid that will handle our logistics needs, I'll need their contact information."

"But of course Mr. Thomas. Jiang is not only a loyal aid but has operational authority when and where it matters. So it seems you need some rice?"

"A boatload, as it happens. We'll also need a bank transfer instead of another check, Mr. Lee."

# CHAPTER III

## *Origins*

Sure, anybody can plan, but doing is what counts in the end, and doing involves people. The first part of the operation was simple, and to be expected. To bang the pirate nails, Thomas thought, bring a bunch of hammers. It wasn't the sexy part of the plan, but even without everything else, it was wholly necessary. There's no nuancing pirates. The sad thing is that some of the pirates don't even want to be pirates. They might have family that is starving, sick, or fill in the blank of what other ailments that might drive you to be a pirate if you're living in the endless squalor of what the classless would refer to as a shithole country. People do what they think they have to do, usually deciding on the least amount of pain, and warlords deal in pain with regularity. Use up a pirate to do the dirty work. If he dies, quits, leaves, drowns, gets AIDS? Get a new pirate, rinse, repeat.

Sob stories aside, with a gun in their hands, they're the bad nails in this plan.

You could do basic boat security with a couple of guys, schedule workers to be lookouts with the armed guards pulling 12-hour alternating shifts, and return fire would likely turn away a masked marauder. They weren't looking to have their little boats shot up and drowned, and executing an accurate firefight against trained riflemen on a stable firing platform of a big ship isn't the way to go either. These pirates aren't the smartest, but a few errant attempts under their belt and they do know how to talk to each other about what doesn't work.

This plan was different. This plan really needed eight hard men: fore and aft heavy-caliber snipers, port and starboard riflemen, and some redundancy. Thomas had business partners in their firm, this is true. But the real truth is that the three men had their own specialties and often ran their own operations. There would be overlapping cases to be sure, but it was rare that all three would be involved from beginning to end. Not every case required a shooter or a gun of any type. Far more often the client's problems could be solved in a way that didn't leave a footprint. That's what made Thomas so desirable – he was a great cause and effect planner. This op would use two of them on the boat and six others they'd contract out for, albeit men they knew and worked with in the past.

Thomas could reverse engineer and manipulate the OODA Loop like nobody's business.

The OODA Loop is an oft-cited military mental application of Observe, Orient, Decide, Act, then repeat. War is an ever-changing environment and one who goes through these progressions the fastest wins. The often hackneyed citation is certainly overused and often misapplied. However, truly understanding its value is literally the difference between life and death. To best understand it, one must look at how it came to be.

It was born of Captain John Boyd, who flew F-86 fighters in Korea. This was really the last of dogfighting jets before the reliance on air-air missiles, the last era of men and machines without computers doing the work. During the Korean war, Americans had a 12-1 kill ratio over those flying MiG-15's of North Korea, though those were often Chinese pilots. Sure, American pilots had better training overall, but 12-1 is a big ratio. *Was the F-86 Sabre such a better jet?* Captain Boyd must have wondered during the long hours flying over the mountains of Korea. Not on paper, which was why he must've pondered this so long and hard. The MiG's stats scream a better fighter. The MiG-15 was faster, could turn quicker, and climb faster than the American F-86, and those are the metrics of a better plane in a dogfight. What did the F-86 have that was better? A bubble canopy. This allowed the American pilot to have a 360-degree view of the battlespace, whereas the MiG pilot only had about 270. Americans could build those bubble canopies, but Russia couldn't as they didn't have the tech and their windows ended up being quite boxy. First to see is first to act. Imagine that. Life as a Russian fighter pilot, flying an objectively "better" plane, yet was almost sure to lose due to the simplest of facts that your opponent had better glass because it resulted in a better view. Yet it's not just the better view, it's knowing you have the better view. You now know how to manipulate the view to your advantage. Deny your opponent from view, even for a moment, and you can observe, decide and act before he can. So the OODA Loop isn't just about what happens when you're thrown into a fight, it's about planning how to use your enemy's actions, and the actions you manipulate to your advantage. That simple concept has profound real-world results.

A modern-day example is the use of the scrambling quarterback. Thomas actually used Vince "Air" McNair as an example in his thesis, at least that's how he tells the story. McNair, he said, always looked like he was about to get sacked; he'd just barely get the play off but got lucky every time. But as a wise man once said, "there's no such thing as luck," certainly not every time. The truth was the scramble was part of the play, not an act of desperation. McNair rolled right coincidentally as the receiver did the same and then the passing lane was different, the defender was out of position and was slower to react. It looked chaotic, and it may have looked messy, but looks weren't the mission, scoring was.

Thomas had his own little version of the OODA Loop: The Marble. It was no clever acronym though, just named after a marble. Picture a marble rolling across the table. Apply enough force, and you know it will go straight across off of the other side. You controlled its destiny.

But what if the marble was self-aware and didn't want to fall off the abyss of the table? It doesn't matter, it's a marble. No matter how much the marble doesn't want to fall off of the table, it's a round ball without the means to deny the one doing the rolling. The point is that if you understand your adversary, it makes him easy to roll. Compel him to follow the path that he'd choose to follow. Create the illusion of choice by design, force, enticement, or misdirection. What matters isn't just the application of chosen pressure, but of equal importance, the will to apply it. If the marble is the sole provider of a family of marbles, the question was could you still have the temerity to roll it off of the table with equal enthusiasm. Invariably the question would come back to "does the marble have it coming." "The important thing to remember," Thomas would always tell the team members, "when you're working for us, the marble always has it coming." In reality, though, there are few absolutes.

Thomas could see where the solution was to be found and how to get there, he didn't care what it looked like.

Thomas's father served to defend the country, and that put Thomas on the path to do the same. The military training he received early served him well. He graduated college early, before being able to justify the officer's uniform. The path set before him was intelligence work, and the War on Terror provided ample proving grounds. He traveled to Afghanistan where there was a great deal of asymmetric operations that had global implications.

It was there that he met the other two men who would make up the three partners of their current firm.

The first was Robert Smith, a tech guy, an obscure expert in hacking that even Thomas wondered if he had changed his name to the Smith just to blend in. But he knew him in the service as Smith, so unless he changed his name as a kid.... While Thomas was a planner and a hammer, Smith had his own specific skill sets. Though certainly capable with a firearm, Smith was the guy who'd look for the chink in the armor from his desk. Hardware's great, but great software makes the hardware useful, and then so much finer. Robert was the software.

*He will not be joining us on the boat,* Thomas thought, and hacking pirates couldn't be worked into the plan if he wanted to.

After his tours with the service, Smith did some anti-hacking work for a few banks and insurance companies. He found a large number of people's insurance policies were hacked before the company even knew about it. Many people aren't aware that their policy has a "cash" value. People can take the cash and close the account, but that kind of defeats the idea of the policy. How about finding out your policy was cancelled afterwards for the few thousand dollars that may have been there? Robert proved his value time and again, and Thomas had no doubt his tech skills would be needed along the way, but Robert wouldn't be needed on the boat itself.

The third leg of the triad was Max, Max Bowman. He was German, very German. Max grew up in Manheim, a working city. Manheim was kind of the Pittsburgh of Germany, but with older homes with only one river, the Rhine. He attended the German Military Academy in Munich and then served as an intelligence officer. While serving, Thomas worked with Max on a number of occasions as Max was a liaison to the US Army Intel. But before the briefing in the tent eleven years ago, their meetings were superfluous.

Herr Leutnant of the German Militärischer Abschirm-dienst (Military Counterintelligence), was part of the Bundeswehr which goes by their acronym of MAD. Curiously, MAD is also known as the deterrence strategy of Mutually Assured Destruction to American servicemen, and that joke by Americans was getting really old. At the time, Lt. Bowman was serving as a liaison in Afghanistan to coordinate intel on terrorist activities that would have an impact on both the German and European theater.

Max cut a uniquely Aryan looking figure with short, well-cut blond hair, and broad muscular shoulders given his thin physique. While he kept the physique when out of the service, he lost the short hair to soften his appeal given the political consulting work he pursued.

Max was going to come along on this mission as he may certainly be helpful in navigating the multiple government agencies this mission would entail. And well, Max was still a hammer.

Years ago, they first met at Bagram Air Base, Afghanistan, in a tent.

# CHAPTER IV

## *War Stories*

Eleven years ago, this briefing in a tent concerned Ghazni Obaidullah. The name wasn't of a man, but a small hovel of not even a village. It was a number of homes with relatives of the same family led by the elder Abdul Obaidullah Khwaja. In Afghanistan, very few use a family name. Obaidullah is in fact his given name, and the common name of Abdul just added before it. Khwaja means "Lord," a part of the name added only after he became the elder of this family. They were within the Pashtun province of Ghazni Zabul. So, unique to this hovel, the last name of what they called their land changed to match the elder of the family, hence Ghazni Obaidullah. It wasn't meant to be confusing, the name honored him, just as it honored his father before him, and would someday honor his son. It wasn't much, but it was theirs.

Captain Robert Smith was there with his boss in Army Intelligence briefing a quick reaction force of a recent attack at Ghazni Obaidullah. Lt. Max Bowman was there as liaison and sat with the Colonel overseeing the brief. Robert lead the briefing by providing an overhead sketch received from an inhabitant family member shortly after a mortar attack on the village. "Three mortar hits, that's it, and nobody was killed or even injured," he said.

There were two homes on the left side of the "road" that had a walled empty space in between. There was an entrance and exit at either end of the walled enclosure, though diagonal from each other. This was used for keeping goats next to the homes. The other homes were perpendicular to these, a little over a hundred feet away, and the Abdul Obaidullah lived there. Robert put a crude drawing of the attack on the screen given to him by the village to convey the mortar hits.

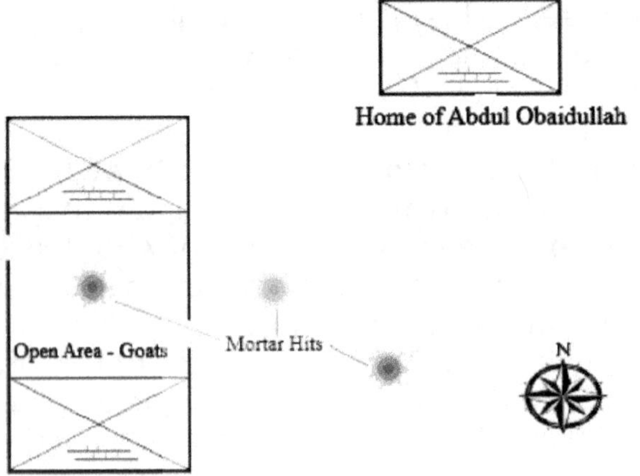


"Not even a goat, sir?" one of the soldiers quipped.

"They didn't mention it, but I'm guessing they lost a few goats," Robert replied as if it was a serious question.

"Well, I was just kidding sir, but ah, why do you guess they lost a few?" the soldier continued, now actually interested in goat casualties.

Robert briefly looked at the sketch. "Because they bothered to draw a sketch. Because someone traveled over 4 hours by car, truck, or slower by horse to get us this sketch. Because if *they* didn't suffer a loss, they wouldn't have bothered with letting us know."

"Woah, well wait a minute sir. If you know they suffered a loss, why a goat? Why wouldn't they tell us that? And how do you know it wasn't a human loss?"

Robert had come to understand intel in Afghanistan needed to be read with nothing short of a Rosetta Stone. "Because if *they* knew who did it, they wouldn't have bothered telling us about the attack at all, and if it was a human loss, then *they'd* have an idea of who wanted to launch mortars at them, and would've taken it into their own tribal hands, even if they guessed wrong."

"And why the goats, sir."

Robert smiled. "They care about the goats, and it hurts them to have them killed. They wouldn't tell us goats were killed so as not to scare us off. Plus, this walled area between the two homes likely had goats, so..."

"So they care more about the goats than us," the soldier laughed.

"Now everybody gets it. To continue. Aerial surveillance after the fact found this man, Mohammed Farid, had visited the Obaidullah family frequently. A drone strike was considered, but denied as too high a risk to the Obaidullah family; the collateral damage was almost certain. Farid uses a variety of caves that cross the small mountain range behind the village, so targeting him in the open with certainty has been problematic."

Robert continued, "Farid visits Obaidullah, Obaidullah's daughter, and then one of his horses. Same pattern. Now, Farid's a Taliban drug dealer, no surprise, and he's been looking to push Obaidullah into his "field" to expand his operation. Part of Farid's problem is that Farid's fairly low on the Taliban totem pole. Intel says he's likely related to higher-ups but hasn't earned *his own* as it were. But he's saddled with a crew from his boss or uncle for all we know. The chain of command here is sketchy. Signals intelligence says he's looking to go out on his own in a big way. The mortar attack was the first attempt. We think he's going to kill Obaidullah, marry the daughter, and expand in the fucking newly named village of Ghazni Taliban Farid."

The weak joke got a laugh as Robert looked around the room. Robert saw the man in the Captain's uniform in the back of the briefing at the start but wasn't introduced. He was sitting with an older man in plain clothes that screamed spook. They were silent, until now.

"Excuse me, uh, Lieutenant Smith," Thomas paused, "but that's not what's happening here.

Robert was taken aback by the Captain in the back row, he knew nobody else had any of the information as of yet.

"I'm sorry, Captain? I'm unaware of any other information, what else do you have?" Robert was feigning an eagerness to learn.

"Oh, nothing other than what you just stated. But, not only can I tell you what their plan is, but I can tell you how to stop it, kill the Taliban men accompanying him, get the village elder to side with our effort to the degree you're hoping for, capture Farid and get him to give up everybody within hours." Thomas said without skipping a beat.

"Oh, and that's it...sir?" Robert said, almost skipping the sir at the end encouraged by the laughter by some of the team members in the room.

Thomas smiled, "Well actually Robert, we're also going to save the old guy's favorite horse"

# CHAPTER V

## *The First Triumvirate*

Thomas raised his hand to Robert as if apologizing for the interruption, but that didn't stop the interruption, "Taliban Farid isn't interested in the daughter, or even the village elder, he's interested in the horse."

The team still in the briefing squirmed as if they just felt trapped in a quagmire from which there was no escape.

"Please, let me explain," Thomas asked, both truly asking and yet standing to insist upon their attention at the same time. "Farid is looking to expand, there's no doubt about it from the communications intercepted, but he's not doing that with the three anchors hanging around his neck. Let's call them Moe, Larry, & Curly."

"The Taliban Three Stooges," Robert quipped.

"Bingo, that they are, and more than they know," Thomas concurred. "Moe and the boys are sent to help Farid, but also keep him in check. Farid has family connections and some wealth behind him, but whether it's his boss or his uncle as you say, he's traveling around with men that aren't his own. So to Farid, they're in the way. They're in the way and so this is Farid's plan."

Thomas walked over again to a large sketch of the mortar attack on the screen. "Three shots fired. This was sighting in a rifle at the bull's-eye. Three hits, and it doesn't matter which ones were first. They're all moving away from the home of Obaidullah. If Farid wanted to kill him, he was firing the rounds in the opposite direction. Farid either started off to the South and moved west, while Obaidullah's house is to the Northeast of the hits, or started off to the West and moved Southeast."

With that, Thomas had the undivided attention of both Robert and the team.

"So if Obaidullah wasn't the target, what's the target? Why sight in mortar rounds to a box with just goats? Because we're the targets. Us, along with Moe, Larry & Curly. That walled area has both a way in and a way out on the other side. Through some manner, Farid is going to know the next time our vehicles roll up on the village. Hell, the sighting of the mortar rounds may have also accomplished that alone. Farid was going to be in that box along with the three stooges, and either fire on us directly, or have them spray a few rounds."

Lt. Max Bowman, who as liaison rarely interceded in discussions that weren't within his purview, was content to stay out of the fray, except it now seemed as if they'd be following Thomas's lead into the fray itself. "That's kind of a big leap. Farid would be stuck in there with them."

"No, I think Farid is planning on giving them arms that

won't work, or will fail, then shooting the three in the leg, leaving them alive, stuck there screaming and unarmed in a small confined space. He's then going to use Obaidullah's favorite horse to skedaddle from the other side of the wall the short distance to where he has the mortar tube set up and already sighted in. Because of the wall, he probably won't be able to see when you guys enter to take the wounded prisoner, and you won't be able to see him. That's why I think he's planning on disabling their weapons, he can't have them shooting at you and scaring you off. He'll want them wounded, and defenseless. And sergeant, what would happen if there were three wounded defenseless Taliban available?"

Sgt. Milone, one of the Rangers in the meeting who'd be involved in whatever action would be taken, thought for a second, being sure there wasn't a trick question involved not knowing this officer. "Well sir, we'd make a slow and smooth approach to make sure they're unarmed and to assess if they're wearing vests, or if there were some other IED in play."

"Fine sergeant, and then," Thomas urged him to continue.

"Well sir, we'd then have our team enter, keeping separation and watching our angles while each man is secured."

"Yes, with how many men sergeant?" Thomas asked.

"Well there's always at least a two-man team to enter, and then we'd have to both secure and cover the wounded while treated," Sgt. Milone finished.

"My point is, you'd end up with anywhere from two

to six grunts in there to secure them with cover, then maybe more involved with treating the 7.62 x 39mm round they took to the leg, along with the requisite tourniquet…" Thomas paused to let everyone get to the obvious conclusion on their own. "Add in a translator," Thomas glanced at Max who served as such, "an officer, another guy on the radio…and then drop in a mortar round, killing everybody."

Thomas pointed to the village on the map. "Farid is not fighting a land war, he's fighting a naval battle. The territory of this village is meaningless to him. He just needs to take pieces off of the board. Wipe off the three men holding him back while simultaneously punching America in the eye with at least a half dozen dead by his own hand? That's a bunch of mail-order true believer followers for Farid. He can parlay that into real power. Farid's play isn't about Obaidullah, his daughter, his land, or even us for that matter, it's all about him. It's all about Farid raising his status."

Everyone in the room looked at the sketch, skimmed the intel and each other. It's an audacious plan by basically a Taliban nobody.

Robert nodded, acknowledging the thought process, but was skeptical. "I'm not saying that's not his plan, but it's a pretty smart plan. It's a really big play for a small guy. Hell, if he doesn't kill his own men, he's not going to live long."

"Great point, but his having to fire the mortar rounds will help us," Thomas quickly added.

"Remember Captain Smith, we're going to kill the Taliban men accompanying him, get the village elder to side with our effort to the degree you're hoping for, capture Farid and get him to give up everybody within hours, and for that, we're gonna have to save the horse."

"What do you mean we have to save the horse? And again, how is knowing he is going to fire mortar rounds a help," Max demanded.

"Well, we're going to have to shoot the horse," Thomas lamented. "I'll show you the rest."

Thomas then laid out the plan the first time around with a basic overview so the team would understand how the parts would all come together. The members of this quick reaction force were Army Rangers, true professionals, and as such, they were certainly paying attention from the beginning. But once they got the idea, several of the men leaned forward, salivating over how it would hopefully play out and it was different, new. New is always exciting. Thomas took time speaking to each of the men individually as the plan depended on certain skill sets that wouldn't be in their legend. This took time. Thomas had to go over the role that each Ranger would have to play, and there wasn't a lot of room for errors along the way as each step relied on the one before it.

They'd be rolling out in the morning, and it was a long drive. It was far enough that flying in on Blackhawks would've been on the table, but that didn't fit with anyone's plans. Farid's plan was better if they arrived by vehicle but still may work if they'd arrive by air. The problem with that is that depending on where they'd land could scare off Farid, plus the quick arrival may deny him the ability to spring the trap.

Abdul Obaidullah Khwaja had previously complained to the Americans that he disliked helicopters landing near his home, as it scared the horses.

The way to building a relationship was to be respectful of his wishes. They could have used Ospreys and just landed a mile away and then drove in to save on time, but as it happened, Thomas needed to spring the trap. So the long slow drive was all the warning Thomas could hope to give to Farid.

The glint of the sun was just trying to broach the horizon as they headed East. There were six vehicles in the group: a Humvee followed by two MRAPs (Mine-Resistant Ambush Protected), followed by two more Humvees with a Toyota pickup truck bringing up the rear. The MRAP costs up to $1 Million per vehicle, but the Toyota was actually more important to the plan. Well, only if it went as planned. Otherwise, the armor would be lifesaving and the pickup disposable.

Thomas made sure to have the men in the right vehicles to help each other go over their parts over the long ride. Repetition, repetition, repetition of the Six Ps: "Proper Planning Prevents Piss Poor Performance." "Poor performance?" Thomas would have none of that.

Outside of inhaling roughly 4.3 pounds of Afghan dust during the drive over the ever dusty terrain along the way, coupled with the feeling of a genteel ride on a wooden rollercoaster built in 1911, the ride there was unremarkable. The dust was an exaggeration, the ride was not.

As they approached the homes, true to the plan, the group of vehicles slowed and actually tightened up, which was not the norm. While approaching the area attacked by Farid's mortars from the south, the lead Humvee turned about forty-five degrees to the east as the MRAPs followed suit forming a slightly curved armored wall while the other two Humvees and the paper thin Toyota followed further to the right. In essence, this view from the doorway of the walled space between the two homes only had a direct view of the lead Humvee and the MRAPs.

Farid received multiple calls of the column, and oh so hoped they were heading straight for him. *The audacity,* he thought. "L'audace, l'audace, toujours l'audace" was a quote of Napoleon he was repeatedly told by his father. Audacity, audacity, always audacity. The quote inspired him in many things he did. Farid later learned that the quote was also usurped by the American General Patton. Despite feeling betrayed after later learning that an American shared his love of the quote, he now found that it fueled him. Napoleon didn't begin as Emperor and Patton's first rank wasn't "General," every great man starts from less, and he was convinced greatness was there to be taken.

Farid saw the column approaching from afar, as the dust revealed their presence long before the engines could be heard. The three men with him in the opening were so carefully positioned. He personally laid hay over a few logs he carried down from the mountain behind him. He sweated and swore to the men that he would make sure they'd survive the attack. Farid had explained his plan to them: "When the Americans drive up to the village, and they will respond to the attack, you'll lie in wait. You'll then fire enough on the convoy to get their attention, and we'll escape through the rear. There's not enough room for them to quickly drive their vehicles around to the rear, so they'll have to pursue you. But as soon as we attack, I'll ride Obaidullah's horse to the nearby mortar and fire as soon as you signal they're inside. The infidels will be slaughtered, and we'll all be praised."

The men assigned to work with Farid never truly liked him. To them, he was a boy with a name who'd never sacrificed. They'd actually die to protect him, there was no doubting that, but their loyalty was to their leader, not him. For their part, they were unknowingly doomed no matter whose plan worked.

Thomas and Max were in the lead Humvee and exited on the passenger side, moving slowly and without concern, but they were very conscious of keeping the Humvee between the opening to the walled space and themselves. Robert remained in the MRAP since he was charged with point man of information as it came in; the situation was bound to be fluid. Six other Rangers exited the vehicles, but all from the passenger side, leaving no easy targets for the men in the hay.

Farid stood behind his three and saw the Americans exit and just mill about. "What are they doing?" he thought. They weren't walking over to Obaidullah's house and they also didn't seem to be paying any attention to his direction. Farid thought he could wait, but one of his three men who was lying prone behind some hay started to slowly move backward.

*He's going to run*, Farid thought, *and none of them can do that*. Farid truly wanted to shoot an American for himself. Even though he would be the only one alive to tell the tale and the tale could always be retold as remarkably as he wanted, he really wanted to fire a clean shot at a soldier; he wanted that part to be true. However, that desire gave way to his fear of failure. He decided a clean mortar shot was the only important one.

Farid stood, taking his position behind them, and ordered his men to fire when he did. Farid raised his AK-47 and fired a burst at the vehicles. The 7.62 x 39mm round struck the armored vehicles to be sure but found no flesh. His three men opened up with their weapons as well, each getting off a solid burst of automatic fire. For that fleeting moment, they felt in control.

Curly's weapon then exploded, killing him instantly; his right jaw, cheek, and eye were torn from his face from the metal of his AK-47 that simply burst. Moe and Larry were fine, but their weapons jammed simultaneously, and Farid shot them in both legs just as quickly. Farid shot Curly in the legs as well, as if losing one's face in death wasn't enough. Farid had cleaned the AK-47's of his men himself, right after he had personally placed the hay. And he did clean the weapons well, as he had to be certain they would function. He had unloaded the magazine as if to check for sand or debris; he meticulously tapped each one as if knowingly looking for a problem. But it was all a show. Farid then reloaded each magazine with 10 rounds of perfectly good ammunition, then a cartridge he had scrupulously marked. These bullets were only that, bullets. He had previously pulled the bullet from the brass, then returned the bullet to the brass cartridge after dumping out the powder. From the outside, it looks exactly the same, and even in weight, it didn't feel much different, the majority of weight coming from the brass and the bullet. Without the powder, the cartridge does still fire. The firing pin hits the primer, and the explosion of the primer causes sufficient pressure to move the bullet from the brass into the bore and barrel of the rifle. The problem is, without powder in the cartridge, there's not nearly enough pressure and power to push the bullet all the way through the barrel. It's just stuck there.

For Moe & Larry, the bullet stopped as soon as it hit the rifling of the gun. The bolt cycled back without enough force and didn't put a new round in the chamber. As they tried to cycle the bolt and put a new round in, they were shot in the legs by Farid, but it didn't matter. With a bullet lodged in the rifling, there was no room for the next round to load, and nothing short of a metal rod and a hammer was going to get it out. Their rifles were now useless.

The reason that Curly didn't fare as well was that he had an older AK, and lots of rounds had been fired through it. After firing a burst from the AK-47 at the American vehicles, Curly then squeezed the trigger, but nothing happened. The tampered cartridge still only had the pressure from the firing of the primer. The rifling inside the barrel was heavily worn, so when the bullet jumped from the brass into the freebore (the short distance of the barrel with no rifling) the bullet traveled far enough into the barrel providing enough room for the next round to chamber. Curly simply assumed that the gun jammed. He quickly cycled the bolt putting a new live round in the chamber and squeezed the trigger. He squeezed the trigger not knowing that there was now a 123-grain hunk of metal firmly lodged in the barrel. The pressure from the cartridge pushed the bullet from the new round into the barrel, which quickly struck the bullet from the previous round causing the pressure to build exponentially in the chamber. The older AK-47, wrought with multiple micro-fractures from years of abuse became a pineapple grenade in Curly's face.

Moe tried to turn his AK on Farid as he lay there screaming but to no avail. The gun couldn't be made to fire, and Farid was out the back just as quickly fleeing on Obaidullah's horse.

Farid gave a quick look back but then turned away, his eyes fixed on the route to the mortar. One wrong spill on the horse and he'd be doomed just as well. He made it around the bend quickly. He had practiced the ride before, under thirty seconds from mount to dismount. He leaped off, tied off the horse, and scrambled up the dirt rise on all fours staying below the line of sight to where his mortar tube was hidden. He tore away the brush hiding it, then peeled off the dark cloth hiding the tube underneath, being careful not to change the position of the tube and revealing the two mortar rounds he had placed next to the tube.

The position of the tube allowed him to look between the rocks and see into the back doorway of where his three men now laid, and out the front. While Farid couldn't see over the wall at all, he could see when the American soldiers entered, then he could fire and run.

Farid assumed the Americans would be slow to enter, but he saw nothing. There was no quick way for the vehicles to get around to the back, but Farid's head was turning as if on a swivel as he was starting to panic. They weren't entering. Farid lifted up the mortar round in a back and forth manner as if deciding to fire then changing his mind just as quick.

Thomas wasn't panicking, but he had expected the rounds to fall shortly thereafter. While still under a minute, it was taking too long, the rounds should have fallen. Farid was surely at the tube already. Somehow Farid knew to wait. Thomas exited the safety of the MRAP and ran over to the team now waiting to enter. They were positioned on the southern side of the home putting the building between them and the suspected position of the mortar round.

"Sgt. Milone, I'm going in," Thomas said quickly and started to move. "Keep your men here however, we can't have everyone trying to spring the trap."

Max grabbed Thomas's arm. "Hold on, I'm going with you." Thomas raised his hand to protest, but Max cut him off. "Unless you speak Pashto, only one of us can yell enough names and orders to make this work."

Thomas liked the idea of adding a layer of deceit. "Good idea, but here's the quick version, we run in, I'll break right, you break left. We quickly decide if their guns are jammed, there's no rule saying they don't have more than one. Dispatch them if you must, but then we quickly zigzag back and forth until we get to the other side. I think he is set up at the right angle to be able to see through the rear entrance to the front and knows nobody has entered. We zigzag going through the entrance to look like many, sprint out the other side before we're blown to bits, and then break right outside the back door to protect us from the blast. We don't have to be the ones to get Farid."

Max was nodding along the way. "Alles gut Max?" Thomas asked in German.

Max smiled, "Let's spring it."

"On me." Thomas turned and took off with Max running in quick pursuit. He was through the door and went right, and was shouting orders to imaginary soldiers as Max checked left. He then yelled in Pashto at the two wounded men screaming in protest, but their arms were raised. They were out of the fight.

Farid raised the mortar round now seeing that at least some Americans had entered, he was ready to fire. Then he saw quick flashes of light back and forth as others appeared to have entered. Farid hesitated. He wanted to kill as many as possible and waited hoping to given the time required for more to enter. He was too greedy. He then saw two American soldiers running out the back, and now feared they were coming for him. He dropped the round and it made the solid thump of the mortar round being launched from the tube, the round was in the air. Farid sprang from his hide, sprinting for the horse. He wanted to turn and watch, but he'd be in the open and in view if he didn't get on the horse and flee.

Thomas and Max both heard the mortar round, which is not as exhilarating on the receiving end. They ran parallel along the wall to the end of the building and both dove to take cover. So long as the round found the intended mark, they were out of the blast radius, but shrapnel, brick, or stone ejected from the blast kills you just as dead.

The round didn't have to go far; it was all over very quickly. It found its mark; Moe & Larry were really having a bad day. They were instantly killed.

Farid was on the horse and thought he was home free as he didn't have to go far to the tunnels; by then he knew he'd be safe. Farid never heard the shot, though. Obaidullah's favorite horse, always so sure-footed, stumbled as if it tripped on a rock. Farid didn't think the stumble was enough to cause the horse to fall, but it briefly slowed, then tumbled to the ground, throwing Farid hard onto the rocky terrain. A sniper with a 7.62x51mm suppressed rifle was pre-positioned on the far side to await Farid trying to flee.

Farid laid there, stunned from the fall. Moments later, a Humvee rolled up to Farid in the dirt before he could gather himself, and he had no chance to reach for his weapon, wherever it had fallen. The Rangers patted him down, removed a knife from his waist, but there was nothing else on him. A couple of zip ties were slapped on his wrists, and then the show began.

Corporal Steffan took Farid, battered and bruised from the hard fall from the horse, and shoved against the Humvee. "You fucking piece of shit. If the officers weren't watching, I'd skin you alive for what you did." Cpl. Steffan turned around and bent him over the hood on the Humvee while another Ranger went to check on the horse. He quickly got a hold of the reins so the horse didn't try to bolt and bleed out more.

"I can't just hold him here, he'll take off. Drive the Humvee over so I can tie him to it," the Ranger called.

"Start walking shitbag," Cpl. Steffan sneered as he shoved him back towards the houses. Another Ranger drove the Humvee down to the horse. They quickly tied him up and put a compression bandage on the wound. They were trained to save a pig that was shot in training, dealing with a live animal provided both the necessary complications and reality of trying to save a living thing. Thankfully, they wouldn't shoot the horse, in the end, the way they did the pig.

The short walk back wasn't wholly necessary, another vehicle could've gotten them. But the delay back was, as it happened, entirely necessary. Plus, Cpl. Steffan continually prodded Farid along the way.

As Cpl. Steffan and Farid rounded the corner of the house into the square. The Toyota pickup was there with the bed facing them and the gate down, and Farid saw several American soldiers looking into the bed with their heads down. The Sgt. facing him had his arms on the back of the truck apparently needing it to stand. Sgt. Rodriguez was an emotional man to be sure, but the delivery of vitriol in Spanish against Farid came across as pure hate. Plus, his natural manner was very animated.

Sgt. Rodriguez grabbed his helmet off of his head and threw it towards Farid as he rushed towards him. "Tu madre, puta puta de perro, debería cortarte las bolas." The rough translation targeted his mother and involved making Farid a eunuch. But Sgt. Rodriguez could've just ordered lunch in a harsh tone and it likely would've sounded the same to Farid, but you just never know who knows what. Sgt. Rodriguez, therefore, made sure his emotional outburst was heartfelt in case Farid knew any Spanish.

Sgt. Milone rushed over as Rodriquez was on Farid, picking him up off the ground as he continued to swear, and then came the joy to Farid's ears. "You killed my brothers you piece of shit." Sgt. Milone pulled Rodriguez off of him, it was a good show.

Farid couldn't tell how many entered the area between the houses, and when he saw the two men come through the other side, he feared he missed them all. Farid smiled believing he'd succeeded in killing the Americans, no matter what the number.

That smile earned Farid a push from Steffan and then that put him in the arms of Sgt. Rodriguez, who grabbed Farid by his clothes, swearing constantly, keeping the momentum going over to the back of the pickup.

Sgt. Gomez grabbed the tarp covering the bodies, exposing most of what looked like the bodies of the American Rangers. The fatigues and boots were certainly American, and Farid took a great deal of satisfaction that one was missing a leg.

With that, Sgt. Milone & Cpl. Steffan intervened very quickly, covering up the bodies. "Put him in the Humvee Cpl.," Sgt Milone ordered, and then turned to console Sgt. Rodriguez who was breaking down sobbing with all the drama of a soap opera star.

Farid did not know what was in store for him. He'd go to prison to be sure, he heard the stories. But he knew the stories didn't end with executions. Usually, there was suffering, humiliation, and then release. Yet he had a victory over the Americans that the village had seen.

He'd come out of this alright in the end.

Thomas and Max stayed out of the fray, just watching from the sidelines for now. "Max, Robert, come with me please."

Obaidullah stood outside his home with his son and several younger men. While they surely had arms, they left them in their homes. As Thomas approached he nodded to Max to relay what he was going to say.

"Abdul Obaidullah Khwaja, if I could have a word with you please," Thomas asked and the elder nodded with a stern look. "While I regret the battle on your doorstep, it appears it was planned by the man we have in custody. Am I correct that the intent to attack us did not come from you or your own"

Obaidullah didn't want to appear weak, but he certainly didn't want to be on the bad side of the Americans. He hated the Taliban, but he had to live with them more than he liked. The Americans hadn't killed any of his people, but like the Russians, he suspected they'd leave and then what.

"He did not attack you at my direction, but he's often a guest here. I can't tell you I'm sorry for his actions, as I was not responsible for them, but I have no intent on attacking Americans," Obaidullah said with the artfulness and demeanor of an experienced politician.

"Regrettably, your horse was shot during the attack as we were capturing Farid," Thomas said, pointing down to his men working on the animal.

Obaidullah saw his favorite horse, his head writhing in pain and fear. "I know you did not come to kill my horse, but my horse will die nonetheless."

"Oh no sir," Thomas smiled. "I have every intention to do everything in our power to save the horse. If it's alright with you, I've ordered a helicopter to come and pick up the horse. A veterinarian, an eh, 'doctor just for animals,' is being flown in to treat him as well. We're going to fly him back to the base where there's surgical staff on standby. Then we'll bring him back if that's alright with you." Of course, the helicopter was already on standby beyond the ridge all along, but since saving the horse was part of the plan, wasted flight time wasn't worth the risk.

Obaidullah was taken aback by their effort to save his horse. He's heard stories about the dead the Americans leave in their path, but that's from those that support the Taliban. He heard very little about American generosity and felt grateful for the effort.

Obaidullah put out his arm for Thomas and they shook. Thomas turned to Max, "Max, if you could stay and see that his horse gets off OK?"

"Absolutely sir." Max was happy with himself, he actually got to be part of the effort instead of just being a liaison. He knew he had contributed plenty before, but being in the field, it just felt better.

Thomas and Robert then walked back to the trucks making ready to depart. Farid was right about one thing, he was going to jail. There was an Afghan prison with a variety of Taliban groups not that far from where they were. Well, a couple hours of a miserable ride. Afghanistan is a big place, but *not far* is relative. During the ride, Thomas and Robert talked about writing to the families of the dead Americans, what specialties they each had possessed, and who they thought they should get for replacements, commiserating about the loss the entire way.

During their ride, true to his word to Obaidullah, and the plan, the helicopter landed. A man ran over to care for the horse, while several of the Rangers prepared a harness to pick up the house and carry him back to their base. The Rangers ran the end of the harness to the helicopter and all got on board. Max approached Obaidullah to say farewell and assure him that they'd do everything they could to save the horse, which Obaidullah genuinely appreciated. He was truly grateful for the attention to his horse. After the men jumped on the helicopter, it slowly rose, raising the wounded animal softly into the air, his legs still moving as if grasping for the earth below.

The helicopter then moved over the homes in the village, circled around, and slowly rose. The point was so everyone could see the Americans taking the wounded horse. The visual is an indelible story they'd tell to each other and to others. The Americans saved a horse for an Afghani elder, for which they went to great effort. The conviction of the story told by other Afghans is worth infinitely more than what any American could promise them. The actions spoke volumes. Plus, Obaidullah agreed to have a helicopter arrive and leave from his village to save his horse. He'd have a harder time denying the Americans arriving by air in the future.

The convoy of vehicles arrived at the Afghan prison, a walled compound away from basically everything.

They all stopped outside. Sgt. Milone, Thomas, and Robert drove Farid through the prison gates in the Toyota pickup. Farid thought that it was his salvation, it was not to be.

Thomas started to needle Farid in the truck with weak pleas to give up information, with throw away lines like "prison can be hard," or, "I can be of help," but "I can be the friend you need" upset Farid the most and he suddenly thrashed about in the truck.

"Let me out you dogs, I need nothing from you." Farid cried. He longed for others to know what he had done. He might be a prisoner, but he'd be respected here. And there would always be later, when he got out.

Thomas opened the door and pulled Farid out slowly saying "you accomplished nothing." Pride erupted and Farid saw his chance for his Taliban brothers to share it with him.

"What have I accomplished! I killed the men in the back of this very truck. It was my plan to kill you all, and I'm sorry I didn't kill more, but Allah be praised. I killed these," Farid yelled for all to hear. The Taliban prisoners were behind gates but in full view of Farid's proclamation.

"What men?" Thomas asked.

"The three men in the back of the truck! I killed those dogs all by myself," Farid sneered with evil glee. "With the mortar I planted there, you saw, it tore the leg off..." and with that Thomas tore the cover off of the top of the three dead men, leaving the lower half still covered. Moe, Larry & Curly.

"Yes Farid, you did kill these three Taliban with the mortar rounds, as you've just said," Thomas said quietly so one else could hear. "And I'll bet a number of these men know exactly who these three are, and I bet they know you weren't thrilled about having them around. But right now, you have two choices. You either come with us and you tell us everything, or we let you go behind the gates, and you can explain how you didn't kill them after you just said you did."

"They won't believe you," Farid said, obviously not considering the ethics of Taliban justice and conviction methods.

Thomas replied, "I only need one to believe me. My advantage is I can talk to every single one of them alone any time I want. The other advantage is... we have the video." Thomas winked.

This was the certain skill the Rangers were interviewed for; acting. Everyone knows Three-card Monte is a carnival act of misdirection, but the Rangers' Oscar-winning performance hid the very game they were playing.

Farid could make it through prison with the prospect he was a hero, but now that was gone. He didn't kill any Americans, and Americans are always taking pictures. Plus, he knew nobody in Obaidullah's village would back up his story, certainly not now after he had stolen the elder's horse and got it shot while he fled. Farid stood there frozen as if, if he did nothing, he'd be saved.

Thomas grabbed Farid, turned him around, and rushed him up to the gate looking into the Taliban within. "Look in their eyes Farid, they want blood, but it's not just mine," Thomas said while pressing his face into the bars.

And then one of the younger Taliban inside, who was staring at Farid, took a slow step towards him, and with that Farid knew, if he stayed, his neck would be slit before the next dawn. Farid struggled to push away from the rails and just said "I'll go, I'll go," closing his eyes so he wouldn't have to see the shame of his own betrayal.

Thomas nodded over to Sgt. Milone and Robert. "He's all yours."

Sgt. Milone put him back into the truck with another Ranger, and Thomas wanted to talk to Robert and Max on the route back to the base, so he got them into the back of one of the MRAPs. It was cramped, but the noise helped keep the conversation between the three of them.

"Max, I have to tell you, I appreciated the help," Thomas said unashamedly. "You saw what I was going for and got that the trap had to be sprung, no matter the risk."

"Well Captain, I admit I was thrilled to contribute," Max said with a great deal of pride, "far too often, as a liaison, I'm left on the sidelines, as you say."

Thomas leaned in towards the two sitting across from him "I'm here to tell you that these sort of problems exist with and without wars. These are problems that need to be solved, and I'm in a position to tell you that once you're out of service, I'd like you to come to work with me." The two men smiled the nervous smile of not knowing what to say. "Relax, it doesn't have to be tomorrow, and I don't need an answer today, but I'm not here on this mission by accident. Rolling Farid and saving Rangers was a plus, but I didn't come here for that. I'm here to recruit two partners for the future."

Robert shook his head, "So wait a minute, you're here to recruit? You're still in uniform, and you get to choose where you go just to recruit?"

"As it happens, I do. And more importantly, that's what I'm offering," Thomas replied.

"The older civilian you were sitting with in the tent, was that your boss, your employer, or your client?" Max was an intelligent intelligence officer that read people as well as intel. "Are we working with you, for you, or for him?"

Robert's eyebrows raised and looked at Thomas like one might respond to an infamous Columbo question hurled just as he was about to leave a room.

"Excellent question. He's a boss now, but would only be a friend later. It would be our firm to pursue the matters we choose to pursue and be paid however we deem to be paid. But like all of the friends we've ever made, he's a good one to have. We can work for whoever we want. The only caveat I would insist upon, as officers sworn to defend the United States, we couldn't take on matters that would in the end harm America, or our allies" Thomas said solemnly in deference to Max. "Robert, you can put your hand down and just speak."

Robert put his hand down, it was an awful habit. "As the one known as a hacker, I just really need to be clear.

If you're saying we're working with....some acronymed American agency, that's all fine and good, but we have to know exactly what's going on. The laws regarding data from just data providers is a minefield all on its own. If I'm to be free to look around someone else's data, as it were, I have to know if I'm committing multiple felonies before I'm working with people who may be arresting us."

Thomas nodded, "more than fair. I can assure you that when I say we'd be able to operate at more than arm's length in the legal sense, we would be."

"Well Captain," Max said with an extended hand, "whenever I decide to get out, I'll at least give you a call."

Robert kind of shrugged somewhat used to hearing the big plans that many in the service speak of, and for the first time was involved himself. "Sure why not. Hopefully less with mortar rounds."

"Well," Thomas demurred, "I can only say probably less."

Upon arriving back at the base, Sgt. Milone was already taking Farid to an area used for interrogating prisoners. They didn't keep prisoners here long, as either they'd go to an Afghan facility,  the CIA would take them to one of their own sites in Afghanistan, or on less frequent occasions, they'd be sent to other countries where the host government wanted them for their own reasons, or if it was deemed more likely to get more information. This was just a layover to make that determination.

Thomas grabbed his gear and extended his arm to the

two men, "Well then, until you give me a call."

Robert was a little shocked. "You're not coming in to interrogate Farid?"

"Nope. You're here, you know the players, which I'm not as deeply involved with by the way. You know Farid's history, so you'll be able to jump on whoever he gives up, the lies he tells, and besides..." Thomas paused getting the last bit of his gear from the MRAP slung over the remaining shoulder, "I was never here."

"Wait, what" Max asked.

"I was never here, this was your plan, you two are going to get the information from Farid, and act on it, then just be sure you get the horse back." Thomas finished.

"But...." the two men said simultaneously.

"But nothing, there's no sense giving credit to a guy who was never here." Thomas turned and left.

Two years later, both Max and Robert wrapped up their service time within the same month. They had, of course, already called the number provided and their triumvirate was formed.

That was eleven years ago, and the missions never stopped. There's never a shortage of clients, and Thomas was also able to line up the clients he specifically wanted.

# CHAPTER VI

## *The Boat*

Das Boot. It was a great movie about men and the sea suffering the turmoil nearing the end of WWII in a submarine from the German perspective. Thomas didn't need a sub, but like all big plans, many little things mattered. The boat had to be both a battleship for defense, but an easy mark for pirates. Lee had a number of ships that were targeted, but to be fair, they were mostly big, way too big for this plan. If the boat's too big, they're not as inviting. Almost all of the attacks came in part because Lee's boats failed to follow all of their own protocols. Attacks would be less likely if his Captains didn't take shortcuts with men and routes to cut their costs, just to boost their own bonuses. A smaller crew lowers costs, a shorter route saves time. But Thomas' plan wasn't to stop the pirates from attacking – oh no, that's the plan of the short-sighted.

The boat needed to be midsized, fairly low in the water, something perfect to invite being boarded, yet with a nice tall tower for lookouts. Having the high tower was just common sense tactically, but in this case, quite necessary if, or when they were overrun.

Max found a container ship recently sold by Oseberg Shipping that wasn't yet in service, making it possible for Lee's people to make a deal. Oseberg is a Norwegian shipping company named after a Viking boat found on the Oseberg farm in 1904. While a powerful name for the brand, the Oseberg ship itself was part of a burial that involved multiple animals sacrificed for the women buried in it.

Max hoped there was no bad luck in the choice, but it seemed to be just what Thomas was looking for. It has a six-story tower at the rear and was just the right size to be both inviting and defensible. It is actually a "feeder ship" of average size. A feeder ship is often used to unload from a large container ship directly and then distribute goods to smaller ports, or making shorter hauls between multiple ports. If one could visualize a container ship carrying about over 10,000 containers that are the size of a trailer pulled by a truck, a feeder ship would carry only about 350 of those. The boat is still over 350 feet from stem to stern and 60 feet wide.

The high tower was there to see over the equally high containers stacked on the deck. Plus the vertical use of quarters allowed more room for storage and fuel below. The boat had a walkway under the main deck which would normally be entirely covered with containers. This was a problem as the walkway would have access to the bowels of the boat. It would have to be blocked off with a steel plate arranged for cover. The great thing about containers is that you can put them where you want, and this boat has its own cranes to move them at will. This trip didn't have to maximize square footage for profit. Instead, it had to maximize the kill zones.

The boat had to be able to protect the operators and the crew, not just from a couple of pirates, but the inevitable attack from a large force, heavy weapons, and of course fire.

After hours of coordinating expectations of what was needed down the to the very last detail with Jiang, Mr. Lee had a car take Thomas back to The Peninsula Hotel, an opulent 5 Star suite on the water. Thankfully this was provided by Lee as part of the invitation for a meeting. Thomas had done well to be sure, but dropping over $6,000 a night on a hotel wouldn't have been his choice. Sure, the $250,000 easily covered that, but wanton needless spending is a bad mindset to get into, especially for things that don't last.

As Thomas entered the Peninsula, there was Max.

"Thomas, I spoke to Jiang about leasing the ship," Max said with an 'I'm so on top of this' attitude.

Thomas replied, "Yeah, and?"

"The ship is heading to Thailand…" Max said before Thomas cut him off.

"Woah, woah, woah, we're calling it 'the boat,' not the ship," Thomas said.

Max, not surprisingly, was easy to read. He had the easily identifiable 'what the hell' look on his face.

"First, Thomas, it's a ship. It's an ocean-going vessel, and infinitely more important, who gives a shit what it's called," Max replied.

"Max, they call submarines boats, and they're ocean-going," Thomas said wryly.

"Yes, submarines have *always* been called boats, and the

name stuck, so why are we calling it a boat Thomas?"

"Because submarines are stealthy and cunning, and they survive against superior odds, and I'd like to think that's us. So thank you, Max. Since nobody gives a shit, we're calling it The Boat, please continue."

Okay, Thomas thought, the facial expression Max exhibited of quizzical and 'fuck you' are difficult to separate. There are in fact facial homonyms.

Max continued. "*The Boat* is heading to Thailand to load up with rice. The ship, *boat*, can hold a couple of hundred containers including above deck and in the hold, but I'll pare that down so we have the defensive flexibility you asked for."

Thomas raised his hand, which he often did with Max, a bad habit learned from Robert.  Max, you see, was always irked to be interrupted, as if he was a professor desperately taking pleasure in getting to a salient point. Thomas also enjoyed interrupting Max.

"Max, there's a wrinkle in your container design."

"What wrinkle?" Max asked, as if he wasn't seriously enjoying designing a fort with containers.

"We're going to have several armored vehicles on board, they'll be able to move around the deck to different vantage points if needed. I felt it would help with flexibility," Thomas said, not being entirely honest. Not even close in fact.

"Armored vehicles? I heard the Marines were doing that on some of their assault ships to deal with smaller threats." Max was clearly thinking about it and smiled adding a "that's a good wrinkle, Thomas."

*Oh, sorry Max,* Thomas thought to himself. *It's going to be a bit more than a wrinkle when you find out.*

Max then went back to the lecture. "I've also secured a number of sales and deliveries for a variety of charities by having Lee subsidize both the cost of the rice and the shipping to fill it up quick."

"I've already scheduled multiple deliveries on the north side to Berbera & Djibouti, but I want to stay away from going all the way up the Red Sea. Bad enough to deal with Somalia on one side, I'd like to stay away from the civil war in Yemen if it's okay with you."

They both laughed the sick kind of laugh, like, *yeah, we know we're jumping over fire, but heaven forbid there's a rock where we need to stick the landing, because "that's" the problem.*

Max paused for a moment while looking over the options. "I also have several in the works for Raysut, in Oman, but again, that's to the North and I want a number of Southern deliveries before I firm those up. Any thoughts?"

Thomas brought up the map of the area on his Panasonic Toughbook, the computer he used in the field so many times. It's not a gaming computer, but it was aptly named. It took a beating and the built-in GPS still worked. You don't always have Wifi in the field. This area he knew, but he didn't know all of the ports to the South. They needed an equal number of deliveries to the South.

They had to basically go back and forth through waters offshore, trolling for pirates. This was easier said than done as the US Navy and others have a general patrol in the area. Little boats they may not see, but a big boat they'll notice, and without bills of lading for deliveries justifying one's presence, they're going to suspect an arms smuggler. While Thomas wouldn't be smuggling arms, they'd have them en masse, and having the boat geared for total war would raise an eyebrow if examined.

So they'd need to find enough valid deliveries North and South so that Max's government contacts wouldn't be needed. Hopefully.

"We can't get the boat into Mogadishu. Way too much attention to the locals and patrols," Thomas said, still eyeing the options.

"Well Thomas, I've had options for all the way to South Africa, but that's too far, we don't want to be at sea that far out of the area for that long. I'd check for UN contracts, but that's more on the radar than we'd like to be. If we were carrying something more valuable perhaps?" Max was getting flustered.

"No Max, rice will be fine." Still looking at the map Thomas decided to sum up the solution, at least for the time being. "Look Max, the boat's going to be leaving Thailand with rice. We're going to Thailand to up-arm the boat and make some preparations before it sails, but I don't plan on staying on the boat for the whole trip. We can't bring the boat into Seychelles with the arms anyway, so we're going to fly into Seychelles, drink some rum, eat some French food, and bone up on the intel. We'll take a skiff out to *the boat,* then start making deliveries and flirting with pirates. Since we're a feeder ship, take orders to Seychelles."

Max's arms went up, "But Thomas, as you just stated, we can't bring *the boat* into Seychelles."

"Max! Anybody can take a 'reservation' to make a delivery, but having the little piece of paper saying you're supposed to, that's all we really need." Thomas smiled in the annoying kind of way only a jerk of a friend can and still be funny. "If we pick up Southern deliveries later, we work them in and you can always toss the Seychelles deliveries later, problem solved."

"Gotcha Thomas will do," Max said, just shaking his head. Thomas always seemed to have an answer. Almost everything just seemed to work for him.

Max got up to walk out to go get a drink, "Oh, and Lee told her to just buy it, said it would be better to own it for later?" Max knew the plan, just not the entire plan. It's not that he'd ever withheld information on operations from Max before, and it's not that he didn't trust him; it was that this was very different. He'd tell Max when the time came, but he just knew Max wasn't going to be happy about it.

"Well Max, I can see how it will be better for later, it'll put the fear of God into pirates, that's for sure," Thomas said with a smile. "And you found a former "Oseberg" boat? You just had to find a German one didn't you."

Max Laughed, "Oseberg is a Norwegian company you heathen. But the *boat* they sold, yeah, *that* was built in

Germany. You want to die on a boat made in China?"

"Oh no, clearly dying on a German boat formerly owned by a Norwegian company is so much better…." Thomas agreed, with great sarcasm.

# CHAPTER VII

## *The Crew*

Thomas was reviewing which men he should bring on this mission, and thinking deeply about it. It would be a harsh mission as they'd be certain to put down a number of pirates; it was not only certain but as it happened, a necessity for the remaining part of his plan.

The problem would be choosing men who would unflinchingly dole out the pain, then also make a choice to take a risk to do what's right. That's a tricky combination to find.

Many of the operations Thomas worked on weren't in board, court, or staterooms, but in the real world of evil men doing evil things. If there's a balance, Thomas believed his work helped keep that balance. And you can't do that by saving everyone. The harsh reality is there's always a choice to decide who you save, and that means dealing with those that have put themselves in the way. Thomas was considered to be well rounded by those that knew him, but that knowledge came predominantly from his work, not his interests. Any familiarity in art or literature, even when it was something he appreciated, was no more than that. In truth, he wasn't well rounded at all, he just wasn't raised that way. Thomas' Uncle raised him, and his Uncle was very single-minded. The term single-minded is often used in a derogatory manner and is often confused with simple-minded or inflexible. Uncle certainly wasn't that.

Uncle Phillip would school Thomas as they traveled, prodding him to solve whatever problem was given to him during their lessons. Thomas would've preferred to play baseball, watch baseball, listen to baseball on the radio, read about baseball, or if there was anyone around, talk about baseball. However, Phillip, one could say, applied the pressure to Thomas as if he was the marble.

"Thomas," Uncle Phillip would say, "You need to finish the school work assigned to you, and Then we can talk about baseball."

"But, I don't always like all this work," young Thomas lamented.

"Well that's why they call it work," Uncle Phillip replied. "Look, Thomas. Think of any baseball player you want, and I bet they're great at just one thing. Sure, some may be good at many things, some may be what's called a five-tool player, but even many five-tool players probably aren't considered to be great players. They're rarely the game-changers. The sad reality is that well-rounded people don't change the world." This was a truism he mentioned more than once.

"Think about that. All of the greatest players in history all went to school at some point, they all went through the grades so that they could get what they wanted..." Uncle said as he looked at Thomas, who was thinking this over.

"Thomas, if you want to play professional baseball, you would probably have to do well in college. That means you have to get into college, which means you have to do well enough in the schooling you're doing now. If you want to change your world, excel in everything you do at all times not because you love all of those things, but you're willing to make that sacrifice to get out of life what you truly want, just like almost every baseball player you've ever known has had to do."

Uncle knew what buttons to push, but even now, later in life, Thomas missed never really having a shot at baseball.

Both he and Max would be on the boat. Robert would not be joining them on the boat, as hacking pirates couldn't be worked into the plan if he wanted to. However, Robert could keep an eye on them along the way and would play a part later Thomas was sure Robert would be of help in front of a computer screen wherever he was in the world, but Thomas put that part of the plan in his pocket. For now, that was his plan alone.

This meant he'd need at least six others.

Of the snipers, he'd go to James Abernathy for certain. A former SAS sniper whose favorite weapon was the M137, which he used extensively in Afghanistan, and expanded his proficiency with the weapon once in private practice. At 44 he wasn't a young man but was in excellent physical condition. Abernathy was of the mindset that if you can't run, you can't fight. While sniping may be thought of as a lazy warrior by the uninformed, lying prone, and going to war only one or two thousand yards away, the shot is a very small part of the job. Abernathy had the skill set and most importantly, the will.

In considering Abernathy, Thomas thought back to a sniper from another era. One of the greatest snipers in history was Sgt. Hathcock, an American sniper in Vietnam. He once crawled over seven hundred yards through a field. That doesn't sound like much, but it had to be done so slowly so that the guards watching the field wouldn't see the movement. It took him three days. Three days of lying there, moving that slowly, never flinching at any sound. The mental discipline to do that is unfathomable to most. Simply imagine making no grand movements for three days and one realizes the bodily functions that occur over a three-day period. Then take a seven hundred yard cold bore shot killing the North Vietnamese General and lie there while the enemy scours the field before slipping away in the darkness alone and on foot. And then think about the fact that he did all that understanding that it was likely a suicide mission from the beginning. Just imagine trying to be perfect at everything for three days with your almost certain death tied to your being successful. If Sgt. Hathcock failed to get into position to take the shot, he'd likely avoid detection and live. Take the shot and miss? Sure the sound of the shot would raise alarm, but without a hit, there's no sure direction of where the shot came from. But those that witnessed the successful shot would have known what direction it came from, and he'd likely be found by the enemy. Torture, wouldn't describe what would have happened to him. For three days Sgt. Hatchock crawled over an open field with the knowledge that success would likely mean his death. The will to perform to that degree? Admiration just doesn't cut it. Sgt. Hatcock did all that and then had the will to survive on top of it.

Abernathy would do fine, despite his insistence on being so British. The man insisted on afternoon tea even on missions. Thomas believed Abernathy did so in the presence of others just to create the air of superiority. Of course, that very act itself is painfully British, so it was undoubtedly true.

The other sniper on the list, Tony Bennett, was an American shooter he'd worked with before.

While Bennett also served in the Army, and in Afghanistan, their paths never crossed while serving. Bennett wasn't a lifer, he was only in for four years.

Thomas looked back on the notations of Bennett's mission reports, the classified record to which he was fortunately privy. He didn't go to sniper school, though he was offered if he re-upped. Sniper school requires demonstrating excellent infantry skills, and wartime affords the opportunity to demonstrate those skills to be sure. During his second year in, an Army sniper and his spotter made their way to an edge of a hill that had cover, which was composed of a much older abandoned structure. The base of the structure was all that remained. It was set back enough so they wouldn't be silhouetted along the ridge. It was a perfect spot to survey the valley below before his unit advanced along the road – too perfect, apparently, because as they entered, the IED detonated, and Bennett could see the two men thrown from the blast.

Bennett scurried up the hill and put a tourniquet on the spotter's leg while the others tended to the sniper. Incoming small arms fire came from across the valley, but shots fell short and because the blast threw the men several feet below the crest, they were out of any direct line of fire.

Bennett moved up to cover to view where the incoming fire was coming from, another similar abandoned building at least six hundred yards away. Well, it was abandoned except for the guys shooting at him. Bennett was a shooter, and would often have the role of Designated Marksman, but anything much over 500 yards with an M-4 is suppressing fire at best. The bullets have velocity, but are light, lose their energy, and have a lot of drift in the wind, something the valley had plenty of.

But the sniper's gun, that was another story. The M-82 Barrett .50 sniper rifle. It sends a round with nearly 14,000 foot-pounds of energy at the muzzle that can kill a truck at over 1,000 yards. To put it in perspective, a 9mm handgun round tops out at about 400 foot-pounds. More than that, anything firing rounds 12.7mm and below is called a gun, and anything 12.7mm and above is called a cannon. A .50 caliber is exactly 12.7mm. Whether shouldering a big gun or a small cannon, the receiving end is just as dead.

Bennett used the ACOG sight on his M-4 to range the target, it was a little over 600 yards, he didn't even finish doing the math, he only had to be close. Bennett wasn't familiar with the Nightforce mil-dot sight, but the beauty of those dots is that they mean the same thing on every scope. The distance between the dots is 3.6 inches at 100 yards, 7.2, inches at 200 yards, and so on. He knew that his 5.56 would land about 84 inches low at 600 yards. Math, ugh. At 600 yards that would mean that he had to raise the crosshairs about three and three-quarter dots and he'd be spot on.

He only had to estimate the drop of the round and knew how many dots to raise if the scope was zeroed to 100 yards. Of course, he didn't know if the sniper zeroed the Barrett to 100 yards or 700, but he had to start somewhere,

The shooters were still shooting from behind cover, primarily clay-like walls, maybe stone-filled. Bennett went through the ammo available and without hesitation loaded a magazine of tungsten-filled armor penetrators. If they're behind the wall, his plan was to just hit the wall in front of them. He laid prone with the rifle, making sure his eye was as far from the scope as the eye relief would allow. He never fired a .50 cal sniper rifle before and didn't want the kick to give him a scar where his eyebrow used to be. He took several deep breaths and then with a solid exhale put the crosshairs on target, raising it the nearly four dots required above the center of the wall. He fell back on his training. Not Basic Training, but how to hunt by his father. "Squeeze the trigger so slow it'll surprise you," he'd say. "Just don't be surprised when it does." The kind of nonsense fathers loved to say. It had meaning. Squeezing the trigger so slowly meant the pull didn't adversely impact the shot. Bennett was surprised when it fired, with a suddenness and violence unlike anything else he'd ever fired before, yet the recoil was manageable. He quickly regained his view and only saw the aftermath. There was no more firing from the several men behind the wall, all he could see was that the wall behind them was painted red. The armor-piercing round hit a wall with such voracity that the carbon in the wall compressed to a hardness approaching diamonds. Those small pieces of flesh-eating projectiles then exploded from the other side, like a conical shaped shotgun blast up close and personal, shredding anything behind the wall. One shot ended three bad guys.

Bennett's actions earned him an offer of a trip to sniper school – his tendency to be called a "gun nut" paid off – but he wanted work that paid more.

Bennett was undoubtedly Italian. He also didn't hesitate to use his fairly good voice to live up to his namesake. All jokes aside, the guy could make any rifle sing and then some. He'd be a good fit.

Marcus Siegfreid wasn't a gun nut per se, he was more like the "nut du jour." He once had a neighbor problem whose cat kept wandering into his yard. Siegfreid gave his automatic sprinkler system a second source of fluid. The cat was bleached white for six months, not that Siegfried ever saw him again. It wasn't bleach, he wasn't cruel to those that didn't deserve it.

Whether it was gun, heavy weapons, or customized explosives, he had a great knack for picking the right tool of the day without preference. Thomas liked having him on board, and on a ship with lots of things that could go wrong he wanted a layer of defense. Siegfreid served in the Marines, right out of high school. He did four hard years in infantry, and without a great MOS to fall back on in the real world, he spent four years "on vacation" using the GI Bill to obtain his degree in chemical engineering. Working hard while drinking beer in college is on vacation by comparison.

Siegfreid's degree in the sciences expanded his tactical methodology. Smoke grenades became smokier, flashing bangs were bangier, and the guy knew how to build a layered defense. Everything you do doesn't have to kill the enemy, it may simply slow each part of the enemy's attack to enable his inevitable slaughter when it gives *you* the advantage. Thomas liked the way he thought defenses through, which he was sure would come into play on this mission. Plus, Siegfried's dedication to speed, surprise, and violence of action was right out of the playbook, so there was that.

Rounding out the team would be Kim Nguyen, Francis Marks, & Gregory Atkins. They had all done security work for their company for a long time. Though their work typically involved security work more than assault work, the men had all earlier served in the military, although Kim Nguyen served in the South Korean Army. Francis Marks did eight years in the Marines in a Trax (an amphibious assault vehicle), while Gregory Atkins served in the Air Force in search and rescue.

There were a lot of moving parts on this mission, and despite his desire to bone up on the assault side, he was still cognizant of keeping everyone safe – not just his eight men, but the crew of the boat. Sure, Lee served them up to be at risk for the mission, but Thomas had no intention of rewarding the loyalty they showed to Lee by serving them up to the pirates. So having experts at moving backward under fire, would be just as important as those moving forward, and in this case, integral to the plan. Thomas just hoped that they felt that way as well.

Thomas put down the folders and emailed Robert the list of men to have them meet him at his home in Thailand. Like Congressmen, Thomas had two homes: one in DC, the seat of power where his clients from all over the world apparently came to spawn, and Thailand, an isolated beach home in Phuket on the west side of the peninsula north of a beach. It was both convenient to the side of the world where so much of his work took place and still so much a fortress of solitude when he wasn't.

The home was very nice, and then some, but he spent most of the time under a covered patio overlooking the beach and the sea. The home was on a hill, a good distance away from the noise and scurry of those enjoying the sand, but he liked the view of those enjoying themselves. That, and the windmill palms surrounding the pool. A local woman by the name of Boonsri kept the house and cooked on any occasion he needed, but he often cooked for himself. A gardener tended to the outside. That would be the place to meet for this mission, somewhere personal, where he could work on expanding the personal connection. He may need it.

Thomas picked up the phone and said "Robert" and it dialed. The phone answered with a "Yello," which was Robert's hello.

"I just emailed the list of names I picked, and I'd like them to meet at my house by the sea two days from now on Tuesday," Thomas said.

"Sure thing buddy, I did just get the email and will do just that. Is there anything else?" Robert asked, seeming a bit curious.

"I want the men to come here to go over the details, it's going to be a hard mission, and I want to develop a bit of camaraderie as they haven't all worked with each other before," Thomas explained.

"A hard mission, Thomas? You seem to be so certain of the outcome, " Robert replied.

"I mean it's going to be a hard mission, in another way. The plan involves putting down a lot of pirates, and we can't afford hesitation or doubt in the middle," Thomas said with far more conviction than Robert could know.

"Gotcha, I get it. You're right of course. It's one thing to have to pull the trigger in some of our security details, it's another to go in with that as the plan en masse," Robert sympathized.

"Remember Robert, when we're tasked with taking out one bad guy, we know how bad he is. We take it to heart, we remind ourselves how we're doing the world a favor because of the horrors he's done, and justify it to ourselves so when we squeeze the trigger it's a silky smooth pull and we then sleep like a baby. We won't know who the pirates are, we won't know what they've done, and more importantly, our guys won't know if they've done anything prior to the day they show up at our boat. But that absolutely, positively can't leave room for them to not put them down and none can escape." Thomas took a pause to consider what he was asking, "That's "our" mission to our men, to take that burden from them so they get it done and stay alive."

"Gotcha Thomas, see you Tuesday,"

"And Robert?"

"Yeah, boss?" "Have them show up any time they're in. They don't have to wait until later, but uh, try for nothing before 10 am, I'm going to sleep in."

"I'll be there at 9." Robert hung up.

"Dick," Thomas said to the dead phone; he knew Robert would be true to his word. *Boss my ass.*

Thomas would meet the men, and the day after they could then drive to the east side of the Phuket Peninsula where *"the Boat"* would be moored to meet with the captain and their crew.

"It'll work," Thomas said to himself, expressing a rare moment of having to console his own fears. "All of it will have to work."

# CHAPTER VIII

## *Home on the Sea*

Thomas awoke to the gentle breeze of the fan a few minutes before his alarm would go off at 8:45 am. He may have been miserable about waking up early but wasn't going to give Robert the joy of waking him. Thank God for the hot shower.

Robert let himself in just before 9:00 a.m. "Thomas!" Robert yelled joyfully hoping to wake him, only to be wholly dejected to hear the shower. That passed as he smelled the freshly brewed coffee. Black Rifle Coffee! Robert loved the symbolism, but the coffee was even better. Robert poured a cup of the dark roasted brew, added plenty of sugar, and walked to the patio.

"Nice view, but so boring. I don't get it." Robert walked back inside and started to lay out Toughbooks, one for each of the crew members. On it, it had the layout of the ship along with the duty schedule, areas of responsibility, and emergency routes they'd all have to memorize. He had the captain of *The Boat* do a video walkthrough and then he converted it to a program that would allow the crew to walk through the entire ship so they could repeatedly familiarize themselves with it before ever setting foot on it. It was like a video tour of a home you're looking to buy, but with less concern for the curtains, and more for learning which way to run, because your life will depend on it..

"Mr. Robert, what a pleasure to see you," Boonsri called out. Thomas had told her to come in and prep for guests he was having over. "Hello, Boonsri, sorry for the extra work, but it is work."

"You're never a problem Mr. Robert," she smiled. "There's coffee!"

"Already in hand ma'am" Robert smiled but passed on engaging in the witty flirtations the older woman seemed to enjoy. While everything was already planned out, it's the kind of mission that he really had to focus on, especially since he wasn't going to accompany them. He didn't want to just go through the motions and leave the rest of them in the lurch if he missed anything.

Thomas heard Robert was there, dressed, and quickly made for the coffee. "Boonsri, there will be a number of men joining us today, if you could make a fresh pot of coffee and keep the carafe full. And if you could play sous-chef today and just prep for lunch with this," as Thomas handed her the list.

"Just prep? Of course." With that, the ever-reliable Boonsri got to work.

"I'll be on the terrace Robert, let me know as the men arrive."

"Gotcha boss," Robert said with just the right amount of sarcasm.

"Boss my...." Thomas went to enjoy the view and the coffee until they arrived.

The men trickled in and took to the coffee, drawn by the aroma, and especially the pastries Boonsri offered. They gathered politely at the table as Robert referred them to their laptop to review the material, their position on the boat, and the layout. It was far easier for Thomas to give a meaningful briefing if everybody already knew their basic tasks.

Some of them knew each other well, some just in passing, some they met for the first time. There was the customary sizing up one's brother before the operations to make sure they had each other's back. But this was an eight-man team (which was sizable in comparison to many other jobs), plus it was Thomas's home, so it was cordial.

After letting the men break themselves in while reviewing the info, Thomas finally got up and came inside.

"Alright, I hope you all reviewed your positions" and the men generally all grunted a "yes." "Good, here's the big picture. The two snipers, that's Abernathy and Bennett" pointing to both, "they'll be on bow and stern during the day, Marks and Atkins will be port and starboard. Max and I will be port and starboard at night, and Nguyen and Seigfried will be bow and stern at night."

"Why am I at night?" Nguyen asked.

"Obviously, because you're a Ninja Nguyen" Thomas replied. It was a bad old joke, primarily because Ninja's were Japanese, and Koreans were less than fond of the Japanese (to put it mildly), but mostly because Thomas knew Nguyen liked to think of himself as a Ninja, but just not the Japanese kind.

“We’ll have a full suite of night vision and thermals so while the bad guys may think about a night attack, they’ll likely be spotted even farther out than during the day. Everybody will be suppressed, I won’t have a lucky RPG shot take anyone out because of an unnecessary flash…”

“Nice of you to think about us,” Max said. “But you’re expecting RPGs?”

“I’m expecting something. But I’d hate to lose anybody Max, then I’d have to work overtime,” Thomas said wryly. “That’s why the goal is early target acquisition, lure them in, be sure we’re in position, then after they’re in range, we end them quickly.”

“ROE is shoot first?” Max wanted to clarify the rules of engagement.

“Unfortunately, yes. But we’re not just going to light up every boat that comes our way, if they’re not pirates, they’re not our target. We ID them early on, we need to see arms and intent. But there’s no water cannons, no warning shots, no half measures. If we see a pirate, we end them swiftly so they lose the ability to communicate that we’re heavily armed. And whatever boat they come in, we put that down as well, I don’t imagine anything sizable. The concept only works if we stay looking like a sheep that’s easy to be sheared. If word gets out that we’re heavily armed, then we’re not a target, we’re Typhoid Mary. And Typhoid Mary didn’t have a plethora of suitors,” Thomas laughed, “and as it happens, we need lots of suitors.”

Abernathy raised his hand, "I see the projected route, as targets will likely come from our due West, if the Captain could be told to never run perpendicular to the Sun, maybe a little zigzag, for us long-range shooters," giving a nod to Bennett as Thomas nodded to them both.

Thomas continued, "We're going to go visit the boat tomorrow. Make a list, check it twice, and go over everything with all of the crew, and especially the Captain. I understand that he'll be ruling the boat with an iron fist, so if you need anything, let him know. I'd say remind him that we're in between the pirates and him, but I think this guy more than gets it."

Abernathy nodded to himself as Thomas spoke, making a mental note to talk to the Captain, "Also, while I see the route planned, I don't see a time frame. Roger said it was an "open-ended mission," but do you have a general idea?"

"We're going to see the boat tomorrow, they'll finish loading the containers of rice, all of the arms will be on the boat. We're going to fly to Seychelles, go over the intel, bone up on response responsibilities, drink a bunch of French Rum, then we'll take a skiff out to the boat when it gets there. No guns in Seychelles, at least on the up and up, and I don't think we need to sit on the boat for an extra six days. Total time? I'm hoping a couple of weeks start to finish, but it could mean weeks more. Right now, the plan is that we're dangling bait. The biggest is how good we are at looking like an easy target."

Siegfried followed Abernathy's lead and raised his hand, "I'll need some time for some of the install, chief."

"We won't engage until we're ready, but that's what a lot of tomorrow is for. You need doors welded to prevent entrance? You mark it and tell them. You need the piping laid for the fire control system? You tell them where and how much. I know you mentioned hanging some extra steel plate from a cable deployed by the cranes along the sides, which I like by the way, so that's scheduled for delivery. Just keep in mind it has to be slung low so it doesn't impede the shooter's line of sight. But if takes a hit from an RPG and saves the boat, it's worth the effort."

"All good sir," Siegfried nodded. He was always happy when some of his ideas were being integrated, and Thomas seemed to always take them all.

Thomas continued, "Our route will skirt the coast, and we'll try to hit the hot spots repeatedly in a short amount of time. While we have paperwork for a number of deliveries we're, uh, gonna be late for some. Hell, the bad part is if we don't have contact, we may even have to make a few. We'll have the routes of the various navies on patrol, but that doesn't mean we can just camp in the paint the whole time."

"Camp in the paint?" Nguyen asked?

"Stay in the same spot without moving," Thomas said. "Sorry, it's a lame basketball reference."

Nguyen followed up. "And how will we know the routes of the navies on patrol?"

"We have an intel unit for that, so we'll be in touch throughout," Thomas said assuredly.

"Oh wow, uh, that's great," Nguyen replied quite reassured. *If we know where they are, then we have the possibility of getting help if we need it,* was his first thought.

"Look, there's no way to foresee how many attacks we'll encounter, or be certain that we'll be attacked at all. But we're over-prepping for a reason. Our goal is to eliminate them. If we eliminate some, that puts pressure on others. The fact that we're putting them down is one thing, the other is that with their boats sunk, they never make it back to port. While that keeps our ship the same as every other, it also means that eventually, we may get a bigger response. We don't know the relationship of any of the pirates – is a brother lost, a father, a son? Will they stop attacks out of fear, or look to make a statement in retribution? Will they know it's us and show no quarter, or blithely approach thinking we're pushovers even if they have superior numbers? There are lots of possibilities, lots of emotions, and we can't guess at all the internal workings of the pirates. While we have information on almost all of the groups, what we don't know is if they're united in any way, and so on. Our goal is to poke the bear, then put him down." Thomas paused to let that singular thought sink in.

"So, since we're poking the bear, I want every advantage. Siegfried suggested hanging an extra steel plate from the cables of the twin cranes. We could deploy that if there's a significant attack, but we also don't want to scare them away too early. With the plates hanging several feet above the water and slung bouncing around as we sail, it will both offer the boat a level of protection against anything heavy and present a problem if they want to board. Getting whacked with a half-inch steel plate will give them pause to think about approaching. Every second of their indecision is an extra one for us. The reason the fire control system is being piped all around the ship, is because I expect there may be a large attack at some point. If we're making a statement against ten groups of ten guys, nothing will come of it." Thomas raised his hand to draw their attention even more, "But if we're making a statement against one group of a hundred guys, the one guy will need to make a statement of his own."

"Hope for the best," Max said, and everyone answered, "prepare for the worst."

"Amen," Thomas finished. "Lastly, since you were so studious about the paperwork Nguyen, everybody needs to read through the contracts, and there's a special addendum in this one. It is what it says it is. Read it, understand it, agree to it, sign it. But there's no explaining what some of the additional payout will be until later. That's just the way it is."

"Now, I'm going to cook us some food," and Thomas began to walk outside to the built-in stone grill outside by the pool. He'd started smoking two slabs of pork earlier in the day and needed to add some more wood.

Siegfried chimed in, "Man, you're cooking, not too manly man!"

"There's fire involved, that makes it manly," Thomas quipped.

"I don't know man, still in the kitchen," Siegfried kept digging.

"It's outside, but that aside. I've rebuilt an engine, I've

designed and built the addition you're eating in, I've designed and built the pool you're swimming in, and designed and built the business that's paying you. Are you honestly saying I can't build the meal fit for feeding you?" Thomas waited patiently as they were all somewhat taken aback.

"Oh no, I don't think he's saying you "can't" build the meal.....just that it's not too manly," Max said in the most annoying of German accents.

Everyone paused not knowing how the joke would land, but Thomas couldn't hold his stern look any longer and burst out laughing. "Well I'm making Bacon Egg American Pie for breakfast, so just don't fucking call it quiche!"

# CHAPTER IX

## *Prep the Rice*

Thomas awoke to the sight and sound of the fan above. That, and the smell of the bacon, egg, and cheese pie wafting into the room. After quickly getting himself together, he went into the kitchen only to see everyone already up. "I'm glad y'all made yourself at home...saved me from making the coffee." The men grunted, smiled and waved good morning. Thomas grabbed a cup and a good size slice from one of the remaining pies.

"Late sleeper?" Nguyen asked.

"Best for last," Thomas replied. "After everyone eats, get yourself together and we'll drive over to the boat. Your personal arms were shipped there, but there are sidearms here for everyone, and there's a rifle in the back of each of the three Land Cruisers."

"Are we expecting trouble here?" Abernathy wondered.

"No, not expecting at all. But if there is, I don't want to lose," Thomas replied.

"And three Land Cruisers for the eight of us?" Siegfried wondered.

"Ever been in the back seat of a truck and been smashed in the face by a guy with an M4?"

"No," Siegfried responded.

"Well," Thomas said, "once was enough for me," and the others laughed the kind of understanding laugh of when shit goes sideways fast in a firefight. Thomas thought about pointing out that if you're sitting in the back seat on the left hand side of the vehicle, a right handed man shouldn't spin to the right to shoot out the back. Not only because you might smash the guy sitting next to you in the face, but because you're pointing the rifle at him and having it go off while bumping around in the back of a vehicle is possible. It's those little things that cascade into major failures under fire, and unlike Call of Duty, you don't get to respawn. "But mostly because there's a lot of gear here we're taking with us, so we don't need to be packed."

"Three vehicles for security, three in case one fails, three because one isn't enough, and three because it's still Thailand." Thomas ate the quiche; it was delicious. "Eat up, then we'll pack up."

Everyone listened and ate up.

Thomas rose and took his dishes over to Boonsri who would have some cleaning up to do. "Alright, when you're done grab some of the gear and load the trucks. The boxes have all the radio coms, sat phones, the night vision and thermals. Make sure you have your personal gear. There's storage on the roof too, but keep the pricey stuff inside. Again, it's still Thailand."

Everybody slowly finished and started packing, doing the grunt work.

The trucks were still being packed for the trip to the boat when Thomas' phone rang. Thomas answered the call as a car simultaneously appeared at the gate. "Hell Thomas, let an ole uncle in."

Thomas went inside and pushed the button. "Boonsri! Uncle's here, if you could get us a couple of bourbons?"

"With ice?" Boonsri asked.

"Naturally," Thomas replied.

Thomas walked to the entranceway as the Mercedes pulled right up to the front. Two smartly dressed men exited the car, looked around, and then one opened the back door. Uncle emerged. Whatever black hair he had once had given way to silver, and some of the barreled chest had moved south over the years, but he still moved as the man in charge wherever he was.

"Good morning Uncle, come on inside." Thomas extended his hand as a firm handshake was always required, and then the two men smiled. "I expected a call, but glad to see you."
"Problem with being able to call anytime from anywhere is people don't get together when they should," Uncle turned, "and it's been awhile."

"Please," Thomas waved him into the library, which Thomas rarely used for reading, but it was very private. He had the walls filled with sound deadening material, and there were two sets of insulated French doors. A white noise generator inside the room coupled with music piped at the windows playing Beethoven's Symphony no. 7 in A major op. 92, part II constantly prevented the possibility of outside eavesdropping from the outside. Plus, he liked the same song replaying while he worked. The background music made work less boring, and the repetitiveness meant it wasn't distracting,

Boonsri entered with the bourbon, Ben Millam, named after a freedom fighter who helped form Texas. "Thank you," Uncle said respectively as Boonsri hurried to leave the room. They got along, but she didn't like that Thomas and his uncle seemed to share secrets, and that made her worry for Thomas.

"Ice, Thomas? Why do you bastardize such good bourbon with ice?"

"Every warrior needs to win a battle, and I think Boonsri needs a little win around you," Thomas smiled.

Uncle laughed, "Fair enough, at least it's still just bourbon. So, the point of dropping by. First, I looked over the two missions. I have no problem with the first, it seems straightforward enough."
Uncle took a sip of the bourbon to thread the needle of his concerns. While legitimate, it was a personal matter, and he didn't want to overstep. "I have concerns over the second part."

"The second part has a number of moving parts, but they're all interrelated. But if you want Ciid Fiidka, it's the best way. The only place he ever goes out of his compound is the refugee camp. You can't drone strike a refugee camp, or should I say, even I won't help with that," Thomas explained.

"Relax Thomas, I wouldn't drone strike refugees either.

I might think about it, rationalize the value, but unless it's refugee camp for communists or Nazi's, it's a no go."

"Look. When he leaves, there's only one route, and that's great. I could execute the first part of the plan to prod him to go to the refugee camp, but he doesn't always go personally. He takes multiple vehicles, and they're garaged, so you don't know which of the vehicles he'd be in. You'd have to hit them all, but if he doesn't make the trip, you'll have missed. And he'll never venture out again." Thomas took a drink and waited, he knew the response.

"All good Thomas, except you could run the first part of the operation as planned, and a SEAL Team could wait for him to leave and then finish him off at the camp just the same. Why are you complicating it with you being the one to finish him? He hasn't hurt our family." Uncle finished realizing he could've phrased that better.

"C'mon. No, he hasn't hurt our family, directly, yet. But he's hurt people our "family" cared about. As it is, I'm likely to have put down pirates *our family* may have cared about, but as you say, I've rationalized it knowing it's the only way to actually solve the problem. The do-good fairy isn't going to solve this, and..." Thomas was about to go on, but Uncle raised his hand in surrender.

"I give, and sorry, that's not really what I meant. I meant I'd get it that you'd want to be the one to pull the trigger if the guy killed *your* cousin. That I'd get, and you'd never get a complaint from me about it. Just because we haven't spoken to him in years, remember who you're talking to." Uncle adjusted himself in his seat, unsettled at talking about it. "My point is, I don't see the personal need for you to be the one to pull the trigger. It seems as if you're adding a layer of complication that you don't need to add. Leave it to the SEALS, or whomever else may need to get wet."

"Look, I haven't talked to cuz' in a while either. But I know the area, I know the people. Starvation, disease, crime, gangs and institutionalized corruption. You're not going to be able to have a SEAL Team hang out without people noticing for too long, especially inside the camp. That information is worth money, and they know it. It's a refugee camp, it's packed. The only way to stop people from giving us up is if it's done with people they trust more than they fear, and there's only one guy there who can do that. Jeremy wouldn't turn the SEAL Team in...probably. But he sure wouldn't go to any effort to protect them over the refugees he's there to help. That's a risk he's not cut out to make. And if he's not putting himself on the line, the refugees sure as hell won't." Thomas hesitated to break some other news to Uncle about who would actually be helping him them at the camp, keep it simple.

"That's his home, that's his family. If I'm there, it changes the dynamic. He won't be happy, certainly not thrilled to see me, and he won't even condone what we're doing, even though it's the best thing for the stupid bastard in the long run. But he also won't risk exposing us to Ciid Fiidka, and his pressure on the refugees inside the camp may be the only thing that will curb the loose lips looking for a payday." Thomas sat back and took a deep breath. He knew what his uncle was worried about, the two of them in the same spot.

Resigned to Thomas, and his plan, Uncle decided to

take a slightly different tactic. "So I'm to believe you're going to leverage your connection to Jeremy to accomplish the mission?"

"No sir. You're to believe that I'm going to leverage my client's desires and funding, to accommodate your missions, to accomplish what I want, just as always," Thomas smiled. "And in this case, Jeremy not wanting me dead serves us all. As it will work out, and no matter how much he'll gripe about it, Jeremy won't stop it."

"I'm obviously concerned, especially because there's a lot of unknowns, and both of you two idiots are the few I want to keep around." Uncle paused to try to find a crack in the plan. "Your client is good with this side plan, won't it put your deal with him at risk. Does he even know about the second part?" Uncle asked.

"He doesn't know, no, and no. But he'll be on board afterwards in a big way, and..." Thomas was cut off.

"Will be? Why would you even tell him about it later?" Uncle asked like so many times before, and by so many clients. It didn't matter that Uncle was used to Thomas having an answer, it was just that he still had to hear it.

"Will be, because knowing after the fact he'll hope it'll make him a rich man. Well, a richer man." Thomas finished the bourbon, got up and grabbed the bottle.

Thomas walked over to top off his uncle's glass, but Uncle first deftly poured the remnants of his ice into Thomas' glass. "Neat please, you can have my ice. What else do you need?"

Thomas had a list, a short one, but it wasn't inconsequential. "Combined Task Force 150 operates in the Indian Ocean, into the Gulf of Aden and the Red Sea. I'll want their ships, routes, and contacts on board if we have to make a visit."

Combined Task Force 150 was a multi-national force of navies that operate to stop terrorism, drug smuggling, and yes, pirating. While many of the ships that rotate service were American, French & British, there were roughly fifteen different countries that did so, making "hey, call my uncle," less of an option.

"To avoid contact?" Uncle asked.

"That, and the wolves attack the herd where the sheepdog isn't. The bad guys must have spotters, and they're not going to hit us with even a French ship on the horizon," Thomas quipped. They laughed, but both knew it was an unfair joke. The French soldiers they both met abroad had as much grit as anyone. They were exceptionally well trained, but often less well equipped.

"You know the Arabian Sea is CTF 152, and that's a little more problematic. There's a lot more eyes in that area, and not all friendly," Uncle wisely pointed out.

"Yeah thought about it, and we'll really be keeping out of that area as best we can. We may have to stop in Oman, but we'll swing up from the South to limit contact there. I'll save that war for another day," Thomas said, referring to the Iranians and their various exports of terror.

"That's it, just good guy travel plans?" Uncle asked.

"That, and phone number and code for an exfil, if it

comes to that." Thomas looked away, a little embarrassed asking for help even though it was part of the deal.

"Exfil? You expecting to need helicopters flying into the refugee camp?" Uncle asked.

"Expecting, no. But the second part of this will be hot on several fronts. I'll have to split my team at best, and that's assuming they all come. And getting them all to come is a lot easier if they have a get out of Somalia free card. Knowing they have US forces that'll send a chopper to get them out of a hot mess makes it easier to wade in, *dumb* as that may sound. Ergo, not just a number, a number and a code. They need to know if they make the call, it's not just me that people are willing to come get." Thomas finished the rest of the bourbon.

"One more thing I may need," Thomas asked. "If we can't avoid being searched by CTF 150, be prepared to make a call for us."

"To search you, with the armed trucks onboard? Are you nuts?" Uncle was more than aghast.

"Ah, that's the rub," Thomas said wryly. "We need to maintain that we're the sheep....*and not the wolf.*"

"Got it," Uncle said with a smile. "I'll get the intel together on CTF 150 and I'll arrange the exfil code, and I'll send everything over to Robert. I'll look into who I can trust on the search part if there are no American boats in the area. Then it's not just the boat, it's down to what officer I trust, er uh, bribe...trust to bribe." Uncle lowered his head and spoke with a bit more seriousness. "Thomas, having a phone number and a code isn't the same as having a helicopter. The more you're avoiding CTF 150, the fewer assets that are in the area. There may be civilian assets available, but sending them into a hot LZ may not be an option, and that's not including the obvious that a civilian pilot will bail at the first tracer round."

"I know. I'll try to keep them close when we have to go ashore." Thomas said, acknowledging the difficulties in coordinating a lot of things that can't be coordinated.

"Relax, let me know when you're going ashore, and I'll be sure they'll be in the area. I'll send them a goose to chase. Never a problem." Uncle finished his bourbon and stood. "I wish I could stay longer. Heck, I wish you could stay longer. But I know you're heading to the boat, and I'm heading to Dubai."

Uncle put his hand out with a smile, "May the road rise up to meet you."
"May the wind be ever at your back," Thomas replied. It was a favorite Irish poem that Uncle would often quote to other men, and Thomas adopted it when younger, though it made Uncle uneasy at first, and he didn't know why. It made him feel older at the time when everyone around him was older, and as he became a young man it made him feel more personally connected to a man who was hard to become really close to. It was like a secret handshake. The poem was short and sweet, but it wasn't until he was actually older that he realized Uncle said it, or parts of it to men going into harm's way.

*May the road rise up to meet you.*
*May the wind be always at your back.*

*May the sun shine warm upon your face; the rains fall soft upon your fields and until we meet again, may God hold you in the palm of His hand.*

It had a different meaning now than it did when he first heard it as a child.

Uncle felt better about Thomas's plan, and Thomas had the other parts he wanted and hopefully never needed. He never had to call for an emergency exfil, and there were times it just wasn't logistically possible. But he really needed to have it for the men who he'd be asking to stick their necks out on a mission that was more than they'd signed up for.

Max approached as the two were about to part.

"Tommy, take care of yourself," Uncle said as he turned. "Max, sorry we don't have time to talk and bend an elbow. Take care of him."

Max waved and nodded to Uncle as he left. He knew the man, and knew the deal. While they talked when required, and quite amicably every time, it was understood that Thomas was the conduit. The bending of an elbow happened, but it was infrequent.

Thomas had gone through boot camp like every other boot, but when he came out, he immediately went to work with Uncle.  He both served with other military units when needed, and led them. Sometimes he "consulted," providing a plan or crucial intel that nobody else seemed to have. There were a number of operators under Uncle, and they often worked as a team. But the relationship Thomas had with Uncle was unique. Not only was he in the military, but he was apart, separate from any chain of command. While he couldn't give orders to Generals, Uncle could, and did. But those kind of orders rarely had to be given. Take the time to explain the best course of action in an undeniable fashion, outline that they get all the credit, with no responsibility for the failure, and everyone seems to follow, no matter the rank.

But years later, they concluded that there was so much more they could accomplish. The deal was simple. Thomas left "service," which was wholly within the authority of the CIA to begin with, along with every other acronym'd entity with which Uncle was connected. He opened his own security company, which was well funded. The missions were his own, and within his own purview to accept and execute. But where American interests could be fulfilled in parallel, or intertwined with the private work Thomas provided, they would be done in earnest. In this way Uncle provided information en masse to Thomas, but that included mission objectives as well.

This enabled Thomas to identify clients who had big problems with the "wrong" people. He'd be able to use the client as a legitimate cover, as he'd always fulfill their objective. But he was also able to glean information from private companies that may never say a word to any government agency. It didn't take long to build a network of clients and sources of information. Thomas didn't raise suspicions of this arrangement. Thomas didn't do freebies, favors or giveaways. If a company needed to recover their stolen proprietary information, they had to pay. By the same token, when he gave information to Uncle, they'd be sure to act on it in a way that would never blow back on Thomas. That arrangement took a lot of trust, and that trust had an origin.

Thomas grew up in the work after his father passed away when Thomas was only eleven. His father worked for Uncle in many different ways, although his was more an academic career than in the field. His father was an expert in international economic politics, a field where the honest "experts" would tell you there's no such thing as an expert. The reality is so fluid that anything could apply, and so much of the field may entail the legal, the illegal, and the yet to be recognized macroeconomic effect.

Thomas once explained it with a story his father told him. "There is a black market for cheese," he'd say. "Not because cheese can't be bought anywhere, at any time, but it's there nonetheless. Small pizza places are audited often, and they're a cash business, so the IRS can tell how many pizzas you sold based on the ingredients you bought. Cheese accounts for 50% or more of their total wholesale costs. So if they know how many pizzas you made, they know how much money you took in. So. If you're XXX Pizza, you buy a $300 box of stolen cheese for $150, not only did you cut your costs, but you cut the taxes that must be paid on your total cost. The very method of chasing tax cheats creates the pressure point where they cheat to avoid taxes. Cheese."

He'd describe, in great boring detail, that this reality incentivizes thousands of pizza places to act in the same way and a need for black market cheese is created. Now think about pizza places as different countries and there's thousands of issues and all those issues involve money. They all have their own interests and ideologies, and what do you have? A mess. A mess, and a lot of motives and ways that money can be weaponized for countries to use in different ways.

Thomas's father was apparently brilliant at following the money, and seeing the micro that created the macro. That brilliance led him to make a connection between an oil deal and a terrorist group. It wasn't a huge deal, it wasn't Bin Laden. Just money that was going to a group that was found to have terrorist ties. But he asked a question to the wrong guy, word got around at the speed of light, and he was killed for it. Killing him was senseless – the information he gathered was already known – but bad guys aren't always judicious in the use of violence when trying to save themselves. Killing Thomas' father brought the house down on themselves, but that was little solace to the eleven year old boy made an orphan. He lost his mother, too, at the age of four, and struggled to remember her.

With no other family, Uncle raised him, and Max knew that despite the "work" connection, they were close, and he did like knowing that the work arrangement involved a guy who cared.

"Tommy?" Max asked, never hearing his Uncle call him that before. "All good with your Uncle?

"Alles gut," Thomas answered, though more wondering aloud. "Are we ready to roll to the boat?"

"*Alles gut* Tommy," Max said with a wink.

"Never again Max. Grab the keys." Thomas grabbed a coffee for the road. He was going to have to navigate a lot more than Thai roads later in the mission, and he was thinking about how honest he should be with Max and when. It was going to have to wait until they were committed.

The trip to the boat was uneventful. Lee's assistant Jiang was even waiting at the entrance to the shipyard to make sure there wouldn't be any problems connecting with the captain. Jiang walked the group of men briskly to the boat

"Mr. Thomas, I've had the boat renamed as you asked, and I arranged a few additional delivery "orders" in the area," Jiang said wryly. "They're for humanitarian agencies that appreciated a lower price in exchange for a fluid delivery date."

"Fafnir?" Max asked.

"It's a Nordic boat deserving of a Nordic Name. Fafnir was a dwarf who became a dragon," Thomas said boastfully.

"Yes, Thomas, I'm familiar with the mythology. But after Fafnir was turned into a dragon, he became consumed by greed, wreaked terror upon man, woman and child, and was then slain," Max pointed out. "You didn't apparently stick around for the rest of the story."

"There's always more to any story. The important take-away is it started out as a dwarf and became a dragon." Thomas said defensively. "Besides, it's the name of the boat, not us."

"Oh, well yeah then that makes all the difference. If the boat is slain on the high seas, I'm sure we'll still be fine," Max said sarcastically.

"Should I look into changing the name of the boat?" Jiang asked worriedly.

"God no, we don't have time for that Jiang. And the two of you. The name of the boat isn't for our benefit, but theirs," Thomas explained. "It's what they get for attacking a dragon."

"C'mon Thomas, you think the pirates are going to be aware of Nordic mythology? Surely they won't be put off by the name of the boat," Max asked.

Thomas looked at Max assuredly. "Dragons breath fire Max. It's symbolic."

"Ya, there's that." Max conceded.

Jiang still wasn't quite sure about the name, and wasn't aware of the significance .

"The name is fine Jiang, just get us to the captain," Thomas said.

"Of course," Jiang said, "you can see the boat is moored at the far end."

"The far end? You couldn't find a golf cart to drive us?" Max asked.

"Well I could see…" Jiang started to say.

"Forget it Jiang, he's kidding." Thomas said.

"I'm not kidding," Max said emphatically, "a golf cart would've been a perfectly nice way to navigate the docks."

"For God's sake Max, let it go. You didn't get the free golf cart with the electric car tax rebate when you could have. Just let it go already." Thomas was thinking about a couple weeks on the boat with Max's non-stop beef du jour.

"Well I was in Kandahar and couldn't take it then," Max said.

"Yeah, and you didn't have your American citizenship then either, an important part of the equation," Thomas said, taking the bait to argue.

"My point exactly. They ended the tax credit before I could take advantage of it," Max gleefully pointed out.

"Still sounds like you were just looking forward to take advantage of the American taxpayer," Thomas said as a crewman of the Fafnir rang the bell as they boarded. "Saved by the bell," he cut Max off.

“We’re here to see the captain,” Thomas said.

The crewman walked the group to the captain who met them on the bridge, which was six stories up. No elevator.

The cranes were actively loading containers, delicately placing them about the deck. The hold was mostly full, plenty of room if they needed to put the vehicles below deck. Thomas had given specific instructions on how the containers were to be placed before leaving port. Instead of the logical pattern of saving space, it left areas in the middle open. This wasn’t just so they could easily run across the deck on the sides from either end without risking falling overboard, but to create an inviting entry to any unwanted guests.

But that arrangement was partially covered with containers until they left port. The arrangement would have been so unlikely to the experts in port that it would have drawn unwanted attention. Despite the fact that nobody would've known why they arranged unusually, Thomas did not believe in underestimating anyone, especially chance. 'Fortune favors the prepared mind' is a saying for a reason, and the winners get to create the sayings. A casual observer would say that surely Somali pirates weren't receiving intel from Thai dock workers, but there was actually no way to know that. In fact, Thailand had a lot of immigrant workers and Somali refugees were often persecuted and taken advantage of in a variety of work. So if a Somali could make a few Bahts for phoning home, why wouldn't they? Never give the unknown a chance to kill you.

Captain Zhao had a big smile. He was a small man, but of big stature. He smiled and opened his arms at Thomas and the men as if they were family returning home. "Welcome gentlemen to my home, and my home is your home," Zhao said, putting his hands together as if about to pray. "I assure you the men on *this* ship..."

Max wanted to laugh at Thomas, but Thomas's glare waved him off.

"are very loyal to me, and even more so to Mr. Lee. If you need anything, you have but to ask." Zhao looked around at the men as if sizing them up, quickly realizing that Jiang was right. It would be a cruise to remember.

"This is a good, well made ship, and I have had the men follow your instructions," Zhao said with pride.

Robert half stumbled in carrying several hard Pelican cases filled with communications gear. "No that's alright guys, I got it, don't bother to lend a hand," he said, but only a quarter joking.

"Sorry 'bout that Robert," Thomas said turning to Captain Zhao, "is there an adjacent room to the bridge where we can set up some communications gear? It needs to be a secure area, from most everyone."

"Of course, my room right behind here. Very secure," Zhao said as he pointed the way.

"Thank you Captain, I'm going to walk the ship to familiarize myself and my men will need someone to accompany them to go over the work that needs to be done until we meet up later." Thomas said.

"Of course, of course. Please, have your men meet them below on deck, right outside of the tower. I'll have the workers meet them there," Captain Zhao said smiling all the while.

Thomas nodded to Siegfried. "Siegfried here needs to look over the fire system you've installed so far. So please have your man that's familiar with the system meet with him."

"Oh, yes of course, Mr....." Zhao asked hoping for his last name as he felt uncomfortable with addressing others he just met with their first name.

"Siegfried is my last name, it's cool to go by that."

"Sorry, *Mr. Siegfried.* Special piping, very smart. Ayden,

you go with them." Zhao waived to one of his men.

Thomas extended his hand, which Captain Zhao grabbed and shook enthusiastically like a car salesman who just unloaded a Pinto at full price. Robert went with Zhao into his room to set up the communications gear while Thomas & Max went to walk through the boat.

Siegfried split off with Ayden, who hailed from Singapore. Ayden's first job was with Lee's shipping company, getting the opportunity solely because his father worked on the docks for Lee. There were a lot of men like Ayden working for Lee Shipping, second generation employees who owed their work to their father's good name. That meant there was a real effort not to embarrass their father, and that work ethic breeds loyalty to the company. This relationship was not lost on Lee, it's long been a way to have employees tied to the company, by their own work ethic not to shame their parents. While most workers wouldn't get rich in his company, he rewarded that good loyal work with a good pay. Loyalty and good pay in the world of logistics is a symbiotic relationship that really pays for the company.

"So, uh Ayden?" Siegfried asked.

"Yes Mr. Siegfried, I followed your instructions on installing the piping, but the final instructions for connections weren't provided, so I couldn't finish," Ayden replied, somewhat apologizing for a task he wasn't yet given.

"No, no Ayden, all's good." Siegfried said with a wave showing he wasn't expected to have finished. "Let's start on deck, show me what you've done and work backwards from there OK?"

"Yes Mr. Siegfried, this way." Ayden led Siegfried back down the stairs on the tower that led to the bridge and onto the deck. He waved for Siegfried to wait as a second, and handed him a hard hat and a vest. "Always wear a yellow vest on the deck, and a hard hat, especially while the cranes are loading the containers." Ayden pointed up to a container being swung from the docks and placed on the far end of the deck."

"Well I get the yellow vest, but what good is the hard hat going to do if they drop a container on it?" Siegfried asked.

"Oh, no good, you'd be crushed. But the hard hat is white, so it helps the crane operator see you." Ayden replied quite honestly.

"Well then I should be able to just wear a white baseball cap?" Siegfried wondered.

"Some men do that, but the seas are windy, and baseball caps blow away. Think of it as "heavy won't blow away not get crushed hat,"" Ayden said jokingly.

Siegfried laughed and put it on, "well at least 'til we're at sea."

Ayden walked Siegfried over to the piping on the deck. The piping was installed tightly against the structure to avoid being damaged by the movement of containers. The sprinkler heads were angled 45 degrees upwards towards the interior of the ship, and while the sprinkler heads were installed in a series along one pipe, another pipe was run in parallel. In this way, if damaged, at one place, it would still operate to some degree. Like Christmas lights, one bad bulb may kill a part, but not the entire strand. And Ayden had the wiring installed all along the pipes as well, just as diagrammed.

"The wiring is finished to the deck below," Siegfried asked.

"Just as instructed," Ayden replied. "Sorry, I should have shown you the controls first."

"No, not a problem," Siegfried said, "I wanted to get a feel for the deck install first, there's plenty of time for me to see the controls."

Ayden then walked him to smaller pumps at the end of the decking where the pressure would be needed to help lift from the deck below. All good. Ayden walked him down to the larger pumps in a hold on the lower deck.

"There are eight pumps, two on each zone, as instructed," Ayden replied, pointing at his work.

"Have you tested the pumps?" Siegfried asked.

"Oh yes," Ayden said, taking pride in his work, "only two of them are new, but the others are all in fine shape. They were tested before they were brought on board, and after everything was connected to make sure we had the pressure adjusted properly for the heads."

Siegfried smiled while nodding his head, showing his gratitude and approval.

"Now what do you want me to do to complete it," Ayden asked.

"Nothing." Siegfried said as Ayden's face frowned, not understanding.

Siegfried looked around and saw the two vehicles Thomas talked about, along with the other gear and materials he needed. The other men on the team were all addressing securing the boat and setting up their own areas of responsibilities to prepare for the mission. This one was his, and Siegfried was very pleased with himself. Horrifying if it came down to it, but still pleased.

"Nothing until I'm back on board. It's all perfect." Siegfried smiled and waved to the man who did all the hard work. "Let's go grab a coffee and take a look at the controls."

"Sure thing Mr. Siegfried," Ayden said, still not grasping what he actually built

◆ ◆ ◆

The men worked on their respective areas throughout the day.

Robert set up communications gear in the room Captain Zhao specified. That gear allowed the bridge to communicate with all of the operatives and them with each other. It also allowed Thomas to communicate with Uncle via computer or the satellite phone.

Besides that, Robert linked the cameras on deck to a local cloud that all of the operatives could access independently. Plus, he was having Zhao's men place thermal cameras as well. While there were a couple covering the deck of the ship, which would show people on deck, the main reason was to have several aimed at the sea. Boats give off heat, and can be easily picked up at night on colder waters. The thermal cameras would provide great long distance early warning anybody approaching. Robert followed the axiom of a drill instructor "wearing a Depends is better than pissing yourself without." This of course was actually in reference to a Marine who chose to piss himself rather than ask for a break to use the head at the wrong time. The point the DI made wasn't that he shouldn't have pissed himself, but that he should have planned for that eventuality, no matter how unpleasant or hopefully unnecessary it may be. DI axioms don't always translate well, but they are often memorable, which is apparently the point.

The two snipers were setting up their hides, both with a lot of similar material. Sandbags were all around, with a steel plate in the middle for extra protection, plus a spotting scope for distance at sea and a low slung lounge chair for maximum comfiness. Tony Bennett had the benefit of setting up his .50 cal Barrett m82A1 on top of the tower of the boat. The only downside was that the increased elevation was another factor in calculating long range shots. The big advantage was he didn't have to plan a route to flee to if the boat was boarded, the tower was it. Of course, the top of the tower didn't leave a lot of options if the tower was compromised. He had a rope to rappel down if necessary, but if it came to that, he'd be at the end of his rope. It would mean the bridge was in the hands of the pirates, and if they had the bridge, they'd almost certainly had the deck. While there were inflatable escape rafts strewn about the boat, those would hardly fare well against pirates. Basically a yellow balloon in the middle of the ocean isn't much of an escape. His advantage was that he was on the top of the tower, a totally defensible position, and the .50 would prevent anyone from getting on top with him. He'd have to be in a tough spot to ever leave under fire, that was his plan.

Meanwhile, James Abernathy was on the bow of the boat with his .338 Lapua Magnum. Abernathy also had a Barrett rifle, hard to compete with the success and proven reliability of the weapon used by the US military for so long. However, Abernathy preferred the newer M107a1 model, and enjoyed the tweaks for accuracy. His weapon used a Proof Research barrel, a seemingly odd name for a barrel company. But their barrels live up to the research part. They're turned down to remove much of the steel that would normally remain on a regular barrel needed to give it the rigidity needed for long range performance. Then, in place of that steel, the barrel is wrapped in a space age carbon fiber, giving it far superior rigidity than the steel it replaced. The added advantage that the barrel dissipates heat much faster than normal, allowing it to stay in the fight that much longer, especially when using a suppressor, which Abernathy preferred. Even better is that it now also weighs about thirty-five percent less. Losing a couple of pounds may not seem like much, but on a big rifle like the Barrett that weighs over 30 pounds with optics, it makes a difference, especially since he may have to run the length of the boat, and then every pound counts. He hand wrapped the grip to make sure his hand found the same spot every time. He even added a small finger guard to help firm hand placement on the handrail. Accuracy of a gun is key to be sure, but it means little if the shooter doesn't do his job. And a key to accuracy isn't all about the "right or wrong" way of shooting, but that it's consistent. Everything from hand placement, cheek placement on the stock, trigger pull, etc, it all adds up to putting the round in the same spot each time.

Unlike Bennett, Abernathy had to plan on making it to the tower if the boat was boarded. From the bow, he had a path on either side of the deck. The problem with those routes was that they'd also be in full view of the water, the very direction the pirates would be coming from. And once committed to either side, you're committed. There's no getting to the middle of the deck from the sides of the boat . So even if the attack came from starboard, a run to the port side was appealing right up until a boat appeared on port. To address that, Thomas had arranged a route up the middle of the deck, hence part of the precious placement of containers. Even the up the middle route had a little zig zag in it to give him cover if he was pursued.

The containers made for providing excellent protection. Each 40 foot container weighed 8,000 pounds on its own, and was made of steel. While most rifle rounds would penetrate both sides of a container, some handgun and shotgun rounds are often stopped after just one. But the containers aren't empty, they're each filled with 20 pallets of rice. Each pallet has forty 50 pound bags. That's 40,000 pounds of rice stacked from floor to ceiling in each container, and there were a number of containers stacked up on either side of the path up the middle. Even an RPG hit to the exposed area wouldn't penetrate all of that, or even move all that weight. The interlocked design gave them Lego like strength.

It was a lot of planning and preparation to lay out the path for his possible retreat, and he appreciated that level of detail and effort by Thomas. It always made jobs with Thomas more appealing. The inherent level of risk that's always there no matter how thoughtfully planned never really seemed to be real.

Abernathy also had a comfy lounge chair, which seemed to make the prospect of work seem less so.

While Abernathy, Bennet, Siegfried and Robert all had specific duties, Nguyen, Marks and Atkins walked the deck round and round with workers on the boat. They pointed to where additional steel plates had to be welded into place, where ropes should be tied, where additional fire extinguishers should be placed, and sand bags piled to create interior defensive positions if needed. Much of the work was already started, getting a virtual walkthrough made that possible. But while Google maps is handy to get an idea of a neighborhood, being there is the only way to truly appreciate the sightlines, the topography, the time it takes to get from A to B. Their work was to make sure they had good defenses to repel possible boarding, and to know the quickest and safest ways to get to the Tower if needed. All the extra hands made the work go faster, but even for a small container ship compared to the full sized ones, it was a big boat.

As the sun was setting on the day, so were their tasks. While a few things would remain for when they boarded the ship in the Seychelles, the workers would have had ten days to place the steel plate and make all the welds. That and the sand bags were the most time consuming. *Better them than us,* they all thought.

Robert tested the coms with everyone on station, walking around the deck and below, and everything checked. Repeaters were placed throughout the boat done to make sure of that. Thomas called them all to gather at the base of the tower.

Captain Zhao approached Thomas as the men gathered, followed by two men carrying a large cooler – filled with ice and Phuket brand beer per Thomas's request – and placed it at the bottom of the tower. While it was a common, well respected Thai beer, he was not above the infantile jokes it would enable. Thomas grabbed a beer and passed them all around. "After a hard day's work, Phuket," he smiled. "Here, here," they all laughed at the ridiculously poor pun.

"Take a break, drink up, if you think of anything

else you need or want done, tell Captain Zhao here," Thomas pointed at the man with the giant smile. "Otherwise we'll be able to pass it along before we join the boat later on." Thomas raised the beer to them all and walked off with Max and Robert.

"So Max, are we forgetting anything?" Thomas asked.

Max shook his head, "Very little, I think. I love the boat, it's perfect for us. The containers make it like toy building blocks, molded to our needs. We can conceal ourselves easily, it will be an inviting target..." Max's mind wandered off for a second, thinking about the heavily armed trucks Thomas included. Total overkill he thought, but far better to have it and not need it than the other way around. "Besides, we'll have over a week of Seychelles rum to think of anything else. Plus, we can call Robert Hood here if we need a hand."

Robert clinked Max's beer with his own "ausgezeichnet" (excellent). "Once they've had their fill, collect them all we'll head home for the night. The flight isn't until 10:10 tomorrow morning, but we have a layover, and it'll be a long day."

"Couldn't have booked a private flight you cheap bastard?" Max joked.

"Could've. But we have the time," Thomas replied.

# CHAPTER X

## *Seychelles Rum*

The flight to the Seychelles was long – flying to places in the middle of the ocean usually are – but it was totally worth it. They were staying at the Kempinski Resort, with excellent food, immediate access to a long excellent beach, and a variety of private areas for them to gather throughout their stay. Plus, it was isolated from the rest of the island, so there weren't a lot of distractions, save those staying there.

The Seychelles is known as "The Land of Perpetual Summer," which is never a bad thing. The resort faced the long open beach but was also surrounded by lush green mountains, remnants of the volcano that created the island long ago. The island was a joy to visit on any occasion. It's natural isolation of distance from anything provides the added benefit of avoiding the overpopulated traffic of tourism that has afflicted so many other previously wonderful places.

The point of having them all stay together for the week in Seychelles wasn't just to avoid extra time on the boat, though that was a good reason all by its lonesome. Keeping everyone fresh and focused with long hot days isn't the easiest to begin with. Even when mild, the humidity in tropical areas wears on people, and tempers shorten. Avoiding 10 extra days of type A grumpy guys in close quarters before even starting the mission seemed like a no brainer. Plus, some of them had worked together before, others had not. It was always good to get to know the guy you're trusting with your life before running into a mess.

Thomas figured they'd drink a bit of Seychelles rum, shoot the shit, tell stories, run in the morning, and fatten up at night. They'd have time to argue out any questions on responsibilities and engagement before it mattered.

Plus, Lee was footing the bill for the time. Soft time paid the same, so it was good for them all around.

Their plane touched down a few minutes early, offset by the wait to get their luggage; their gear was already on the boat. A shuttle bus was sent by the hotel for their arrival, and they didn't have to share the ride with any other tourists.

"Alright everybody, listen up," Thomas asked. "Tomorrow morning, get up, have breakfast wherever you like, then plan on meeting at 11:00 am. I have a private area reserved for us in the Café Lazare right here at the resort. Now that you've seen the boat and have a better feel for what the set up is, I want to give you a bit more details on what to expect."

Everybody wearily nodded; it's amazing how tiring 15 hours of doing nothing can be.

"Max, I'd like you to join me for breakfast, however. Buzz me when you're up," Thomas said.

Max smiled. “Great, you’re so much fun in the morning.”

The morning came faster than desired. Max buzzed and said he was on his way to the café. There was no way Max was going to be up after Thomas and then listen to Thomas bust on him for sleeping in. Thomas realized he should have just set a time, as he could have used the hours to sleep a bit more. Thomas hustled and figured he could skip the shave.

“Kaffe please,” Max said as soon as the waitress was in sight and Thomas raised a peace sign indicating the same.

“Came a little early. I still hate long flights,” Thomas said, equally desperate for the first cup.

“So the meeting today, any highlights?” Max queried.

“Given the nature of expected targets, and what we’re asking of the men, I felt it would help to give them a brief on the head honcho leading the other team,” Thomas replied cryptically enough. They weren’t around anyone, but the area wasn’t swept as it would be later.

“Head honcho?” Max asked. “There’s just one?”

“Always more than one,” Thomas laughed, “but there’s one that’s been almost exclusively involved with our client’s ships”

“Ships?” Max laughed. “I haven’t heard that word in a while.”

“Fuck you, Max. I love calling our boat “the boat,” and

you're not ruining this for me. And shut up, here comes our coffee," Thomas said, pointing to the waitress.

"Thank you miss," Thomas said politely.

"Thank you so much, you're a life saver," Max said with a big smile. The girl turned and smiled back as she walked away.

"You see that," Max said eagerly.

"Oh yeah, a beautiful young Asian girl who has a tourist flirting with her politely smiles back hoping for a bigger tip. Shocking," Thomas opined.

"Hey, you want to say 'das boot' for your pleasures, indulge me mine," Max snapped.

"Fair enough," Thomas said apologetically, "is the marriage to Ute off?"

"Not fair Thomas, I didn't do anything. I just smiled and observed her smiling back. What's wrong with that?" Max said a hair defensively.

Thomas sat up, leaning on his elbows about to impart wisdom upon his friend. "Ah. The ole 'I didn't do anything' defense. You're not blind, so obviously you will see beautiful women once married. That said, confessing to that observation once married may not be the best idea, and taking pride in the response, Max? How'd you get engaged with that kind of blindness to dealing with the female species?"

"I'm awesome, I have a nice flat, and she loves me…obviously," Max said exuding pride in himself. "Und du?

Thomas had been dating a lovely girl named Molly in

DC. She was in the financial sector in DC that handles complex financing that typically involved companies who had government contracts. New York may have the Stock Exchange, but the biggest spender in the country is the US Government. The biggest money-makers in the Gold Rush weren't just the few that hit it big finding the mother lode, it was the guy that sold the shovels to all the losers. Fund businesses with upfront cash covered with the payment guaranteed by the US government, minus the commensurate percentage for making the loan, and you have a well-paying profession. Molly was a good fit for him, in both personality and dating style. She wasn't in government or politics per se, despite the vast political connections of her work. She wasn't military or connected to the intelligence community. But stories from both their work overlapped, and while many of her contacts had the appeal of being desirable to Thomas, he shied away from trying to make any of that happen, which she appreciated. Nevertheless, she mentioned his name to several of her clients during their time together without ever telling him she did so.

Yet their dating was a bit flat of late. He knew he was coming up on a time where he had to make a decision on whether to tell her more about his work before getting a lot more serious. He couldn't marry her and then tell her, "oh by the way...." and hope for the best. And too soon? He couldn't tell her too much until he trusted her to bite her tongue if they split. While it was not a crossing the Rubicon moment, it was close.

During the height of the Roman Empire, for a Roman commander to enter Rome itself at the head of his Legion, the penalty for him was death, and the same for all those that followed him, no matter how many thousands that may be.

When Julius Caesar, then the Governor of Gaul, crossed the Rubicon River at the head of his Legion, there was no going back, hence the creation of the phrase. But what would you call it when Caesar first talked to his Tribunes about entering Rome to try and overthrow the Republic? The die was not cast with that conversation, but the conversation couldn't be taken back. Thomas imagined the trust Caesar must've had in the Tribunes that served under him and the faith they had in Caesar. This wasn't that, but Thomas didn't want to screw it up just the same. Uncle of course was zero help: "don't tell her anything, simple" was his advice. It was 1950's advice and yet Thomas had little better for Max.

"Given our uh, work, have you talked to her about security needs of potential blowback, however, unlikely?" Thomas asked.

"Romantic to the last aren't you?" Max quipped. "But yeah I had Robert talk to her. Since he's the one cleaning up her social media and giving advice on metadata, I figured let the smoother talker smooth it over."

"You had Robert break all that to her, sounds like you cheated," Thomas said.

"I would say that I was Sun Tsu smart to avoid conflict. We're all not as good as you at planning, but I can pass the Deutsche Mark with the best of them," Max said.

"It's pass the buck, that's the phrase. You don't get to substitute Deutsche Mark for a turn of a phrase,"

Thomas admonished.

“Said the guy with a “Boat” obsession,” Max joked, “the women will have to wait a bit.”

“I’m happy for you,” Thomas said. But for his own, he would have to wait for now. He’d think about it after all of this was over.

They later gathered again in the same Café, but in a sectioned off area away from the rest of the crowd, not that there was one. Most of those staying at the resort were out and about the island; those that weren’t were down by the beach. Trays were placed on a table so the men could serve themselves buffet style, there would be no servers during their meeting. Kim Nguyen arrived early, not out of being the most punctual, but to sweep their area for any bugs. Not that there should be any, but maintaining operational security from start to finish eliminates a lot of worries. The men wandered in and engaged in meaningless small talk to pass the time. Nguyen wasn’t finding anything but wanted to set up a short-range jammer.

“Here boss,” Nguyen handed the device to Thomas. It resembled a walkie-talkie, but with extra antennas. “If you could set this up for me.”

Thomas looked at the device. “How do I set it up?”

“You turn it on and place it in the middle of where you’re going to talk,” Nguyen winked. “You got this.”

Thomas shook his head and smiled. A sense of humor, everybody had to have one.

It would only affect a radius of about 50 feet, so none

of the tourists would be wondering what happened to their cell phone, but their little area would be transmission free.

"All clear boss," Nguyen simply said.

"Alright people, grab your food, grab a chair and listen up," Thomas said, finishing his own plate giving the men a moment to settle in.

Thomas stood and took a deep breath. "I know we covered the basic rules of engagement earlier, but I wanted to go over it in greater detail, and especially more about the main bad guy."

"Main bad guy?" Francis Marks asked.

"Yeah, main bad guy," Thomas responded. "The intel we've been able to obtain indicates that almost all of the pirates targeting our client's ships are from one group led by Ciid Fiidka. He's a Somali "warlord," for lack of a better title. His crews appear to have good information on who to target beforehand. While it could be tips from crews, there was no pattern found to indicate that as the source. We think they may use drones from small boats at a distance, look for vulnerabilities, lack of armed guards obviously, lack of lookouts, ease of boarding, etc. That's why our defenses have to hide all that. Abernathy and Bennett, your lounge chairs are great, but you're going to need a low slung tarp to keep it hidden."

Thomas took another deep breath. "But back to Fiidka, the main bad guy. He's not just leading pirates, he's not just a drug dealer, arms trader, thief, crook, etc., he's responsible for political assassination, corruption and bribery, and even human trafficking. But even worse, he's a pedophile that uses aid camps to cull children for his own use." As the men all squirmed a little in their chair, Thomas paused to let all that sink in.

"So. When I'm asking you to put down the pirates, I'm not just doing so to send a message to stop theft at the high seas for a billionaire. I don't want you to waste any empathy for this gang. More to the point, the more that this gang led by Fiidka is degraded on the sea, the more he's degraded elsewhere. To serve our client's interests, we're going to pick off their spotters and pick off their attackers. This will leave him with three basic choices. The first is he keeps sending out elements the way he has, hopes for the best, and just keeps refilling the ranks when they don't come back. This goes to the "enroll pirates, lose pirates," repeat model. This would be the smarter thing to do for him if he was just a pirate. He has no personal connection to them, and their loss doesn't diminish him so long as he can keep replacing them. It's not like there's a Mogadishu News alert on pirate death, there are always job openings. Given the control issues he has personally, all of the other parts of the business, and his intertwined corruption politically, he will likely feel that he can't lose face, or lose elsewhere," Thomas said, starting to pace about.

"The second option is that he takes a break from piracy. He stops sending out elements, puts those assets into other endeavors. You can't lose if you don't play. This may weaken his overall business, but he could justify taking the breather with the thought of laying low and starting up months, or a year from now." Thomas looked around and shook his head. "Yeah, I don't buy that one either. Money and power are as addictive as heroin. This guy isn't just giving up on such a big revenue stream. And it's not just the money. Being THE guy who attacks foreign ships is part of what puts real fear into his rivals. Being the guy that bails is what gets you killed by the competition, or it may embolden a subordinate who now sees you as weak. I don't see a pedophile pirate warlord just giving up and willing to look weak," Thomas finished just shaking his head.

"No. This isn't a guy to de-escalate when the only risk would appear to be to his pirates. Why throw them away piecemeal not knowing what's happening? The fact is he has a lot to lose with his other endeavors, so he'll want to know. After taking a lot of hits, why keep doing the same losing thing? That's literally the definition of insanity, and even the criminally insane aren't totally stupid. No. If we cause him enough losses, I see Fiidka sending out a large force looking to either make whoever is killing his guy's pay, which from his point of view could be a competitor or a boat like ours with armed guards. Well, not a boat like ours, but you get the idea. If it's some naval force, he wouldn't plan on engaging them, but then he'd at least know. Not knowing will bother him, a lot. He'll assume that by sending a large group, whether they're successful or not, they will be able to determine what's happening and report it back to him at the very least. At best, that large group will kill the competition, or take a boat. And if that boat was killing his men. Oh boy, will he make them pay, so you know his instructions to his men will be..." Thomas looked around the room, "...which is why we're preparing for the worst-case scenario. Our goal is to take out the pirates, by looking like a target, that doesn't look anything like a threat."

"Here's a packet of information about Fiidka, including some pictures. Look at it, pass it around, and get it back to me before we're done with lunch." Thomas looked about the trays and the smoked barbecue pork was making his mouth water. "We're here for over a week. Run, stay in shape, but eat well and get plenty of rest. We're going to meet every day to talk over scenarios and the planned responses. It'll be boring, but I want the repetition to sink in. Feel free to do the same if you're just hanging out otherwise, but no 'shooting the pirate in the head' quips. Don't talk within earshot of any of the guests. Let's not ruin the guests' stay."

"Now, if you have any questions," Thomas waved his hand as if to stop, "let me eat first."

The week passed on Seychelles quicker than they all would have liked. Each day the men met, and Thomas would go through the on-duty schedule, reviewing the varying routes to be taken on the boat, and even the different methods of scanning the waters. After only 15 seconds – maybe less – attention span diminishes measurably. So a different route resets the clock. Alternating between visual, binocular and a thermal scan resets the clock. Overlapping routes so the guys at least have someone to nod at to reset the clock. No security is perfect, and no man is perfect all of the time. Layered security and challenging the attention span goes a long way to improve both. Far better to be bored during the planning stage while drinking rum in the sun when it doesn't matter. One of the finest Seychelles Rum is St. Andre made by Takamaka. It's aged for eight years in American oak, while gently stirred by a virgin dressed in white while the heavenly music of a harp resonates among the casks. Well, it's aged for 8 years in American Oak for certain, the rest just fills the mind in the idle time in between. It's still amazing that they ship American Oak to the Seychelles for genuine Seychelles Rum. The men made much faster work of it, even Marks, who isn't much of a drinker, though he bastardized it by mixing it with Diet Coke.

One more day until they'd take a ride to join the boat and Thomas poured over intel supplied by Uncle. To his pleasant surprise, there were targets already routinely spotted. They were tracked leaving the beach just North of Merca in Somalia, which made sense for Fiidka. His "home" was in a remote area close to the shore between Merca and Mogadishu. His home was in what would be called a compound in America, but a remarkably common arrangement in the Middle East. A walled outer portion with a series of interlocking buildings. This compound includes the peak of a small hill, which meant there were multiple stories. Even if some unnamed country sought to put a Hellfire missile in his bedroom it would mean bringing down layers of the buildings on the countless servants and their families below. Some terrorists hide among civilians to prevent being killed, Ciid Fiidka stood on top of them.

Thomas sipped the rum, comforted by the heft of the glass, the coolness of the ice, and the warmth of the setting sun. He felt less so while the rum touched upon his emotions. He had put so much in motion that so many lives depended upon. This wasn't the first time the lives of his men were at risk, not even close. Hell, he couldn't count the times if he had to. But this was the first time that it was truly personal, and he wished he was a lesser man. A lesser man wouldn't give these good men a choice. He'd arrange and pay for those to follow him, unleash his personal hell upon Fiidka and sleep well. But it was personal. How could he claim any moral high horse by killing for his own, if he tricked others to die for his purpose? For all he'd done in the past for Uncle and country, this was different. The rum-filled emotions faded, the steel conviction and force of will returned quickly enough.

Thomas looked at the intel. Targets aplenty.

He'd make it work.

# CHAPTER XI

## *Pirates Ho!*

Thomas woke to his daily alarm, the sweet sound of "Toss a coin to your Witcher, Oh Valley of Plenty," from his phone. The wake-up call from the hotel followed a minute later. He still laid there gazing up at the ceiling fan, wanting to fall back into a sound sleep where nothing mattered. But of course, everything mattered, and a day long-planned couldn't just be slept away.

Thomas poured himself out of bed and into the hot shower. He assumed the boat would always be able to provide a hot shower, but never asked, so he relished it all the more. He put on an outfit consisting almost entirely of white cotton, which was not his usual fare. But for the last morning in this tropical paradise, it seemed that a festive tone would be the way to go with the men. Besides, the soft cotton was remarkably comfortable. The only thing more so would be his pajama pants, but wearing them to breakfast probably violated the most liberal of dress codes.

The men were scattered across the Café', and the secrets du jour weren't being discussed, so there was no need for the security of isolation. Operators aren't "on" every moment of every day, there's the reality of friends, family, and many of the same daily struggles.

One of Thomas's friends from serving years ago in the War on Terror was now a Tier 1 operator in a SEAL Team. He was a great guy – very funny – but still a real professional when it counted. His mother had cancer. He was operating a world away and dealing with the reality that his mother was going to die. He previously went home to see her after the diagnosis. Problem was, she had months to live. There was a fight, but this was the second time around for her and they all knew it was a token effort. Needing a week off really isn't a problem. Needing a month? For your mom, sure, that could be arranged, they treated operators well. But what month did he want off? The month where she was still herself, and only moderately down, or the last month in the hopes of being with her, watching her suffering and languishing in pain before she passed? It was a tough question, impossible really, since "the last month" isn't written in stone. Wait too long, and you're not home to say goodbye and spend the rest of your life kicking yourself for kicking in doors instead of being with maybe the one person in your life who you truly have to be there for in the end. Visit too early, and maybe miss the end. Thomas' only advice was to ask her what she wanted and swear to abide by her wishes beforehand. He'd make her happy for honoring her wishes, and wouldn't beat himself up afterward. Thomas' advice wasn't really for his friend, but his friend's mother. There's no way to end the pain of those that survive, but her son giving his mom the sense of control over going out on her own terms in the smallest of ways was the only meaningful gift left to give. The worst part was that Thomas hadn't kept in touch with him over the last few weeks.

Thomas took a deep breath to forgive himself for the lapse and looked about the room. The men were scattered across the Café', along with their own hardships large and small. Thomas hoped they'd have thought about those they haven't been able to give enough time to later in the mission, then they'd be quicker to understand his unique tale.

Max came up behind Thomas and slapped him hard on the shoulder, which made Thomas almost knock his coffee off of the table. "Guten morgen meine hund," Max crowed with his big German smile. Max was way too vibrant and awake in the morning. "Ready to go, buddy?"

"I don't think I've ever been more ready," Thomas said. "After I get to refill and finish my coffee you perky bastard."

Max banged the table laughing. Max was as thick-skinned as they come, and he loved everyone else who got it.

The men finished the last of the really good food they'd have for weeks, checked out, and made their way to the beach. A 35-foot skiff was arranged to take the eight of them to the boat. It wasn't that big of a boat to go to sea with eight men and their luggage, but they'd meet the boat only twelve miles offshore. The twin engines made it a fine ocean-going fishing boat, so it would serve as a Taxi.

"Alright men, vacation's over," Thomas called out. "The only easy day was yesterday."

"Here, here," Abernathy cheered with the SAS enthusiasm of his youth.

Bennett looked over at him, "well, I can't say I share your enthusiasm, but I share the sentiment," and laughed.

The ride took a solid forty-five minutes, but the view of "The Boat" parked and waiting made the end of the ride go faster. Instead of a stairway being lowered, one of the cranes lowered an empty container. The stairway was chained and locked. They didn't need some intruder getting lucky by being able to get on board and lowering it. Eliminating luck was Thomas' forte. Of course, nobody is ever thrilled being in a metal box hanging fifty feet over the water either. There were ropes inside to hold onto if tilted, to prevent dropping everyone into the water. Captain Zhao was thoughtful, not that it would matter a lick if the whole container fell. Some anxiety of riding in a less than proper elevator aside, the lift up went fine.

As the men stood on the deck looking around at their home for the foreseeable future, the lax mood of their brief stay in Seychelles passed. Captain Zhao hurried to meet them with the never-fading big smile, "Mr. Thomas, please come, we'll get you to your rooms."

Thomas extended his hand, "That's great captain, now let's get underway."

Thomas tossed his luggage in the corner of the room, he'd sort himself out later. He made a beeline for his bed. Not to nap, but to sort through his arms laid out. The first thing he did is pick up his favorite sidearm, a

Sig P229. He put in the extended magazine, racked the slide, dropped the hammer, and holstered it. Thomas had felt naked walking around without a sidearm and the weight on his leg was welcome.

The P229 is a little smaller than the venerable Sig P226, but the P229 fit his hands perfectly. And since it accepted the P226 magazines, it meant the smaller gun still took the 20 rounds of 9mm. His version had night sights of course, but it also had a Viridian light & laser. The flashlight is a really important part of this equation. At night, at close distance, a handgun is even more of a just point and shoot weapon. The light lets the shooter know what he's shooting at, preventing shooting a friend, as opposed to the intended foe. Plus, a handgun is used far more to stop an aggressor than to start the aggression. A 178 lumen blinding light from a handgun may go a long way to stopping the common criminal from continuing an attack. If not, the laser on the chest adds to that. But this engagement didn't involve common thieves, there wouldn't be a lot of negotiating or warnings by either party out here on the seas. None on his part as it happens.

Thomas then put on his vest with front and rear plates. They weren't anywhere close to expecting an attack or needing them, but from here on out, the routine of being prepared to go had to begin the moment he woke. The plates would stop rifle rounds up to the 7.62 NATO rounds. Sure, it may knock you down, break your ribs, or the bullet may disintegrate and you would take hot metal shards on your exposed arms, hands, legs, or face, but you'd be alive and still in the fight.

Thomas had a separate vest for extra magazines, which

he put aside for now. The vest also had a holster for another P229. Thomas often caught flack for donning the extra guns. In a straight-up battle, they'd be right. Extra ammo and concentrating on using your primary weapon is key. In a battle with soldiers or marines, you worked as a team. In operations where you were working alone, where nobody may be able to cover you during a reload, the quickest reload is a second gun. He always preferred taking the jabs over not having a loaded gun when he'd need one. Sticks and stones may break my bones, but an empty gun can get you killed.

His rifle of choice was a custom M4 chambered for the 6.8 SPC. The round packed a bigger wallop than the standard 5.56 round, and also had an extended range of lethality. There were other cartridges more accurate, but reliable and lethal mattered more. Thomas would certainly have that handy when engaging any of the pirates as they approached. He then picked up the M4 suppressed pistol he'd carry around while on the boat. At half the length of a regular rifle, it was better to work the corners in the tight space inside the boat, and with the suppressor, it would be a lot easier on the ears.

Thomas put in his earpiece that linked all the men by radio on the boat and made his way to the tower. He settled in and reviewed the intel Robert had been gathering on boats that may be pirates or their spotters.

Robert had been a busy little bee. Pirates of old would raise the Jolly Roger identifying them as pirates. Not so much today. Today, they're small boats, sometimes several working together. There are no markings. They don't sail along brandishing AK-47's for all to see, especially when leaving or entering a port. In fact, using a port at all is risky, many use the shoreline. But avoiding detection also means not having a Pirates Cove. They can't use the same place all the time.

That fact helped Robert a great deal. What legitimate boater leaves from one place, and returns to another....repeatedly? Robert, using the satellite access that Uncle graciously arranged, used a program to graph the track of every boat in view up and down the Somali coast. The satellite info wasn't even an American one. India had an ISR capable Satellite (Intelligence, Surveillance, and Reconnaissance) that covered the Indian Ocean, and how Uncle got that access, he could only imagine. He'd never ask. But a pattern of boats not returning from their starting point became apparent after just a few days. All the bigger boats were quickly discounted, they're not pirates. Fishing boats that circled the same area in a grid search pattern for days that ignored shipping lanes that also ended up back from whence they came were discarded. They weren't trolling for ransom.

After a lot of painstaking work, Robert saw a pattern emerge. Small boats that would go straight out for nearly a day, park for a day, then take a direct ride back to shore returning to a different spot. Once they returned to shore, they'd leave shortly thereafter, probably with a different crew. Robert had access to the total overview, with no ability to zoom in and redirect the view of the satellite. Once targeted, however, the tracking was automatic. Robert simply tagged the moving target as a pirate boat and tracked it over the days Thomas was relaxing. With each additional boat identified as a potential pirate boat, a pattern of routes taken by these small boats created a woven scene over the water. Like fingers stretching from the shore, each line of the boat reached out to the sea looking for prey, then returned to another spot nearby. The multiple fingers emerged with thirteen identified boats making a similar pattern. They weren't all going out at the same time, it varied, and there was no specific pattern to that. Each one may have simply been following the "go out, hang, come back" pattern without a watch so they weren't coordinated that way. Robert didn't know if others had tried the same thing. The advantage Robert had is that his method wouldn't have been really useful to anyone else. Identifying who may be a pirate or spotter isn't enough for the US Navy to sink it. Again, sailing around with a rifle isn't a maritime crime, and the small faster boats wouldn't approach a US Destroyer. Robert's advantage was the lower bar of verification, and the ability to draw them in. With every passing hour, he was more certain he found a shortcut to trolling for pirates.

Robert couldn't see for himself, as he couldn't zoom in, but he believed the intel regarding them using drones. That was what they were probably doing when they parked: launching a drone, going high for a better view, and scouting for prey. Then they'd decide who could be attacked.

Thomas saw that the recent boats to the South were on the return trip, which meant he had time to get to where they'd inevitably hope to "park" to look for prey. He decided that he'd be the one eyeing the prey.

"Captain Zhao," Thomas called out.

"Yes sir," Thomas heard in reply, only picturing his ear to ear grin.

"Make way towards Mombasa for twelve hours, then head due north, but then slow it down. We'll start trolling from then on."

Thomas went down to the deck to pass the word in person. He walked into a conversation where Siegfried was drilling into a metal cone while others were looking on.

"A Hail Mary?" Nguyen said questioningly.

"A Hail Mary is when they throw the long bomb in football Nguyen," Siegfried said dismissively as if South Koreans don't know the game, "and this looks like a football."

"I know what a Hail Mary is, *Marcus*. Just because I'm not a basketball fan...forget it. It's the last-ditch play, that's what I don't like about the name," Nguyen fired back.

"Oh yeah, that's no good," Siegfried realized.

"What does it do?" Marks asked.

"It's basically a fat pipe bomb." Siegfried put down the part he was working on and picked up a finished piece." Conical ends on one side have been drilled to cause fragmentation. There's a simple lighter attached to plenty of fuse in the rear. Light the fuse, throw the long bomb, a high arcing pass from the ship," Siegfried caught himself turning to Thomas, "uh from the *boat*, towards the bad guys below. Because we have the high ground, even though it's heavy it'll reach a boat coming close enough to board. The explosive charge will burst from the fragmented cone first, plus, as a bonus, there's a little thermite grenade on the inside, to set things on fire." Siegfried finished proudly describing his creation.

"Sounds more like a Fuck You Mohammed than a Hail Mary," Marks quipped.

"That's not right," Nguyen replied, attempting to feign being serious. "You shouldn't make fun of a religion."

"I wasn't making fun of a religion," Marks replied, "a lot of pirates in the area are probably named Mohammed."

"Yeah but "Hail Mary?" Pretty sure that's a reference to Christ's mom, so substituting "Fuck You Mohammed" doesn't sound good," Nguyen said sternly.

Marks just went apoplectic, "well it's a "fuck you Nguyen" then. Hell, you can't throw a football anyway."

Siegfried started to interrupt them, but Thomas had enough of the show. "Call it whatever you want, don't blow anybody up on the boat. Make sure it goes that-away," Thomas said pointing to the sea. "And the word from Robert is that we have about twelve hours to contact..." Thomas looked over Siegfried's creations, "...so finish this up, whatever all this is, and make sure you're up on your schedules."

Siegfried responded with a "copy that," and the other men nodded and went on their way. They passed the word to the others who armed up, and they knew their scheduled times for walking the decks, which meant that half of them went straight to sleep to reset their body clocks.

◆ ◆ ◆

The ocean was so peaceful. The ship gave off a hum from the engines, but that became white noise to the endless view of the water all around them. Captain Zhao had headed towards Mombasa as instructed and started to head North for the last hour. Thomas was eyeing Robert's targeted boats planning to intersect with the first one who was still making its way to its peak, wanting to make contact before it parked and sent up a drone. Thomas assumed they didn't fly the drone while navigating the seas. He figured the pirates would wait till they parked to launch their drone, assuming these pirates had one. Timing was everything and he had originally thought that darkness would be his friend while engaging the spotters.

But it was nothing but sunshine for the first boat they'd encounter. He was thankful that the first boat they'd engage would provide plenty of light. The little pirate boat was close to 230 miles offshore and certainly out of range of communicating with anyone on land.

The dots on the screen were getting closer. One of them was their boat, the other, hopefully, a target. Remarkably, you can only see just under 3 miles on the ocean. One would think you could see further, but the whole curvature of the Earth thing is real. Three miles is only three minutes at 60 miles per hour. No, his boat didn't do that, but two boats at 30 mph equal that in closing speed. Thomas figured he had that amount of time until visual contact, plus one minute until engaging. "Alright people, we have a dot just over three miles out.

Get your eyes peeled at 10 o'clock off the bow, and stay concealed in case they have a drone up."

Thomas went to get his 6.8, but that was just routine. One little boat. This was going to end fast and out of the range where the small arms were needed.

Thomas returned to the deck, smartly concealed between the arranged containers. He raised a pair of ATN Thermal binoculars to scan the horizon. They didn't have a big magnification, but this wasn't about reading a license plate, just eyeballing where they were, and a hot engine shows up on a cold sea like a flare in the dark. Contrary to night sights, thermals work equally well during the day. Which was the other reason for heading North. Heading into the setting Sun isn't the best play when using thermals, and it would surely keep the snipers happy.

Sure enough, the dot emerged over slight swells in the distance then disappeared. The gentle waves intermittently concealed the smaller boat for the next few minutes.

"Captain Zhao, adjust your heading to 20 degrees." They were heading due North as instructed, and this would ensure they'd be ahead of the approaching pirate, but just as important, he'd have Zhao slow to help the shooters.

Bennett and Abernathy were already communicating. Normally, a spotter would call out the distance, which some of the other men could have filled in for that role. The problem with that plan would be that if those men were otherwise engaged in repelling borders, then they'd have to do something different. Thomas was a firm believer in practicing the shot as it would be taken in the game. He'd see basketball players taking lazy practice shots and then they'd be surprised to miss the under pressure shot in a game. Muscle memory is a thing in sports, it's real in all things. Practice the shot as you'd do it when you need to make the shot. Doing anything less is only teaching your brain to do less. So the two snipers exchanged wind readings. They timed the pitch of the boat. They now had an eye on the boat and ranged the target including its speed to intersect.

"Captain Zhao," Thomas asked calmly over the comms, "slow her down to ten knots, to a crawl if you have to."

The little boat had spotted them as well. While they had only just changed direction, the pirates likely spotted the boat a little earlier. They probably hoped to have sped in front of the boat, but Thomas had the original angle on them, and they surely didn't know that Thomas was going to hit the brakes. They turned a little to their right, obviously hoping to intersect the back of the boat and go from there. They were already less than 1,500 yards out. That's not an easy shot to hit a man on land with both target and shooter in a fixed position by any means. However, they really didn't have to hit the men, just the boat.

And the first encounter with these pirates was also intel.

How close would they get before either attacking or turning away? This was key information to know, and likely would be the same for them all. Thomas was in no position to chase them if they turned tail and ran.

His boat didn't have anywhere near the speed of the smaller craft. He thought about having a deployable speed boat to give chase in these situations, but math dissuaded him. Even if they had their own small boat and men hooked to a crane and concealed it, deploying it to the water would take time. And once the pirates saw that, they'd turn tail and run. Or worse, shoot at the dangling boat. Time meant that they'd have to pursue beyond visual contact with the big boat, and then a whole lot of other unknown variables would come into play. Other boats, engine problems, etc. There were way too many risks. He'd fight on home turf.

Thomas now watched as the pirate boat approached him in a straight line. Though it didn't turn aside, it slowed. Whether that was out of caution or the fact that Thomas had slowed their boat he didn't know, but they were at 800 yards.

"Easy everybody, don't engage until ordered," Thomas reminded them. "We need to know how close they'll come."

The now slower closing speed stretched into the annoying. "C'mon," Thomas thought, as the men must've universally been mumbling to themselves. They dare not speak as it may have drowned out the apparent Bennett Abernathy competition of who called out the newest distance first. The possible pirate boat was at 500 yards, but the bow lowered. They were slowing to a stop.

At that distance, all the men had eyes on. There were two men in the small boat, along with several gas cans. That and a sandwich was their only likely cargo. There was no purpose for these men to be this far out on a single-engine boat, they didn't even have fishing poles to fake a reason.

The men appeared to be talking and one reached behind him and put something on his lap. Thomas couldn't see it, but likely an AK. The other picked a small black box, likely the controller for a drone. Thomas didn't doubt Robert's analysis, but he wanted to see more before going down the path of no return. Sure, flying a drone around a boat 240 miles from shore doesn't prove you're a pirate in court, but this isn't that. The man on the bench moved to the side and raised the rifle on his lap, not aiming at the boat, but just pointing it upwards. That was enough.

“Hit and sink,” Thomas called out and moments later Bennett & Abernathy coordinated on taking the shot; the two rounds went out almost simultaneously. Abernathy sent the round from his .338 Lapua and hit low in the torso of the man standing. Because the little pirate boat was approaching them perpendicularly, the round exploded through the first man and finished the second man seated behind simultaneously. They both fell into the boat. *Accuracy*, Abernathy thought.

Bennet's 50 BMG round went over the bow but deep in the stern right at the waterline. The explosion of debris from it continuing through the boat was mixed with the men falling from Abernathy's round. The plume of water arising from behind the boat let everybody know, “the boat's going to sink.”

Thomas watched, pleased with the outcome, but not as much as he'd like to be. “Bennet, you were a little high.

Abernathy, you were a little low."

Abernathy laughed, "Usually it's the other way around. Bennet's always depressed, and I'm, um, not."

"Funny," Bennet demurred.

Thomas was glad they took it in stride, "Work on it. The ocean moves."

"Captain Zhao," Thomas called, "Come around."

The boat maintained its now painfully slow speed to turn towards the doomed little boat. As they approached, the mild swells were enough to be wafting over the sides of the little pirate boat. The gas cans were floating to and fro, not yet able to escape the bodies doomed for the deep.

Thomas was now at the side of the deck looking down into the boat, and a little white plastic cooler popped up too. Thomas briefly wondered if they had already eaten their last meal, or what pitiful meal it was, then smartly put two rounds in each of the gas cans leaving the cooler for last.

With the last two rounds in the cooler, the evidence of all their existence was consumed by the sea, and with a wave, the boat and the men were gone.

"Cold," Max said on comms.

"Ice cold," Thomas replied "Reap what you sow."

Thomas returned to the tower to watch the new dot emerging from shore.

"Captain Zhao....."

◆ ◆ ◆

While miles out, contact with the next boat on Robert's list was assured. Just as before, this boat was heading in a straight line away from shore.

"Hey," Max called out as he approached Thomas dedicated to watching the dot approach.

"Thomas, I was thinking, and did a little math."

"Impressive Max."

"Fuck you, little man." Max was about a half an inch taller than Thomas, but to Max, it was a mile. "I was calculating the speeds and paths of all the other boats. I'd be shocked if we can hit all of them before they know the first was missing. The intercept course to each, given their routine, is at least 900 miles. That's a solid 45 hours of zig-zagging and not allowing for engagement time."

Thomas nodded, "yeah, I can see that it would be tight, but honestly, I expected weeks of going up and down the shore just hoping to get lucky and be attacked. Robert did too good a job finding all the targets, and their variation in times meant there's no way to choose the best time. I'm hoping for the best."

"Hoping for the best? Since when? You plan for the worst if your bottle of Gin is low. The problem is that the routine of the last three will put one just coming to shore, the next will be all the way out, and the other will be on the way back. The one we just engaged was already a day out from shore. They had to be close to just parking and deploying that drone. They only hang around for about twelve hours, then go back in. That means in 36 hours, They'll start to wonder."

Thomas again nodded in agreement, "yeah, but if we can finish the three in the remaining nine hours, it won't matter. We don't know if there's anyone actually waiting for the boat to come in or do they just refuel with supplies there. These guys aren't punching a clock, and how quick will anyone onshore be to call it in? Hopefully, they won't want to be quick to hang their pirate buddies out to dry."

"Hopefully?" Max's eyebrow raised, "since when do we do hopefully?"

"Think of it this way," Thomas said trying to assuage Max's concerns. "Worst case scenario, 36 hours from now, the group waiting for the first boat calls it in. They inform everyone up the line and let's assume that they can get in touch with each boat. Problem for them, by then, we'll have taken out ten of these little boats. We'll have the last three as you say."

"Yeah but the first of the last three will be close to shore by the time we can get there," Max implored.

"Right," Thomas said. "Close, won't be safe. Even if they know. Even if All three boats know. They won't know soon enough. 40 hours from now will be night time for all three. The first one heading into shore, we can intercept without lights and engage. The other two, even if they scatter, remember, we can track them with ISR and remove them from the board."

"Cutting it close with sending a message," Max offered.

"It'll work Max."

*It's part of the plan*, Thomas thought.

They were hours out from the next target, and Thomas did some more math. Their newly discovered pattern of pirates vastly shortened the time between the time frames they'd be engaging the bad guys. Thomas's original schedule of patrols with alternating shifts was now a little out the window. Having both Abernathy and Bennett awake to engage at the range they'll likely approach to make it easier. They couldn't just lay there for 40 hours awake, however. Thomas decided to call an audible early.

"Listen up people," Thomas called out over the comms. "We're going to be engaging way quicker than expected and with quicker frequency. We now have twelve remaining targets that will take forty hours, with two to four hours in between. Abernathy and Bennett, take a nap. Marks and Atkins, each of you go spot from their posts and wake them up and call it in if you spot anything. I'll alternate time on the screen with Max. Siegfried and Nguyen, get eight hours, then relieve Marks and Atkins. We'll do that through the targets we find; rather, the ones Robert found for us."

Minutes later, Max showed up on the bridge in the tower and poked his head through the door as Thomas watched the screen. "Hey, want me to spell you for a while."

"Nah. After the next one. I want to make sure there are

no twists in their routine," Thomas said with his eyes glued to the graphed lines of the boats on the screen.

"Can't Robert do that?" Max wondered.

"He is, as we speak, doing the same thing. He's also doing quite a bit more. He's still looking for other boats that fit the profile, especially those that may be nearby. I don't want to be complacent and think the only ones we have to worry about are the ones we're tracking. I want to make sure the ones we're sure of don't change up the routine."

"Alright, I'm gonna walk the deck till the next one, after that, I'll take the screen," Max said, turning to the stairs.

*Sure thing,* Thomas thought. He was way too fired up to sleep now anyway.

Time passed and Captain Zhao kept adjusting course to keep in front of the dot. It was now just over the horizon.

"Alright guys, wake up Bennett and Abernathy," Thomas instructed. There was no time for a coffee, but they could get their eyes adjusted. It was still light out.

And there they were, moving a bit faster towards them than the last boat. "Eyes on, at 11 o'clock, moving a little quicker."

"Copy that," came over the airway simultaneously from the others.

"I spot three targets," Bennett called out.

"Confirmed," Abernathy followed. "One up, one prone, one on the bench looking at his laptop."

"Prone?" Thomas asked. "With a weapon?"

Abernathy replied, "I'd say yes on the weapon, and I'd say the laptop is controlling a drone. I have a small thermal contact at 3:00 o'clock. And the prone target is now pointing our way, definitely a weapon."

Thomas scanned their 3 and sure enough, there was a small white dot. That's a drone. "Range the boat."

"Under 900 yards," Bennett chimed in.

"Keep under wraps," Thomas implored, "the drone is way closer than that."

Thomas could see the dot of the drone on the thermal binoculars moving around the boat in a circular direction, not truly moving closer. The boat slowed slightly. just under 800 yards, and it hit Thomas. If this stinkin' drone had a thermal camera, hiding wasn't much of an option.

"Forget the hits, prepare to go for the sink," Thomas announced. This meant "forget shooting at the individual men, sink the boat."

"They're still coming towards us," Bennett asked. "We should wait for them to be closer to get a cleaner shot."

"I'm on the deck in 30, everyone get ready to unleash hell. B & A, don't miss." Thomas called out. Thomas grabbed the 6.8 and slid down the flights of stairs quickly turning on the landings in between. He paused at the bottom exit from the tower, knowing that if their drone had a thermal camera, the second he exited, he'd be spotted running to the perimeter. That would be a sure sign of a problem to the spotters.

"Bennet, Abernathy, Marks, Nguyen & Max.... is everyone set?" Thomas said with only the mildest amount of being out of breath.

"Set," came over the comms in a simultaneous voice, yet he knew it was all of them. There wasn't a "no."

"Unleash on my call. I'll break and you fire." Thomas instructed. "three, two, one, fire," and as Thomas ran for the wall of the deck, fire rang out. It only took a few seconds for Thomas to make the wall, but he already heard "Hit" coming over the comms. That was just the boat he assumed. Thomas pushed the 6.8 against the top of the wall at the edge of the deck. The bipod mount wasn't opened or extended, but the mount to the bottom of the handrail provided a solid purchase. He quickly picked up the boat with his scope and raised the center dot high above the little boat. The scope had multiple marks indicating an approximate range, known as a BDC scope (bullet drop compensator). By raising the scope, the corresponding dot matched the corresponding range. It wasn't perfect, but Thomas was just trying to hit the broadside of a boat. As he put eyes on the boat, a few flashes erupted. They were firing back, but that ended quickly. He let loose a few rounds nonetheless. The little boat skidded to a stop as if it hit the brakes. This wasn't the boat wanting to stop, that was water pouring in the front making it less of a boat. It just sat there.

“Hold fire,” Thomas called out. “Captain Zhao?”

“Coming around Mr. Thomas,” Captain Zhao responded, anticipating his request.

Again, the slower speed was painful during the approach to the floundering boat. The actual shooting lasted only seconds, so in the immediate aftermath, the adrenaline flowing is almost intolerable. For all the talk of “calm under fire,” and Thomas was, it didn’t stop the fact that his left leg would shake afterward. No matter how effective the mental composure, there was still a physiological reaction. Thankfully, it never affected him during, but he always felt it afterward, no matter how truly calm he was. It wasn’t embarrassing per se, it was just something he couldn’t control, and that’s what bothered him.

As they came up on pirate boat number two, this one had two outboards (far better for going so far offshore). Perhaps with three men, they decided to use their drone while driving. Now, the three men were all horizontals, twisted, and flopping in the water that had swelled over the bow. Again, there were gas cans, and he didn’t want to leave them floating as evidence of anything. He waited until the boat got closer, and called out to plink the cans. He fired off a few rounds at them despite the others starting on command.

Again, with one last swell, the boat and the men disappeared from view, they were alone on the sea once again.

Thomas hustled back up the stairs in the tower past the bridge to look at the dots of the others targeted.

“Captain Zhao…next.”

◆ ◆ ◆

Zhao brought the boat around towards what was thought to be Pirate boat number three. Thomas thought about examining the boats and the bodies for any clues if they were from the Fiidka’s clan, yet he didn’t foresee Somali Pirates being a treasure trove of CSI usable information on them. They may have radios, but cell phones filled with the numbers of co-conspirators or data that could be used against anyone higher up seemed unlikely. Pirates aren’t arrested daily, but it’s not uncommon for them to be questioned, and a criminal such as Ciid Fiidka isn’t sending proof of his guilt to sea with men who may need to trade that info to save themselves. Time was too valuable to bother with recovery.

While Thomas was thrilled with how quickly contact was made, he decided to call the guy who made it all possible.

“Yello Thomas,” Robert answered, “I see you’re making short work of what I sent you.”

“Eternally grateful for the great intel, but the time in between the boats and the fact that there’s a total of 13 is anything but short.” Thomas then got to the point. “I have some other homework for you.”

“Great, don’t you have enough work on your end?” Robert asked.

“Sure, but while the pattern suggests that all these

boats are the same clan or group, there's nothing about them that will tell us if they're with Ciid Fiidka or some other group," Thomas asked.

"Hmmm, oh I agree. I'd say that they're almost certainly with the same group. The odds of two groups using the same pattern while fairly evenly spaced has got to be a low number," Robert offered. "Although I don't think there's a code on pirate territories. So what are you thinking."

"Well, since you tracked the boats for the week before and saw where they landed, then went back out, and repeated the process. Can you look at the vehicles that were there, at the time, and then see where they went afterward?" Thomas asked hopefully.

"Sure, if there's one vehicle that left an isolated spot and then drove on an open road without any tall buildings blocking the view to another isolated spot....yeah, no problem," Robert said with a reasonable amount of sarcastic tone.

"I get it! You're watching on the big screen and really can't zoom, so if it's obscured in the city, the idea is toast," Thomas conceded. "But Fiidka's place is along the shore. There's one main road on the shore. I'm liking my chances."

"Alright Thomas, the boats are on autotrack, so I was only really looking for other boats that might fit the profile right now, so I have the time." Robert liked the work, but only when he'd find something of value. The chase wasn't exciting if there was nothing there. Finding the boats he was pretty confident of, the cars, not so much.

Thomas added, “And I don’t expect them all to be identified. We only need one. If one is his, then they’re all likely Fiidka’s men.”

“Will do Thomas,” Robert replied.

“But two would be better, by the way,” Thomas deftly added.

“Hang up the phone Thomas,” Robert quipped. “I’m busy.”

“Captain Zhao! How long?” Thomas asked.

“2 hours, 26 minutes,” the captain was eagerly replying when Thomas cut him off

“Great Zhao,” Thomas was momentarily thrilled.

“Sorry Thomas,” Captain Zhao, “there’s more.”

“Oh,” Thomas replied.

“2 hours, 26 minutes, given distance and speed,” the Captain explained. “We’re heading North, and the ocean current here travels South, and there’s a headwind.”

“So how long will it really take?” Thomas asked.

“More,” Captain Zhao offered. “We have to change course periodically to make sure we intercept in front of him. Our speed and distance to travel are both dependent on what their little boat is doing, and it’s not going to sail in a straight line.”

“How much more Zhao,” Thomas asked. “Roughly.”

"Ten to Twenty minutes?" Zhao said apologetically as if he was explaining a failure on his part.

"Don't worry about Captain, I'll worry about the time, you just get us there," Thomas reassured the experienced Captain.

Zhao was spot on, it took ten minutes more. As before, the two little men in the boat headed straight for the feeder ship. The shipping containers must look so inviting. These men didn't stop, or even slow. Thomas watched the boat as it came well inside the 500-yard perimeter. Bennett and Abernathy continued to call out distances, and now the probable bad guys were at less than 400 yards.

Thomas started to wonder if they were blown and was this little pirate boat that was going to do something different, like launch an RPG at them in vengeance. The pirates then slowed, still appearing to be clueless of the loss of the other two boats. They were then verified to have nefarious intent and were summarily dispatched.

The pirates had established a pattern, and now so did their demise.

"Captain Zhao!" Thomas called out worrying about the extra time that was needed due to currents, "Next!"

The pace quickened. Robert continually updated course corrections by using maritime software to give realized projections to Thomas so he could plan intercepts accordingly. Of course, Dolphin Maritime Software is more from one location to a second fixed location, whereas the pirate boat tracking projection was from one known location to a guess of one based on the patterns Robert had observed. While they all followed the same "pattern," they certainly all varied.

Some stopped short, limiting how far out they'd go, and just sat there. They likely wanted to cut the risk of being at the limits of their fuel, but it also meant that they knew Fiidka couldn't see where they were. That would be a risk they definitely wouldn't take. Those pirates that sat around were just using up the time they knew they were supposed to be out there. So they were on a clock, and there was a pattern to be found there too.

So with pirates making continual changes, Robert had to do the same. Thomas got more updates, and Captain Zhao more course corrections. That pace quickened, and the effectiveness of taking out the pirates followed. With each boat they intercepted, the men hid better, reacted to the boats turns quicker, and stayed smaller. With each command to put the pirates and their boats down, the bullets were sent with even more effectiveness. Anticipating the ebb and flow, the rise and pitch of the boat became second nature. The brute force of the big sniper rifles were now both obtaining the pinpoint accuracy they were accustomed to on land. The snipers had their sea legs.

They'd gone through the five of the pirate boats. While the boat performed each time, that doesn't mean there wouldn't be a few hiccups.

Boat six was flawless. The pirates approached their

boat to within three hundred yards, both men stood up, one in front, one behind. The man behind spread his legs to stop it from swaying, while the man in front held binoculars to look at the boat. Yet the sun was in their eyes, so God knows what they were hoping to see. Both the boat and the men were pitch-perfect, as it were, allowing Bennet and Abernathy to take the shot concentrating on the movement of their own boat alone. The perfect targets obliged and they went down hard.

Boat seven was not a lucky number at all. The pirate in the back of the boat was little. A teeny, tiny build of a man. So much so that Bennett & Abernathy quickly chimed in that they were all for killing pirates, but ten-year-old boys was right out. So getting closer to identify him was imperative. The little man in the back didn't sit on the rear bench to steer. Instead, he laid on the floor of the boat with his right arm fully extended just to reach the control of the motor. The wide-brimmed hat that appeared to have come from down under didn't offer a great look at his face. Not only did the position look uncomfortable, but it was also a poor position to keep a straight line, and the little man couldn't see over the bow. The other pirate was up-front by the bow sitting low and draped over one side, periodically putting a hand in the water for no apparent reason. He'd wave to one side or the other, and the pilot of the boat would then oblige, turning either too much, or too little. It was a constant dance and neither seemed to care. Their lax behavior didn't scream pirate at all.

Finally, they were in the range of Thomas being able to

use his spotting scope to get a clear view of those on the boat. And he so thanked the fact that it had image stabilization, one of the things you don't really appreciate until you don't have it. Thankfully, the tiny man was just that, the little beard gave it away. While a few gray hairs would've been too much to ask for at that range, his scraggly face was that of an old man, not of a child. The tiny man then brought a cigarette to his lips, though still apparently yelling at the waving man in front.

Then their route made sense. The tiny man took a slug from what had to be a whiskey bottle. He not only washed the flavor of tobacco from his mouth, but he also drowned it. Then the man in the bow did the same but from his own bottle. These little pirates were smashed. Their guns were on the seats nearest them, and they just kept on coming.

By this point, Bennet & Abernathy could see enough of their behavior to come to the same conclusion.

"Yo, these guys are hammered. Are we sure they're pirates," Bennet chimed in?

"Robert pegged them. They're following the routes and the same repeat pattern. They're armed, and there's no fishing gear." Thomas said, trying to convince himself as well.

"I think they're pirates Thomas. But I know they're drunk off their arse," Abernathy added. "How about we let them get closer and make a move to be certain?"

"Hold fire," Thomas quietly called out over the comms.

Thomas knew what the men were thinking this wasn't close to being fair. Even if they were pirates, even if they could verify after the fact, it would nag at them. Heck, it would nag at him. Thomas would justify it to himself over time, as they likely would as well.

Thomas's memory had a timely reflection. He hunted deer on occasion, and a friend of Uncle knew this. The man asked Thomas if he could come to his home, where he had ample acreage to hunt some of the deer. The man complained that the deer would come and dig up the bulbs his wife had planted, and even eat the cedar shingles off of the side of his house. "They're pests," he said. Okay, Thomas thought, he'd dealt with pests, and deer (despite their cuteness) can be just that. So Thomas asked about the property. Was it open terrain? Or was it wooded? He was contemplating what weapon to bring. A shotgun with slugs in heavy forest, or a .308 Winchester if they were to be taken at a distance. "Oh, I don't think that matters, I feed them, you can walk up to them with a .357 and just shoot them in the head," the man said casually.

"No thanks," Thomas said. "But hey, if it's that easy, you can do it." The "easy" part isn't always as easy as it sounds.

You could just walk up to these drunks and just shoot them in the head. Thomas would save the second story for the men after this played out.

"Alright look," Thomas said with conviction. "These are the guys, we're going to prepare to put them down. But given their condition, if they just turn around and don't engage us, we'll let them sail home. Robert has the boat tagged and will track them throughout. Hell, we can get them on the way back. Everybody copy."

"Copy that," the men acknowledged on comms.

"But that doesn't mean anybody sticks their necks out," Thomas commanded. "Those drunks still have AK-47's in their laps."

Another "copy that" rang through their earpieces.

All their eyes were on the drunken sailors, and as the tiny man turned the bow the wrong way into every swell, the boat tossed about more than it needed to and veered ever farther away from where the pirate captain pointed. Yet, with each sway, they were closing in on the boat. They were well within four hundred yards and didn't seem to even consider slowing.

As they approached three hundred yards, the closest that any were allowed to come, they plowed forward. The man in the bow kept waving his arm, clearly looking towards the boat. The man waved a bit more to the left as they would have passed behind the boat, clearly still looking to intercept.

"They're at two hundred yards boss," Bennet chimed in, now with a little more concern for themselves than the drunken pirates.

"Is there any sign of a bomb on board?" Thomas asked, all too used to the IEDs of the recent conflicts.

"I see a small tarp in the middle covering something," Abernathy offered. "But I can't tell from the shape. And inside one hundred yards I'm going to have to move closer to keep them in my line of sight."

"Warning shot?" Marks offered.

"And have them report back," Thomas shouted. "If there's one shot, by anyone, it ends here."

And with that, the man on the bow stood up with his AK-47 and started spraying the boat with bullets.

Thomas's cynical mind first thought he fell into a trap, acting as if they were drunk as a ploy just so they could get close. But right then, the man stumbled while still firing and fell into the water. Tiny man let go of the motor controls without tying them off. He stood with his hand outstretched into the air towards his pirate buddy, despite now being no less than twenty feet away, and with that, the boat hit a swell. Then the boat turned while the unsecured motor didn't comply as quickly and the boat turned suddenly and Tiny man fell back into the boat.

With that, the small tarp flew into the air, flung off by a third man who was hiding, or sleeping. underneath. The third man came up firing his weapon at his pirate buddy in the water believing him to be the threat that woke him. Tiny man pleaded with him to stop shooting, pointing at the much bigger boat behind him. Too late for the pirate in the water. Unloading a thirty round magazine from twenty feet away makes it hard to miss a man-sized target, even if plastered. He did, however, quickly reload, obviously intent on shooting at a good-sized ocean-going vessel to get revenge of his dead friend, even though he was the one that sent him to the bottom of the ocean.

"Hit and sink," Thomas finally called out.

The shots rang out from Bennet & Abernathy as drunk pirate number three started to fire. He fired toward Tiny man, not hitting him as Abernathy had already put him down. Although the rounds rang out striking metal about the motors, the damage and sparks lit the back of the boat on fire. It would sink surely enough as Bennet put a hole in the boat after the shooter, yet the fire wouldn't be put out quickly enough. Black smoke from a fire can be seen at quite a distance at sea.

"Zhao, bring us around now!" Thomas screamed. "Get us next to that boat and men on the deck to put out that fire with a water hose."

Zhao screamed out the orders just as quickly with no time for a smile. The big boat shuddered as Zhao did all he could to slow the behemoth as quickly as possible. The engine fire spread quickly, and it must have reached several less than adequate gas cans, as an explosion followed, pushing the black plume higher. The men on deck hit the little boat with as much water as they could; the water did more to sink the boat than put out the fire directly. With the boat underwater and the fuel diluted, the flames disappeared into the sea with the men.

Thomas looked around the horizon. There were no other ships in sight. He'd go inside and check with Robert to see if others were near, or if they changed course. His plan was not to be seen, at least not this early. But to the task at hand.

"Now for a story. During Vietnam, a number of heavily armed US Marines were in a superior position atop a Machine Gun Nest. They had the high ground, they were dug in, and they had shooting lanes lined with sandbags for protection. The land was cleared, with a nice field of view. Then, in broad daylight, six Viet Cong emerged from cover and charged the machine gun nest, yet all they had were machetes. The Marine on the M-60 froze. He'd fired at charging Viet Cong before, it was sadly routine. But this? It didn't seem "fair." It felt un-American. The Sergeant, either sensing the sentiment of the men, or accepting the challenge of the Viet Cong, then ordered the Marines to fix bayonets to their M-14's, and the men spilled over the security of the nest and engaged the charging Cong. The Marines killed all six, and only one of the Marines sustained a minor injury. This engagement, undeniably a proud moment highlighting the fighting skill of those Marines, also led to the realization that our inherent sense of "fair play" was a flaw that would inevitably be exploited by the enemy, and it resulted in a major re-education of American fighting men to never fight "fair" when you're fighting for your life."

Thomas finally appeared to take a breath. "If you haven't heard that story before, let it sink in. Because for the rest of *this* mission, this was the last time."

There was silence on the comms.

"Captain Zhao," Thomas yelled. "Next."

The next four pirate boats were sent to their watery graves without note. Again, the "routine" became routine. Thomas sat looking at the screen. Robert had stayed on top of scouting the last two boats, number twelve and thirteen.

Twelve was already on the way back from the farthest part of its leg, while pirate boat thirteen was just arriving at its farthest point. For at least a couple of hours, thirteen would just sit there.

Thomas was about to have Zhao make the course corrections when Robert called on the Satellite phone. “Thomas, you have a problem with intercepting the next boat,” without even so much as his typical *Yello.*

“Well that’s a fine how do ya do,” Thomas joked, “what’s our problem?”

“Combined Task Force 150,” Robert replied.

“Where and who, specifically?” Thomas asked. *Perfect timing,* he thought to himself.

Northwest and heading Southeast right into the area of intercept, and the who is the French Frigate Surcouf.” Robert replied.

“The French,” Robert said, remembering his earlier joke to Uncle.

*Fucking karma,* Thomas thought to himself, not exactly “perfect” timing after all. “Alright Robert, Uncle?” Thomas asked, hoping for a solution.

“Uncle says he can’t sway the French in time, he needs us to avoid contact for at least four hours. He’ll be able to get his contact on the ship in the right position by then. But that’ll put both of the other boats on the return leg, and we know what that means.”

"It means those waiting on shore have to know something's up by now and if they're close enough to get a call or reached by radio, we won't get close enough." Thomas spelled out the problem he knew he had to overcome and use it to provoke Fiidka.

"Robert, this is what I want. I want a route that will allow us to intercept CTF *after* the four hours, and I want to be boarded. Arrange that with Uncle," Thomas said.

"Boarded?" Robert asked, "you can hide the gear, but can you hide the trucks?"

"As I said, arrange that with Uncle. If getting a passing grade isn't possible from the French, then it's a no go," Thomas replied.

"Alright, but why?" Robert asked knowing there was more.

"Because that's not the tricky part. The tricky part is you need to find the intercept course that will have the French intercept us but also then be in view of boat number 12 that will be returning to shore. Whatever they hear, or have heard, they'll see our boat being boarded, and cleared. That tells them two things. The first and most important is that we're obviously not a government boat. 150 doesn't inspect government boats. And heavy arms wouldn't pass inspection. Whatever those on land suspect about us, seeing us pass inspection will be less threatening than their imagination. In fact, that makes us both a target for piracy and revenge." Thomas said, expecting this moment would come to pass.

"Well, aren't you giving the pirates reason to suspect

you had something to do with the other boats? They might not know anything at this point," Robert rightfully wondered.

"It's a great point Robert," Thomas said. "The fact is they're not sure of anything. To take out so many of their boats would have taken a month or more if we were just trolling for pirates. Instead, it took us only a few days. That sudden of a hit has to have caused alarm by now. The men on shore who know their friends haven't been coming home will be suspicious of *any* boat from this point on. We've been on a great run. Your ability to use the intel to identify their boats, and target their operation; it changed our entire plan of just lingering trying to draw them in, to chasing them down. We only know of these last two boats. Beyond that, the pattern is likely gone. So we're going to risk not getting these last two boats. Instead, we're going to turn that loss into an advantage. By letting them go, they can deliver a message, and that will be what we want them to see. We're going to let them know that we're *not* connected to any government by being searched. We're going to make sure that they don't see any lookouts. We're going to look like easy pickings. As a bonus, we're going to put on a show of how unarmed we are."

"So are you thinking those pirates are going to try to hit you after they see you pass a search?" Robert asked.

"No. At least I hope not," Thomas mused. "They're on the return run and low on gas, they'll go to shore. But after they find out what's happened, Fiidka will likely want to know what they saw. Fiidka will want revenge for his boats being eliminated. We're giving him an easy target. Sure, he can attack other boats too, but he won't be sure about them. His first revenge will be against a sure thing, and we want that to be us. So hopefully those boats go right back to shore, and when they're asked if they saw any wolves, they'll only have a story about a poor little defenseless lamb."

"That can work," Robert said. "That could work out well. Hope it doesn't work *too* well. I'll work on the intercept course and call Uncle."

"Perfect Robert," Thomas ended the call. *Perfect.*

While Thomas's boat was heading in the general direction of an intercept. Robert ran a variety of projections, but none were going to line up to ensure the little pirate boat was going to be in view when an intercept could be arranged with the French Frigate. According to Uncle, the officer that would board their boat was "on board," but beyond instigating the search once the boat was spotted, that officer couldn't arrange to change course. Despite being right in the same area, they were at a distance that the pirates may not initially spot them because of the ocean swells. The ocean may be flat, in general, but the Earth is curved and the swells mean their view to the horizon may be significantly reduced.

Robert wished he'd have figured out a solution before calling Thomas, but it couldn't wait anymore. Robert grabbed the sat phone and made the call. Thomas was patiently waiting on the other end.

"So give me the good news," Thomas answered.

"Well, I can give you a course and speed to get you close, but the fact is that even with the mild ocean swells in that area their visible range may be limited, they might not see you," Robert answered. "So no good news."

Thomas thought for a second, "nonsense Robert, send those instructions directly to Captain Zhao. That will ultimately work out better for us."

Robert, expecting at least a mild joke at his failure, Robert certainly didn't expect Thomas to be happy about it. "How is that better?"

"Well, the solution to them being too short to see at distance is to make ourselves taller. To do that, we blow smoke. Nice big plumes of thick smoke, that'll get their attention. That will also lead them to *find* us. They'll think themselves smart, it'll explain what attracted the French Frigate, and not only will we look like the little lamb, we'll look injured."

"So what will you burn to make the smoke?" Robert asked.

"Same thing to give your car a smokescreen," Thomas replied. "Put coolant right into the exhaust. Big thick white plumes of the burning coolant also have a distinct smell, if they get that close. Send Zhao those instructions Robert, now we have a plan."

"Were you going to put up the smokescreen anyway," Robert asked, "or did you just think this up?"

"As they say, Robert, 'Necessity is a mother.'"

Robert winced, “I think the saying is “necessity is the mother of invention.’”

“I like my way better,” Thomas replied.

“Copy that Thomas,” and with that Robert ended the call with a click and sent the instructions to Zhao with a second one.

“Captain Zhao!” Thomas bellowed.

“Yes, Mr. Thomas,” the very cheery Zhao replied as he popped his head into the doorway.

“Prepare to run coolant into the exhaust of the engines, at a point where it won’t damage any of the systems, but still hot enough where it will still burn,” Thomas instructed.

Captain Zhao didn’t get the reason, “but that will make a lot of smoke.”

“Yeah, it will. It *really* will.” Thomas grinned.

“Ahhhh, very good.” Zhao beamed, though not yet getting the why. “Very good!” And Zhao took off yelling instructions to get it done.

Robert had forwarded an email address received from Uncle that could be accessed by the French officer who Uncle “arranged” to board their boat. Thomas used that to send the officer his part in the play, which also required a few props. Thomas hoped that wouldn’t be a problem.

Then Robert called when it was time for the smoke. Captain Zhao used the boat's intercom to yell the instructions to the bowels of the boat. Almost immediately, large billows of white smoke spewed from the stacks. Unlike steam, the white burnt coolant hangs in the air, carried aloft by the heat of the air around it. Robert also planned for the boat to slow dramatically before being intercepted to give the pirate boat plenty of time to see it and correct their course. This also helped with the "poor little lamb who lost its way" story.

Thomas stood by Zhao on the bridge, Robert continuing to give subtle directional changes based on the trajectories of the French frigate and the little pirate boat. The frigate maintained a steady course, whereas the pirates were a little less than reliable.

Thomas took off his shirt, leaving only a white tank top. "Captain Zhao," Thomas asked, "alert your crew to wear only white shirts, tank tops like this are better if they have them."

"Yes Mr. Thomas," Zhao unquestioningly replied.

Thomas then alerted his own men, "Hey, listen up. I want everybody in a white t-shirt, or a white tank top if you have it. If you don't have either, borrow one from somebody."

Max replied, "Sure, I have plenty if anyone else needs one, but do I want to know why?"

"This is a show for the pirates, remember? If you're wearing a white tank top, you're not wearing body armor of armed guards. We're going to look the part of unarmed and weak," Thomas explained."

"You think the pirates will be even able to see our shirts? They'll have to get closer than the horizon," Max rightly asked. "And I never look weak."

"I have no idea how close they'll come, or if it will matter. But if they do come in close, I want to take every advantage, as usual." Thomas then went on, "and no weapons in sight! Everybody copy that? Get everything hidden."

The men all chimed in that they got it, and Marcus asked to borrow a shirt from Max. It was a little big on him.

The smoke billowed and continued to rise, surely the French Frigate Surcouf spotted it first. Thomas had Captain Zhao slow, and drift off slightly away from them and more towards the approaching pirate boat. They had to extend the amount of time they were advertising their presence to be sure they'd be spotted.

The French Frigate hailed them over the radio, rightfully asking if they were having an emergency. Captain Zhao was as cheery over the radio as in-person and cheerily cursed his repairmen for the coolant leak. However, Zhao deftly asked if the French could hang around while they came to a complete stop to seal the leak. The French agreed and announced they'd be sending an inspection group aboard. The French were tough on pirates and were going to make sure that their boat wasn't billowing smoke for another reason.

Captain Zhao slowed the boat per their instructions

and called down to the engine room to increase the flow of coolant. They'd have to shut it off before the search. Thomas had told Zhao about having a ringer in the search, but that didn't include everybody, so he wanted to get as much smoke out as he could.

The boat slowed, and shortly after the French Frigate Surcouf slowed alongside. Though commissioned in 1997, it was a sleek ship of modern design. The frigate didn't have a large crew, but a wide array of arms. From Exocet anti-ship missiles to the 100mm gun on the bow, just because were on pirate patrol, there was no doubt that this was a serious warship. Zhao had been through searches before and would put on the same happy face. He scurried down the tower's steps to meet the approaching inspection team coming over on a skiff.

There were only six men on the skiff, five came up the stairs that were unchained and dropped for them, the other stayed on the boat. This was far fewer than would normally board for a warranted inspection. CTF-150 had the authority to search ships in international waters for drug interdiction as well, but the French policy was not to respond to distress calls with the same voracity. They didn't want to dissuade calls for assistance.

The five French sailors were greeted by the smiling Captain Zhao as they came onto the deck, "Thank you for coming, thank you so much," as if they'd saved him.

Lieutenant Audric Marchand suffered through the vigorous handshake from Zhao, "Okay, not a problem, we are glad to wait until you make your repairs. If you don't mind, my men and I would like to take a quick look around the ship to make sure all is well."

"Of course, of course," Zhao responded, "please take one of my crew to find your way."

Lt. Marchand eagerly accepted the offer, "Excellent, but we'll be splitting up, so we'll need four." And without skipping a beat, Marchand pointed to Thomas standing to the side, "I'll take that one, you three, take a man, search the lower decks, and you stay with Captain Zhao." Marchand started to walk to the opposite side of the deck not even waiting to see if Thomas followed, which he was. Zhao waved them off and returned to the tower with his appointed Frenchman in tow.

After Lt. Marchand was well out of sight and sound of his men, and the sea "I'm your man. I am told to say 'your uncle sent me.' "

Thomas smiled and shook his hand "glad to meet you."

Marchand frowned, "seems like a weak codeword, 'your uncle sent me?' "

Thomas raised his hand about to explain, but just let it go.

"So, I kind of brought what you wanted for the show, where should we do it?" Marchand asked.

"The show is for the approaching pirate boat, they're coming from this side of the ship, and may even be in range to see us now. We'll have to wait in hopes they get closer, otherwise, the show's no good." Thomas then realized Marchand said "kind of." "What do you mean 'kind of?' "

"You wanted the pirates to see me throw guns taken from you overboard yes?" Marchand asked.

"Yup," Thomas replied, "that simple."

"Oh yes," Marchand replied, "simple for Americans. We French don't have extra guns lying all about to just throw away without anyone noticing."

"Well then what did you bring?" Thomas wondered aloud.

Marchand looked around to make sure none of his men returned too soon, then knelt down taking off his backpack. From it, he pulled two black Uzis. "Here, I brought these," and handed them to Thomas. Plastic squirt guns painted black.

"They look just like the real thing," Marchand said proudly. "At least from afar."

"Well they're better than nothing to be sure, but Lieutenant, these will float," Thomas said, eyeing Marchand's reaction.

"So they will," Marchand replied then realizing if the pirates see the guns floating it would really defeat the purpose.

"Here," Thomas said, "over here is a cigarette tray for the men to smoke. Take a knife, break out a few parts, and fill yours with sand."

So the two stood over the tray, scooping clumps of sand out of the filthy tray to weigh down the toys. Successful operations are often built on the smallest and dirtiest of details.

"You know, we don't normally just throw guns overboard," Marchand pointed out. "Ships at sea are allowed to have them."

"I know that, you know that, maybe even they know that, but they'll see guns being tossed overboard," Thomas pointed out, "and that's the message I want to send."

Marchand managed to fill his fake Uzi quite quickly, shaking it in his hand to get a feel for the weight. "There, this is good, it will make a nice splash too."

Thomas agreed. "Wouldn't have been my first choice, but it is a show after all. Isn't it odd that you brought over a backpack?"

"Ah no," Marchand patted the pack. "There is a bottle of French wine for your captain. My captain likes to make friends with all the merchant captains he can, his business card is taped to the bottle. I don't think he plans to stay in the navy for a long time. I'm to give it to him as we leave, assuming there are no problems."

"Nice that he shares the wealth," Thomas said.

"He shares it by using wine meant for men on board," Marchand pointed out frowning. "So, when do we go on deck for the show?"

Thomas held up a finger as he radioed Max on tower duty. "Max, how far out are our friends."

"Too far, they're still approaching, but they've slowed," Max said. "They can likely see the French ship on the other side."

“How far out,” Thomas asked.

“To see what you want them to see?”Max asked rhetorically. “I don’t think they’ll ever be close enough by the naked eye, but almost 30 minutes at their present speed with a decent pair of binoculars.”

“That’s too long,” Marchand said. “My team won’t take that long on just a walkabout.”

“Everybody, listen up,” Thomas called. “I need a distraction in the bowels of the boat. Thoughts?”

Siegfried chimed in “flashbang in the engine room?”

“Will that be loud enough for the French to hear?” Max asked.

“Two flashbangs?” Siegfried replied.

“Whoa, ease up on the bang,” Thomas chimed in.

“Notice his ideas always go boom,” Max laughed.

“Alright people. Siegfried, find out where the Frenchmen are, make sure you’re not on top of them, drop one in a circulation vent,” Thomas ordered. “The noise should carry, the casing will be hidden, then call out over the boat’s comms that there was a noise in the engine room asking others to come. If they all hear it fine, but we only need one to hear it to really sell it.”

“Got it, boss,” Siegfried replied. He took off down the stairs being sure not to run into the French sailors. He found a good vent he could use. It was above eye level, but he could access it fairly easily by standing on a pipe that ran along the wall. He put earplugs in, pulled the pin, and tossed it in covering his ears as well.

While somewhat prepared and concealed, the concussive force in the confined space of the boat was still enough to rattle his teeth.

“Captain, Captain,” Siegfried called out over the ship's intercom, “I heard an explosion, I think it came from the engine room.”

Captain Zhao wasn’t aware of the plan, so his expression of yelling at the men to get down there came across as undoubtedly genuine. Two of the French sailors searching the ship heard it too and called up to their fellow sailor waiting with Captain Zhao. Max came out of the other room and just winked at Zhao with a subtle head nod to the side indicating they should go take a look. Zhao’s shoulders lowered in relief, knowing there wasn’t a real problem. He then realized he was to put on a show as well, “Well c’mon sailor,” Zhao waved to the Frenchman, “let’s go look,” and the two took off down the stairs.

Max took a quick look out the door and confirmed they continued down the stairs, “They’re off to the engine room Thomas, you got your distraction.”

“Great Max,” Thomas said relieved, “get eyes on our pirate friends and let me know when the show should start.”

“Copy that,” and Max used the mounted spotting scope in the bridge to get eyes on the pirates whispering to himself, “Come for the show my friends, we won’t kill you….today.”

The pirates on the little boat were still approaching. They saw the French frigate on the far side but knew it wasn't there because of them. They were also low on fuel and didn't want to go far out of the way. These two pirates at least had fishing poles and even a net on the back. They'd actually fish while offshore trying to take dinner back with them. They put the lines in the water and decided to continue nearby trolling. *Just a couple of fishermen, nothing to see here* they hoped. They had seen the white smoke high in the air from afar, which was now all but gone as they approached. They saw no one on the deck. The pirate in the back told the man in front to lie down and look through the binoculars as they approached to get a closer look. Even with the calm sea, the vibration of the motor made getting a steady look difficult. He moved about to try to support his arms on the boat in a way that they'd absorb the shimmy as their boat skimmed across on sea as he'd done in the past, but it was never comfortable.

As time passed, they were finally getting close. "Alright Thomas," Max called out on comms, "They're getting close enough that they should be able to see you, better get out there before they take off."

Thomas and Marchand walked towards the door while Thomas was still trying to outline what he wanted the show to look like. "Relax," Marchand said confidently, "I'm French, the land of pantomimes, and I can have an emotional tirade like nobody else."

"Everybody hates mimes," Thomas said as he opened the door to the deck.

"That's true, but everybody watches," Marchand said in rebuttal.

Thomas walked out onto the deck with his hands raised to his shoulders, not so much signifying he had his hands up at gunpoint, but in the apologetic disarming manner one might expect of someone caught doing something wrong. They weren't going to yell at each other out of concern another French sailor may hear, and the pirates were too far out to hear anything anyway.

"This is me being sorry," Thomas said as he turned to face Marchand.

Marchand held one of the squirt guns, "Uzi's," in each hand on the receiver, not on the pistol grip. With his right hand, Marchand pointed one towards Thomas and held it steady so the silhouette of the gun could be seen, while his left hand waved around frantically while Marchand mouthed various French expletives. "And this is me being really, really pissed," Marchand said, "and don't laugh."

Thomas lowered his head for a moment to avoid doing just that. Plus, it surely looked contrite.

The faux tongue lashing went on for nearly thirty seconds. With that, Marchand took a step towards the rails extending his right hand overboard while Thomas reached forward without taking a step, giving the appearance that he didn't want Marchand to drop what he was holding.

"See," Marchand said with a scowl, "mimes can tell a

compelling story." With that, he let go and the toy fell towards the water bouncing the hull as it fell. While it made a convincing splash, the sound of the plastic hitting the hull didn't sound like the all-metal Uzi should, but since they could barely hear it, there was no way the pirates could have.

"Just toss the next one a bit further anyway," Thomas said while appearing to plead for the other.

Marchand stood up tall and straight showing clear defiance to Thomas's visual plea and tossed the second toy over the side. This was the one Marchand had fully packed with sand and it made a significant splash. Marchand brushed his hands off to say "that's that," and motioned for Thomas to go back inside. Thomas lowered and shook his head, opened the door, and went into the boat and out of view of their two-man audience. "End scene," Thomas said to Marchand.

"I was good, yes," Marchand smiled.

"Perfect, now wrap it up, give Zhao the bottle of wine, and hit the road," Thomas asked. "We have work to do, thanks."

Marchand took the hint, and it wasn't personal. "Of course." Marchand radioed his men to meet him on deck. On the other side of the boat and totally out of view of the pirates, Marchand handed the bottle of French wine to the smiling Captain Zhao and ushered his men to get back to his own boat. He wasn't given all the information from this man who contacted him, but he knew there was only one reason to make oneself look defenseless. "Poor fools," Marchand thought about the pirates, "they are in for a rude awakening."

# CHAPTER XII

## *Aarg Udasho*

The pirates made their way to shore, low on gas, lower on water, and they were happy the French Frigate was more interested in the big ship than their own. From a distance, they could see the men on shore waiting for them to arrive. Ali counted at least four men waiting. There were multiple vehicles. It was odd, as there were usually just two men with a vehicle to tow the boat. Ali was in the front and instinctively laid down to try to steady his view, but this was impossible this close to shore – the ripples in the water from the wind coupled with their movement made it far too bumpy – so he signaled the other pirate, Abshir, to stop the motor. The boat quickly slowed and Abshir steered the boat to ride along the waves rather than straight into them. Something was wrong, and they both wanted to make sure they weren't sailing into a trap. The pirate steadied the glass and could now count five men, two of them waving their arms frantically to come in, while the other men were heavily armed. As Ali squinted through binoculars pressed against his eyes, he recognized the two men waving; they were often there to greet him, but he did not know the others.

"No way, I don't know the other men," Ali insisted, "the other men are armed, so we should go quickly down the shore where they can't reach us from the road." Before the second pirate could chime in, his radio cracked with the familiar voice of a friend.

“Come in! What are you waiting for, come to shore,” the voice called out.

“Who are those men with you? They’re armed... are you ok?” Abshir called out.

“They’re Mr. Fiidka’s men. They’re fine, we’re fine. They’re here because they were worried about you,” came the reply.

“Worried about us?” Abshir was confused.

Ali picked up the radio and asked, “Why would they be worried about us, we didn’t do anything.”

“They’re not worried about you doing anything,” came the familiar voice on the radio, “they were worried because none of the other boats have returned to shore.....for days.”

“What? Are they dead or captured?” Ali now signaling his fellow sailor to start to steer his way to shore.

“No one knows, none have returned, all may be lost. You need to come in now, Mr. Fiidka insists.”

With Mr. Fiidka insisting, Ali now signaled his Abshir to hurry to shore. Whatever the reason, survival was dependent on not angering him.

The two pirates rode in separate vehicles and were told not to talk to each other. Each knew they did nothing wrong, but both knew that it may not matter with their boss. Not knowing what happened to other boats may not save them. The caravan of the three cars made their way to Ciid Fiidka's "home." The large walled complex was near the sea, isolated from others, a lone road that splintered off towards his home had no other destination. If you drove on that road, you'd better have a good reason to be there, or his security teams would shoot first, then not care about questioning you.

The beginning part of the road was only dirt, and the dust from the lead car was obscuring their view. Ali squinted to see two large arched metal doors that pierced the walled structure allowing the vehicles to enter the compound. As the three cars passed through the gates inside, they turned to go under a roofed area into the complex. Men were approaching the vehicles before they had a chance to stop. Fiidka's men quickly started to question the two pirate underlings inside the cars, making each tell them everything they knew, and everything they saw. Their trip was uneventful, they saw no other pirates, and the only military unit in the area was seen to be a French ship inspecting a commercial ship.

The pirate Ali said, "although the French threw their weapons overboard. Does that matter?"

Both pirates provided exactly the same story, and both were equally nervous. The men doing the questioning grabbed the pirates and roughly hurried them out of the vehicles. The open area inside the walled complex was quite large. Cantilevered roofs were covering the many vehicles and trucks inside the complex, protecting them from the hot Somali sun Ali thought. There was even a garden on the other side of the complex where the laughter of children was heard, if only for a moment. They were led into the buildings which had many twists and turns. The structure was very old and appeared to be added onto over a long period of time. Much of it was sparse, clearly inhabited by guards, and there were a lot of guards. Ali was paying attention if he and Abshir had to make a run for it, but it became apparent there would be no chance of escape. There were far too many armed men throughout the complex. Ali realized that being of value would be his only salvation.

The two ultimately entered a nicely decorated room, with plenty of books, pieces of art, and odd trinkets. Though it all looked as if none of it went together, like a museum of pieces collected randomly throughout time. The guards manhandling them stopped.

Ali had been there before, and this room was much nicer than any other parts of the residence he'd seen before. Ali spoke of being there in the past to Abshir, as a badge of honor. Then he felt privileged, but now that feeling quickly waned as he had the feeling that this invitation may mean something else entirely. Abshir was younger and, as his only knowledge of it was Ali's tales, his only sense of the place was that he'd be silent and let Ali speak first. He was also obviously the smarter of the two.

Ciid Fiidka burst into the room flanked by two of his men and stopped on a dime, his head unmoving with his eyes fixated on his two pirates. Though over a dozen feet away, Ali took a step back, as if unnerved by being so close to Fiidka, as the guard behind him was prodding him to stand tall.

"Enough," screamed Fiidka at the guard, taking a few

steps forward, "don't touch this brave man." The guard felt slapped and now it was he who shuffled back in deference. "These men have faced our enemy, and they are the ones to lead us to avenge our fallen brothers." The words inspired the two pirates. They served for years going to sea, paid a pittance, often in food, or select medicines needed for loved ones...paid in many ways that were a life for a life. Theirs for their families. And now, they were spoken of as heroes to the man who had virtually enslaved them all this time, pretending that choice was an option. Brothers? They never were, yet they both suddenly loved him for it. They felt as though his concern for them was authentic and saw their ability to help him as a means to further feed and protect their own family. The choice wasn't theirs, they simply didn't know it.

"How can we help General Fiidka," Ali quickly replied, Abshir nodded in agreement, but stood quietly saying nothing.

"You can tell me exactly what you saw involving the ship with the French," Fiidka asked while sitting casually on the edge of his desk.

"We spotted smoke from a mid-sized container ship, white smoke," Ali began. "We were on our way back in, and low on petrol, very low in fact. But we felt...we both felt, Abshir and I, that we should find out all we could." Ali saw Fiidka's gaze locked on him, his eyebrows raised feigning sincerity, Ali too naïve to know the difference.

"So we approached, and then saw a French warship approach and stop next to it."

Fiidka then interrupted Ali, "Did the French ship fire upon the container ship?"

"No, well, not that *we* could see," Ali said, now looking at Abshir sensing not knowing wasn't a good answer. "We were far away at the time, but we headed towards them as fast as our small boat would take us."

"And what did you see Ali, the French swarming the ship, gunfire?" Fiidka asked.

"No, at least, nothing on the deck that we could see," Ali again looked to Abshir, as if seeking verification. The truth is that the only men on deck I saw was a French soldier and a shipmate."

"Sailor," Fiidka stated.

"Sailor?" Ali asked.

"You said you saw a French soldier on the ship, but it was a French ship. Am I to assume you saw a man in a uniform and assumed he was French, but that you don't actually know what he was because you're too stupid to know the difference between a sailor and a soldier?" Fiidka explained.

"Well yes, I..." Ali began.

Fiidka slammed his left hand down on his desk hard, "Then stop telling me what you think, which is wrong, and tell me what you saw."

Abshir breathed a sigh of relief, content that his decision to remain silent was the way to go.

"I'm sorry sir Fiidka," Ali looked around for some help but found none in Abshir who turned away, and the guards offered looks far worse. "You're right of course, a sailor. And you're right of course, I could not tell what flag his uniform flew, but that same man was seen, by both of us," Ali explained, looking now again at Abshir because what he was saying was true, "that the same man we both saw throw the guns overboard, Uzis in fact, returned to the French ship with other sailors. Well, they were in the same type of uniform as well. Then the French ship moved away."

"Uzis?" Fiidka asked. "Are you certain?"

"The French *sailor* held them out while yelling at the man on the ship," Ali said confidently. "If they weren't Uzis, they were a copy. The weapons definitely looked like Uzis," Ali said, again looking at Abshir for confirmation.

However this time Fiidka did the same, and Abshir could no longer be silent. "It was as he said, they looked like Uzis." Abshir then winced at his own comments. *Why did I say "it was as he said,"* he thought? *Just keep quiet.*

"And what did they say!" Fiidka demanded from Abshir.

"We could not hear," Abshir said, shaking his head with absolute conviction. "There was the noise of our motor, the sea, and we were too far away."

Fiidka lowered his head nodding in understanding.

"But the Frenchman, the man in the uniform, was very animated, and appeared to be very angry with the man on the ship," Abshir explained. "Whatever reason he threw the guns overboard, he wasn't happy."

Fiidka nodded at them both, then turned to sit at his desk. He paused to think about it. He didn't know why the French would just throw weapons off a ship. It didn't make sense. Guns weren't allowed into certain ports, this was well known, but this was an area where "little" guns were common. And Uzis were little guns. These were not the weapons of attacking men like him, used in the big open distances of the sea, but the weapons of criminals in cities. Fiidka realized that whatever this ship did to infuriate the French sailor to throw the guns overboard, it didn't involve the loss of his men. It surely wasn't the French that had attacked his men. If not them, then who. It left him wondering who to blame.

Fiidka's thoughts wandered while the men stood before them, Ali was longing to help.

"If this ship killed my friends, I'd like to repay them," Ali spoke out bravely. Abshir had nowhere to hide. Fiidka looked over to him and despite the obvious pause, Abshir nodded as if in agreement. The truth was Abshir wanted nothing to do with being in the middle of any of this.

"No, my dear Ali, I do not think this ship was involved in whatever happened to our brothers," Fiidka said as if they were truly kin. " No, the men on this ship did something to upset the French, that's all. But, whatever they did, we know they have fewer guns on board than they did before. We know the French aren't fond of them, and they may then be slow to respond."

Fiidka stood. "No, this ship had nothing to do with the death of our brothers," without actually knowing of their demise, "so we will absolutely attack this ship, and we'll make them all pay for whatever was done!" Fiidka was now in a froth, turning while talking as if rallying a crowd of thousands despite there being only seven of them in the room.

"We'll ransom them?" Ali chimed in excitedly.

"No you fool," Fiidka snapped. "The French surely were able to see your boat as it went by. If the disappearance of all of our boats was being done by the military ships patrolling our waters, they would have chased you, or just sank you without even moving." Fiidka turned towards his guards. "No, this was not the work of the police of the seas, but the work of a criminal."

"But what criminal?" one of his guards asked.

"Ah, that's the question" Fiidka smiled. "And who do you get to catch the criminals?" Fiidka paused. "The police of course." The confused look on the pirates' faces caught Fiidka's eye, "Obviously this was done by someone looking to unseat our efforts at sea. They systematically destroyed my boats, killed my men, all to grab power from me for themselves. But who, which group? There are several."

"Let's kill them all!" one of his guards said, supporting Fiidka's desire for revenge.

"Oh, we will, my brother. We will attack them all. But that won't finish them off, that will start another blood war. We do not want to fight them all at the same time just to find the ones responsible." Fiidka paced the room. "No, we'll attack every competitor, quietly without revealing ourselves, but we'll let the police finish them. We won't ransom that ship, we'll attack it, and kill them all. One dead foreigner on a ship will garner far more attention than the thirty of our brothers who have been sent to the depths. But kill the whole ship's complement and the foreign press will demand justice, and the search for their killers will be epic. By killing everyone on that ship, it will compel the international forces to stop at nothing to find their killers."

"But that will be us," Ali said sheepishly.

Fiidka shook his head. "And this is why I do the thinking. We'll take items from the ship, and later plant them at locations that belong to our competitors. We let the *police* know about the items, and they'll finish off our enemies. While they think they're doing their job in getting retribution for the dead on the ship by sharing that information with the international police, they'll be doing our job in finding out who killed our men. One of the groups will talk if caught, and then we'll know who was responsible for starting this. Then I'll know whose families must die so that it doesn't happen again. We will kill many birds with this one stone."

Ali now nodded his head in agreement, as if fully grasping the plan, but not yet realizing what it meant for him.

"Now Ali, you and your man here will go with my men to lead the attack. Good hunting," Fiidka said.

Ali's eyes opened wide. He'd spotted for boats to pirate, he'd even boarded several smaller boats brandishing the AK-47 and acting like a wild man to compel the crew to hand over cash and valuables, but he was no soldier. "Yes, but..." the words failed him. Ali didn't know how to say "Why me?" and not incur Fiidka's wrath for questioning him in any way.

Fiidka smiled, "You and your man have seen this ship,

so you know this ship with your eyes. Your eyes then go with my men to make sure they attack the right ship. This is important, you two will be first on board. They're unarmed as you have said."

"Of course Mr. Fiidka, we understand," Ali said, looking at Abshir hoping for support. Abshir just stared back at him thinking how to get out of this but knew that was hopeless.

"Good," Fiidka said, patting him on both shoulders, "you two will lead the attack on board. Bring back radios from the ship, electronics with serial numbers that can likely be traced back to it...and you'll bring back all the valuables you find of course. If this goes well, I'll see that you're rewarded. Now go. Other spotters will be sent out immediately to try and find the boat you described."

Ali and Abshir walked out of the complex with the guards to the cars. "Wait here, we'll leave in the trucks," the guard said to the men and walked off.

"So now we're *leading* an attack, Ali?" Abshir complained, stomping his feet in the dirt wanting to scream, but instead whispered, "We should've stayed silent."

"Oh, how did I know that seeing the French stop a ship would mean we'd have to attack it?" Ali complained. "If we held back and he knew more, we'd be in even worse shape."

"Worse than leading an attack on a large ship and having to kill the entire crew?" Abshir asked.

"Better them than us," Ali now said boldly. "Besides,

they don't have any guns, we'll be fine."

"Sure Ali, sure," Abshir said accepting their fate, but truly not understanding it.

Inside, Ciid Fiidka fumed. Colonel Xirsi Omar, formerly of the Somali police, was second only to Fiidka and stood by patiently listening. He knew to allow General Fiidka to tirade unabated; he was a patient man.

"So Colonel," Fiidka finally started to ask a question, "besides sending those men to make a statement, how do you propose to let our enemies know how upset I am?" Fiidka always called him Colonel, so Omar would always respond with "General," which Fiidka never was. But he was family, a cousin, and blood family meant service and respect.

"General," Omar began, "I understand you want blood. you want your enemies to know it was by your hand, and you want them to be vanquished."

"Good, you know," Fiidka impatiently replied, "but what are you going to do about it?

"I'm going to draw their blood, but like your idea of planting devices on our enemies to attract the attention of the foreign *police*, my men will take steps to make it appear as if it was the act of others," Omar explained calmly. "Then their revenge will be against our enemies."

Fiidka seemed to forget his own plan. "But I need them to know it was by my hand. Otherwise, they may try this again."

"General, if we want to plant devices from the attack on the ship on our enemies, then use that to get the police here to bring in foreigners to finish them, we can't let any of them suspect it was us," Omar pointed out, reassuring the fact that his plan hinged on them not knowing.

Fiidka raised his arm in protest and was about to speak, but the Colonel knew how to placate him, "General, they'll know, but only in the end. And in the end, they'll be weaker from attacking themselves, and whoever did this will be weaker still after the foreigners are through with them," Omar said confidently. "In the end, we'll be stronger than ever, and then we'll know which group did this to us. Then they'll know when we show up at night, and slit all their worthless throats."

This was the kind of reassurance Fiidka needed to hear. He wanted blood, he wanted to know he'd get them all.

"Good, good," Fiidka said putting both hands on Omar's shoulders in praise, "I know you still have good sources to make this work." The Colonel smiled and nodded in agreement.

"Since those worthless dogs are going after the ship may take a few days or more, how soon should we hit our enemies?"Fiidka wondered.

"We'll hit them immediately," Omar said confidently. "Many of the other groups have men that are split up, all over the place, it may take a while for them to figure out they're being hunted and killed. And we want them to attack each other before the ship is attacked. Once the slaughter on this ship is known, they may not be as eager to attack the others. Plus, the worthless dogs provided good information on the location of the ship, I think our spotters will enable an attack quite soon."

"Do what you feel will work Colonel," Fiidka said. "Order however many men you need, but you oversee the attack on this ship yourself. Everything depends on slaughtering this ship. Fiidka's gaze meant that he meant it.

"Yes General," Colonel Omar said with a salute and a smile. Omar left the room to get their attacks in motion.

Fiidka walked towards the balcony, but not onto it, and he didn't even reach the window. He'd been the target of strikes before and bore several scars to document the near-hits. He'd seek the pleasure of looking out the window from a few feet back, down into the neatly trimmed open garden in the center of the square residence. The boys played in the grass.

# CHAPTER XIII

## *Kill the Grackles*

With their boat underway, Thomas stood atop the tower as twilight gave way to the night. The clear skies and a half-moon provided plenty of light for the sea to shimmer. Outside of a periodic flight far above, there was nothing. Thomas had Captain Zhao stay on the same course and at under half speed. Unaware of any confirmed pattern, now they were trolling.

Thomas walked down the steps of the tower to the communications room adjacent to the bridge. It was time to call Robert. Thomas picked up the handset to the satellite phone and pushed the requisite numbers; an antenna was wired to the outside portion of the boat.

"C'mon Bobby, pick up," Thomas to himself after it rang only once, his lack of patience due to his hopes of getting good news. "Yello Thomas," Robert answered on the third ring.

"So give me a good word," Thomas asked. "Any sign of bad guys coming our way."

"Well, there's a lot of boats in the area, but none that I'd say are coming for you," Robert said sensing Thomas's disappointment. "But it's early. There's a lot of small fishing boats out, compared to last week, but that doesn't mean any of them, are 'them'"

"None of the boats are making a beeline for us?" Thomas wondered.

"Some are heading the same general direction, but none with any speed or purpose. There are the bigger commercial ships that I hope aren't involved, and even a big sailboat that's not even going in a straight line." Robert wondered what else to say. "If any get close, or look threatening, let me know, I'll go back in time to see where they came from, maybe that would help. If any change course to intercept, you're my first call."

"All's good Robert, it'll happen," Thomas said hopefully.

"Well, you certainly did enough to get their attention," Robert replied. "If I was a pirate, I'd attack you."

"Awe, that's nice. Call me with good news, I'm out," Thomas said.

"Copy that," Robert replied, ending the call.

Thomas needed Fiidka's men to attack; he needed to drain him of his men even further. Much further. Thomas was buoyed by Robert's "If I was a pirate, I'd attack you" assertion. Thomas poured a cup of coffee, put his feet up on the table, and tried to lose himself in his thoughts. What else could he have done to get the attention he needed, and not scare them off? Nothing. Sadly, nothing. As it was, with the disappearance of the many pirate boats, it could easily scare off Fiidka from doing anything else at sea for weeks, or longer. He could retreat, stick to his land base rackets, then go back to work months later after he restocked his clan of pirates. That would be smart, safe. He preyed on the knowledge that Fiidka was likely to be neither.

Thomas stayed up to the wee hours hoping for new news, but nothing. He finally surrendered to sleep hoping murphy's law would result in an immediate attack.

Regrettably, it did not. He slept to the early morning, checked in with everyone, and still...nothing. He had food sent to his room and scoured the same screen Robert was watching hoping to see something different. A number of contacts, nothing exciting was found.

He showered hoping the hot water would wake him from nothing happening. He toweled off hoping to be interrupted by an attack, still nothing as the day moved boringly along.

*Enough wallowing and waiting,* Thomas thought. He decided to make the rounds. He went to the top of the tower, hovering around Bennett's perch, now empty as the snipers recommended alternating their schedule. Thomas descended from the tower to the deck and walked up the middle to the bow. This is the path Abernathy would have to run through to make it back to the tower if they were boarded. There was simply no place for Abernathy to hide on the bow. Any real opening for him to get to, to hide in, would be an opening for those that boarded the boat. And there was no way Thomas was letting any pirate inside the boat itself. On top of... well, that was part of the plan.

Abernathy was sitting low in the lounge chair, with the binoculars around his neck, but reading.

"Hey boss, what's the word," Abernathy said casually.

"Nothing yet, at least according to Robert," Thomas said as if Robert had control in the matter. "What are you reading."

Abernathy then realized it may have looked like he was distracted, and closed the folder exposing the colored binder. "I was just going over your mission plan, and if we're coming up on the bigger attack from the pirates you hoped for, I just wanted to make sure I'm on top of the time for me to bail," his head nodding at the path between the containers that lead back to the tower.

Nguyen rounded the corner on his rounds and approached not wanting to interrupt their conversation.

"Rest assured I wasn't slacking. I've been scouring the horizon between sentences," Abernathy assured Thomas.

Thomas smiled, "not a problem, I'm sure you are since you'd be the first one they'd shoot."

"Thanks, that's *great*?" Abernathy laughed. "But while you're here," Abernathy asked, "I meant to ask, why'd you title this part of the op as "Kill the Grackles?"

"People think about crows as a big threat to corn crops. The fact that everyone knows the name of the mannequin crucified in so many cornfields gets that point across. But Grackles are, in fact, the number one threat to corn crops. But it's not just that Grackles eat corn, it's that they travel in large flocks. So if they show up, it's not just a bird pecking at an ear. They're locusts wiping out whole areas of crops. While scaregrackle doesn't exactly flow off of the tongue, they're also not afraid of scarecrows, they're bold. They steal worms from robins and raid the nests of other birds. They're the scourge of the little old lady with a bird feeder, who somehow doesn't understand that the Grackles don't know it's not a Grackle feeder, like the guy who goes nuts that squirrels won't stop eating all of his bird food."

"So it's just a metaphor for a pirate?" Nguyen asked.

"Yeah Nguyen, that's the short version," Thomas replied.

"I didn't realize you were an ornithological expert," Nguyen said, "I enjoy birds, I...."

Thomas cut him off, "Not an expert Nguyen, just a guy with a bird feeder tired of it being ravaged. I see similar patterns in vastly different things and enjoyed using the comparison."

"So you kill the grackles at the feeder?" Nguyen asked, almost aghast at the thought.

"No, I just run around like an old crazy lady trying to scare them away," Thomas said as they laughed at the visual. "But the metaphor is there for a reason. They're bold, and they'll come in waves. We may only have a lot of rice on board, but make no mistake, they're going to be coming for us in the end."

Abernathy looked back at the path between the containers, then turned back to Thomas, "don't worry, I can make the run. I've practiced, under twenty seconds easy, start to finish."

"With your gear?" Thomas asked.

Abernathy patted his heavy rifle, "all the gear I need anyway."

Thomas nodded. The path had the twists and turns intentionally laid out to prevent anyone from getting a straight bead on him during the run from the bow to the tower. Twenty seconds for about a hundred yards doesn't sound that fast, but this isn't a track meet. That's in boots, carrying a fifteen-pound rifle and a side-arm, along with ammo having to make a few sharp turns every so often. The containers were slightly staggered to give him protection. Under twenty seconds from the word go isn't bad at all, it's just that twenty seconds can be a lifetime in a firefight. "Alright, but practice taking the turns, I want it to be under fifteen seconds."

"Sir, I've pushed it when timing myself, I don't think I can shave off five seconds," Abernathy said thinking about the run.

"Simple, then leave five seconds before you're told," Thomas said smiling.

Abernathy crooked his head in wonder.

"It means don't wait for me to tell you to start," Thomas said. "If they're that close that we need everyone in the tower, your targets are likely to be out of view from your vantage point anyway. So as soon as you can't see them, don't move to the edge to get an eye on them, just call it out and bail."

"Got it, boss," Abernathy appreciated the instruction to make the call himself. "I can always join Bennett on top at that point, he'll share."

"Where's he now," Thomas asked.

"Sleeping, he's got the late shift, so he's got a few hours."

Thomas nodded and moved about the edge of the boat peering out to the horizon. They'd seen a few boats come and go from afar, but nothing had shown them any interest, and Robert would've known if they were interested. He'd have seen them change directions, parallel their route, something. He and his men had night gear, the snipers both had thermals, but he hoped the attack would come during the day. His men would have the advantage of being able to target what they were looking at during the night, but darkness is an inherent advantage to the attacker.

Just then as Thomas was wondering when it would come, his portable satphone rang. Thomas dug it out of its pouch and answered, "Go."

"Get your 6.8 Thomas," Robert replied. "Several of the *fishing* boats just acted fishy. Four of them just changed direction and sped up. They'll intersect at your 4 or 5 o'clock depending on speed."

"ETA?" Thomas asked while turning around to head back towards Abernathy's perch.

"About an hour," Robert hedged, "assuming they attack right away, they could slow to wait until dark."

"Yeah, I don't want that, hold on." Thomas thought for a second. He grabbed the microphone for the radio on the boat. "Captain Zhao, cut our speed to half what we're doing now, got it."

"You got it, Captain Thomas," Zhao yelled through the radio.

Thomas then went back to the satphone. "Robert, just so you know, we're slowing down, we're inviting them in during the daylight."

"Well, I guess I hope you get what you want," Robert replied. "And one more thing. The lazy sailboat is also on an intercept course now, it'll come in at your 2 o'clock depending on timing. I wouldn't figure a sailboat to be part of their plan though."

"I appreciate the heads up," Thomas replied. "Try working their routes backward, see if that helps to ID them."

"Will do. I'll call with what's around if and when they approach. Robert out."

"Copy that," Thomas said while coming back up to Abernathy's spot. He continued without skipping a beat. "Gear up for a major attack, we have multiple boats that will come in from about our 4 o'clock, and a possible sailboat from our 2."

"A sailboat?" Abernathy said looking up quizzically.

"I'm only reporting what Robert spotted," Thomas turned to go get his rifle from his bunk, "Whoever else is on coms, wake everybody, and gear up. We might just have that attack we were hoping for."

The others replied coordinating who was waking who. With the other boats still over the horizon and approaching, they'd have plenty of time, even given their slowed speed. If Thomas needed more, he could always have Zhao speed up to buy a little extra time. In his cabin, he put on the vest with front and back armor plates. He checked the Sig P229 strapped to his leg. It was loaded of course, but it only takes forgetting once to be fatal. He put a second vest over the top that held extra mags, and a second Sig P229. He slung the AR-15 pistol on a single point sling over his back. That held a 60 round Surefire mag, and he had a second one in a pouch on his left hip. Thomas used the extra-large magazines for two reasons. The 6.8, having visually identical magazines to a 5.56 is an easy way to be stupid. Loading the wrong caliber ammunition in a firefight is a good way to get dead. Having the two different magazines size-wise ensured he didn't make the mistake of grabbing the wrong one for the wrong gun. It may have seemed like overkill, but he provoked a big attack, he had in fact hoped for it. The whole point of the big attack was to obliterate them, not just firing a few rounds and scaring them off. The other point of course was surviving the attack, and "gee, we had too much ammunition" said nobody, ever. He also had a couple of flashbangs and two frag grenades. Thomas finished checking all his weapons, made sure everything was where it was supposed to be, and as he turned he caught himself in the mirror. The mirror wasn't clean, it appeared weathered by time, but it worked. "Just like me," Thomas thought and headed out the door.

As he made it to the deck of the Fafnir, he could see dots on the horizon, closer to three o'clock. Since their boat slowed, the pursuing fishing boats overshot their intercept, but they must have corrected. They were still coming towards him. Thomas made his way to the bridge, "Captain Zhao, time to get your men into the tower where it'll be safe. Have the few you instructed to stay in the engine room start to seal everything up."

"Yessir Captain Thomas," Zhao said enthusiastically and yelled the orders throughout the boat in his native tongue. Zhao turned back to look out the window with Thomas, bouncing slightly from side to side.

“Nervous?” Thomas asked.

“Uh, no,” Captain Zhao responded.

“It’s okay to be jumpy, the body produces adrenaline when it knows something’s coming, it makes everybody twitchy. It’s a normal bodily function, can’t be helped,” Thomas said trying to calm the captain.

Zhao rolled his eyes, then admitted, “It’s a different bodily function I’m concerned about ... I was about to go hit the head when you called.”

Thomas looked at him briefly, which Zhao took for not getting what he meant.

“I have to go pee,” Zhao said.

“I know what ‘hit the head’ means, Captain,” Thomas said with a laugh,” you have a minute, go pee.”

“Oh no, not when we’re under attack,” Zhao said waving his finger at Thomas, then turning his attention back to the approaching dots. “Besides,” Zhao nodded to his left, “I have a bucket.”

These moments are like minutes on the sea. The boats approaching from afar appeared to be converging on their position; it was the slowest of slow-motion train crashes. It was coming, and with every moment of doubt that came before, nothing changed, they were coming towards their boat. Thomas squinted through the large binoculars mounted on the bridge. The fishing boats were non-descript. There were nets mounted on the side. Each had a man on the bow, no weapons were observed. Fishing boats traveled in groups, but the only fishing boats that would risk their nets going across the screws of another ship were deranged reality TV anti-whaling boats peeved at the Japanese for abusing the international rules on whale "research."

"What's the word chief," Bennett asked on coms. "Are these our guys?"

Thomas thought about the answer for a moment. "Let's hope so since that's the plan. That said, as odd as these four boats may appear, I don't see any arms. Stay buried, and no shooting until ordered." Thomas squinted through the binoculars at the boats closing in. Had Thomas maintained their speed, they would have been approaching right out of the setting sun. At least now they were off a few degrees. "Remember, we want them to commit to boarding the boat. So we're sheep until then."

"Should I move the plate steel with the crane?" Captain Zhao asked.

"No sir. You leave it where it is. We may yet use Ziegfried's idea, but I don't want to scare this group away," Thomas decided.

Marks was nestled in by a door just below the deck at one end, the sandbags lined the floor and the area around him out of view from the sea. "So we take the hit 'til they board? Four fishing boats are a lot of boats."

"Yup," Thomas answered simply, though turning his gaze further South towards the approaching sailboat Robert talked about. "Maybe five, keep an eye on the sailboat coming in at 1 o'clock."

"Aarg" Max chimed in over coms.

"Why do pirates say that?" asked Bennett, who was simultaneously eying the sailboat. It was a good size sailboat, offering its port side as a view. But all Bennett could think was that a few of his .50 caliber rounds would sink her; the fiberglass hull was no match for his gun.

"Aargudasho in Somali means revenge," Thomas said.

"What?" Max said.

"Aargudasho in Somali means revenge," Thomas repeated. "There were pirates all over the oceans for many years and if a Somali pirate boarded a British ship in the 1800s, do you think the British sailor remembered the screaming Somali pirate wielding a machete attacking him in sufficient detail to get the entire word of Aargudasho, or did he just remember the 'aarg.' "

"But why would a pirate scream "revenge?" Marks asked. "They were the pirates."

"The British, and most others, would automatically hang a pirate," Thomas said. "Heck, they'd hang the pirate, the pirate's family, the pirate's children. Revenge doesn't mean who's right, it just means what side of the ledger you're on at the time."

There was a silence in thought after that. Most of the men on board knew revenge at one time or another. They got it. Thomas didn't want that to linger for too long, however.

"Alright," Thomas said. "Find your cover, dig in. If we're going to take the hit from these jokers, let Lee's boat take it. Everybody copy," Which they all did and in short order.

Thomas took the satphone and called Robert, Captain Zhao turned to look at him. "Just checking in with home before any fireworks." Zhao nodded like he did this daily.

"Robert, anything on the intel side," Thomas asked as soon as he could tell Robert answered.

"I don't know," Robert said, "but I'm guessing."

"Guessing is great in Vegas, right?" Thomas replied.

"Fine," Robert said with a big exhale. "The four fishing boats closing in on you didn't all come from the same harbor, which one might guess if they were all one owner. They all came from different ones, but that doesn't tie them to anything, or anyone."

"Anything more definite?" Thomas asked.

"Oh yeah, I just finished tracking all four back in time and overlaid their traveled routes," Robert added."

"Okay, where did that put them?" Thomas asked.

"Not so much where that put them, except they were all pretty random in their travels until all of them turned for you, right at the same time," Robert added.

"So our four fishing boats are clearly connected… they turned for us at the same time?" Thomas asked. "That sounds possible, but I'm still not sold that they're definitely our guys."

"Yeah, about that," Robert started to add.

"What else?" Thomas asked.

"So did that mother fucking sailboat," Robert said confidently. "All five of those boats turned to to intersect your boat at *exactly* the same time. Maybe the fishing boats are fishing and got a lead on a school and turned together if you want to keep deluding yourself that they're not coming just for you. But c'mon man, a fifth boat, a sailboat that wasn't part of the pack, now doing the same thing? You've got a couple of minutes left tops."

Thomas breathed a sigh of relief. "Thank God."

"Well, Thomas, I'm extremely appreciative, but to be honest..." Robert tried to continue.

"Fuck you, Robert," Thomas laughed, "and thank you, it helps."

"Keep that big head of yours down, call me when it's over," Robert finished.

Thomas didn't even waste the courteous comeback but went straight to coms with the men. "Listen up. We got four forty-five foot fishing boats coming from our 3 or 4 o'clock and another large sailboat coming in at 1 o'clock. Our intel puts all of these five boats moving in concert towards us. They're coming."

The men all got settled into their prepared spots. Part of the plan was to absorb the blow if multiple boats attacked, entice them on board, then finish them. Picking off and sinking small boats one at a time was one thing, sinking multiple large fishing boats from afar is another.

Bennett and Abernathy already had all their sandbags surrounding them for their daily work.

Thomas would remain in the bridge until just before it started. He wanted to see them from above to judge how they planned to attack so he could direct the others if needed.

Marks and Ngyuen were both just below the main deck on the starboard side of the boat, tucked into corners by a steel door that allowed them inside the ship. When it came time to get to the tower, they'd enter and seal the door. The pirates wouldn't be able to get inside even with grenades; they saw to that with the extra plate steel on top. Then they could both run to the tower on the inside, out of the line of fire, and away from fire.

Max had his setup on the deck near the entrance of the tower. He'd be sure to hold the entrance since this was at the end of the run for Abernathy. It was up a short flight of stairs from the containers, and couldn't be fully concealed by them. There was cover using the walls of the ship that were three feet high in between the two flights. Max built what looked like a snow fort of steel and sandbags that allowed it to be hidden just behind the wall of landing. The extra inch of steel would stop the heaviest of guns the pirates might have.

Atkins drew the boring job, the weak side of the boat, currently on the port side. Whatever side the main attack would come from, Marks & Ngyuen had their spots at the ends of the lower deck. Atkins was to be in the middle of the other side. The eyes, and gun, for anyone who tried to flank them. He'd unload on whoever would come around the bow, or the stern, and be able to call out support from either sniper for help. If the attack would start on one side, but then flip to the other, Atkins would hold from his center position only until Marks & Ngyuen entered the boat, closed their doors, then raced to the other side. Atkins would then do the same back to the weak side. Marks & Ngyuen would have superior firing positions in the concealed corners with overlapping fields of fire.

This way all the men could train for their position, they'd keep most of the guns on target, but all of their options open.

And Siegfried would remain inside by the pumps with the fire system he installed. His gun would be missed, but knowing he had his hand on the switches might mean everything in the end.

Siegfried, not entirely happy with being relegated to remaining inside and out of harm's way, made sure that Marks, Nguyen, and Atkins were ready.

Siegfried got their attention over coms, "I may be in the hole, but remember, I left ya'll the Hail Mary if you need it."

The radio crackled, "I thought we were going with "Fuck You Mohammed?" Marks chimed in.

"Not this again," Nguyen said.

"Just stop," Siegfried commanded. "I built it, I name it. It's a Hail Mary. It's not a last-ditch weapon implying you're in trouble, but it's the last thing you do before you seal up the door. Light it, throw it, get inside. Even if it's ineffective as a lethal weapon, it'll be a distraction to give you cover."

"Well, Nguyen's will be ineffective, the boy has no arm." Marks said.

"Bottle to the man who lands one on a boat," Thomas intervened. "So cut the chatter on how weak Nguyen's arm is. This will happen fast."

And the coms were clear, their eyes now fixed on the approaching boats.

The sailboat was coming in as if it was planning to cut across their path. While there's the never-ending war between sailboats insisting their right of way to powerboats, that skirmish is limited to inside the port. It would be suicidal on the open water. There was no indication that the sailboat had nefarious intent, as there were no armed men visible. Still, this kind of approach is risky anywhere, and on the open sea far worse.

The four fishing boats were another story. They were all on a linear path to intercept their boat but were originally spread out. Now, their parallel paths narrowed, fixated on a single point. Same thing though, there was not a gun in sight. Thomas wouldn't risk firing the first shot, no matter how sure he "thought" these were the bad guys. They'd have to prove it first. While the men kept scanning all the boats coming in, they concentrated on the four fishing boats. While never considered speedy, the powerboats were going much faster than their boat laden with containers purposely plodding along at a slower speed. They were the ones who could close quickly if they wanted to. Instead, they just steadily got closer and closer, and when they were within a hundred yards and nothing yet happened, Thomas worried that one may be intended to ram their boat and detonate at the waterline. *That* would be a problem.

Fortunately, that was not the pirate's plan. The sailboat acted first. The sailboat was a catamaran, a sailboat with two hulls separated by a dozen feet with a deck connecting them, and an empty space between the deck and the sea. Three small speedboats suddenly appeared, as if shot out of the bow of the sailboat. Their presence was concealed from view between the hulls of the catamaran in the space below the visible deck to the sea. The men in the speedboats were armed and heading to cut across the front of their container boat. This attack was designed to draw whatever defenses there were to the starboard side, while the speedboats raced around to attack the port side before men on board the containership could adjust and get to the other side.

Moments after the speedboats launched from the catamaran, men emerged from the fishing boats. They were simply hiding behind cover.

Thomas didn't see the RPG's but instinctively called out, "Take cover and brace for the attack," just moments before each of the fishing boats launched the deadly rockets. The closest fishing boat was too close, it hit the outer hull about a dozen feet below the top of the deck. Even if it poked a hole inside, it would be small and not have an impact on the ship, it was well above the waterline. The second rocket struck a container, which caused it to rain rice all over the deck. The third rocket glanced off a container and impacted too close to Max's position for comfort, near the bottom of the tower. While Max felt the heat from the blast and was fortunate none of his fillings fell out from the shockwave, he was otherwise fine.

Thomas saw the trail of the rocket rise from the fishing boat and strike near the entranceway on the starboard side below where he was positioned. "Max, you good?"

"Still here, but a little toasty," Max replied.

"Everybody else good?" Thomas asked, and everyone chimed in that they were.

"Then hold until they commit to boarding. We'll be your eyes and ears everyone." Thomas ordered. "So keep your heads down."

Nobody wanted to just lie there surrounded by sandbags waiting, letting the enemy get closer isn't a natural response. But that was the plan, and they trusted the plan because they had the utmost trust in Thomas.

None of the pirates on the speedboats had RPG's apparently, at least they didn't use them. They sped to the port side to try to board during the attack. They used simple but effective tools, a four-pronged metal hook at the end of the rope. The three speedboats lined up and sped right into the wake coming off the bow. The pirates threw their lines and two men started to scurry up each knotted rope.

Atkins still had the boats in view, he saw the hooks come up, yet the curvature of their boat meant he could only assume the pirates were ascending. Once over the top, they'd be on the same landing as Atkins, yet cut off from Abernathy on the bow without scaling another level and getting around the containers placed in the way. All the other doors on the same level as Atkins were sealed from the inside, the only entrance was the one behind him. Two of the fishing boats moved in to do the same thing on the starboard side.

These two boats threw up a number of lines, they'd be boarding on the same landing that Marks and Nguyen were on. While the pirates would be in the open and caught in a crossfire between the two, they had to be sure they didn't fire at each other as well.

Marks called out on coms, "I've got at least six hooks coming up, but I can't see how many men."

"Keep your head down Marks," Thomas ordered. "That's what the cameras are for. Hold"

Thomas could see the six men scaling the ropes on the port side, the three speedboats stayed close. Each boat only had one man remaining onboard steering. They were perhaps staying close in case one of their own fell back into the water. They were just as likely to try to stay so close to the boat to remain out of the line of fire from anyone on their boat.

The starboard side was different. There were no fewer than eight lines and there were already two men on each line, with a third ready to go. There were knots and loops in the line to help the pirates ascend. Three men on a line would normally require a thick rope too heavy to toss far. This looked like mule tape, an ultra-strong polyester used in industrial applications. Slippery for climbing, Fiidka didn't care too much about that, he wanted the ship to be overwhelmed. A third man got on one of the lines, the same thing for the next.

"Get ready to unleash hell on the boats," Thomas ordered. The men brought their weapons up, each readying to spring like a Cobra into action.

As soon as the last of the men got hold of the lines, the fishing boats started to move slowly away from the containership, without a shot being fired thus far, they just casually moved over as if on a gentle cruise.

"All fire," Thomas ordered and the symphony of gunfire erupted from all around them.

Abernathy was already centered on the catamaran that had slowed to unleash the speedboats in front of them. Now knowing it was a catamaran, he fired into the front of its starboard side hull right at the waterline. Round after round of the accurate .338 Lapua Magnum hit all around the same spot. The pirate captain of the catamaran, now feeling the impact of taking heavy fire, instinctively went full-throttle on the small in-board motor and then turned to his left not wanting to risk cutting in front of the oncoming behemoth. The beauty of the catamaran is the speed of the two hull design and the increased stability of its width. On a hard turn, one of the hulls can even come out of the water, balancing the boat like a car on two wheels. That's why Abernathy chose to decimate the starboard hull. While the damage from his rounds could sink the catamaran over time, the pirate captain, now turning to his left, which put more of the starboard hull underwater. He put far more pressure on the hull now being fractured by Abernathy's fire, and by trying to speed up, he increased the pressure of the water on the hull forcing in even more. The catamaran shuddered from the front of the hull buckling from the damage and the increased weight of the water now inside.

"Zhao," Thomas pointed at the catamaran now semi-dead in the water. "Finish her."

Captain Zhao barked out the orders to turn on the fledgling sailboat. This is where their slower speed helped. The turn to the right over a short distance would have been very difficult at full speed. The catamaran was quickly out of view from the bridge, blocked by the bow of the Fafnir. Captain Zhao then relied on the front camera to make sure his heading was true.

As soon as the order was given to Zhao to change course, Thomas barked another command, "Abernathy, your ass better already be running,"

"On it," he replied. He wasn't running yet but was starting to make his way. He turned and crawled flat after putting enough rounds into the catamaran that he knew it wasn't going to go anywhere. He could've turned to fire on the fishing boats to his right, but they were already spraying the front of his ship. The shots flew all around, mostly pinging off of the containers above him. He decided if he was going to make the run, he didn't want to be slowed by getting shot. He quickly crawled with his weapon until out of their line of fire, then rose and began to sprint. He felt good about the run.

Zhao's turning to the right was also to help the others. On the port side, it provided enough separation between the three speedboats that Atkins didn't have to expose his whole upper body over the side just to see them. The turn to the right also closed the distance of the fishing boats for Bennett and the others.

Because Atkins couldn't see the men climbing in front of him, it also meant they couldn't see him, so he didn't have an immediate threat from them while engaging the speedboats. A US Navy SEAL can climb a rope at 6 feet per second. Atkins figured that these pirates weren't going to hit too close to that on a moving vessel with gunfire all around. Since they were ascending in front, they had more than 18 feet to climb. He had the seconds he needed. Atkins popped up enough to have the speedboats in view and targeted the lead speedboat. He opened fire hitting the pilot who fell hard to the left, the pressure of the pirate's body fell upon the handle on the outboard motor, which made the boat take a hard left turn. The remaining two pirates, seeing their lead boat decimated by fire, were confronted with the reality of there being no one else on board to shoot back. Either they take their hands off the engine to return fire, thus slowing and out of control in the ship's wake, or try to elude the gunfire.

The second boat's pirate had less time to think of what to do in response because the first boat turned quickly to his left, instinctively trying to avoid the traffic accident, he turned hard to his right. Too hard. His boat hit the wake and a wall of water hit the pirate almost knocking him off the boat. He then turned hard to the left, sideswiping the giant ship. He hit full throttle while being battered by the blasts of the wake then against the hull.

The remaining pirate probably had the best idea. He turned slightly to his left, then took his hands off of the throttle and reached for his weapon. He raised the AK-47 to fire at the general area where the shots rang out at his comrades. He hoped it would keep the enemy at bay while the big ship moved far enough away to save him. It worked for a moment, the rounds hit on the steel walls and roof of the deck where Atkins was hidden. Even a ricochet could be a problem. Atkins had already planned on moving out of his sandbagged fort to his left on the deck. With the second speedboat speeding up, he wanted to move left to put the speedboat in front of him. That way he would be firing on them from behind. They wouldn't have a chance.

But the pirate in speedboat number three wasn't cooperating. By slowing down he'd be engaging a pirate to his left and his right at the same time. So Atkins grabbed the Hail Mary and scurried quickly down the deck to his left, concealed and protected by the metal walls. He popped up enough to get a bearing on the third boat, which was already farther behind him than he thought, and the pirate immediately altered fire on Atkins' new position. Atkins quickly darted even more to his left, lit the fuse, and threw the pass over the side of the boat in the direction of the pirate boat without even looking over, thus not exposing himself to the pirates suppressing fire. The rounds pinging off the ship stopped as the pirate saw the incoming device. While he didn't know what it was, he rightly assumed he was in trouble. There was no time to move, the throw wasn't that far away. The Hail Mary didn't detonate in their air. Instead, as it was a short throw, it landed in the water in front of the boat, and then exploded, lifting the boat into the air with a plume of water, blasting off part of the bow. The pirate went flying, landing backwards into the water. As soon as the explosion was heard, Atkins popped up over the side, seeing the decimated boat and the pirate in the water, he fired off a few rounds and it appeared he hit him in the leg. Atkins then immediately turned to his right, seeing the second pirate in front of him finally able to free himself from the beating he was taking from the wake of the ship. Atkins took a breath, then fired at the clear steady shot set before him. The bullet hit home, revealed by the explosion at the top right part of his head, and the pirate's body fell off of the boat. Atkins then emptied his magazine into the boat. Atkins gave no more thought to the pirate in boat number three. Whether he hit the other pirate or not made no difference if there was no boat to get home. There would be no help for any of them.

Atkins quickly ejected the magazine and popped in a new one as he ran back towards his sandbag fort. However long he took to engage the speedboats, it took him just a couple of seconds too long, as two pirates simultaneously flipped themselves over the side of the boat onto the deck like the catch of the day. Atkins fleetingly thought of engaging them but knew others were following them and he had to stick to the plan. The pirates flopping on the deck were trying to bring their AK-47's to bear on the man they saw running towards them on the other side of the sandbag fort, which was awkward being prone. They both just started shooting, not even seeing Atkins in view, firing some rounds into the sandbags and others overhead. Atkins was just trying to time it right. He scrambled on the deck using his sandbag fort as cover. As he approached he then threw a flashbang well over the fort diving short of the near side of the fort. Right after the blast, without hesitating to check out the results of the flashbang on the pirates, he lifted himself up just enough and dove over the sandbags and into the sandbag fort itself, landing flat so he was exposed for the least amount of time. One of the pirates opened fire without being able to see while lying on the ground, the rounds just peppered the sandbags.

Atkins was turning to his right to get inside the door. Just get inside and lock them outside on the deck and he'd be clear. He finished turning and was out of direct view when he heard the clang of a grenade behind him. The second pirate, despite being blinded by the flash-bang, just threw a grenade hoping not to blow himself up? "Is he nuts?" Atkins thought as he dove through the door landing hard just as the grenade went off. While the blast was only ten feet away, none of the shrapnel hit him directly. There is a steel wall a foot off of the floor beneath the hatch, meant to keep water out, which protected him from the direct blast. He was a second slow in getting up from the concussion of the blast but kicked the door closed nonetheless. Atkins fumbled around to close it but did so forcefully. He used the steel bar designed to prevent it from being opened from the outside, forcing it between the handle and the floor.

Atkins then stumbled away, looking back at the door hearing the pirates banging on the outside, feeling as if the boat was shaking beneath him. "What was that? he called out on coms.

"That was the catamaran," Thomas called out. "You good."

"I'm great," Atkins replied.

He then realized the other reason he was stumbling around wasn't just the possible concussion from the blast, but his hand came up with some blood on it from the back of his leg. He felt again. Not the back of his leg, but his left butt cheek stung with pain when he found the spot. Some of the shrapnel, or other debris inside the doorway dinged him, a small flesh wound. Thankfully, there was little blood, and he could still move quickly. He'd be happy to just be embarrassed later he thought and continued to hustle towards the tower.

Bennett was in the sweetest position of them all from the word "go." There he was perched on top of the tower, farthest from the enemy. The initial explosion from the RPGs rocked the containers in the middle of the boat. As shocking as the visual of that may be, it didn't slow him to his purpose

He wasn't watching Abernathy send the catamaran to the depths. While Abernathy sent the rounds that made her dead in the water, it was the Fafnir that finally finished her. Bennett was free, in the realm of shooters. He could see all, yet he appeared unseen by others. His rounds rang like artillery, while the rounds of his enemy fell like the faintest mist, pinging on the metal below. Bennett was charged with not letting any of the boats get away. That meant the farthest boats were his. The two fishing boats that didn't approach to put the boarding party upon their container ship were kept running side by side parallel with their course. As soon as Thomas ordered to rain hell up them, and turned right into them, the two farthest fishing boats reacted quickly to move away. While they had greater speed than the big ship, it wasn't much greater, they weren't speedboats. And with the containership turning into them, their horsepower was expended on making a sharp turn rather than generating distance between the two.

Bennett could have aimed for the bow along the waterline, like Abernathy did, hoping the rounds would create enough damage to force in enough water to either sink the boat or stall the aggression. Or, Bennett could have fired at the rear. Damage or destroy the two inboard engines and the fishing boats would be sitting ducks. Bennett, however, preferred causing chaos within the ranks of the enemy first, then he'd concentrate on killing them and then on sinking the boats. Bennett fired at the pilot of the boat, intent on both killing him and destroying the controls. Bennett wanted to kill the pirates' idea of attacking him, to remove that from the enemy, and then slaughter them wherever they remained. Bennett fired into the contower of the farthest fishing boat, one of the two that didn't approach to board men onto the containership, laying waste to whatever and whoever was there. The first few rounds hit true, but he fired more to be sure.

Bennett's Barrett .50 BMG was the ultimate soldier operated field weapon. Power to stop a truck, or shoot down a helicopter, but light enough to be fielded from anywhere a man decided to plant it, and accurate to over a mile. The downside, likely the only downside, is that all that power and accuracy only existed in 10 round mags. The .50 BMB is the fire breathing dragon whose only weakness is to take a breath in between leveling everything before it.

Bennett swapped the mags of the Barrett to unleash the next round of hell into the next fishing boat when he saw a trail of white streaming from the fishing boat he had just fired upon. The white plume meant a coolant leak, and that boat could no longer get far enough away.

Bennett immediately sent all ten rounds of .50 into the bridge of the second fishing boat, whatever lived there before was no more. Bennett quickly reloaded. Stopping the fishing boats was one thing, killing all of the men that may be on them was another. Since these two fishing boats didn't unload anyone to board, these had shooters still on board. These were not little speedboats, and then there were still the boarders to deal with.

Nguyen and Marks had the toughest job from the start. In football terms, they were little cornerbacks who had to roll up and stop the fullback at the line. They had to stop the most, with the least, and in the shortest amount of time while being at the most risk. Nguyen could easily see the two fishing boats that were off to the side from his vantage point. That wasn't his concern, those would belong to Bennett. The other two fishing boats moved in close to their boat to put men on the deck in front of him. Both he and Marks had to sink or slow the first and second fishing boats. They weren't launching small artillery rounds like Bennett, both relied on sheer firepower. While Nguyen had used the Surefire 60 round mags in the past with confidence, Marks used a 60 round drum. Their coordinated concept of defense was to overwhelm the first and second fishing boats towards the front with small arms fire while Bennett could concentrate on, and finish, the two slightly farther away. One could say they "executed" their jobs flawlessly, as they coordinated their burst of attack. Just before Thomas gave the order to fire, the two confirmed their plan.

"Marks, when I pop up to fire on the first boat, you follow suit on the second" Nguyen radioed.

"Why not the other way around," Marks asked? "I'm closer to the first boat."

"The overlapping tracer rounds will confuse the shit out of them," Nguyen rightfully pointed out.

"Got it, all fire on your go," Marks replied.

As soon as Thomas gave the order to fire, Nguyen popped up and fired at the first fishing boat. He was on the back portion on the starboard deck, so the wall above the deck protected him from the view of the other two, but left him a clear shot of his target. Nguyen braced the front grip of his rifle against the rail on the outer portion of the deck and squeezed the trigger. Every third round was a tracer, which meant that everyone could see the path of the bullet from the moment it left the barrel to the moment it hit home, or if it missed. Nguyen aimed and fired all 60 rounds from the first magazine, and they all seemed to hit home. He couldn't tell if the boat slowed. After expending them all, he dropped to the ground to reload, preparing to repeat the process.

Marks did the same thing. Looking back, he was protected from gunfire from the left but was in a good spot to fire on the boats running parallel to the ship. While he positioned himself so that he couldn't see the lead boat, he could see the other three behind it. Marks fired all 60 rounds from his rifle into the bridge of the second ship. Despite Marks being slightly more exposed than the others, as the fishing boats were facing him, the pirates on the boats were overwhelmed. With the overlapping tracer rounds falling up on the first two boats and Bennett's .50 BMG eviscerating the two that were farther away, this wasn't going as the pirates had planned. "Just get the men on board, then stand by," they were told. With so many men on deck, the best the containership could muster would be a water cannon they were promised. But instead, it was raining lead, and the men trying to board were still struggling to climb up the sides, and the pirates in the fishing boats were being slaughtered. "Where was the boarding party on the other side," they thought?"

Right after Nguyen and Marks finished expending their extended magazines into the first two boats, it was Max's turn. He was concealed behind the sandbags when the RPG hit earlier as Bennett was engaging the two fishing boats a bit farther away, now at his 3 o'clock, while Marks and Nguyen were engaging the boats that just unloaded other pirates onto their boat. Max then popped up and alternated fire between the two boats at his 2 o'clock. The coordinated continuous fire would give them no reprieve, no time to think, no time for them so survey what was happening. The continuation of the onslaught gave the artillery piece, otherwise known as Bennett with his .50 cal, time to methodically decimate the farthest boat, to the closest, so that there would be no escape. Small arms fire erupted from the fishing boats as the pirates, tired of being shot at, raised their AK-47's above their heads and fired from the protection of cover, not even looking to see if they were firing in the right direction. After expending his magazine, Max dropped back down and just called out "Max reloading," and that was all that it took for the cycle to start over.

Nguyen and Marks then both resumed firing on the closest two boats, now trying to turn away from their position. They were late to turn, late to realize the container ship was turning towards them at all. Seeing the steel bow go over the catamaran like a tractor-trailer over a leaf must have left an impression that "being too close," may not be a good idea. And they were now way too close. So while they were now putting a little distance between themselves and the containership, they were too slow to react, and simply had too much ground to cover to make a difference.

The farthest of the fishing boats, which wasn't all that far away and the one Bennett opened fire on first, burst into flames and a blue burst of smoke erupted from the back. Oil from the engine was pumping onto the exhaust, a round from the .50 must have cracked the block or worse. That boat wasn't going anywhere. Bennett then concentrated on boat number three, while Nguyen and Marks continued to fire at the two fishing boats in front of it.

Boat number three then actually did something really smart, it turned hard in towards the containership. The pirate piloting that boat must have been fired upon from big ships before, it's all about the angles. A heavy-caliber rifle can easily hit a boat sized target from a half-mile away with accuracy. Yet if the shooter can't see the boat, he can't shoot it, and snipers in real life are rarely hanging out over the edge. They're recessed, buried back in a high position exposing themselves to the very least degree. Bennett was perfectly positioned, way up high on the tower several feet from the edge. That made him the smallest of targets to the pirates below. It also meant that after the fishing boat turned in towards the containership, it was moving inside his view from his vantage point quickly.

“Marks, Nguyen,” Bennett called out. “Check fire on the first two, concentrate on the boat turning in, I’m losing him.”

Both Marks and Nguyen heard him, not a big change in aim for Marks, both were in his line of fire. Nguyen, however, would have to move significantly to his left to turn around the wall on his right to target the turning fishing boat. This would put his left side and back to the pirates on the first two boats.

While Marks was able to quickly fire on the boat attempting to get away, he could see the return fire towards Nguyen was going to keep him pinned down, or vastly increase his risk of being hit if he stuck his neck out. “Hail Mary,” Marks thought.

“Nguyen, Hail Mary,” Marks called out over coms. “He’s turning towards us, I’ll throw in front of him, he’ll have to keep turning, putting him closer, then you throw, he’ll be close.”

“Copy that,” Nguyen replied while the pirate’s rounds rang off of the steel above him. “It’s better than sticking my neck out.”

Bennett simply replied, “Go for it, I’m on the front two,” and just as quickly altered his firing accordingly. While those two boats were close to the Fafnir, they were well in front.

Marks picked up Siegfried’s creation, it was certainly heavier than a football. While the idea of standing tall in the pocket throwing the long bomb, in this case literally, appealed to him, standing up with incoming fire was out. Then it hit him, "Bernie Fucking Kosar." A sidearm throwing quarterback from the Cleveland Browns that made slinging the football cool. Marks popped his head up to get a clear line on the boat, backed up a bit so he remained concealed behind the wall to his left, lit the fuse on the Hail Mary then took a quick spring dropping to his knees sliding forward, and slung the metal pigskin sidearm over the side of the boat. He was concealed the entire time, but the high arching toss flung with a perfect spiral, looked as if it was fired from a cannon. Whether it caught the attention of the pirate captain Nguyen couldn't tell. But the pirate saw Marks throw, and since headed straight for the pirate fishing boat he continued to turn in towards the Fafnir. Nguyen wasn't as confident of his throwing ability, so he stared too long at the pass Marks made at the boat that was approaching just trying to gauge how far it would travel. The Hail Mary Marks threw then detonated squarely above the pirate fishing boat, the shrapnel hitting home as bits of their boat seemed to explode all around.

"C'mon Nguyen," Marks called out, "throw it."

Nguyen never stopped looking at the pirate boat, parts of it smoking from the blast, or, more likely, the thermite grenade that was inside. He took a step back, lit the device, and heaved it over the side like a shot put. It looked lame. It was a duck, tumbling end over end. There was no arch and was only by definition a throw by the smallest of margins, it was that fraction of effort greater than a drop. To be fair, Nguyen never thought about it as a pass or a throw. He saw the target and put the muscle behind the device he anticipated would be required to get it from A to B. It became the kind of story that would be retold for many years, as the Hail Mary didn't explode above the fishing boat as Siegfried had intended. It didn't spew shrapnel and thermite over a flammable boat as Marks had proven could be done. No. Nguyen's was a throw in the game of football that would be seen as a feeble pass was, however, perfectly adept at getting A to B. The short drop/toss fell onto the boat just before the pilothouse. It didn't land on the decking, typically constructed in a solid manner to allow one to walk upon. No, it didn't land there. Instead, it fell onto the fiberglass hatch covering an entrance to the cabin below. Why didn't it explode earlier? Time. Nguyen didn't throw it as Siegfried anticipated, and Siegfried included enough fuse to ensure the thrower had enough time to make the throw to help prevent the thrower from blowing themselves up. Nguyen's previously described weak arm only appeared to be true. The "drop" meant that from the time Nguyen lit it, until the time it reached the boat was much shorter, while the fuse was just as long. The Hail Mary crashed through the fiberglass hatch and into the floor of the cabin below. It did not penetrate the 105-gallon fuel tanks. It didn't have to. The explosive charge was only moderately significant; designed to send shrapnel over a large area to slow the pirates. Fuel tanks on military vessels are hardened to protect the crew from an errant projectile. These were pirate fishing boats. There was no protection. The small blast shredded the tanks, momentarily projecting undetonated fuel into the air. The thermite grenade, however, left no chance for the fuel to remain a liquid. The 4,000 degrees Fahrenheit explosion from the grenade made the air-fuel mixture from the explosion of the Hail Mary become a blast that disappeared the boat. Its fragments instantaneously traveled in every direction from the blast, a circular flame erupted, and in a moment, the recognizable parts of a boat that seemed to just be expanding were then suddenly gone.

"Whew, that'll get their attention!" Marks cried out over coms.

"I don't know who this "they" are you're referring to," Nguyen replied while popping up from behind cover firing more rounds into the two remaining boats, "cause they're gone."

Marks went to fire on the two remaining boats in the fight and immediately drew substantial return fire hitting all around him so that he dropped to the ground to avoid contact. "I don't think they're dead yet," came his cheeky reply.

Bennett was still methodically sending rounds into the front two pirate fishing boats. "I'm still workin' on two big boats, so, there's still a "them." They may not be sunk yet, but they're not going anywhere. Shouldn't you two be out of there?"

Thomas had made his way down from the bridge to just above Max's position and the entrance to the tower. He would provide cover until the last man was inside from the deck above before they sealed the door. Knowing that the boarders would soon actually make it on board, and the damage already done to the pirates only means of escape, their boats, Thomas agreed. "Marks &

Nguyen, seal it up and head for the tower,"

"Copy that," Nguyen said, "I'm in a hurry to collect my bottle." Nguyen spun to his left through the entranceway and closed the door with a bang. He rigged the door shut with the same device that Atkins had, thus ensuring there was no quick breach from the outside.

Marks, still lying on the deck after taking fire, just pushed himself backward through the doorway behind him. There was no reason to take any extra risk while fleeing. "Copy that, but whoa there Nguyen, my throw was on the money, the bottle's mine." Marks then sealed the door and braced it to prevent the pirates from entering as well. He then bolted to run to the tower.

"Thomas said a bottle to the man who landed the Hail Mary "on a boat," Nguyen paused for dramatic effect while making his way through the ship to the tower's entrance. "Yours exploded "above" the boat. Mine landed "on" the boat."

"That's bullshit," Marks said, actually stopping while making his way down a corridor in the boat. "My toss was exactly what Siegfried intended."

Thomas came out onto a landing overseeing the main deck, he could see that at least a couple of the pirates scaling the side had made it onto the deck by the bow, others likely had too, they were simply out of view due to the containers. Bennett continued to fire on the fishing boats, but they're not small and easily sunk. Their very design is not to sink, even if flooded. "Jesus, you both get a bottle, so long as you're alive to collect it, hustle your asses to the tower." The pirates were able to tell they were taking fire from high above. Thomas moved to the right and fired several rounds at the first fishing boat, the tracer rounds would give them another target. He then immediately crouched down and moved to his left, using the angle of view from the boats and the containers to offer him cover. Thomas could still cover the deck leading to the tower's door, however, the pirate's rounds fired in response pinged harmlessly off of the white tower only leaving splotches of the gray primer underneath.

Marks and Nguyen both ran to the tower, neither honestly caring about the bottle itself. Bragging rights mattered, and both laughed at their own idiocy along the way, while they both swore this wasn't settled.

Then it hit, the unexpected chaos always does. It's unavoidable.

Abernathy was making the run of his life. After basically sinking a catamaran single-handedly, he was pretty high on himself as he ran through the corridor created for him within the containers. The adrenalin that he could always contain within him as a sniper had been released during his run, and it was as if he was floating through the containers. Then he saw it, with twenty feet to go until the next turn, rice everywhere.

Abernathy slowed on the corner, slipping slightly on the granular rice covering the slick steel floor. As he stopped around the turn, his path was buried in the rice.

"Boss, hey, I've got a problem," Abernathy said, then realizing Thomas's hearing may not pick up on who it was, given the gunfire, even on coms. "It's Abernathy."

Thomas looked all around instinctively expecting to see a threat, something they hadn't seen or planned for, but nothing. The two fishing boats were still firing and taking fire from Bennett, and those that had boarded were already making their way towards them on the starboard side, he couldn't see the port side.

"I've got a ton of rice blocking my path," Abernathy said while starting to try to climb up it, which turned more into through it. The lightweight granular rice was no longer in bags, but loosely filled the path, and it was giving way to his body weight with every movement. "I'm having a hard time getting over it, I'll need more time to make it to the tower."

"Fuck," Thomas replied, not exactly what Abernathy was hoping for. "How high is the rice?"

"It's high, the RPG's fired by the pirates must have blown the containers to shit and the rice dumped into the corridor we created," Abernathy replied. "If only I could get a footing on the bags that are still full, but I'm not finding much of anything."

"Genius," Thomas thought. "Stop right the fuck where you are right now. You have a flare?"

"A signal flare?" Abernathy asked. "Yeah in my vest, but what.."

"Shutup, don't move more into the rice. Get your flare ready," Thomas commanded. "Zhao Goddammit, you better be listening,"

"I'm here Captain Thomas," Captain Zhao responded as if there was any doubt.

"You can control the crane from there right?" Thomas

asked.

"Yes, of course," Zhao said assuredly.

"My man is stuck in the corridor in loose rice, and can't get through. Pick up a container 'cause you're going to drop it inside so he has something to climb over. He's going to shoot up a flare so you know where he is, drop on this side, the Tower side of the flare got it?" Thomas asked hurriedly.

"Got it," Zhao responded, not thrilled with dropping a container anywhere near a person with nowhere to go.

"Abernathy, you got that?" Thomas asked as he was heading down the stairs to the main deck.

"Yeah, I get the idea, I guess," Abernathy responded, not liking being on the bottom and hoping the pirates couldn't identify where the flare came from.

"Get somewhere you can back up from, call when you're launching the flare, then back up to a defensive position if any of the boarders come your way, tell Zhao when you're clear to drop," Thomas instructed. "And I'm going to buy you some time."

"Sounds good," Abernathy took comfort that Thomas was going to be sticking his neck out for him. Not just because "the boss" took a personal interest in putting himself on the front line, but because it always worked out for him.

Thomas slid down the railing of the external stairs on all fours and hit the deck running. "What do you mean you're buying him time," Max asked, seeing Thomas blow by his position.

"Cover the door," Thomas yelled, "keep hitting the

boats."

Abernathy helped the little flare in his gloved hands not fearing any burning blowback, he'd used signaling flares before. He was more concerned with shooting it straight up the middle and not bouncing it off a container. "Firing the flare," he took a brief pause, "firing!" The maritime emergency flare wasn't much bigger than the size of a Sharpie, but it sent the bright ball of light straight up. Zhao quickly picked up flare rising from in between the mountain of metal containers. "Got it," Zhao exclaimed, excited to be part of it all. "Moving to drop." Captain Zhao had started the process of grabbing a container with one of the cranes, he'd already dropped the spreader to the container starting to lift it before Abernathy fired.

After firing the flare, Abernathy quickly moved back around a corner and moved to the second corner in a defensive position. It wasn't the best, it was to his left. Being right-handed meant he swapped shoulders and would make do with firing at any pirates that came his way. It's something that they trained for, and after all, fifty percent of the corners on Earth are the wrong ones. It wasn't like he had to be perfect in the accuracy department. There was only about a 72 foot straight shot to the next turn.

Thomas's plan was simple. Attack. Attack with voracious speed and surprise to draw fire, and to give the pirates that boarded a reason to pause. Maybe they wouldn't even bother going down the middle corridor, they didn't know Abernathy was there. But since they were not shut off on both sides his plan to draw them in meant there was a good chance some of them would end up there. Bennett was still firing at the first two fishing boats. They weren't finished firing, but they were done. Both had tried to outrun the Fafnir, but they couldn't outrun the 3,000 feet per second rounds that were popping holes through the boats from stem to stern. Black smoke was emerging from both, and the slick hulls that were used to gliding over the water were now like a cheese grater. With every foot forward the force of the water through the holes added weight and the boat sank lower slowing it still more. Those on the boats were still firing aimlessly, they had to hope the boarders succeeded because it became apparent that was their only hope.

While Thomas needed the distraction to save Abernathy, he couldn't attack the boarders first, he couldn't fight them all on two fronts. He raced to the deck and braced his 6.8 rifle against the deck wall using the collapsed bipod as a metal hook for a strong purchase against the steel wall. He took just a moment to put the red circle inside the scope around the men firing and squeezed off several rounds. There was a small illuminated dot in the middle for accuracy which simply wasn't needed. Hit them in the left shoulder or their balls, just as good. The first man went down hard, flailing as the force of falling backward caused his rifle to fly upwards, attracting the attention of some of the other pirates who then ducked from the new attack, and Thomas moved on to fire and hit those that didn't have the sense to hide. They were previously hiding from the less frequent rounds from the tower, which to them, seemed to be targeting the pilot and engine area more than the men on the boat.

"Max, Bennett," Thomas called out. "target the shooters, I don't have time for this."

Max leaped over the safety of the sandbag cover to the rails farther to the right where Thomas was and laid down what would be called suppressing fire, a never-ending barrage of automatic fire quickly alternating on each boat. Bennett's task was now to just kill the pirates, and we'll come back and kill the boats later if we have to. If he saw a pirate, he fired. If a pirate ducked behind a wall, he'd shoot the wall. The debris exiting the other side would be like a claymore mine, exploding outward on the other side, which would kill what was behind the wall. He just loved the .50 BMG.

They all benefited from the delay and indecision of the pirates that were boarding the boat. They were told that they were going to go onboard and slaughter the crew. That was the plan. Go on board, slaughter the crew. How hard did that sound? There was no plan for watching their friends slaughtered on their boats, and then see them explode, or sinking, all while they climbed up the side. The first few that made it on top on the starboard side could've attacked right away. They should have. Their attack may have saved a few pirate lives on the boats. The boarders would have been the bigger threat and demanded the attention of those doing the defending. But when you're the first pirate on board and the shit is hitting the fan, "attack" isn't the first thought. Instead, they hid behind cover, they looked around, they waited as each group of pirates made it to the deck. Ali and Abshir were among those first on deck on the starboard side, and *they* had no idea what the hell was going on other than they weren't going to be the first ones to attack.

They waved to each other about fire coming from the top of the tower, not that they could see the shooter themselves. They pointed at positions around the boat yelling about what to do now, and wondering where the boarders were from the port side. Omar was leading the attack as Fiidka instructed, but leading from behind. He was one of the last to board the ship. He was third on one of the lines, sending the sheep first if there was a problem. But the sheep had to then wait for the big dog. They were bunched together not knowing what to do. Omar ordered them forward a couple at a time. Omar's orders were out of fear for himself. It wasn't the worst strategy, it was just that's often not how one wins.

The containers were staggered on the side of the deck, zig-zagging cover along the way. This of course was because the center corridor of the containers was alternated to give Abernathy cover from the front to the back.

Thomas reached the main deck, separated from the boarders from the alternating containers, and instead of bothering to reload the 6.8 after expending the mag on the boats, he dropped it to the ground, swinging the suppressed SBR with a red dot sight slung over his left shoulder into firing position. A red dot sight is a marvel in its function and simplicity. A small tube sits atop the rifle, there is no magnification on his, though some may be magnified. When looking through the tube, a lone red dot can be seen. Where the red dot appears, that's where the round will strike. This was ultimately the first big improvement of the basic concept of aiming a rifle from having to align two iron sights first used in 1450. While looking down the tube, if the shooter moves his line of sight, the red dot moves too. There is no perfection needed by the shooter, proper alignment was very forgiving. In the heat of a battle if a soldier is on his back, looking through this optic, around a corner, at night....the red dot appears where the gun is aimed and that's where the round will strike.

Two pirates, with no such optic, however, came around a corner just as Thomas had. They raised their guns and fired spraying the deck. Thomas had pivoted on his left foot to turn his body around the corner of the container offering him protection from the rounds. Four other pirates simultaneously turned the corner from about thirty feet behind only to see them firing at nothing.

Thomas took a fragmentation grenade from his belt and pulled the pin, and waited. The pirates kept firing, he'd let them have their turn, then the shooting stopped. Thomas didn't know if they fired all 30 rounds from their magazine, but given their length of fire, it had to be close. He tossed the grenade to the ground on the metal deck. The clanking sound bouncing towards them did not leave any doubt, and the two pirates moved to their right hoping for cover around the corner, which would have been fine, except the grenade detonated past the corner killing them both instantly in the blast.

The blast also signaled Thomas to pivot on that same left foot around the corner firing at the four pirates originally believing it was a six on nobody. One fell dead, another wounded, and two moved to their right for cover around an outstretched container. Thomas didn't see it, but the sound of the container crashing down in the corridor was unmistakable and everyone heard it. Everyone.

The six pirates who boarded on the port side couldn't get inside the boat. So they made their way to the main deck, went towards the bow intent on joining the others. Not knowing which way to go led them to the belief of safety in numbers. They heard the shooting, they heard the grenade, and then they heard the crash of the container as they passed the center of the bow. They all looked up fearing a container was crashing down upon them, but that wasn't it.

The "leader" of the six pirates seeking the safety in numbers during a firefight wasn't going to split his forces and send three down the corridor. Several pointed down the path, but he shook them off. "Did you hear that? A container fell and you want to go in there? Are you crazy?" Thankfully, the very thing that may have attracted them scared them off. He led them over to the much larger boarding party. He'd let Omar order his men.

As Thomas was firing at the fleeing pirates, he rounded the corner to cover the distance to the next container quickly. "Abernathy, are you over the container yet."

"Working on it," Abernathy replied as he still had to wade through several feet of rice just to get there, and he really wasn't happy with having to turn his back on the pirates that may be pursuing him while he was trying to climb the container. "I'll be hitting the container in ten seconds, then I should have a clear shot to the tower. So whatever distracting you have left, do it and run."

Thomas made it to the corner, quickly enough, but only had one other grenade. He took it out.

The pirates around the corner didn't have a lot of places to hide from incoming fire, there were even fewer places to fire from a defended position, but there were lots of them spread around the deck.

Then the clank came from around the corner, the pirate's eyes widened in horror. The two who'd seen the previous grenade blow their pirate comrades blown apart scrambled away hoping that distance could save them. Those that had cover saw the bouncing grenade, saw their comrades in panic, and ducked behind whatever piece of metal they had to avoid the blast yet to come.

Instead, Thomas rounded the corner, shot the wounded man on the ground in front of him, shot and wounded three of the pirates simply ducking for cover, while diving for the grenade he rolled across the deck, which still possessed its pin. While on his back, he pulled the pin and flung it back over his head towards the concealed pirates while using the body of one of the wounded pirates as cover.

The blast was now moving closer to Omar's position. *How many men were his men dealing with*, he thought. Omar saw Abshir and Ali cowering on steps to the lower deck, which enraged him. These two, who reported this ship as an easy target! He wanted to shoot them both himself. "You two, up! You're coming with me....lead the way," Omar pointed towards the sounds of the shooting and Omar thought *I can always shoot them myself later.*

Thomas was temporarily exposed. The blast had kept their heads down for a second, but that wouldn't last. Instead of taking the time to reload his suppressed SBR, he drew the Sig P229 from his vest since he was still on his back. He rolled over to his left and opened fire non-stop on every pirate he could identify, still using the wounded pirate as cover. Thomas expended the twenty rounds quickly, then rolled back behind the pirate, he dropped the empty gun and drew the fully loaded one from his leg. The pirates returned fire, mostly spraying the area from cover without really aiming. Their bullets ricocheted off the steel deck all around, the wounded pirate waving at his allies to stop until several struck him while lying there. He was only wounded no more. Thomas continued the roll to the other side and opened fire as he'd done before, but kept rolling and firing the two more complete rolls until he was back behind some cover of the container. He reloaded the handgun and holstered it while feeling fire in his left chest.

"Abernathy, where are we at?" Thomas called out, as he was using his hand to check for a wound.

Abernathy was finally through the loose rice, had climbed up the container, and was just lifting himself on the top of the dropped container. "I'm on top now, I'll have a clear run."

Thomas pulled what looked like the remnants of a bullet from where the pain was coming from, there was pink, but there was no real blood. One of the rounds sprayed at Thomas ricocheted off the steel deck upwards, but was caught by the curved end of the ballistic steel plate he wore on the front. The mangled bullet only had enough energy left to run along the inside of the curved plate, tearing through the material of his clothes, and ended up becoming trapped between his skin and the metal and his skin. Thomas knew that bullets were heated to over 500F when fired, which is relevant if you're using it to start a fire, but damn, they burn too. The lack of a lot of blood meant it was a contact injury, he could put a bandaid on that later. Bandaid wounds are a win.

"Then run brother, because I'm doing the same thing. Get ready at the door Max!" Thomas held the reloaded SBR and fired a volley aimlessly around the corner, the pirates responded in kind, then Thomas fired again. Then he ran like hell. Letting the pirates think that there would be a continued exchange of fire would give him the seconds to cover the rest of the open deck without having to look back. So he hoped.

Atkins, Marks, and Nguyen all arrived on the deck by Max's position by the tower at about the same time. They took positions to cover Thomas and Abernathy. There wasn't any fire coming from the two remaining fishing boats. During Thomas's attack, they'd slowed from Bennett's continuing fire; their engines no longer working and their hull no longer seaworthy. The two vessels were adrift behind their ship and out of view of the men on deck anyway.

Siegfried, forced to remain inside the ship and worse, compelled to listen to Abernathy in need while he had to stay at his post, was killing him. "How close Thomas," he called out over their coms.

"Abernathy" Thomas simply asked.

"Seconds out" Abernathy replied, huffing from a much harder run than expected.

"Close, get ready, we're almost there" Thomas replied.

Max looked around at the three, "You three, get up the tower, I got this, we don't need to get backed up getting through the door."

The three men looked around and at each other, there were no bad guys to justify arguing the order to retreat, so the three jumped to their feet and hustled to the door. Nguyen and Marks went through the door and started to run up the stairs. Atkins, being the last man, figured he'd get the door for the three remaining men making the run. So he pulled on it, to get it started and hold it, to be ready. It didn't move. He pulled on it hard, then threw his foot on the wall pulling with all his might. Nothing. He looked behind, it wasn't secured to the wall at all. Then he noticed the doorway, there was some pitting from a blast. The RPG fired over Max's head and hit the corner of a container, it took the brunt of the blast. However, some of the molten copper that's spewed forth to defeat armor ahead of it had struck the upper hinge on the door. It was welded in place.

"Shit, we have a problem," Akins called out turning to Max, and everybody heard over coms. "The door to the tower is welded open, it won't close."

Siegfried stated the obvious, "It has to close."

"No time," Thomas replied.

Siegfried, not liking what he might be asked to do, "Thomas, it really has to close! Trust me."

"Max, grab a frag grenade, wrap three fire extinguishers

around it, and head up the stairs and wait," Thomas instructed.

Max turned and bolted through the door to the tower.

"Wait, what?" Atkins asked Max.

"You cover them," Max replied, grabbing the first fire extinguisher then turning to head up the stairs. "Somebody get me some fucking duct tape!"

Captain Zhao had duct tape. He tossed it to a crewman who simply ran with it towards where Zhao was pointing, out the door and down the stairs. Marks and Nguyen were on the third level and took an extinguisher off the wall. They looked down at Max who must've instinctively felt their gaze and just yelled out "stay there, I'm coming to you." Max grabbed the second extinguisher then moved up the stairs.

Omar, now reinforced with the six men from the port side that made up for the six he lost, moved them all forward. He moved slowly at first. There were still thirty of them on board. And so far as he could tell, there were only a few shooting back at them. They may have walked into a trap, but with thirty men on board, he was determined to take the ship. That determination was even stronger now that he had no boats of his own. There was no retreat "Our boats are gone, this ship is our only way home. Live or die! Your only chance for life is to take the ship!"

After rounding the corners without taking any fire, he felt motivated to push faster and overwhelm whoever is left on board. Looking up, he also didn't want to be victim to a falling container. "Run, run now," he ordered. Omar looked at both Abshir and Ali, who looked back at Omar, "you two, run" he motioned with his AK-47. The two took off ahead of Omar, but not with the speed or enthusiasm as the others in front of them.

Abernathy was first to the stairs and saw Atkins waving him on through the door. Thomas was nearing the top of the stairs as the pirates turned the corner. Several of them raised their weapons to fire, but too late, their shots went over his head as they lost the angle. Omar caught sight of Thomas running for his life, and he wanted blood. "Run, run now" commanding that his men sprint ahead, desperate to catch this man alone.

As several of the pirates made it over the top, they fleetingly saw Thomas run through the doorway, then another man returned fire briefly, but he too quickly ducked and spun inside, disappearing through the doorway.

Thomas looked back as Atkins followed. "Keep moving up."

"Keep moving ole man," was Atkins' reply.

Thomas looked up and saw Max holding three fire extinguishers over the gap that would fall between stairways.

Omar paused, the door was still open. There was nothing between them and the inside. He looked up expecting a container to be dangling above, but there was nothing. There were no shooters seen. He stood up bravely, looking back at Abshir and Ali, now behind him on the lower deck. Their advancement was slowed by the gunfire of Atkins as he turned to enter the tower, and the two would not be quick to pursue. He shook his head, he'd deal with them later.

After Thomas and Atkins were up a few flights, Thomas paused, letting Atkins go by, "Siegfried."

"It's time, turn on the pumps," Thomas ordered.

Siegfried had checked the valves a thousand times in the last few minutes, he flipped the switch. "It's on," was all he said.

The fire system previously installed had nozzles piped all along the deck of the metal ship. The methodically designed sprinkler system worked as exactly intended. The aerosolized gasoline was being sprayed onto the outer deck.

The pirates all stopped in their tracks, looking at each other in horror. Omar ran for the open door, looking back at Abshir and Ali who were already running in the opposite direction. *Nowhere for them to go* Omar laughed to himself, *at least they'll burn.*

Some of the pirates started to follow Omar, hoping for the open door. Others ran towards the side, thinking about jumping overboard but stopping realizing there were no boats left. Instead, they looked in vain for safety, and a few seemed frozen, becoming more awash in the aerosolized gasoline particles now soaking the clothes and clinging to their skin, perhaps believing this was just a warning.

Omar's sprint to the door briefly slowed as he approached just outside, he viewed something appear in front of him. As if in slow motion, the red fire extinguisher was lowering itself from above. In the most fleeting of thoughts, he thought it was there to help.

The blast of the grenade ripped through the three pressurized extinguishers, propelling the metal through Omar's face, removing his head from his body in pieces while his body fell forward and to the floor due to the inertia from trying to jump inside.

Immediately after the blast. "Spark it," Thomas called out. The system was simple. Spark Plugs wired around the ship, their tips exposed to the air. The aerosolized gasoline didn't take long to ignite at various points around the ship and the "whoosh" of the flame was an explosion all around. The pirates in the middle of the blast were set ablaze, but there were no screams from them. There was no air to breathe and the first breath of the liquid flames destroyed any ability to call out in whatever agony they surely felt.

Some were close to the edge, thinking they'd wait and see to decide if they should jump. They should've jumped. The igniting gas just set them ablaze quicker than their ability to decide, much less move. The blast propelled them towards the metal wall serving as a railing. Most were mercifully rendered unconscious from the blast, as they were then consumed by the relentless fire. The Fafnir lived up to its name.

Captain Zhao watched out from the bridge. The gas sprang forth at slightly different times around the ship, it had to flow from point A to point B, so some appeared to scramble clear of being soaked before it eventually caught up to them. He didn't see any that survived, and none seemed to jump overboard. There was no escape. Zhao thought to himself, "I'd have jumped, boat or no boat."

Thomas had made it to the top and saw Zhao shaking

his head, saying, "Nobody left" before he even got in view of the deck below. After immediately seeing the carnage, and agreeing with Zhao that nobody could be left, he said "Siegfried, hit the water."

Siegfried killed the switch sparking the fuel, moved the gate valves that lead to pumping the gas to pumping seawater. The seawater line was already primed and the pumps were set to operate on maintained pressure, so the change was immediate. Saltwater now sprayed over the deck, outing the flames and turned the cool water to hissing vapor as it fell upon the hot metal. The white plume of steam erupted from all over the ship, billowing forth a cloud that engulfed the boat. The slowed speed allowed only the bow of the boat to be seen, it appeared as it was continually emerging from a cloud gliding across the water. It was a cloud of death for the pirates.

The explosion of the fire extinguishers had prevented the fuel from being ignited at the bottom of the tower and stopped the fire from spreading inside through the open door. A fire would have erupted quickly upwards, the smokestack like tower drawing in air at the bottom sending the heated smoke and heat upwards to where all of the crew was supposed to be safe.

None of them realized that the blast designed to make the bottom of the stair non-flammable also killed a pirate directly. That grisly discovery would be made by the boat's crew when they "cleaned up."

# CHAPTER XIV

## *Wrath of Dusk*

Omar was smart. General Fiidka valued him above all others, which was why he was his second in command. The Colonel had the command of the men while Fiidka had bullied his way to the top over other factions. Omar was the tactician that kept him there, which was why Fiidka sent him to personally oversee killing the men on this ship. Omar's plan of blaming other groups with equipment from this ship was brilliant, it could have more than made up for the loss of a dozen little boats. And the loss of the men? Those were easily replaceable. Besides, new blood was always hungrier. But now he couldn't contact Omar. Fearing the worst wasn't just based on fear, the GPS trackers he had on his four large fishing boats and especially his catamaran had disappeared from view, and all around the same time, some of the blips circling aimlessly before going dark. He didn't have GPS tracking on all the small boats, whether any of the three small ones were lost, he didn't know. Yet with four forty-five foot fishing boats gone, it didn't bode well for the smallest to have survived.

With Omar gone, and the boats are gone, then all those men are gone. Was there fifty, or sixty? He didn't know. There were sixty-two in all, but he never truly counted or cared. He thought about the twenty, or twenty-five or so were previously lost on all those small boats. It was about to get worse.

Magan was one of his lieutenants, he'd been executing Omar's plan in his absence, and was on his way up to see him. It wasn't good news.

"General Fiidka, I've heard nothing new about Omar and our men. There is still no contact with the boats." Magan stood there strongly, not even wanting to appear in any way responsible for this loss.

Fiidka nodded but was less concerned about the boats, or even the men, than the future of their plan, which now seemed impossible. "What about the attacks on the other groups?"

"I've had a number of the other groups attacked, as Omar ordered," Magan added.

"And our losses," Fiidka asked.

"Twenty-three, or so, as I'm aware so far," Magan replied. "I used mostly younger, less experienced men, as Omar ordered sir" Magan made sure to add again. "Omar felt that using men that weren't connected to us was better, though they were less experienced and therefore suffered greater losses. Several are wounded, and well, we don't know yet."

"And with Omar's failure, now we won't have the proof from the ship to plant and blame the other groups. We'll be the targets of both the others and whatever foreigners that sank our boats if it's found out that we were the ones responsible," Fiidka said aloud.

Magan wasn't sure what to say. "They won't say. I'm sure."

"If you want to be Omar, you'll make sure," Fiidka replied. "How many are left that know it was really us? I mean how many even have a clue?"

"About a dozen others, they're young men, trying to make a name for themselves, it seemed good to give them a chance to earn their place," Magan offered, not realizing what was to come.

"Then kill them," Fiidka said. "If you want to be Omar..."

Magan didn't blink, he knew it just as easily could be him. And besides, he so desperately wanted to be Omar.

"Of course, General Fiidka. I'll take care of it myself." Magan felt his dream was coming true. "We'll need more men General, many men."

"We'll get more." Fiidka stared at Magan. "Tomorrow, you take care of those who might betray us. Then we'll go to that "savior of the poor and pitiful," and take the cream of the crop like we always do."

Magan was a local recruited by another local who'd worked his way up as an enforcer in the local drug trade. He was noticed by Fiidka years ago and joined his men directly. He didn't know what Fiidka meant, better to ask quickly. "I don't know what you mean, General Fiidka."

"Ah, yes," Fiidka remembered seeing him as a younger boy, wanting him around, even though he was too old for him personally. "The refugee camp. There is a foreigner that attracts many people from all over. Lost families, men with no future, young boys looking for *adventure*. I pay the right guards. We can always get more men.'" Fiidka smiled and walked away.

"Of course General Fiidka. The next day then." Magan called out as Fiidka walked down the hall.

# CHAPTER XV

## *The Twist*

On the Fafnir, the men celebrated. Not with a party, but with the relief that comes afterward, with the adrenalin that makes holding in laughter hard and sitting still impossible. The quick recounting of stories, the joke of Abernathy's accomplishment of climbing MT. Rice, a story destined to be retold ad nauseam.

One of the stories would be Atkins, who suffered the only real wound. While in the stairway to the tower, after the fire, the other men saw the blood on Atkins. They saw it on the back of his left leg. All of a sudden they turned, genuinely concerned, Marks pulled a field dressing stored in one of his pants pockets. "Relax buddy, I got you," Marks said.

Atkins recoiled, thinking about trying to get out of identifying where the wound was because he didn't want to hear about it, but seeing their concern – their genuine concern – he relented and said, "Just give me the bandage, I got hit in the ass."

"I thought so," Marks said jokingly. "I was just hoping to grab your ass."

"Fuck you, I'd rather bleed out," Atkins replied. "Give me the dressing brother, it's nothing."

"Seriously, if you need someone to take a look, Nguyen is available," Marks replied, not letting go of the ribbing. The otherwise small wound would surely turn into a never-ending story.

Captain Zhao's men were "cleaning up the boat," which meant they were dealing with the dead pirates. It wasn't a thankless job, Thomas's men did offer to help, but the help was refused. The crew saw the aftermath, they heard from others on the bridge the carnage that the pirates had intended for all of them. They may have signed up for this, but the second they were the targets and Thomas's men saved them, they felt saved nonetheless. Plus, Captain Zhao pointed out that whatever they found while cleaning up was theirs to keep. The pickings were sparse, the fire saw to that. One of the pirates must've had a gold ring, there was a molten piece of gold found in the area of a hand. While it had condensed into a blob, it was still gold worth keeping. Others took the remnants of the firearms found, hoping to clean them, but most were a lost cause. The steel parts survived, many aluminum parts did not. Still, they preferred only having to clean the deck than having to be the ones who had to fight on it. The scene was apocalyptic, and still smoldering.

Thomas walked up to the bridge immediately after the fireworks were over. He didn't want to be congratulated by his men; he didn't want to face them. Not yet. Captain Zhao came over, beaming an even bigger smile, if possible, and shook Thomas's hand with the veracity of Keith Moon on the drums. "Thank you, Captain, if you don't mind, I need to go sit for a few."

"Oh, of course Captain Thomas, of course," Zhao replied. "Don't you worry, I'll take care of..." and Zhao paused, not knowing how he should phrase it, "...all this mess. Including the containers."

Thomas nodded, walked into the room adjacent to the bridge, poured a good-sized glass of bourbon, not bothering to get ice, and sat at the small table in the center of the room. "Now comes the hard part," he thought.

Max stood at the bottom of the tower. He stared at the gruesome remains of the hand grenade slash fire extinguisher bomb that kept the fire from roaring into the stairway of the tower. The headless corpse was no longer threatening, no longer seeking to take all that Max had. Max reminded himself of the necessity, as all the men did at one time or another, often in different ways. They all knew they operated in a gray area. The ability to compartmentalize wasn't good, or bad, it was just necessary.

One of Zhao's crew caught Max's eye on deck, and he waved him over. The man came running.

Max looked down at the headless corpse but pointed to the melted hinge that prevented the door from closing. "Fix this first, the door has to be able to close..." he said, briefly looking down at the corpse again. "Then get rid of that."

The man looked at Max as if the instructions were out of order.

"If we're attacked again, we need to close the door. The dead can wait." Max turned to go back into the tower stepping over all that was left of Omar.

Max climbed the stairs slowly, he was in no real hurry despite his foreboding tone to the crewman. The other's were patting each other on the back and Max just reminded them to get back to their posts on the off chance there was more to come. Thankfully Robert was still looking over them so he wasn't worried about an imminent attack. There were no other boats in the area.

Once onto the bridge, he was given the same hero's greeting from Captain Zhao. Max was looking for Thomas, and Zhao pointed to the room inside.

Max walked in. The lights were off. Max turned on the light and saw Thomas sitting at the end of the table with his head slightly bowed, a drink firmly in hand.

"You okay?" Max asked.

Thomas briefly looked at Max with a faint smile but had to look away.

The hesitation and regret quickly passed, replaced by the normal conviction, "Sorry Max, but I'm not done yet." Thomas threw the red binder onto the table. It was new to Max.

Max didn't say a word. He picked up the red binder and started to read. Thomas always broke down missions this way. A summary of the overall mission objective, then with steps along the way. But along those steps of how Thomas expected things to go, were branches of possible alternatives and solutions. It was like an inverted tree that started as the bottom of the trunk, grew into a tree, then ended at the bottom of a trunk. In reality, their missions most often looked like the straight line he'd planned on, but there are always bumps.

Max only glanced at the tree, and read the beginning of the summary: "The land-based mission will involve landing the two Flyer Defense 60s, establish overwatch on the route from Ciid Fiidka's compound to the refugee camp, while the rest would travel to the refugee camp and eliminate Fiidka there. Then..."

Max didn't bother to keep reading and slammed the binder hard on the table, "What the fuck, Thomas?" Max pounded both fists on the table staring at Thomas, then just as quickly threw both arms in the air, "Land-based mission? I don't even know where to start!"

"I know," Thomas said, "I know this is a problem, but..."

Max cut him off, "No, no, no, you don't get to explain first. Speaking of first. Forget we brought eight guys for defending a ship... a *ship,* Thomas. Which, worked out as planned, eight guys attacking a warlord on land is a bit light. Forget that I didn't know that this is what I signed up for. I know the men we contracted earned every penny of their pay already, and they sure as hell don't owe us anything more than that. *Us,* Thomas. Me, you and Robert. Which again, forget all that, *us.* How the hell do you spring all this on me in the middle of an operation....did Robert know?"

"No, Max, nobody knows," Thomas replied.

"Well that's excellent, at least you're a selfish jerk to everyone," Max replied.

"You're not wrong," Thomas said. "You're not wrong about how I'm handling this, but you're wrong about the why."

"I'm thinking I should explain it to all of you, all the men at the same time. Don't you think that's best?" Thomas asked.

Max was nodding his head up and down while staring at Thomas angrily, but that followed with "No! Are you nuts?"

Thomas wasn't arguing the latter part, but didn't expect the "no."

"Look, I know you. That's what's annoying me on so many levels. I know you're not a selfish jerk, I know that you've treated our partnership as *that* at all times, even when you're clearly the one doing the leading. I know that I'm worried about eating my words here, because you always have a plan." Max stood up straight. "So if I'm eating my words, I'm not doing it in front of anyone else, and if you're going to convince them of going ashore to attack a warlord on his home turf...you're going to need my help to convince them."

"You're too good to me," Thomas said.

"Don't get too excited, I'm going to stay pissed at you for not bringing this up, earlier." Max was turned away from Thomas shaking his head, thinking, *I know he's going to convince me.* Max then said, "Fine, let's get this over with, and I don't want to read the long version. Tell me what the hell's going on."

"Well, it all has to do with Uncle," Thomas began. "More to the point, family." And Thomas explained everything.

Max then exited the bridge and started to gather up the men, having the crew posted as lookouts. He was sure some of them would have preferred that job to the "cleanup."

They all gathered in the room off the bridge, it wasn't roomy, but Max had Robert on the satphone so everybody could hear everything.

Max turned to Thomas, "your show."

Thomas sat with red binders for all the men in front of him, the fingers of his right hand tapping over them.

"These binders are for each of you, but only if you want. You've fulfilled your obligation of what you were contracted for, and then some," Thomas said with an appreciative nod and smile. "So after you read through this, you can accept, or... or you can stay on this ship as the security detail until we dock in a few days. Either way, *either way,* I want you to know how grateful I am for the work you all did here. The reason we're all still here is because we all did the heavy lifting at some point."

The men nodded, still pumped from the adrenaline still flowing in the aftermath of combat.

"But before you read the mission, I need to share a few things about myself, personal things. I'm not telling you this to sway your decision, but so that you understand *my* decision. My decision to do it at all, and also my decision on how I decided to handle it in this way.

Max & Robert were just as unaware of it as the rest of you." Thomas paused, but of course, he didn't share enough yet to warrant a response, the men nodded and were all ears. Thomas rose to sit on the side of the chair, slowly taking total command of the room.

"When I was eleven, my father died. My father worked for Uncle, doing this work for God & Country, at least that's how he described it to me. Not that I knew much of anything about his work, he was away a lot. But there were weapons in the house that I dare not touch, papers in boxes I dare not read, and people who'd come to the home that I dare not see. We moved around a lot, and my mother had died before I could have a memory of her, so I didn't know how odd my life was..." Thomas took a pause and looked as if he was trying to find a memory that just wasn't there.

"So, my father died. What then? A man came to my home, and he was one of the few men I'd seen before. Once, when a neighbor mentioned him to me, my father quickly replied it was my uncle, from my mother's side. I accepted that as true. This man came to my home and promised to take care of me, promised to raise me, promised to let me be what I wanted to be. I told him I wanted to be like my dad. While it was a normal response for an 11-year old, I think I gave him an idea. How to make an 11-year old be like his dad. Look at us, what do you see?"

The men casually looked around the room, not knowing exactly where he was going with this. "Experience. We're all experts in something. We're all accomplished in our jobs, and not just because we're strong, fast, and can endure, and not just because we're smart. We're experienced. That experience makes all the other tools we have what we are. Look at some of the best operators in the world. They're not twenty when they're at their peak physically. So many of the best ones – the best at surviving the chaos that is almost guaranteed to happen in battle, or in a mission – are the ones with the experience to foresee how things are going to unfold, and who take the chaos in stride when it's sure to come."

"Shame of it is, as we're all finding out, 'you can't put the wise experienced mind, in the body of the young.'" Thomas rose pointing to his own. "At 35, I'm in great shape, and intend to be for many years yet to come." Pointing at Max, "we've been running some great operations."

"Uncle got the idea of letting me be like my dad, without waiting. He took me in, and involved me in missions from day one." Thomas paused for that to sink in a second, but raised his hand to stop an obvious question, "No, I wasn't armed in the field at 11. Uncle would describe the problem, and then the mission plan. He'd tell me about previous missions, my schoolwork was to review previous missions and point out the flaws, to question how it was done, and try to come up with better ways to have executed the plan. Between personally sharing his thoughts and knowledge I had access to a massive amount of classified information that a Congressman wouldn't be allowed to read. Then, as time went by, Uncle introduced me as 'working for him.' Despite my obvious young age and a periodic odd look, nobody ever questioned it. I didn't talk much, usually only sharing my thoughts with Uncle, letting him use them when needed. For me, it was homework."

"Homework, until he had me go through basic training at Parris Island at 16. Nobody knew. Nobody was to ever know. Being big enough and muscular for any age helped. Having worked with some of the best interrogators in the world made dealing with the mental knives of the drill instructors palatable, nobody could ever say easy," and they all shared the laugh with their own memories of hardships at the hands of their own instructors years ago. "But by that time I already had five full years of on-the-job intelligence training."

"I had private tutors for schooling, and their paperwork is what got me into and out of college with a degree before remote learning was a thing, all while I traveled the world with Uncle. The reason I know I've done well isn't just me. While the 18-year-old grunt may serve four years before really starting an intel career at twenty-two, I was given at least a ten-year head start on experience. And not just run-of-the-mill busy work, but the kind of real-world dirt that set up black missions for years. That kind of head start helped set up our company, our success rate, and resulted in the very liquid quid-pro-quo that still exists because of it. Our cooperation with Uncle, doing the work we do often overlaps with the work he'd like to do, but can't. This is why we have help when we need it."

Thomas paused again so they could take all that in. "Help. So, how help applies here. Uncle has a son, therefore, he's my 'cousin.' While we grew up together, Jeremy did not want to follow in his father's footsteps, so while I spent most of the day with his father, he did not. We all know lots of people who are built differently.

We can do this job, we know others who can't. Jeremy not only couldn't, but *wouldn't.* He was repulsed by the idea of even being a soldier, and even more so the idea of working in the shadows. So Jeremy didn't want to follow in dad's footsteps, and his dad – to his credit – didn't force him to. He instead paid for him to go to an Ivy League school, where he shared his Ivy League ideas with his Ivy League friends, but Jeremy didn't choose a soft, cushy Ivy League life."

"Fast forward in time, and Jeremy is now the head of a refugee camp," Thomas nodded in the general direction of land, "in Somalia."

Things were starting to come together with the men.

"Jeremy's a great guy, selfless. While to us, to me, he's grossly naïve of reality, that naiveté has allowed him to build something that's saved thousands in a land where most would never try, and some of those that do are killed for it. He just can't protect it."

"Ciid Fiidka has, for years, used the camp to attract men to pirate for him, or work the drug trade, or whatever other criminal endeavors he's involved in. For the most part, he only took those willing. While the willing may have seen the life of a drug lord as their only escape, even if true, that was their choice. But since Fiidka's a pedophile, he also uses the camp as his personal supply of young boys. And those boys are not going willingly. They're taken. If the mother fights, she's beaten, or worse."

Thomas stood, putting the folders on the desk in front of him with his hand held in the fig leaf position, displaying what little vulnerability he had. "So I plan to eliminate Fiidka, eliminate the cycle of terror for this region from one of the largest criminal organizations that both feeds off desperate young men, and does far worse to others."

"So, *this* is personal to me. I'll adapt and carry out a plan whether anyone wants in, but this is my mission, not the company's mission. There was no point bringing this up if the first part didn't go as planned. And don't beat yourselves for wanting to ask, there is additional pay. You'll see it at the end of the binder. Some of it is a bit creative and you may have some questions on that as well, but either way....I'll be on the deck." Thomas stood and walked out.

Max could be heard saying, "Read it, you'll see."

Thomas stood on the deck of the container ship, the smell of the sea mixed with the distinct smell of a doused fire. The sunset containing a beauty that could never be created by Man hung above the scene of the burnt corpses the crew was removing. It was surreal. Thankfully, the crew was methodically getting rid of the remains over the side, but the memory would be indelible. To Thomas, there was a sense of failure in this victory. The only solutions that work are sometimes regrettably the worse ones. His thoughts pulled him to think if he was doing the right thing as the men emerged from the base of the tower, with Max leading the way.

The men stood like a jury around him, and he was the one waiting for the verdict.

Max took a step back. “This isn’t my show. The men have some questions.”

Bennett took a step forward, as if it was required to take the floor, “I read the overwatch portion, where Abernathy and I, along with another one of these yutzes,” Bennett said pointing at the group, “would be the stopping force for any vehicular response from Fiidka’s compound to the refugee camp.”

“Yes, that’s correct,” Thomas said matter of factly.

“Well I don’t see why we’d need a third,” Bennett pointed out.

Abernathy chimed in. “I think he means if we’re a’ hammering vehicles of evil, we’re not waiting ‘til they’re close enough to spit on. So a third man seems like he should be tagging along with the group at the camp. After all, if you fail what’s the point?”

Bennett nodded but wanted to clarify: “I’m saying that Abernathy and I can hold any group off that they throw at us. A third guy is a waste. The two of us can spot for each other. And if the vehicles are approaching, we’re going to shoot them, how much spotting do we really need?”

“Okay, so your spotter can go with us,” Thomas meekly agreed. Thomas was concerned with addressing fears in the plan, and instead he received good advice to be bolder.

Bennett and Abernathy nodded as if that answered all their questions.

“That’s it?” Thomas asked.

“Not quite,” Nguyen interjected. “The additional payment methods."

"Yes, what about them," Thomas replied.

"It seems as if that's operating against the client," Nguyen said questioningly.

"Ah yes," Thomas replied, then catching himself. "And by "ah yes" I mean I understand your reason for the question. The client is aware of the first, and wholly on board as he's the one financing the second."

"The explanation left a lot of leeway for the final dollar amount," Nguyen added.

"There's no doubt about that," Thomas said convincingly. "The first, I expect, would be no less than around $50,000. It may be more, but Robert is still working on that part. It'll be an equal share irrespective, and that includes Max and me"

"And Robert," Max chimed in, "to be clear," he said, shrugging his shoulders.

"Yes," Thomas admitted. "The second part is hard to say. It could be nothing, or as you see, it could be quite a lot. Honestly, the second part with Lee sounds ridiculous. While I'm confident he'll try to make it work, I have no way to guarantee how it will play out in the end."

"So basically $50,000 extra, up to a lot more?" Bennett asked.

"Could be less than $50,000," Thomas pointed out. "But I wouldn't put it less than $40,000 if that makes a difference."

Nobody spoke. Thomas assumed there were reservations, and he wanted to say he understood it was too much to ask.

“Relax, Thomas. We’re in. We’re all in,” Max said.

# CHAPTER XVI

## *Infil*

Thomas beamed a big smile that would've put Captain Zhao to shame. "Then come with me to check out our rides." Thomas waved the men to follow and they all descended into the bowels of the containership. The two armed vehicles brought onboard were described as being possibly used against attackers, they're heavy armaments could be quickly moved around the deck if need be, but obviously wouldn't fare well if the deck was set on fire.

No one was aware of their real purpose, until now.

The vehicles are Flyer Defense 60s, a lightly armored off-road vehicle that can be heavily armed. The Flyer is a tubular design, which gives it the strength it needs to travel quickly over any terrain. The design also provides a lot of protection and they're incredibly adaptable depending on the mission.

One of the vehicles was armed with an M2 .50 BMG machine gun mounted on the top of the vehicle, with a SAW light machine gun mounted for the guy riding shotgun. SAW stands for Squad Automatic Weapon and fired the same 5.56 round as the M4. The difference between it and the M4 was that it was belt-fed. This means 200 rounds of uninterrupted fire from the gun capable of firing 725 rounds per minute. While that sounds impressive, sustained fire will eventually melt any barrel.  After 400 continuous rounds, the barrel should be swapped and Thomas hoped the battle got that heated. Thomas liked the idea of two machine guns mounted to the vehicle. While both could fire simultaneously, the logical deployment is that both open fire to suppress the bad guys, then the M2 does the heavy work while the SAW targets in short bursts, or until the M2 it needs to swap a cartridge belt, then the SAW takes over suppression.

The other flyer had a Mk 19 40 mm automatic grenade launcher mounted in place of the heavy machine gun on the roof. While it looks similar to a machine gun, it is not. While it has a high theoretical cyclic rate, in practice, the 48 round belt is what's fired per minute. With a real-world range of over 1,500 yards, and killing anything inside fifteen feet of impact, it's a devastating weapon. With a usable targeting range of nearly a mile, it's a fantastic weapon for mobile assault. One of the benefits of having Uncle is both vehicles and weapons like this. The vehicle is reported as out of commission somewhere, and arms are reported destroyed somewhere else. Either way, Thomas ends up with some nice arms. And not only the arms. DARPA was looking for real-world testing of the SAGM grenade fired from the launcher. It uses a laser range finder so that the round will detonate above, behind, or next to the intended target, wherever the guy is doing the launching commands. The airburst round is twice as lethal. Uncle apparently promised usage. The only downside was that Thomas had to write after-action reports of weapons like a Yelp review. It was a small price to pay to get advanced weapons. There was no machine gun on this rig, the guy riding shotgun would be free to fire his service weapon wherever he saw fit.

Thomas went over the highlights of the vehicles with the men. It doesn't matter what career you have, cool toys are cool toys.

"So not only will we be heavily armed, these are off-road beasts that can hit 70 mph on the open road," Thomas continued. "So it can get us in and out quickly, and it packs a lot of punch."

"Speaking of "heavily," Max asked, "how heavy are they, and how are we getting them from the ship to Fiidka's?"

"They're over two tons, without arms, us or our gear. Walk this way, and you'll see how we get them to shore," Thomas replied.

Thomas opened a container and inside appeared a mess of a vinyl blob.

"What the hell are we looking at Thomas?" Bennett asked.

"You're looking at a couple of ferryboats," Thomas replied.

"More like "fairy" boats," Nguyen joked. "Those will hold the trucks? On the ocean?"

"Ferryboat, is the company name," Thomas corrected ignoring the joke, "a European company, they're unique. They'll carry up to 11,000 pounds, which we'll be way under. They're not meant for heavy seas, so ship to shore could be tricky. Thankfully, there is a spot where a sandbar juts out to the ocean, meaning that the waves there are minimal."

The men looked at them not being wowed with confidence.

"You'll see how durable they are once inflated, I've taken a ride with one before," Thomas said, trying to assuage any concern.

"When?" Max asked.

"I took a test drive in Budapest," Thomas replied as if it should have been obvious.

"To put your minds at ease, we'll have a couple of small

Zodiacs and life jackets. We won't need'em." Thomas assured them. "The crew members will drive them back to the boat, then they'll head to port at full speed. Robert will make sure they're not near any other boats along the way. When it's 'over, we'll be able to drive right into port and up and onto the boat."

"Man, Thomas, these things just look like bigger versions of my pool toys," Atkins said.

"These aren't made of cheap vinyl, they're made of Hypalon, a synthetic rubber. Plus, they have multiple inflation chambers, so if one starts to leak, the rest are still intact, just like your pool chair," Thomas added.

"Yo man, comparing it to a pool toy really isn't helping," Seigfried said, clearly not liking this part of the plan.

"I can't believe you guys." Thomas looked around at all of them. "So a plan to provoke a mass armed pirate attack, where our survival is built upon being on the *inside* of a gas grill, that I then parlay into attacking a Somali warlord in a multi-pronged land attack with only eight men, and this is the only issue you have?"

Abernathy raised his hand, "Thomas, it's a blow-up toy on the ocean that's going to carry us, that's fine, I'm good with that. But a two-ton vehicle? Honestly, it seems a bit unlikely that'll work."

"It'll work. Once it's filled," Thomas started to explain.

"You mean, once we blow it up," Max joked.

Thomas laughed, shaking his head, "you're not helping."

"Laughter is the best medicine," Max replied, "I read that somewhere."

"Fine, once, we blow it up," Thomas continued, "we have the cranes on the boat to lower it to the water. The Flyers are driven to the deck, the cranes then lift them and place them slowly into the Ferryboats. There will be ropes dangling from the vehicles so those in the inflatable can line it up for an easy insertion. The cranes can lower them as slowly as needed. Then, after you see it floats, we'll all get on board, and head for the shore."

"Fucking Bennett will be the straw that breaks the camel's back," Nguyen joked.

"You sure as hell won't, not with your girlish figure" Bennett replied.

"Ouch," Nguyen laughed. "Just don't eat a big breakfast please."

"So Thomas, when do we set sail?" Max asked.

"Well, there's one big unknown. We won't know when he'll go." Thomas pointed out. "Information collected in the past found that he does go personally, but they haven't ever discovered the trip beforehand. If they did, they would've used a drone strike on the vehicles if they knew he was in them."

"Does Jeremy ever know beforehand?" Max asked.

"No, at least I don't think so," Thomas replied. "I've been in touch with one of his aides for years, making sure he was okay. I've garnered more specifics recently, under the guise of being more concerned, which wasn't entirely a lie. I know what guards are on Fiidka's payroll, that's how I got the pictures you saw in the binder. And I know that once we sneak in, there's a place she can hide us from view. Fiidka likely has informants on the inside as well. Well, even if he doesn't have any, we should assume it."

"I figure we blow up the Ferry's, and leave under the cover of darkness. Drop off Abernathy & Bennett outside of the entrance to Fiidka's place. Hopefully, they'll see vehicles leaving that look like a Fiidka-worthy excursion. We then take up concealed positions inside the camp, so we're not overexposed for any length of time and wait for their arrival. Whatever threats they fear, it won't be inside the camp of unarmed refugees. Also, Robert will still have eyes on us, so that'll help. So if it's going to happen, it'll be today, tomorrow, the next day." Thomas concluded.

"You trust this girl, the employee?" Marks asked.

"Yeah," Thomas replied. "If she's not Jeremy's girlfriend, she wants to be. I previously mentioned some things to do, including a place to hide in case I had to come to rescue Jeremy, along with her and the staff. She seemed comforted by that. I don't think she's as naïve about the area as Jeremy is."

"Look, it's not perfect," Thomas said. "That's the plan, but if we have to bail, we bail. At least we're not on the boat, it's not the Alamo where we have to make our last stand. So check all your gear, and get some sleep."

The men all responded in the affirmative and made their way inside. Thomas went up to the tower and told Captain Zhao to get the inflatable Ferries ready and when to wake him. Thomas didn't bother going down to his room, but went into the office off the bridge, shut the door, and crashed on the cot. It was a long day.

After the men were awakened, they went onto the deck and saw a Flyer suspended by a crane being slowly lowered over the deck. The inflatable Ferries were already in the water. Captain Zhao's crew had the inglorious task of awaiting the truck's arrival, the ropes dangling beneath them. The crewmen grabbed the ropes to help line up the rectangle truck to fit into the rectangular inflatable ferry. The crane operators, used to moving containers around at speed, moved a bit slower, but fit the vehicle in on the first try. The crewman secured the vehicle, while the men on deck took some confidence in the fact that it didn't sink straight away.

Thomas, still looking to add a bit of confidence to this arrangement, "Guys, keep in mind the Marines use an amphibious assault vehicle that weighs 26 tons. They go ship to shore."

"This is a truck on a big pool toy," Nguyen replied. "Nice try, it's still weird."

Once the trucks were loaded on board, each with an abundance of additional ammunition, a small zodiac was loaded as well. It wasn't tied to anything, if there was a catastrophic failure, it would stay afloat. Thomas called down instructing the crew to tie a small anchor to the inflatable. If they capsized because of high seas, that usually meant high wind, and winds can blow an inflatable faster than a man can swim. While the anchors wouldn't touch bottom, the drag should give at least one of them a chance to reach the boat, then drive it to pick up the others. But if it came to that, it wouldn't be roomy. The boats were small and the mission would likely be scrubbed. Even if they saved all their ammo, even if they could take out Fiidka at the refugee camp, they needed the firepower and mobility of the trucks to destroy the response from his compound. Sure, they may be able to get away, but the refugee camp couldn't. And if Thomas's men didn't end them, untold numbers of innocent refugees would bear the brunt of the response by Fiidka's remaining men.

Thomas and their men were lowered to the boats on a platform attached to the crane the same way the trucks were. Once onboard, the men all donned life jackets. Thomas made sure Zhao's crewmen did the same. They didn't seem to share any of the concerns for the trip the way his men did, and he half expected them to have a bit more respect for the trip given their profession on the sea, but their calm demeanor seemed to help.

Thomas's "test" flight of the inflatable ferry was on a lake with a truck, and the only waves were produced on purpose by a powerboat they had sail by to demonstrate the stability. These one of a kind inflatables seemed to be the most viable solution for his mission all things considered. Getting an actual ferry on board wasn't in the budget, nor practical, but he quietly hoped he didn't put too much faith in them. They cast off into the darkness. Somehow not being able to see made how alone they were easier.

One of the greatest inventions is GPS navigation. Glove boxes, stuffed with maps have become a thing of the past. Stopping to ask for directions in places where you should never be to begin with, was no more. But the impact wasn't just on the tourist, the delivery guy, or law enforcement and ambulance response, but both maritime and aviation. They use GPS navigation as well. So while Thomas and his men were plodding along from the Fafnir at the surprising pace of close 20 knots in the inflatable ferry, the navigation should get them exactly to the right place to get to shore. The need to navigate from the stars was lost Thomas thought. While a GPS may not be handy when needed, he could only navigate in general directions. The stars were always there, sans clouds anyway. Yet knowing how to find East, or North by the stars isn't the same as finding an exact spot in the darkness. The Ferries were built to handle a nine-foot swell, but not nine-foot-high crashing waves at the shore. Waves coming into shore at morning tide can vary. That's why the long sandbar jutting out into the ocean like a spear into the oncoming waves was their target. It jutted out far enough into the ocean that the waves were just swells. He was sure the inflatable ferries could manage that far better than the breakers.

Thomas climbed atop the Flyer to have a better view of everything around them. There was no reason to believe they'd run into a problem traveling to shore, but reason, chance, neither mattered. If it could happen, Thomas worried about it. Not worry, as a helicopter mother might, but more like the queen mother responsible for the next ruler. The risk was always in play, and it was always life or death. His eyes were not only straining to see the shore but looking for the white crests of waves, something to be avoided. He had night vision goggles and would put them on when they were closer. It was a clear night and the beauty of the stars was worth the strain to see without them.

The sounds of the surf ahead told them that they were approaching the coordinates entered into the GPS for the sandbar. Thomas donned the night vision goggles, viewing what was in front. There was no sign of the sandbar, the white water from the crashing waves appeared as a straight line continuously in front of him, and the gentle swells were quickly becoming higher and shorter in duration. Thomas called out to the crewman in front to throw him the rope that was tied to the flyer. He looped it around a mount on top of the vehicle so he could stand as if riding the vehicle like a surfboard. Not that he could control the movements, but holding on to the rope stopped him from falling over. He stood to get a broader view. The waves towards shore were in front of him, he spotted the sandbar no less than a hundred yards to their left. The GPS showed that they should be right on it. "Fuck," was all he said when he realized the truth. The sandbar moved.

Thomas pivoted to face the crewman steering the inflatable and dropping to his knees to avoid being tossed over in the increasing swells. "We need to turn hard left now, the Sandbar's to our left."

"But we'll be cutting across the waves, that's no good," the crewman protested.

"No choice," Thomas yelled as the crewman was then quick to turn. "We're too far in to turn back, and if we go forward the waves are too big for what she's made for," Thomas continued to be certain the man understood the predicament before doing something else on his own.

Thomas had previously obtained the GPS coordinates from whatever source map he viewed at the time, and they were likely spot on, at that time. He's sure he meant to have Robert check using the current satellite view he had access to, but simply forgot. The problem with keeping the plan from others is that you miss things. Sandbars are formed by the ocean current and waves, and therefore obviously move somewhat, sometimes quickly in a major storm."Shit, fuck'n, damn," Thomas quietly beat himself up with the oversight.

The inflatable rose gently with every passing swell but began to crash violently to the right as the inflatable met the breaking part of the wave. The breaking part of the wave is where it turns over on itself, violently. "The breakers," Thomas thought. He didn't like the name.

"Everyone, to the port side," Thomas yelled. "And brace yourselves so the wall of the inflatable doesn't smack you into the Flyer." Thomas jumped down as well but retained hold of the rope for stability. Four mean with gear only added on thousand pounds, plus or minus counting the crewman that could move about the boat. It wasn't a lot, but he hoped it would be enough to prevent the inflatable from rolling over on its side after a severe break in the wave. Thomas hoped the men in the other inflatable could hear him on coms over the sounds of the crashing waves.

Water splashed in as the walls of the inflatable bent from the forces in play. The weight of the Flyer kept much of the inflatable rigid, but the forward part of the inflatable was forced backward from the force of every plunge, lowering the protection from taking on water. Yet after every wave, the inflatable sprung back to its original shape.

The water was accumulating inside, which could be a real problem in the long term, even with the onboard pump meant to get rid of water that made it inside. Thankfully, there wouldn't be a long term, and in the short term, it actually helped. As the inflatable dipped to the right, due to going over the breaker, the water on the right was temporarily suspended in the air, while the water on the left held the boat lower in the water, thus lessening the twisting force that may overturn the boat. This dance wouldn't last in their favor, as once the water was deeper, a wave inside the inflatable would eventually have enough of the wrong inertia and that could end them.

"There," Thomas pointed ahead, "there's the sandbar. Turn to the right to get close to the sandbar, and follow it to shore. Go full throttle to overcome the riptides that may be in play here. They'll turn us around quickly and flip us, so let's plow through." Thomas climbed up on the Flyer to look back at the other boat to make sure it was following. It was. "So they got a little wet," he thought.

The crewman piloting the inflatable grazed the sand-bar several times, obviously intent on making it to shore. At this point, there was no real danger of not making it. Even if they sank, it was shallow enough to wade to the sandbar and walk to shore. But ensuring the Flyer made it to shore, that's what was important to him now.

"Stop hitting the sandbar," Thomas yelled at the crewman. "Full speed to shore!" He ordered as the crewman skimmed off the sandbar yet again, causing the inflatable to slow and pivot to the left even more. "Get away from the sandbar and hit the beach," Thomas yelled as the Ferry did just that. It hit the beach hard, the sound of the rubber sliding on sand unmistakable. The Flyer lurched forward as the momentum stopped far more suddenly for the Ferry than the occupants, with nothing but sand before it.

After seeing Thomas's Ferry skip at parts alongside the sandbar, the second boat wisely moved to the right to avoid the same problems, but the breakers did cause more water to land inside. The second inflatable was following the movements of Thomas's ferry almost too intently, the crewman didn't allow enough space between the two. The problem was the pilot never saw the beach. He only saw the first inflatable hit the beach hard. He turned to the right, but too late to avoid contact. The second ferry slid on the water like a car on ice, the left side of the inflatable clipped the right rear corner of the first. The sideswipe action knocked Marks and Nguyen across the boat, and one of the crewmen unconscious. The Ferry then continued full speed onto the beach before coming for a stop. There were burbles in the water. The bubbles were one thing, the sound of the pressurized release left no doubt. It was obvious, it had a leak.

"Okay move," Thomas shouted. "Let's get the trucks to dry sand asap."

On Thomas's boat, the men disconnected the overlapping front part of the boat, which in doing so, turned the inflatable into a landing craft. The connections to the Flyer were disconnected, then driven onto the beach.

On Max's boat, while they disconnected the overlapping front part of the boat, they tended to the unconscious crewman by first getting him to land. Their Flyer came off shortly thereafter. Abernathy ran across the sea strand and while donning his night vision goggles, scanned up and down the beach. They were alone.

"Thomas," Nguyen called. "I think our boat has a leak. Bubbles."

They both looked over at the two empty inflatable Ferries. Thomas waved for one of the crewmen to come over to him while pointing at the boat, "this one has a leak. Deflate it, put it that one along with the other Zodiac in the good one. The four of you will be light enough to have a much easier time getting out along the sandbar than we had coming in with the heavy trucks, just stay far enough away from shore so you don't run into any rocks."

"Should we turn it around first?" the crewman asked.

"No, you don't want the propeller in the sand when you start," Thomas replied. "Back out along the sandbar, then spin it around just like you would if it were a big ship close to shore. Just spin around early, the breakers will give you a bumpy ride." Thomas turned to see the other crewman was now conscious, and otherwise uninjured. "Just make sure you help him through the ride, he doesn't need to get knocked out again.

"Got it," the crewman replied, now barking orders to the others.

"One more thing," Thomas said with a loud voice, and all the crewmen turned, giving him his full attention. "Thanks for your help, but be gone before it's light." The crewmen all understood that. They had sidearms and weren't fixing for a fight. They assembled and inflated the boats, so the reverse would be easier. They were hustling nonetheless.

"Alright men," Thomas called out to his crew, "check your weapons and gear, you'll dry off during the drive." While Thomas loved his 6.8 M4, this mission was going to be much closer contact than the boat, and the suppressed SBR would be a better fit for the job. He had the 60 round mags for the SBR, not just because of the benefit of more rounds, but because when he was on the boat fielding both weapons, there would be no mistaking which mags were for which rifle, as the 6.8 used a standard thinner version that's externally the same as the M4. He lost one of his SIGs to the fire. One pistol would have to do. This mission would be a quick hit and run, or so he hoped. The men got into the two Flyers, Thomas took one last look at the crewmen as they scurried to take down the damaged inflatable hurrying to depart and hoped they'd fare well on their return. *Well*, Thomas thought, *they're going to have it a lot easier than Fiidka's men*. The Flyers drove over the beach, pausing to make sure there was no other traffic before entering the highway. He didn't want any unscrupulous passersby to be aware of their entry, or draw attention to the crewmen on the beach.

The drive to the refugee camp would have been easy enough, it was located on the outskirts of town, intentionally far away from any populated area. Plus, the vehicles don't need roads. They do need to be concealed, however. They couldn't just park them and take a walk. For this, Thomas cheated. He contacted Uncle looking for a parking spot nearby to hide the vehicles from view. There wasn't one. But just as shipping containers are made for living in refugee camps, they're available elsewhere. He first thought of contacting Mr. Lee, he knew he had containers, but Lee could then pull the plug on the rest of the mission, whereas this was the part Uncle wanted most, and not just for Jeremy's sake. Fiidka had been a thorn in their side for years. This part of the mission was one of the reasons they got the support from Uncle, so it's only fair to utilize it.

Uncle had a trustworthy contact that transported a container to an obscure pile of dirt close enough to the refugee camp for the men to walk, yet far enough away that it did not attract any attention. The two men that Uncle sent would be guarding the vehicles while Thomas and his men were inside the camp. Thomas was never fond of trusting people he didn't know, and he didn't know these men. When Uncle said they were trustworthy, did that mean they were paid enough to be, or did he honestly trust them? It was the same in the end, there was no valet at the camp, so there was no choice but to use them anyway.

They turned off of the road and proceeded up a dry river bed to get around to the back end of the camp, but they were still more than a half-mile away. If people wandered around, it would be between the camp and the road, not back here. This time, the GPS coordinates were spot on. The container was tied down to a low flatbed, metal ramps were already in place in anticipation of their arrival.

The two trustworthy men were standing outside of the truck, one by the door to the cab, the other at the rear of the container. Both were armed with AK-47's. The man at the rear didn't ask for names, who else would be showing up like this. He waved Thomas's Flyer forward to drive inside. Thomas and the men exited, and Marks drove slowly up the ramp. He then exited the Flyer with his gear, and Nguyen repeated the process with the second Flyer. The man shut the back of the container and locked it. He showed Thomas and the men the key, and showed how it unlocked the lock, then handed it to Thomas without a word. Thomas took the key and appreciated the effort to appear trustworthy anyway, they could still drive off with it. However, the gesture was that "we're not going to touch your stuff" was better than nothing.

Thomas and the men huddled up to get a bead on their way into the camp. Thomas had been in touch with Hanna, the aid worker who would hide them. She was reluctant, of course. She thought she was giving Thomas information on how to come help if *she* called him, not the other way around. However, it didn't take much to convince her. He assured her Fiidka was coming to the camp, not only to take men but boys. Also, he informed her, Fiidka had suffered a terrible defeat and may do much worse. Gunfire in the area wasn't uncommon at all, but there had been a lot more recently, so that did make sense to her. Thomas left out the part that the loss was both at his hands and by his design. The men knew to keep that to themselves as well. They were "fortunate" to be able to get there in time.

Thankfully, Hanna had been planning this for some time. Over that time, it allowed her to move things around piecemeal, so it didn't seem suspicious. There was little cover inside the camp as a whole. There were tents, there were open containers, there were large open areas. Very little was private, and the very nature of feeding, and treating the people staying there meant they had to be able to move around the camp. There was fencing around the outside, with barbed wire. There were guards at the entrances, and others at certain places inside the camp, but that was more to guard the stores than the people. Hanna found that the guards would "check" on the supplies quite often, looking for things to steal and sell themselves, as they could pretty much come and go as they pleased. While they couldn't access the medicine, the most basic things have great value where abject poverty and war destroy the most basic of necessities.

The one place they really couldn't go was the makeshift hut that housed the "women's" supplies. There was no real reason for them to enter, they distributed none of it, and there was something in the culture that was "unmanly" about a man having anything to do with women's personal hygiene products. The hut couldn't just abut the fence however, then it would be too easy to be robbed from the outside. So she stored unused cots and metal stands under a tarp next to the fence. Things that would be too unwieldy to carry over a fence, and impossible to sneak out the gate. Piles of tent poles and rolled canvass were placed strategically, over time. Then the haphazardly thrown tarp over the material to protect it. By doing this, there was a path from the fence, to the supply hut, totally under a tarp and unseen by all. While a sudden need for tent construction could happen at any time if there was an influx of refugees, this happened infrequently, and there was no news to believe this would happen soon. Plus, immediately after speaking to Thomas, she had several additional tents put up with extra cots. She told Jeremy with all the recent additional gunfire, it would be smart to be ready for a few, just in case. Jeremy thought it was a great idea, and thanked her for being so involved. She felt a pang of guilt, but it was fleeting. Despite being at great risk herself, she couldn't stand the idea of anything happening to Jeremy.

Thomas looked for the piece of cloth she said she'd place on the fence to identify where to enter. While they could've thrown a blanket over the barbed wire, that would've made a lot more noise and would risk waking others in the camp. Instead, she removed the steel ties to the bottom of the fence and left them under the tarp for his men to reinstall later. Thomas's men could lift the fence, crawl to the pile of junk, and under the tarp and up to the hut. To help keep others out of the women's supplies, she then had her own tent placed adjacent to the hut. Hanna told him that she could easily enter the hut unseen by others, especially at night when there was no activity.

Thomas spotted a piece of cloth on the fence, hoping it wasn't just a piece of garbage that would lead them to the wrong spot. There were tarps over items beyond the fence there, so it seemed like the right place.

Max had a thermal optic, he raised his rifle to scan up and down the fence line. If it was alive, it would appear as bright white on the gray/black dirt or the variety of manmade objects in the area. The only white objects he spotted were horizontal, and nowhere near their targeted entry. Wherever the guards were, they weren't nearby.

Max signaled all clear, and the group walked slowly and while crouched towards the fence. Silence was more important than speed. Nguyen arrived at the fence first looking it over to make sure it was unattached at the bottom as promised. It looked loose. Nguyen held onto his rifle with his right hand, and by putting his back to the fence, grabbed the bottom with his left and lifted. Thomas immediately approached the other side to help, and while he also kept his SBR in his right hand, he remained facing the camp and lifted with his left. This way there was a nice big hole for the others to crawl through without the risk of snagging their gear on it or creating metal on metal sounds that would wake the neighbors. It also had both men keeping a proper lookout all the while for strays.

The men crawled through one at a time and made their way under the tarp to find the hidden path Hanna had created.

After only Nguyen and Thomas were left, Nguyen looped a piece of rope through the bottom of the fence where he had been holding it, then through it over the top to Max. Nguyen lifted the fence while Max pulled so he could hold it in place, then looped another piece of rope where Thomas was holding it, and tossed it over as well. Now Max held open the outside of the fence while already inside. Thomas and Nguyen then quickly went through the gaping hole, but then held the bottom of it as Max silently lowered it. Seigfried returned with the metal straps to secure the bottom of the fence. A diligent guard would notice the missing pieces, raising suspicion and a thorough search. When done, Seigried withdrew to the tarp brushing dirt destroying their footprints. No trace.

Thomas crawled through the tarp to the end, passing the other men along the way.

"Worst fort *ever*," Max whispered as Thomas passed.

Thomas laid there under a tarp in the Somali heat at night texting Hanna they were in position. The response was simple, "clear."

"Okay, Max and I are going to go inside to make sure everything is clear. Nguyen keep an eye on the outside while we're in," Thomas instructed.

"Ready to get out of the fort Max?" Thomas asked.

"Absolutely, the hut sounds awesome," Max replied.

Thomas poked his head out to make sure it was clear. "Let's go," and the two crawled to the back of the hut. The word "makeshift" applied, and that allowed part of the back to be opened without looking like a door. Thomas slowly looked inside to see the lone female and climbed inside with Max following suit.

Hanna was a petite light-skinned black female and spoke English well with a slight French accent. She didn't know where she was from, who her parents were, or even a last name. Her earliest memories were in a refugee camp, and whoever was taking care of her then, they weren't her parents. They passed her on to others, sometimes they traveled, then seemed to end up in the same camp, yet with other people. It wasn't the same camp, and in several cases, the people were tricked into watching her. "Can you watch her for a second," then they'd be gone. Her heart broke with each "parental" change, but she was incredibly fortunate throughout. Though it was obvious that some weren't as attached as she was to them, luck or humanity found that none of them treated her poorly. She was never abused, and while sometimes hungry, so was everyone else.

She reached Somalia as a young girl, brought there by another woman from another camp, who then simply said "I have to go," and was gone. After spending most of her life in refugee camps, she was used to the life. She was also used to others helping her along the way. So for the first time, she was alone. The first thing she did was to help others. Ultimately her effort was repaid by being hired for the job helping at the camp. A young man had taken over, and the life in the camp improved. The young man saw how much she contributed and approached her. "Where are you from?" he asked. She looked around shaking her and shrugged her shoulders, "nowhere," she replied. Jeremy said, "No, you're home." His life had become her life ever since.

"This is it?" Hanna asked. "Just the two of you? That's not enough at all," she whispered quite loudly.

"Shhh," Thomas implored. "There are four more men under the tarp."

"Twice not enough, is still not enough," Hanna replied angrily.

"Okay, calm down. Your math skills notwithstanding, it's more than enough," Thomas assured her. "First, you said he never comes here with more than a dozen men, and after what's happened, it'll likely be less. Even if it's a dozen, we'll be fine."

"First?" Hanna asked.

"What?" Thomas said, a bit confused.

"You said first. And your first statement wasn't reassuring. Telling me he'll have twice as many men, isn't assuring. That's the opposite of reassuring, in fact, it's just twice as bad," Hanna replied. The young lady was fired up.

"Shhh, relax" Thomas replied. "They don't know we're here. They don't know anybody is here. They won't feel threatened here. Plus, you said how nice Fiidka is when he's here, how friendly they all are, how all his men act like they're everybody's pals. Nobody has guns in here, they know that. Fiidka is going to keep to the script. The same casual routine inside this fence means they will not have their guard up. All I need to know is where Fiidka goes when he's here. Does he walk around the camp, or stay in his car?"

"That's *General* Fiidka to you," Hanna said, rolling her eyes mocking Fiidka. "He gets out of the car, and usually just walks around this open area over here," she said pointing to beyond the first several tents past the entrance. "They park their vehicles by the tents, his men move in a circle around that wooden platform that houses the large water bottles that the people use throughout the day. Sometimes he walks among them, sometimes he stands on the platform to look them all over."

"Then you have us perfectly placed to act Hanna, you did great. I know it's easy for me to say, but relax. When it happens, it will happen fast. They won't have a chance, I promise you."

Hanna felt better, this man was certainly confident. She knew they were family and it hit her that he was in as much danger as anyone if he was wrong. "Fine. I arranged places for many people to hide in here, so six is easy. There are holes in different places of the hut to look out, but that means people may be able to look in, I don't know. I can't tell when I look around from the outside, but I'm the only one that comes in here, so there was no way for me to tell if movement can be seen from the outside."

"We'll move slowly," Thomas assured her.

"Don't move at all," Hanna demanded. "There's a porta-potty in the back. I've blocked off access from the front, so others would have to climb over crates of supplies to get to it, and the front door will be locked, only Jeremy and I have the key. He never comes in here, so nobody else should bother you." Hanna then started to wave her finger in Thomas's face, "but remember, this is a refugee camp, not a shooting gallery. And refugees wander around. I've done the best I can to prepare, but that doesn't mean I know what everyone else is doing all day. Don't shoot my family."

"Which are your family, miss?" Max asked, not getting the point.

"They're all my family," Hanna said strongly. "All of them except Fiidka and his men."

"And the guards?" Thomas asked. "You identified the three that have been letting him in."

"They're forced to," Hanna said. "If Fiidka didn't force them, they wouldn't..."

"Sell children to a pedophile?" Thomas asked.

"No, they're..." Hanna was grasping.

"Good people? No, they're not." Thomas said clearly. "And when Fiidka's gone, they'd sell children to someone else."

"No, they'd be happy to be free of him," Hanna insisted.

"Oh, so they've confided in you what Fiidka's forced them to do?" Thomas asked as Hanna's eyes widened, not wanting to accept that the men that she's worked with could also be so complicit. "No, of course not. Have they ever warned any women to hide their children before Fiidka visits? Have they ever hidden any children themselves? They know Fiidka's coming beforehand, they have to. There are over a dozen guards that work here, yet you've said there's only three that have been here every time Fiidka comes. To only arrive when three out of twelve men are on duty on multiple occasions? C'mon, Hanna. You have to know they know beforehand, and you've never seen them do anything to save anyone. They don't care about the refugees. Those three may not be the heart of darkness that Fiidka has become, but they've sold their souls to him."

Hanna shook her head not wanting to agree that they are to be killed.

"But, if you think we should leave?" Thomas said, floating a bluff.

"No," Hannah thought over her options, again. She's been thinking through them non-stop since Thomas started to call more often about the threat to the refugees, about the threat to the camp. About the threat to Jeremy. She tried to see how everything would be fine, that Fiidka would come, take the men who agreed to go. But what about the few boys who didn't want to do, the most innocent who surely deserved not to be taken? "What about them," she thought.

"Hanna, you know it won't ever stop." Thomas took her by the shoulders and looked her squarely in the eyes, "what about the guards Hannah?"

"Why are you asking me if you know so much?" she replied.

"I'm asking you because if I'm going to kill all these men, I'm looking for the smallest semblance that me and my men aren't throwing away our souls for nothing," Thomas replied. "If you can't stand and at least say "it has to be done," are you going to just let other men do the same when we're gone? Will you hire and pay other guards to sell children afterward? If we're not going to make a difference, maybe we don't want to be the ones killing men for no reason?"

"No reason?" Hanna struggled not to scream. "No reason? I live here, this is my home, I feed these people, I care for these people, they're my family, I nurse them, I see them born and I lose some of them. And it never ends," Hanna cried. "I'm only me, I can't stop all of this, I can't change the world."

"One man," Thomas bit his lip, "one woman can change the world. Single-minded people can change the world. All I need from you is to say that if we solve this for you tomorrow, or whatever day he shows, you're going to solve it thereafter. You're going to at least try, and that starts with admitting what needs to be done."

"I will," Hanna said unflinchingly. She looked around looking at Max, really for the first time. She looked into the eyes of a man she never met, she had never spoken to, a man she had no knowledge of who he was, who he loved, or what he believed. She thought about the other men crouched underneath a tarp, in the dirt. She knew nothing of them. And all of these men suddenly appeared to risk their lives, to give the most of themselves and take the lives of others, all to preserve that which she loved so dearly. She also then realized what Thomas was doing. He needed to see if she had the strength to continue after they left. No, not just that. He was fostering that strength, creating it, demanding it.

“As I said before, Jeremy isn’t to know we’re here until afterward,” Thomas reminded her.

“There’s food and water behind you, plenty for days, weeks as I counted on more men,” Hanna turned away to leave, checking outside the front door. “Do whatever you need to tomorrow or the next. I’ll do whatever I have to do after that. I’ll check on you later.” and with that, she was gone.

Max looked at Thomas shaking his head, “Think she’s good, Thomas?”

“I think she’s great,” Thomas replied, praying he was right.

# CHAPTER XVII

## *Head of the Snake*

It was hot on the boat, but Thomas' men now missed the boat. While the porta-potty was necessary to have, the men didn't seem to need it often despite how much water they consumed. In a land where drinkable water is still an issue, the camp had an ample supply. This was thanks to a desalination system donated to them by some company who relished spending ten times as much on advertising to remind consumers how wonderful of a company they were than they did on the system itself. Nobody donated protection. Protection isn't as noble as "renewable resources," at least not to people who never worried a day in their lives for protection.

The men slept in rotations, to keep watch if any of the camp's inhabitants showed too much interest in the hut. They also had no idea what time of the day Fiidka would arrive. While Hanna said it was always during the day, that was before an attack of this scale. That may cause him to alter his patterns. Thomas had previously thought of other things to do that may prompt a visit. He could have delivered information to Fiidka's rivals, attacked other areas of Fiidka's operation, or simply provided information to authorities that may limit his capacity to function. Actions don't happen in a vacuum, therefore there's always a consequence. The more Thomas would've done, the less predictable Fiidka's response would be. The cause and effect here was a simple equation. Fiidka visited the camp for more men, mostly. Eliminate a bunch of his men, stands to reason he'd get more men to refill his ranks. The additional fighting in the area may have been caused by Thomas's actions, and that's the sort of unintended consequence that's hard to control. What if some other group senses that Fiidka's power has waned. What if *they* now feel safe to visit the camp to recruit. Thomas would then be helping to eliminate Fiidka's competitor. When situations are fluid, the fewer ripples in the pond you create, the better. At least that's what Thomas was telling himself as the salty sweat continued to drip off his brow and into his eyes while waiting.

Thomas didn't see Jeremy throughout the day. He saw Hanna several times, busy scurrying about, she cast a furtive glance their way on occasion, and that was the only notice the hut received. She picked a good place.

Robert still had eyes on the area, so if a large caravan of vehicles either left Fiidka's compound or approached the camp, he'd see them and report to Thomas. With Bennett & Abernathy already dug in on Fiidka's route of departure, Thomas was confident they'd get some kind of warning. As the day dragged on, however, it seemed as if it wasn't going to happen today.

Later, in the day, after much of the daily work was done in the camp, after everyone was served dinner, Hanna approached the hut alone. She unlocked the door, came inside, and closed it. She wasn't able to see any of the men, so she quietly approached her stack of boxes first and then said, "it's only me, I'm all alone."

"Hi, Hanna, any problems?" Thomas asked.

"No, except I don't think they're coming today, it's getting late," she said. "And I didn't want to come in at night to turn a light on again."

"That's fine," Thomas replied. "We knew it may not be today," he said reservedly, "the next few days will tell."

Hanna smiled, and nodded her head, looking for the words. "I'm sorry if I seemed a bit off last night. I know I planned for all this, for you to come if I called and needed your help. I just always assumed I'd be the one calling you for help." Hanna looked around the boxes, seeing the hidden figures of the other men. "I just never thought to myself that this might happen without me calling. I... I wasn't prepared, I wasn't ready for this to be real. There are so many people who I care about and need us to care for them. I'm afraid that if any are hurt because of what I did... I'm just afraid."

Thomas smiled a disarming smile, "Don't worry about my feelings Hanna, I can't imagine what you've been through all this time. It's a miracle that you've done so well. It'll work out, I promise."

"Well, Jeremy is why we do well," Hanna quickly added. "I don't want to let him down either. When two elephants fight, it is the grass that gets trampled," Hanna replied, feeling her concerns weren't being taken seriously. It wasn't just her, but everyone in the camp that may be caught in the middle.

Thomas certainly wouldn't be mentioning that it was his actions that hopefully would be what triggers Fiidka's visit. "We'll get you through this, all of you."

"Good," Hanna said. "Also, there's an outlet back by the porta-potty, but don't plug too much into it. If you pop the breaker, it's right there. And if I'm not around, then Jeremy would come in, or he could give someone else the key."

"Got it, go light on the electricity." Thomas smiled.

"Do you need anything else, I'm going to lock up for this evening and won't check in on you until tomorrow?" Hanna asked.

"We don't need anything else, thanks," Thomas replied, "but we didn't get to talk at length last night, and I do have a question. Are there any women in the camp who've lost children to Fiidka? I mean, are there any of the mothers still here?"

"Mothers? Oh yes, sure. There's mothers, fathers, grandmothers, sisters, brothers, relatives of all kinds." Hanna responded, not certain of where this was going.

"How many of just the female relatives?" Thomas asked.

Hanna squinted her eyes looking at Thomas with thoughtful suspicion. "Anyone who asks for 'just the female' anything in a refugee camp, is going to have to explain themselves."

Thomas didn't think about how this started to sound. "No. No, no, no. Nothing like that. Grandmothers count if that helps. Just an approximate number, and then I'll explain. Trust me."

"Ten, at least. Maybe fifty. I'm sorry, but I hate to say I don't know for sure." Hanna's face shared a sorrowful realization. "I remember all the boys he took, but I never wrote down their names. Why didn't I do that? They shouldn't be forgotten."

"If you remember the names, can you check the records of who is here to identify the female relatives of those boys taken?" Thomas asked.

"Sure, I could do that," Hanna replied. "Now tell me why."

"Well, this is what I want you to tell each woman you find that's still here." Thomas leaned over the box and whispered into her ear for a few moments. "But only the one's you're absolutely sure you can trust. If not, they'll have to wait until the time comes. Then, when it's in motion, then they can decide."

Hanna stared at Thomas. It's said that up to sixty percent of human communication is non-verbal. Thomas couldn't tell if her stare was that of agreement or horror. She looked away for a moment, apparently thinking it through.

"Unless you don't think that they'll be interested?" Thomas asked.

"No. They'll be," Hanna paused, "interested. They'll be glad."

"And you?" Thomas asked.

"I'll be glad for them, especially for them" Hanna took a few moments as if feeling she should ask another question, or have a better reply.

Thomas decided to give her an out if she wanted it. "If the number is too small, it may not be a good idea."

"No," Hanna said. "I'm sure there will be enough," and

turned to leave.

"Thanks, Hanna," Thomas said as she closed the door, and locked it.

Thomas went back to his own little cubby hole to hide in across from Max.

"Do you really think she's good with that?" Max asked.

"After she tells the first woman who lost a child to that monster, she'll feel that woman's reaction," Thomas said. "And that will fuel her fire for the rest of our visit."

Magan had spent the previous day visiting the men who he'd hired to attack rivals in the area. While he paid them little beforehand, as he told them their performance was an audition for greater things, these poor men were eager to prove themselves. So it was with no surprise that they were all excited to hear from Magan afterward. With each call, he began, "You did well, I have a bonus for you, and more work, when can we meet." With each call, the lie evolved with more inflection, more feigned gratitude, his voice pretending that they had a bond of camaraderie. Each visit was the same, Magan killed them. There was no bonus, there was no future for them. Magan's day of visiting all the men took him well into the night. He was exhausted and bruised. He wasn't wounded by any of them but cursed them for fighting back after plunging a knife into each of them. Magan believed he was doing a good thing, protecting Fiidka from Omar's mess of a plan. Surely this would ingratiate him more with Fiidka. Surely Fiidka would appreciate him now.

And he did. When Magan returned to Fiidka's compound, Fiidka welcomed him with a smile, placed a hand on each of Magan's shoulders, eager for a report from the day.

"So my friend, is it done?" Fiidka asked.

"Every single one General Fiidka. I'm ready for more." Magan replied earnestly.

"Ah, of course you are. You're sure that's all them, there were no witnesses or anything that could tie them to me?" Fiidka asked.

"There were no witnesses, and there was never anything to tie them to you," Magan replied.

"You did well, you deserve a bonus," Fiidka began with the biggest smile he'd ever seen General Fiidka smile, and Magan's smile faded as quickly as it came.

Instead, it was horror that filled Magan's mind as Fiidka began with virtually the same words that Magan had used the day before on the men he killed. Magan's horror, mixed with disbelief, meant he was slow to act. Fiidka plunged a knife into Magan's stomach and raised the blade, eliminating any chance of survival.

"You lied," Fiidka said looking into Magan's eyes, "there is someone who ties the men to me."

Fiidka then let Magan fall to the ground. Not able to say a word, he only thought of the men he killed the day before and those that said "I don't deserve this." Magan was unable to say a word.

"Erasto! Get rid of the body. Have it dumped at the police station with a note that he was a traitor that renounced Islam."

“Yes General Fiidka,” Erasto replied. Erasto was also a lieutenant enforcer of General Fiidka for years. However, he was smart enough not to be too eager. He also didn’t ask any questions. He was content with where he was.

“That way, nobody will investigate his death, no one will question his disappearance, and no one will bother with who he was meeting with over the last week,” Fiidka offered nonetheless, clearly eager to describe how smart he was. “Not that anyone bothers with the dead here anyway.”

Erasto nodded while dragging Magan’s body to one of the pickup trucks.

“But first, we need to go visit the camp for new recruits, so cover the body, we don’t want that to be the first thing they see when we get back,” Fiidka instructed, his concern for employee feelings seeming surreal.

Erasto had visited the camp with Fiidka in the past. They had always used three vehicles. Ten men and General Fiidka. If there were more vehicles, it may draw the attention of others, too few, and there wasn’t enough to protect him if attacked, especially if one of the SUV’s broke down en route. And, on Fiidka’s orders, the same number of vehicles would leave for everything. This meant if Fiidka needed groceries, he’d send three vehicles. Need to pick up money, three vehicles. If they needed more men or more vehicles, it was in groups of three. Every activity included three vehicles so that three vehicles were the norm. “Nobody will ever get me,” Fiidka would often boast before he’d get into a car to leave while under the cover of the garage.

Today was no different. "Nobody will ever get me," Fiidka said boldly to Erasto as he stepped into the back seat of the nicely appointed Toyota Land Cruiser.

The three vehicles slowly emerged, none of his men were to wave or salute. While he insisted on being called General Fiidka, he was well aware he'd be targeted by satellite surveillance at some point, by someone. With that in mind, he didn't want to be the victim of a drone strike because a man saluted him. He valued the illusion of being a General, but not that much.

The road began with beautifully laid stone outside of his compound and then transitioned to just dirt and rock. Though the entrance to his property was guarded at the main road, and he could certainly afford to pave the road nicely, in the land of the poor, opulence attracted unwelcome guests, and increased the costs of bribes, so he'd suffer the bumpy road.

Once their column of three turned left onto the main road, they were in view.

Bennett and Abernathy were nestled into an accommodating group of rocks. While not the easiest walk up the ridge, there were enough large rocks and crevices to alternate positions throughout the day to avoid most, but not all of the sun. While they were at the ridge of the small stone-filled hill, the abundance of rocks meant that they weren't silhouetting themselves at all, so their movements were easily concealed. There was a light breeze that offered some relief, but at 95F, this wasn't a cool breeze, it was like a hairdryer and the humidity was brutal. Bennett and Abernathy continually checked the breeze, the wind's direction, and humidity. It all factored into their equations. The breeze was consistently at their backs, from about their 7 o'clock, so their rounds would only be pushed mildly to the right, and end up a little high. It was ideal shooting weather.

"Bennett, wake up," Abernathy called out.

"Are we shooting?" Bennett asked, sitting up slightly.

"No. Not sure this is even him." Abernathy replied.

"Well, wake me when you're sure," Bennett said and laid back down.

"Three SUVs just left the compound heading this way," if they end up at Thomas's doorstep we have to be ready. Abernathy was already pushing send on the sat-phone.

"Go," came Thomas's simple answer at the other end.

"Three vehicles just took a left out of the compound heading our way," Abernathy replied.

"Our guy?" Thomas asked.

"Checking. They're still out a bit, not flying. Hold." Abernathy asked. He squinted through the glare of the day, the reflection off of the windshields, the shimmering landscape caused by the rising heat and distance. Eventually, all he could see was a driver and a man in each of the passenger seats. The tinted windows negated identifying anything more.

"Sorry boss, can't tell." Abernathy finally conceded. "Just two guys in front are visible, the rest of the vehicles are too heavily tinted. They'll be crossing our point in about ten seconds now."

"Got it. I'll phone home and have Robert track them.

And wake up your buddy. If this is them, it'll happen fast." Thomas ended the call.

"Did you hear that?" Abernathy turned to Bennett. "Thomas called you a lazy no-good bastard."

"Who's no good?" Bennett laughed. They both laughed. Bennett rolled over and settled in behind his scope. The sun was high in the sky midday. He probably didn't need the sunshade from this point on and thought about removing it from the scope. A sunshade for a scope is like a honeycomb without the honey. The matrix of plastic in a tube that extends beyond the end of the scope prevents sunlight from reflecting off of the glass to give away the shooter's position. At this time of day, it would be unlikely to cause any glare to give away their position. Outside of the added weight, there was no downside, for now, so he'd leave it on.

Abernathy was also setting up behind his rifle, the spotting scope now moot. If this turned out to be the real deal, the vehicles would likely come at them fast. He wouldn't have to bother trying to identify any passengers, the vehicles would be the only thing he has to see.

Both men had cleaned and cleared the area on the ground in front of their rifles as best as they could. Abernathy had solid rock, so he only had to brush away some dirt and stones. Bennett had a bit more plain dirt, so he laid out any flat stones that he could find to build a mural of rock over the dirt beneath the barrel of the big .50 BMG rifle. When it came time to fire, the recoil from the big caliber rifle is made tamer by muzzle brakes, which are just a slab of steel at the end of the barrel that diverts gas slightly backward on the sides and up. This redirection of gas reduces recoil for quicker follow-up shots, lessens muzzle jump, and makes it easier on the shooter. The consequence of that action is a tremendous pressure wave of expanding gas that hits the ground and throws a ton of dust in the air. The first shot will be the worst, for both. After that, Abernathy's placement on the stone should lessen the amount of dust on each of the following shots. Bennett was hoping that his stone creation would eliminate the problem. Whatever came, he thought he'd be fine, he'd made plenty of shots in the dirt.

Bennett watched Abernathy pull out a spray bottle that he'd been using on himself and sprayed down the stone in front of him to also lessen the dust.

"Hey, that's a great idea, here I thought it was just for cooling you down. Mind if I borrow that?" Bennett asked.

"Would you believe I carried it around Afghanistan for more than six months, using it solely on the dirt on the ground in front of me before I even thought to use it on myself," Abernathy said seriously.

The two laughed. They'd prepared all they could, now they settled into the ground and waited.

Thomas dialed Robert as soon as he got off of the phone with Abernathy.

"I was expecting your call" was Robert's voice on the other end.

"Well, three potential Tangos on the move, do they look like they're going to be our Tangos," Thomas asked.

"They have a little ways to go until they should turn

left on the main road towards your home," Robert replied. "How's tricks?"

"Well, a warmer reception than I'll likely get from Jeremy, which is why I had her keep him out of the loop. Problem is, she's into him so I don't know how long that's going to last," Thomas answered honestly. "I think all that's keeping her quiet is she believes Fiidka's going to eventually kill him and she knows Jeremy would never approve of my solution. She knows Jeremy will push back too much, eventually, even though there's nothing he can really do against a guy like Fiidka. Fiidka tolerates Jeremy because he gets what he wants anyway, and Jeremy keeps bringing in people. If Fiidka ever thinks he can get recruits anyway, the guy is toast."

"Boy, and my biggest family problem is my brother's a drunk," Robert replied.

"To be fair, outside of surreptitiously contacting Hanna over the last several months, and looking at his Facebook pages for years, Jeremy just hasn't been a concern. He wants nothing to do with Uncle, his father, and probably less to do with me. I've had it easier."

"You're in a fucking sweatbox in Somalia, bro." Robert laughed, "that's easy?"

"Well, fact is, I could've done nothing, which is what I've been doing with him for a long time. Recently, however, ah shit. I just didn't see that this could go on forever the way it was." Thomas then realized he was hogging the misery. "So what's up with your brother?"

"DUI, rehab, DUI, divorced, DUI and jail, parents paid for rehab, and I recently paid for rehab because I hacked his everything, and when I saw him driving 35 mph on I-95 at 3:00 am I knew it wasn't rush hour traffic," Robert replied summing up nicely.

"Wow, he went to jail for being drunk, and you willfully committed any number of felonies there," Thomas jested.

"Yeah, but I have good intentions, so it's a wash," Robert replied.

"Oh well, good intentions. I have to remember that one," Thomas laughed. "Speaking of intentions, how're our boy's travels?"

"Coming up on your turn...and" Robert paused. "They went straight. Sorry man."

"Ah, keep an eye on them," Thomas asked. "Nobody else has left the compound since we've been in, maybe we're the stop on the way home."

"Nothing else to do to entice them to come your way?" Robert asked.

"Nah, anything else more overt may result in a much harsher response. I don't want to get everybody killed here," Thomas lamented.

"I could send him a coupon for a free tour, I have his email," Robert joked.

"I don't even want to know what kind of sick coupon you'd have to send this fuck, he..." Thomas said before being cut off.

"Hold on sparky, they just took a left on a side road several turns down," Robert said excitedly. "This trip ain't over yet."

"How far till the next turn?" Thomas asked.

"They're on a side road, it's slow going. There's several left turns they could take to get to take a right on the connecting road to your location. Or, they could go about another half mile, which would also take them to the same main road," Robert explained.

"If they don't stop anywhere before the main road, they're coming here," Thomas said. "They're just making sure they're not being followed here."

"Well, you're going to know in a few seconds, they only have a short way to go. Hold on," Robert said.

Max was listening carefully. All the men were listening carefully, but Max was slowly inching closer to the conversation as it progressed. Max was suspecting it was soon time for the men to deploy. Max inched up further to get Thomas's attention. In catching his eyes, Max raised his eyebrows and tilted his head. The question was conveyed was "should we move now?"

Thomas raised his hand with his index finger raised. Max understood that to be '*wait,*' though with the intensity of '*wait, you over-anxious bastard.*' Max got that a lot. The other men in the hut stood to their feet slowly, stretching their legs, getting their blood moving throughout. Laying around for hours in a hot hut would make it hard to go from zero to sixty without loosening up. And they all sensed they were about to go full speed.

"You'll have a couple of minutes to move if they make the turn into the camp. There's a gate, then a short drive, and another gate. Then after they park, it's a short walk until the actual entrance to where you are, we'll know in a few seconds," Robert replied, then changing to the play by play. "Alright people, here we go. They're coming up to the intersection connecting to the main road they passed on earlier. They're taking a right, all three. There's another vehicle behind them, they're speeding up. They're coming up on the turn to the camp, not slowing, wait, they're slowing, they're making a hard right into the camp. Thomas," Robert finished. "These are your guys."

Thomas raised his right hand and flashed a "thumbs up." "They're here, get to your stations. Remember the plan."

There were only six of them, the plan was simple. Kill all of them, try to keep Fiidka alive. With him alive, Fiidka could call for help on their terms, giving Abernathy and Bennett the all-clear to shoot at anything that left his compound thereafter, which would likely be a lot. With all the bad guys dead, they could hustle in the open to their vehicles. The quickest distance between two points is a straight line meant they'd skip getting back to the main road. They'd simply use the Flyers' off-road ability and cut across open land coming in behind Bennett and Abernathy's position. If they were early, they'd hide behind the cover of the hill until needed. If they were late, and Fiidka's men already made it past where the road cut through the hill, they'd engage them there with Abernathy & Bennett shooting at them from behind. A crossfire.

Thomas and Max would remain in the hut. The various holes Hanna created to look out worked for shooting too. They had placed various boxes in front for support and a modicum of protection if anyone shot back. Marks and Nguyen exited out the back, then moved quickly to the rear of Hanna's tent to the right. There was nobody in view behind them, though it was entirely in the open, especially during daylight. If a guard walked the fence, or an errant refugee wandered around, they'd be spotted, and there would be a bloodbath if there was no surprise. They quickly cut the back of the tent and entered fast causing Hanna to scream a short scream.

Nguyen put his finger to his mouth and she nodded. She hadn't seen him before, but he was dressed like Thomas. Plus an armed Asian man sneaking into her tent hadn't happened before. "They're here," Nguyen said briefly, "It's time, so get down,"

"No. I have to be out there to welcome him. We always are, I'd be missed. It's disgusting, but we have to," Hanna said and moved out of the tent before Nguyen could even think about stopping her.

"She's right man," Marks added. "If her not being there would raise a red flag, his guards get an itchy trigger finger, and things'll get hairy fast," Marks said nodding his head.

"Fuck," Nguyen said. "I should've told her to be sure to duck."

"She lives in Somalia man," Marks said looking at Nguyen. "Ya figure she already knows that better than most."

Nguyen nodded. "Pick your spot."

Marks quickly flipped Hanna's bed on its side by the window, holding it together while moving it so there was little noise. The window in the tent was just made of a mesh material. Marks would've liked to cut the mesh away. Once the shooting starts, just like Bennett and Abernathy were concerned about the dirt from the blast of the gun, Marks knew the mesh of the tent would dance around. He could only hope it wouldn't be a problem, in the daytime, it was essential to leave it in place to conceal him. Marks decided to step on the bottom of the tent to help keep the mesh window tight.

Nguyen grabbed one of Hanna's duffle bags and dropped it by the entranceway to her tent. He didn't know what was inside but it was packed solid. He slowly unzipped the entrance up the middle only, and only a small amount at the bottom. He took the tie connected to that side of the cord and tied it to the strap at the end of the duffle bag. This would keep the small opening open. Nguyen then laid down behind the duffle bag. The small open slit up the middle gave him a good view of the open space while only having to move side to side.

"What are you doing," Marks asked.

"With what?" Nguyen answered.

"Her duffle bag. What if there's something valuable inside," Marks demanded.

"We're in a refugee camp in Somalia, there's nothing of value." Nguyen joked. "Besides, you're going to get her bed shot up."

"First, it's just a bed, there could be significant memorabilia or items of sentimental value in a duffle bag, there's nothing sentimental in bed."

"Your phrasing aside, whatever it is, I'll buy her a new

one. Just get ready." Nguyen laid prone watching the few people in sight now. A guard, five refugees getting water, and Hanna.

Siegfried and Atkins got to the fort. They had also exited out the back of the hut and darted to the tarp-covered fort disappearing beneath, then following the clear path created underneath which would give them shooting positions on the open area from the left of the hut. They had to move slowly and quietly, careful not to cause any wave in the tarp that would attract attention. This part of the old equipment Hanna had compiled over time would be visible to many. Thomas aided in her original design. There were two paths that cut back to face the open area were Fiidka would ultimately have to cross to enter the camp. Siegfried took the first, Atkins the second. The air under the tarp was dank, the dust-filled their noses. For a moment, Atkins thought he might sneeze. He pressed on the trigeminal nerve on the bridge of his nose hard, which stopped him from sneezing, but he made a weird noise nonetheless. Siegfried saw a few people look their way, then over the tarp as if it came from afar. Whatever they thought it might be, it wasn't worth rummaging under a tarp through junk he thought. "Atkins," Siegfried whispered on coms, "keep the shit down, whatever that noise was, caught some attention, but nobody's concerned enough to move your way. Yet."

"Got it."Atkins nasally replied with his fingers squeezing his nostrils closed to be sure that was it.

Thomas and Max had taken up their positions inside. Thomas connected the satphone to their coms for the duration. The three shooting positions of the six men gave them a 45-degree angle of coverage for the open area. While all of their weapons were suppressed, that is not to say they're silent at all. A suppressor on a .22 Long Rifle cartridge can make it quite silent, even more so on with a .22 Short. A suppressor on a 5.56 round, turns the sound of a jet engine into a jackhammer. The first is deafening, distracting, and can cause permanent hearing damage. The latter is workable, doable, and controllable. It also vastly reduces muzzle jump, meaning the shooter's eyes can stay on target, and deliver shots on target faster and with more accuracy. As it does not suppress the sounds of the guns of others, meaning the bad guys, electronic earpieces were worn by all. The earplugs inserted in the ear kept enough of the sound out to make any shot manageable, and actually amplified the volume of ambient sound around them, like the whisper of those you're with, or the snap of a twig behind you. Plus as they were connected to their coms link, they were now on a seven-man conference call around the world.

"Everybody good on position?" Thomas asked.

"All good," came the general reply by all.

"They're parked," Robert chimed in. "Their walk to your position won't take them that long."

"Number," Thomas asked.

"I count ten... no, eleven," Robert replied. "I think there's eleven, none remained with the vehicles. There's a guard from the camp that remained there."

"Which is it sparky, ten or eleven," Thomas asked.

"I'm looking at a pixelated picture from space that I

had to hack to get temporary control and it's Indian," Robert replied. "I counted ten, but they're in a group, I think eleven."

"Keep an eye on the guards, and try to ID if they're the three Hanna indicated are dirty," Thomas asked of his men in the camp. "Robert, I don't know how much you can see with all the tents, but if you see anyone running towards us when the shooting starts, give a heads up on the direction. For a point of reference, I'm on the south-east side. So our six is the southeast, use that as your compass."

"Got it. They're walking around the side of the first tents, fifteen seconds out tops," Robert called out. "They'll be coming around at your 1 o'clock then."

"All hold on my go," Thomas instructed. "I want all clear shots. And we have ten targets that have to go down fast"

"Marks and Nguyen," Atkins called out. "Siegfried and I will have straight shots of any guards that head your way, that will be the 1 to 3 o'clock, you should have clear shots of those that head our way and off to our left, 7 to midnight."

"You got it," Nguyen replied.

"Atkins' is right," Max whispered to Thomas. "So long as all of the guards stay in this open area and don't go walking through where all the refugees are."

"They're rounding the corner, now, and once they're under the tents...." Robert cut himself off, there was nothing else he could do but watch.

"Got'em," Thomas said. "Talk it out who's got who as

they spread out, Max and I will take the middle."

The first three men that rounded the corner had their heads on a swivel and armed with AK-47 rifles. They stopped, still looking around, one of the camp guards joined the three. They spotted Hanna, and the guard called out to her to come to join them.

Hanna turned and saw them. She reflexively turned her head towards the hut, and then back realizing her mistake.

"Oh shit," Thomas said, what everyone was thinking.

Hanna then turned back towards the hut and called out, "Hani, it will have to wait, I'll come over later," and started to walk to the group of men.

Hani, the Somali woman who was just walking back after refilling a water jug turned to Hanna and waved, not understanding what Hanna was talking about and continued on her way. Hanna had recovered perfectly.

Fiidka's guard asked simply "Where's the other one?" referring to Jeremy. Apparently using his name would have been to give respect.

The camp guard jumped in, eager to please, "he's coming, my other man is with him." The guards kept an eye on Jeremy when they knew Fiidka was due to arrive. If he wasn't there or acted strangely, they'd know, and warn Fiidka. Or worse. A good idea, but they were shortsighted, and picked the wrong person in the camp to watch.

Another of Fiidka's men rounded the corner, this one carrying an AK-47, but without a stock. A pistol version to signify he was in authority. Maybe a good weapon if you're in a truck, but a rifle without a stock is not a rifle. He'd just be spraying and praying. He'd have to be one of the first to go. Erasto didn't know it, but his choice of weapon garnered attention nobody in the field ever wants. *First targeted.* Those targeted second always have a better chance.

Jeremy and the guard were now approaching from Thomas's left. Several of the other refugees in the area were starting to walk away, casually. The camp guard walking with Jeremy put his hand up and told everyone to "stay where you are. It would be better." Better for who they thought.

Erasto with his AK-47 pistol turned and waved for the rest of the group to continue in. It was safe they thought. Jeremy and the girl were here. Everything looked the same. Everything still smelled the same. Everyone still looked scared, they looked beaten. Hanna's head was bowed. Good, he thought. It was good that he couldn't see her eyes, for the first time in a long time, they had resolve. He only saw what he wanted to see.

There were four men that surrounded Fiidka, but thankfully not too close. They walked like the number five appears on a die, with Fiidka in the middle. The four guards always looked away from Fiidka. The amount of space made him look unafraid, yet he was surrounded by armed men at all times. Two more guards then followed from behind. That's eleven.

"That's all of them," Thomas called out, "call out your shots."

Nguyen and Marks replied that they had a good line

on the first three of Fiidka's guards, who continued towards the refugees but stopped out in the open. The one farthest to the left was the biggest problem, the shot would be towards the area where the refugees were living. Nguyen told marks that he'd take him first. As Nguyen was lying on the ground, he'd shoot high. If the round missed or continued through the body, it would sail over the rest of the refugee camp. While this guard was getting quite close to Siegfried's and Atkins' concealed position, they'd have to emerge from that concealment for a shot. Far better they all remained concealed.

Atkins called out the two trailing guards. They were in view of everyone, but if they backed up slightly, they'd be out of view of Nguyen and Marks.

Siegfried called out the AK-47 pistol-wielding guard and said he could then pivot towards Fiidka and the camp guard.

Thomas and Max discussed taking out the four guards surrounding Fiidka. They'd shoot the two guards closest to them first, not because they were closest, but because they'd be facing them. With the other two not facing any of the shooters, they'd be looking away when the shooting started and the slowest to react.

"Remember, as soon as the guards are down, the rest of you have to pop up fast so Fiidka doesn't draw and start shooting," Thomas reminded them. "We want him alive, but don't get killed doing it." Ergo, don't hesitate to shoot him if we can't.

"Call out who's clear and who's not," Thomas ordered. They all were. All except Thomas and Max. Hanna, Jeremy, and the camp guard were inside the five die guard formation. Close to Fiidka was fine, in front of one of the guards, and intermittently behind the other was not. Things weren't lining up.

Fiidka was smiling to Jeremy and Hanna, talking about how wonderful the camp looked. He put his hand on one of the large water bottles patting it as if taking credit for their good fortune, or so it would look to the refugees that didn't know better. What it actually meant was "it would be a shame if something happened to your water supply."

Hanna sensed what was about to happen, and she didn't want to make the same mistake again, so she dared not look back to the hut. Yet she knew exactly where the hut was. She could tell she was in the line of fire, and therefore so was Jeremy. A moment of concern that these men cared more for killing Fiidka than for her Jeremy, caused her to make a bold move. The only way to get out of the line of fire of the guards was to walk closer to Fiidka. After what Thomas instructed her to tell the women in the camp, she knew he wanted him alive anyway. So Hanna firmly took Jeremy by his right arm and pulled him with her, closer to Fiidka. Thomas was right, she wasn't worried about the camp guard.

"General Fiidka, please take a closer look at the water system, and you'll see how wonderful it is," Hanna beamed for all to see.

"Why thank you dear," Fiidka smiled. How wonderful that this girl is playing along. She knows what's good for her, she'll keep his *savior* of the people in line, and this will last forever.

It must've been shocking to have been so terribly wrong.

With her first step, Thomas called out "ready," seeing that her movements would clear all of their shots. With Hanna's third step, and Jeremy firmly in tow, "fire."

The muffled bursts of rifle fire rang out simultaneously at first.

For Atkins, the shots on the two guards were too easy. Bang, Bang, adjust target, Bang Bang. With that, he started to emerge from concealment.

Nguyen, who was prone, fired at the guard closest to the camp and the planned headshot was easy to confirm from the explosion of the man's skull and he fell like a wet noodle. Marks simultaneously put down the other of the three guards on their end, then both he and Nguyen fired at the guard remaining in between the two, they never had a chance. Nguyen, already prone at the entranceway of the tent, then began to emerge from concealment, Marks followed suit.

Thomas and Max each had equally easy shots. The two guards facing them were under 75 feet away. Because they were all looking away from Fiidka, they didn't yet see Fiidka start to move with Hanna and Jeremy. They remained stationary. Both Thomas and Max fired a double tap at the first guards, then at the second set of guards with their backs to them. Thomas recalled seeing the second guard turning his head ever so slightly as if startled by the sound but not fully realizing that they were under attack. If he realized it, it didn't matter, they were all down. With the first shots fired,

Hanna used her strong grip on Jeremy to pull him to the ground. She meant to fall on top of him, to protect him. However, since Jeremy didn't know what was going on at all he tried not to fall. While Hanna was strong for a thin Somali woman, she was hardly muscular enough to easily pull a man down who didn't want to fall. Hanna hung onto Jeremy, suspended in the air not letting go. In the briefest of moments, Jeremy understood there was gunfire, and what Hanna was trying to do, so he let himself fall, landing hard on top of her, with both of them holding onto the other.

Siegfried put three rounds into the guard with the AK-47 pistol, on the off chance the chief guard may have had a bulletproof vest concealed under his large loose-fitting shirt, he didn't. But because he had such a stronghold on the grip of his pistol, he did squeeze off a few rounds as he fell. The distinctive sound of the AK-47 was even louder than normal due to the shorter barreled version. Thankfully, because it was a pistol, he carried it pointing to the ground, the burst of rounds punched holes in the dirt and sand throwing dust in the air with not even a chance of a ricochet. The man was dead by the time he hit the ground. Siegfried pivoted towards Fiidka. The camp guard that was eager to please went to pull his weapon crying "I'll save you General," and Siegfried put him down with one round, falling at Fiidka's feet.

The remaining camp guard in the group saw all of Fiidka's guards gone in a second, his friend shot dead, and multiple men emerging from all around instructing him not to move. He did, he put his arms in the air.

Hanna, still stuck under Jeremy, struggled to rise. "Let

me up," and Jeremy obliged, then slowly rising himself. "Don't shoot him," Hanna cried out to Thomas's men, referring to the guard. "Get on the ground," she told him and the camp guard complied, shocked, believing she was in charge.

Fiidka remained upright with his hand on his pistol, still in its holster, but it was no longer strapped. One pull he could kill this bitch, how could she do this, also believing she was somehow responsible for all of this. Yet as Fiidka slowly looked around, seeing all of his men dead. *How can this be* he thought?

"Hand off the gun, we're not going to kill you," Nguyen instructed.

"Not going to kill me? Then you're fools because my men will kill you all," Fiidka screamed. "And you two," Fiidka said looking at Jeremy and Hanna. "They're going to do much worse to you two traitors, they'll burn this camp to the ground," Fiidka said shaking his head and spitting as he spoke, the fury and anger inside him about to burst.

"Hand off the gun, or we are going to kill you," Nguyen instructed once more.

"You better believe it," Marks said from behind.

Hope, even the worst of men have it. Fiidka stood up straight and slowly took his hand off of his gun.

Atkins approached swiftly from behind and removed Fiidka's gun, throwing it far out of reach. Fiidka just stood calmly and smiled.

"Weapons?" Atkins asked.

"Weapons? You took it," Fiidka replied smiling.

Atkins raised his rifle pointed at Fiidka's head. "Weapons," Atkins demanded.

"There's a small knife, on my back," Fiidka surrendered.

Atkins found the straight blade in a scabbard strapped to Fiidka's belt. Atkins removed the blade from the scabbard stepping back. Fiidka never cleaned the blade, the remnants of red blood turned black filled the crevices on the hilt, and stained the steel. Fiidka saw Atkins looking at it, "dried blood causes more fear than the blade. The fear means I have to use it less." Fiidka stated as if he was merciful. Atkins tossed the knife further aside, and performed a quick pat down making sure there Fiidka had no other concealed weapons. No weapons, just a phone. Perfect.

"Marks, Max," Thomas called out. "Go get the other guard." Thomas caught Hanna's eye "Bring him back here peacefully, if possible."

Thomas then motioned her to move towards the refugees and away from Fiikda. "Come, Jeremy, come with me," she told him.

Jeremy still had no idea what was going on, he couldn't even spit out a full sentence, then he caught sight of Thomas and froze.

"Jeremy, why don't you stay here," Thomas asked. "Hanna, go on then, get the rest."

Hanna looked at Jeremy not wanting to let go, and Jeremy looked at her confused that the two knew each other. "I'll be right back," she said and darted into the camp.

"What the hell is going on here Thomas?" Jeremy yelled, turning back to him.

"Oh, so you do know this man," Fiidka yelled. "How could you do this, to all your people."

"Me? I didn't *do* anything," Jeremy said, still exasperated and spinning from the suddenness of everything that happened.

"He didn't do anything Fiidka," Thomas interrupted. "Jeremy, good to see you, but go stand over there and I'll explain later." Jeremy swelled with emotion, his arms moving as if talking, but no words were coming out. "Go stand over there," Thomas pointed towards Hanna's tent, away from Fiidka, away from the bodies, and also away from where the refugees would be coming. Were already coming. "Stay there," Thomas said again with certainty.

"So you want me alive," Fiidka said. "What do you want, money? I have money. You want weapons? I see you men like weapons," he said while turning around looking at the armed men smiling. "I have weapons. Hell, I have rockets, even mortars. You want drugs, eh? I have drugs, white people always want drugs, they pay top dollar," his voice failing as he turned. The refugees were emerging and surrounding him. "Fine," he yelled, sensing the need to take command of the situation. "My men will pay your ransom. But if I don't leave here alive, neither will *any* of you. They'll kill you, and everyone you've ever known."

"Call them," Thomas responded.

"What?" Fiidka replied.

"Call them," Thomas calmly said yet again.

"What do you want them to bring you?" Fiidka asked, still believing this was a negotiation.

"Call them, with your phone. Tell them where you are, your men are dead, you're under attack, and that they should all come to your aid." Thomas replied.

"You don't want money," Fiidka asked. It wasn't yet fear, but Fiidka didn't know what to make of this.

"Call them and tell them to come as I instructed, or you'll have no chance to survive," Thomas ordered.

Fiidka nodded, he didn't have to understand what his chances were, or why, but he understood Thomas meant it. Fiidka slowly reached for his phone and pressed a button to make a call. Thomas leaned in to hear the call. "I'm at the camp, men are dead, we're under attack, send everyone," Fiidka ordered.

The voice on the other end of the line was silent, he was there but taken aback by the order. Thomas removed his knife, Fiidka's performance needed motivation.

"Do you hear me, send everyone to the camp now!" Fiidka yelled.

"Yes sir, General Fiidka, right away," the startled voice on the other end of the line replied.

Thomas took the phone and made sure it was hung up.

"That's seventy-five of my finest men on the way to me," Fiidka said proudly. Thomas just smiled without a response.

Marks and Max came around the corner with the other guard, his hands zip-tied behind his back. Thomas tossed the phone landing in front of Max who buried his boot on it in stride. Marks went and put restraints on the other guard.

"Now what the hell is going on Thomas!" Jeremy demanded.

Thomas raised his finger to wait. "Abernathy, they'll be coming, get ready. We'll be leaving shortly."

"Yes, what the hell is going on here," Fiidka asked.

Thomas looked around, the crowd of refugees now surrounded them all, yet at a good distance. He found Hanna, only raising his eyebrows to say "Well?" and she simply nodded yes.

"Okay then. Jeremy. Here's a phone. I'll call you, we have to go." Thomas said.

"Wait, what? No! You can't leave me with this... this mess! His men will kill me, kill everyone. He'll kill me, Thomas!" Jeremy yelled.

"He'll kill you, Jeremy?" Thomas asked. "He's unarmed, he's alone. The camp guards are tied up, what you do with them is up to you, I wouldn't let them back into the camp, since they were selling you to the likes of him," Thomas said, nodding towards Fiidka. "How's he going to kill you?" Thomas asked again.

"What, do you want *me* to murder him, Thomas?" Jeremy asked, "Is that what this is? Are you just here to force me to be like you? I'm not like you, and even if I do kill him, his men are now on his way thanks to you," Jeremy said pointing angrily at Thomas, and then at his men. "Thanks to you."

"No Jeremy, I'm not going to kill him, and neither are

you. That would be murder, and I know you're not a killer. I'm not asking you to be a killer," Thomas said with empathy. "But I do want justice for what this man has done. Not just to you, you're alive. I want justice for all of the murderous acts he's responsible for, and damned sure for what this monster has done to all of the children he's taken," Thomas said looking into Jeremy's eyes. "Don't you want that Jeremy?"

"Of course I want that Thomas, but..." Jeremy said, but Thomas cut him off.

"Then stand there while justice is served, we have to go kill all of his men." Thomas turned to Hanna, "you got this."

"Yes," was all Hanna could say. Yet she said that one word with more conviction than had been in her voice for years. Thomas bent over and whispered in her ear. Thomas then backed away. "Sorry,"

Thomas patted Jeremy on the shoulder, "don't lose the phone," and he turned and ran behind the hut with his men following.

Fiidka lowered his hands, turning around in a circle in utter surprise. "So now what?" Fiidka laughed. He looked all around, now surrounded by hundreds of people from the camp. Men, yes. But it was mostly women and children. He turned to the direction of where his gun had landed, now located behind the group of people who had emerged.

Fiidka extended his hand, "come, give me my gun, and maybe I won't have my men kill you all." A lone woman stepped forward, all she held was a long sharpened stick. It was taken from the side of a cot and sharpened at one end.

“Oh,” Fiidka exclaimed and laughed, “a woman with a stick. What are you going to do with that when my men arrive, you think that will save you?”

“No.” Hanna replied. “Your men won’t arrive.”

“There are over fifty men coming for me...” Fiidka started to tirade, Hanna cut him off.

“Fifty? It was seventy-five moments ago, now only fifty?” She smiled.

“If you only knew what’s going to happen..” Fiidka tried to scare her, again she cut him off.

“No. You don’t know. You don’t know that the man who just left is the one that killed *all* of your pirates, sank *all* of your precious boats. He’s now going to kill *all* of your men. Do you know why?”

The reality that the man, the source of all his troubles had just done all of this, then ran? “No, why?” Fiidka asked.

“Justice,” Hanna replied, and the lone woman moved slowly towards him.

“What? By a woman with a stick!” Fiidka stepped forward towards the woman and she tried to poke him, but he just batted the stick away.

Fiidka stared at the woman, “What have I done to you.”

“You monster, you, you took my boy, you killed him, you took everything from me,” she cried.

“Stop, I feed hundreds, I turn boys into men, if it wasn’t me, it would be someone else, you think these people are your saviors?" Fiidka asked, waving at Jeremy and Hanna. "What I take is there to be taken."

"Well I'm going to take from you," she cried. Again, she stepped forward and lunged trying to poke him. Yet again, he simply batted the feeble attempt to stick him away and started to laugh. His back was instantly in pain, and he turned around swiftly to see that another woman had approached from behind. She was holding a long pointed stick as well, the tip red with blood, a drop falling gently to the sand below. He brought his hand from the wound. Blood. He went to swipe at her, but the first woman's attempt to poke him now hit home. It wasn't nearly as deep as the second, but it hurt nonetheless.

The two women were not alone. Fiidka finally paid attention to the crowd, whose circle had closed on him. There were dozens of women, now fully emerged from the crowd, all holding sticks. They'd be viewed as a pitiful lot, except for the fact that he was fully surrounded, and had no shield. What few men there were, they weren't in front. They stood behind the women only as a reminder that there was no ease of escape, even if he managed to fight his way through. The movement of the crowd stopped, for a moment he thought there was going to be a reprieve, but then came a sharp blow to the back of his head.

"Hey," Fiidka cried. "I will kill the next bitch who, aaaah," he cried again and flailed after being stuck again in his back, and then his hip. Fiidka flailed wildly, slapping at the multiple sticks aimed his way, and then turning to try to prevent being stabbed in the back. He took a step forward towards a group of women trying to expand the circle, swatting their stabbing attempts aside, getting them to retreat ever so slightly, then one of the thrusts found home, catching him solidly on his left arm. As Fiidka recoiled from the blow, the woman followed up with a second thrust landing around his left armpit, causing him to recoil again.

"Now wait, wait. Just stop," Fiidka asked. "If you think that I'm so bad, I'm so wrong, then call the police," Fiidka said nodding his head as if it would cause them to agree.

"Cadaalada," a woman whispered. Fiidka turned to the whisper. It was just a whisper, but it was strong, and he thought he recognized the voice.

"I remember you," Fiidka smiled as if the memory was a fond one. The smile faded when the memory caught up with him. He remembered seeing her lying on the ground while one of his men had their boot on her back while. He recalled he was taking her son, and she cried "cadaalada." Justice.

With that, the woman forcefully lunged with the spear aiming lower than Fiidka thought, and she caught him firmly in the stomach. Fiidka bent forward trying to absorb the blow, then another stick caught the left side of his face going through his cheek and into his mouth, tasting his own blood.

"No. You can't do this," Fiidka muttered, his speech now slurred from the wound in his mouth. "Please."

"Did my son say please," the women yelled. The other women may not have said it aloud, surely in their own minds they had joined in chorus. Fiidka was poked and prodded by some of the women who'd yet to have delivered a blow. The ones who even now were so afraid of this monster, for the years of misery he caused, and the lifetime of memories they'll still suffer. They too, still wanted justice, the lunges now with more force, and Fiidka's ability to deflect them diminished, more landed home. His pants and shirt now speckled with blood from all of the impacts, some of the circles growing larger.

Hanna reached over to Jeremy, sensing that he may want to stop it. He sensed it too. Jeremy turned and smiled at Hanna, "this isn't the justice I would have chosen," he said. "I know," Hanna replied.

"But it's the justice he deserves," Jeremy finished, turning back to watch the women continue to stab the beast with their sticks as he fell to the ground crying for help, which only enraged the women more. Their aim now centered on his head and neck, to end the voice that haunted them. The only sound then heard was the sound of the sharpened sticks landing on his crumpled body, which went on for some time.

Cadaalada.

# CHAPTER XVIII

## *Desert Rats*

Thomas and the men ran off quickly through the fence. There was no longer any need to worry about being seen, the camp guards were all accounted for, and they had no time to waste. They didn't have to crawl and instead now sprinted for the Flyers. The run wasn't long, even with their gear and the heat. It felt good to move after being boxed up for two days, the adrenalin fueling their speed. They reached the container in good time, and praise be to Uncle, the trustworthy men were just that. They were there, their container was there, and far more importantly, with a turn of a key, so were the Flyers.

Nguyen hopped inside and started the first one, backing it a good distance to make room for the second. Nguyen's Flyer had the 40mm grenade launcher, Marks hopped in the back eager to operate the launcher while Max hopped in the front to ride shotgun.

Atkins darted into the container to back out the other Flyer as soon as Nguyen was clear. They all knew the timing of this plan, and they all knew they were going to be cutting it close. There would only be so much time in between Fiidka's call, and when Abernathy & Bennett would engage Fiidka's men coming to his rescue. The two snipers would be able to deal any attackers quite a blow, but even they could only do so much against numbers, numbers that could eventually attack from multiple sides. So Thomas instructed them not to engage at too long a distance. From afar, if fired upon, the pirates racing to Fiidka could split up, go their separate ways over the cover of various terrain. From there, they could outflank the two men set up on a fixed terrain, unable to flee, for lack of any vehicle.

Instead, the plan was that the two masterful snipers forgo proving how accurate they were at a distance, and instead need to prove how lethal they could be at a closer range. Their role would now be how fast they could prove themselves in unleashing hell upon Fiidka's men, to hold them until the cavalry arrived. By holding them, even if they didn't inflict heavy casualties themselves, they'd hopefully disable the vehicles for the turkey shoot to follow. That was the plan.

Thomas jumped in the front passenger seat of Atkins' Flyer, manning the SAW 5.56mm machine gun, while Siegfried hopped in the rear manning the M2 .50 BMG. Thomas stood up in the flyer, grasping the tubular frame of the vehicle donning goggles to tame the dust and sand about to follow. Thomas looked back at Max in the other Flyer as he did the same. Max gave a thumbs up, which Thomas responded in kind. Siegfried gave the M2 charging handle a swift pull with a big smile.

"Let's go," Thomas said, smacking Atkins on the leg.

"Woooooo," screamed Marks, a mix of enthusiasm and the still flowing release of adrenalin.

The two Flyers screamed across the open sand and dirt that would intersect with the road those leaving Fiikda's compound would have to travel.

Abernathy and Bennett were patiently waiting, which was exactly what they're trained for. Patience.

They'd been only waiting for a few minutes. They didn't yet observe a vehicle to exit Fiidka's compound.

"I'm bored," Abernathy said.

"Bored, I thought you were a sniper?" Bennett joked.

"I can be both a sniper, the most proficient at my job, and still be bored at the task. The two are not mutually exclusive," Abernathy replied, simultaneously causing Bennett's reticle to jump from laughing.

"Knock it the fuck off you limey dick. If I miss a shot because you're making me laugh, I'm going to tell," Bennett replied.

The calm before the storm.

"Tell?" Abernathy. "Pray tell, who?"

Bennett spotted the fleeting view of dust rising above the horizon, the kind of dust created by vehicles driving fast on a dirt road.

"Take a breath pastor, I've got dust from a vehicle on the horizon," Bennett interrupted Abernathy's act. "I'm guessing we're moments from spotting the vehicles."

"Got it," Abernathy replied, taking a large cleansing

breath. He'd inhale and exhale nice and long, so the first shots were sure to be true.

They were both locked in on the exit. Then it happened. An SUV came screeching to a halt near the road, nearly hitting another vehicle, sending a small cloud of dirt into the air, and nearly rear-ended by another SUV behind him, and a third SUV briefly turned to the right to avoid them all. All three turned left onto the main road towards them. They were followed by two pickup trucks with machine guns mounted in the bed, then several box trucks. Three cars exited, followed by three more SUVs, which were then followed by three more pickup trucks.

"Thomas, we have a small convoy of vehicles leaving Fiidka's compound," Bennett called out over coms.

"How many?" Thomas asked.

"Uh, all of them," Abernathy replied.

"Exactly, how many?" Max demanded to know.

"It really doesn't matter boss," Bennett replied, "when you get here, shoot at everything you see, and it's them."

"How long until they reach your time to engage?" Thomas asked.

"Under a minute," Bennett replied. "How long until you're here?"

Nguyen looked at the GPS and then at Thomas shaking his head. "More than that, buddy. Can you hold?"

Bennett looked at Abernathy for the nod, the acceptance of 'I'm in if you are' nod, which was quickly given.

"Don't make it over five minutes, that might be a problem," Bennett replied.

Thomas just looked at Nguyen who was already nodding confidently that they'd make it.

The timing wasn't as bad as it sounded for the two lone snipers. Even if Bennett and Abernathy would start to take heavy fire, and have to withdraw to the safety of cover on the other side of the hill behind them, the pursuing pirates would have to drive up the road, assuming they had a vehicle still running, and drive the couple hundred yards inland to be behind their location. All of that took time and covered a lot of open ground. Plus, as far as the bad guys knew, Fiidka was still alive and being attacked. The worst-case scenario would be that the pirate convoy would just blow past and head for the camp, leaving Thomas and the Flyers to have to pursue to save potentially thousands of refugees from their deaths. This would also leave Bennett and Abernathy all alone.

"Call it when you're engaged, and if any vehicles make it passed you," Thomas asked. "And keep your head down, good shooting."

Abernathy quickly glanced at Bennett prone looking through his scope, "Keep our heads down, he says. If we keep our heads down, how are we going to do any shooting?" Abernathy slowed his speech. "And if it's good shooting we're after,...." as the vehicles were approaching the point where the two had agreed to engage Fiidka's vehicles. Bennett, with the .50 BMG, would concentrate his fire on stopping the vehicles themselves on the road. A single well placed round from his Barrett would kill the engine. The armor-piercing incendiary rounds, wouldn't just crack an engine block causing it to slowly die, it would poke a hole into it causing instant, catastrophic failure. The rounds are designed to both penetrate steel, or armor, and ignite what it could along the way. They didn't expect any armored vehicles to be used by Fiidka's men but did expect lots of vehicles, and vehicles have gas tanks that are a lot easier to penetrate than engine blocks.

Abernathy would work on containing the vehicles, especially those who might try to get around the road to the left. There was nothing but mostly flat open dirt to the left of the road. Fiidka's men could cross the open terrain to the left to try to get around the ambush. However, the ridgeline of rock continued far East of the road to the sea, so Fiidka's men would still have to come back to the road, easily in the range of Abernathy and Bennett, or they could travel all the way down to the Sea to try and cross there if the tides allowed.

Fiidka's men could also turn to the left across the open terrain, but there was no way to get to the refugee camp from there, at least not via their vehicles, or traveling for hours. Fiidka chose his compound in part because of the natural barrier the ridge afforded him, helping limit routes of those wanting to approach. Now that choice funneled his men on one road.

Of course, they could turn straight towards them over open terrain too, which was the other reason the two worked to limit the dust being thrown into the air. It wasn't just to help their vision, it was to hopefully conceal their position for as long as possible. Bennett and Abernathy had the advantage of being concealed along a long ridgeline and weren't directly in front of them.

The disadvantage was that they were in a fixed position, and would be grossly outnumbered.

Abernathy started to count down. "Targets time to engage in five, four, three, two...sending." They both fired.

It was easy to see where Bennett's first round landed on the first SUV. The radiator exploded with a plume of white smoke as the bullet went through, releasing the superheated coolant onto the hot engine and exhaust. The combination of the damage done and the pressure of the released coolant separated the hood from the latches holding it down. At speed, the unlocked hood snapped back towards the windshield with the suddenness of force like a mousetrap, destroying the windshield. The SUV shuddered to a stop as the round made it to the engine block, seizing the engine entirely. Blue smoke from the oil sprayed over the very hot exhaust now puffed out as well.

Abernathy had targeted the driver of the second vehicle, which struck home. The round was aimed to impact the driver's midsection after going through the driver's side door. While the .338 Lapua round fired by Abernathy's gun does not have the sheer force of the .50 BMG, it's sufficiently powered to go through a car door with ease, and then some. While he couldn't see where the round hit the driver, the driver slumped and veered off of the right side of the road before overturning, causing an eruption of dust to be thrown into the air. The natural reaction of the vehicles behind them was to slow to a stop, as they only saw a sudden violent accident occur in front of them. The third SUV and the two pickup trucks, moved into the left lane as the lead SUV was still on the road. As they were coming to a stop next to the crippled wreck, Bennett landed another round squarely through the radiator and ending the vehicle's life. More white smoke burst forth, but with the vehicle stopped, there was no dramatic separation of the hood.

Abernathy's second round targeted the driver of the pickup truck, which must've just missed as the driver turned to avoid the SUV now going up in smoke in front of him. However, the bad guy in the back of the pickup on the machine gun must have caught the round as he suddenly dropped into the bed of the pickup, and didn't get back up.

Just a couple of rounds each, and it was going perfectly. The problem was, Fiidkas' men were now fully aware that they were under attack. The machine gunner on the second pickup truck immediately began firing along the ridgeline where it intersected with the roadway ahead, fortunately far East of their position. They assumed that the shots were coming from the ridge along the road up ahead, as opposed to significantly West of the road.

The three pickup trucks that were last in the convoy, turned off the road to the right. For the moment, Abernathy couldn't engage them as his view of them was blocked by the crippled vehicles in the road and the box trucks. The drivers of the box trucks didn't seem to want to risk driving them over open terrain, at least not yet.

Abernathy concentrated on the left side of the smoking SUVs, expecting to engage the pickup trucks trying to make a mad dash around them.

Bennett sent a few rounds into the engine of the first box truck, taking the burden of deciding what to do with that driver, who then literally fell out of the driver's side of the truck face-first onto the pavement. He then scrambled under the truck for cover. The front of the other two box trucks was blocked by the position of the first, and the three cars now making up the rear, had simply pulled off to the right side of the road, also denying Bennett an easy target.

Some of the men poured out of the box trucks looking to take cover on the East side of the road, as the grade of the terrain was slightly lower. Three others exited the box trucks and crouched onto the road as if crouching gave them any additional cover. They were all holding RPGs, clearly looking to find a target, but had no idea where to fire. Another of Fiidka's men had emerged from one of the cars pointing at the ridge, clearly directing them to fire anyway. They unleashed their rockets, which all flew into the stone ridge at a blazingly fast speed. The three nearly simultaneous explosions shook the ground and threw debris all around, but again, it was far to the East of their location.

Bennett targeted the man from the car, surely a leader, and squeezed. They were only 200 plus yards away. At that distance, the round was still delivering well over 11,000 foot-pounds of energy. By comparison, the standard 5.56 round from a US Soldier's M4 would deliver only about 1,000 foot-pounds of energy at that distance, which is still plenty enough to be lethal. It was an easy shot. The bullet would only drop a few inches at that distance, and the mild wind would cause even less drift. Firing at a stationary target, the size of a man, the shot was a reflex for an expert like Bennett. It was beyond lethal. The bullet struck his soft midsection with an explosive force that tore the man in half. His innards fired backward towards the canvas of the white panel box truck, speckling the sides like a demented Jackson Pollack painting.

It was a solid shot, and while it was wise to take out a leader, in this instance it was a mistake. It revealed their position. From the remnants of the body in the road to the stationary white wall of the box truck was a conical painting of death that pointed towards the shooter. It didn't point with laser-like precision, but it was pointing a full 100 yards further to the West where the RPGs were fired. They reloaded quickly and were pointing towards the location of their attackers to the others.

While all this happened very quickly, it was unseen by the pickup trucks driving around the other side of their position. Abernathy had been patiently waiting for these few seconds, expecting them to emerge to try to make a dash to the road up ahead, and they did. As soon as the first pickup truck emerged, he fired. Abernathy then gauged their speed and fired more rapidly at the lead vehicle. Contain, they only truly needed to contain he thought. Hit the lead vehicle, scare the others to hold. Therefore, Abernathy was aiming to target the driver, not the engine. The near-miss on the driver wasn't that for his passenger, who was obliterated. While lining up the follow-up shot targeting the driver, Abernathy was seeing and hearing bullet impacts all around their little area. They weren't as concealed as they used to be.

The machine guns on the pickups were all spraying the surrounding ridgeline where they were concealed. Concealed, not fully protected, and not fully behind cover. Abernathy molded himself just a little tighter, just a little closer to the ground, and his next shot killed the driver and the pickup struck slowly turned away, coasting to an eventual stop. The gunner kept firing closer to their location nonetheless.

Bennett realized his error after seeing the driver under the truck pointing towards their position, he then saw the other three men reloading their RPG's. Bennett targeted the man nearest them and the proof of the bullet hitting home was another layer of blood contributing to the artwork on the side of the box truck. This was not in time to prevent the other two other men from letting loose their reloaded RPG's towards the ridgeline where Bennett and Abernathy were located. The first rocket hit below them, sending a plume of sand and black smoke into the air. The second was about seventy-five feet to the left. They were at the far end of the accuracy that could be obtained by the RPG in the hands of Fiidka's men.

"What the fuck," Abernathy called out. "I think they got a bead on us, how?"

Bennett saw the driver, still under the box truck, feverishly pointing in their location.

"Yeah about that," Bennett said. "That might have been me. Enough of this." Bennett targeted the external fuel tank on the second box truck. The fifteen gallons of diesel were in a black external tank located below the rear box immediately behind the driver's side door. "Boom," he said as he sent the round. The description was accurate. The small hole punctured the tank when it entered, and then exited the other side of the tank causing a larger "exit wound" to the tank, along with the diesel fuel being spewn forth out the back and aerosolized. Whether the incendiary round ignited the fuel on impact or as it was leaving the tank couldn't be determined with the naked eye, yet the two RPG rocketeer's and the driver underneath were instantly immolated.

The rounds were still coming their way from the machine gunners on the pickup trucks. They circled away after Abernathy took out the lead pickup, but they were unrelenting in firing on them and were coming back around. The many other men that left the box trucks had moved on foot along the roadway and began firing as well. The higher grade of the road versus the terrain to the east would continue to give them cover as they approached.

The incoming fire was intensifying. Abernathy and Bennett had blocked the road, they'd stopped the convoy and destroyed several of their vehicles. Yet there were still plenty of Fiidka's men remaining, and they'd only be lucky for so much longer under the withering fire.

"We have to fall back to a more protected position," Abernathy said.

"No argument from me," Bennett replied and fired off several more rounds before reloading again.

"Thomas, we have to fall back now," Abernathy said on coms while both he and Bennett were slithering backward under the protection of the raised rock. "We'll still have some view of the road ahead of them, then that's it. If they come for us, we have to bolt, because we're in trouble."

"We're close," Thomas replied.

"How close," Bennett asked.

Abernathy and Bennett, after moving back behind the raised rock that offered them some protection, then moved quickly to get even further around the back to a slightly higher position, however, it offered no direct view of where the vehicles were stopped during the firefight. They'd be able to see if Fiidka's men moved further North on the road approaching the ridge, leaving only a limited time to fire. As they started to position their sniper rifles on the large rocks in front of them, several of the pickups were already on the road at high speed. Both men put themselves behind their scopes quickly and started to squeeze, and with that, the pickups were out of view. They had gotten by.

"How close?" Bennett asked again, "they got by us."

"I was hoping to time my response better," Thomas replied.

"What?" Bennett asked.

"This close," was all Bennett heard from Thomas before the sound that the cavalry had clearly arrived.

The two flyers had traveled directly towards the position of Bennett and Abernathy along the ridge, instead of the slightly more direct route of intersecting the bad guys at the road. If his men were in trouble, Thomas wanted to support them first, kill the bad guys second.

After hearing that Bennett and Abernathy withdrew to

cover, the two flyers turned East, driving parallel to the ridge, but on the Northern side while Fiidka's men were on the Southern side.

Fiidka's men in the pickup trucks were flying through the gap of the ridge, believing they escaped the fire from the snipers and were racing to save their boss.

The Flyers, still on the sand, moved enough to the left so they could maintain some speed while making the turn to go through the gap. The two Flyers turned hard, the stable vehicles staying on course nonetheless drifted in the sand, the rear end of the vehicle sliding to the left in the tractionless desert. Thomas turned to look at Atkins enjoying the drive just a bit too much. While in the middle of the turn, Thomas turned back and saw Fiidka's men in the pickup trucks come flying through the gap with men manning the machine guns mounted in the back.

"Shit," Thomas exclaimed. "Max hit'em!" Atkins then turned even more to the right to allow Max an unimpeded view.

Max didn't need to hear the words. He was already aiming the 40mm grenade launcher towards the gap when the pickup trucks emerged. He only had to adjust for the truck's speed to lead them and the launcher's distinct thumping sound was quickly repeated, followed by what looked like the trucks hitting a minefield. Explosions along the road, the sand, the rock were nonstop and all-consuming. Their gunners were instantly overwhelmed, couldn't get off another round, and the smoke and debris made even getting a good look at them difficult. Max's rounds were close from the start, which was followed by direct hits on the vehicles that obliterated them and the men. Fire from the gas tanks added to the mix, as the trucks skidded to their end in the sand. Max fired off about half of the 48 round belt as a hello.

As they rounded the corner, Siegfried had yet to fire from the M2 as Max had unleashed hell on Fiidka's trucks sprinting towards the camp. Siegfried saw the sporadic fire of rifles from the vehicles destroyed on the roadway, and several cars were now trying to drive around them on the terrain to the left, while a box truck and a the three remaining SUVs chose to try to go around on the left, but intending to get back to the road. Siegfried targeted the box truck first.

"I got the cars on the left," Thomas called out and opened fire on the vehicles with the SAW. The small caliber fast firing light machine gun sprayed a number of rounds all around the lead car, but many were hitting in the dirt and sand all around that threw a ton of dust in the air.

"They're the big shiny things," Atkins joked at Thomas's aim as they jumped up over the road.

Firing a 750 round machine gun from a vehicle moving 45 mph while going around a curve on bumpy ground covered with sand at a car moving the same over sand, is almost always going to look less than accurate. Once on the road, however, Thomas's fire decimated the lead car, and then the second. The third car turned to avoid the carnage of the other two and flipped over, landing on its roof. Thomas was about to fire into the vehicle to end the occupants when something struck it and it exploded.

"I could still see him from cover," Bennett called out over coms. Their fall back position gave them cover from the main body but allowed some view of the battlespace as Fiidka's men traveled North on the road. The .50 incendiary round through the flipped car's gas tank served its purpose.

Thomas then directed his fire along the Eastern portion of the road where a good number of Fiidka's men thought they were safe from the snipers on the ridge. The relentless fire left them nowhere to hide, and many fell quickly. The remaining survivors laid close to the ground as if hugging it for survival. The tight embrace served them no better. While prone, they were still in view of Abernathy and Bennet, who simply picked them off before they made another decision equally doomed to fail.

Siegfried fared better with his aim as he came around the corner. Fiidka's men in the three remaining SUVS with machine guns were firing as well, the rounds danced in the sand all around them. They too were moving, experiencing all of the same difficulties as Thomas, with far less training, and virtually no real experience of this kind of a moving battle. And they weren't on the road. They had decided to follow the box trucks who in a panic decided to try to make an end run to the right and were still driving over a washboard-like terrain.

Siegfried hit the box truck with such a large volley from the M2 that it appeared to have been disassembled by an A-10. The A-10 is a simple straight-wing jet where the pilot sits in a titanium tub to protect himself while the GAU-8A 30mm cannon unleashes 4,800 rounds per minute of uranium densified rounds that will literally disassemble a tank. This wasn't that, but on the ground, that's what it looked like. After the box truck, Siegfried altered fire to the SUVS, as Thomas joined in, followed by Max with well placed single shot rounds from the Grenade launcher.

The mix of unrelenting machine gun fire from multiple points while the explosions from the few grenades eliminated all of the vehicles still running and any of Fiidka's men foolish enough to stand upright.

The return fire from Fiidka's men lessened, but the Flyers didn't let up the barrage as they pushed forward. The Flyers took several hits from the small arms fire and kept going strong. The fire from Max on the grenade launcher was too much for Fiidka's men. The explosions forced those still in the fight to lay prone and stationary, only hoping for the best, while the two machine guns repeatedly strafed their positions around the damaged vehicles.

Thomas and Max's Flyers exited the road to the left to flank those still firing, and that ended the threats. There was no more return fire.

Thomas waved for Max to come to a stop next to him.

"One more thing," Thomas asked.

"Mein Gott, now what Thomas," Max said, shoulders shrugging in exasperation.

"How many rounds are left on that grenade launcher?" Thomas asked.

Max looked, ran his fingers up the string of 40mm grenades. "Only a few, but I have another string." Max bent over to raise the new string of grenades from the ammo box to the MK19 grenade launcher.

Thomas marveled at the loyalty and felt guilty about deserving it. Thomas asked how many rounds were left, and Max, without hesitation, was starting to arm up as if to go into another battle without question.

"No, Max, don't reload the belt, we only need a few," Thomas said confidently.

"Only a few?" Max asked as Thomas wasn't one to go into any altercation with an unloaded gun. He had always planned on overwhelming victory, so the victors could all go home at night.

"Just one more door to knock on," Thomas asked, and waved Max to follow.

Thomas dialed his phone, and thankfully, Jeremy answered. "I didn't expect to hear from you so soon, or maybe ever again."

"Fair enough, thanks for answering," Thomas replied.

"Well, seeing as the caller appeared as "Most Awesome Cousin Ever," it seemed a shame to swipe left." Jeremey said, "But I'm still not cool with all this."

"Not looking for cool Jeremy, I'm looking for transport," Thomas corrected.

"Transport? For what?" Jeremy asked. "If you need a ride, with your men, I don't know that I should be..."

"Jesus, Jeremy, you wouldn't give me a ride," Thomas bemoaned. "After all this, not a lift?"

Jeremy started to explain that a refugee camp can't seem aligned to one group or another, or it would be sullied by one of them and attacked by all.

"Relax Jeremy, I don't need a ride," Thomas stopped his painful dissertation on Somali etiquette vis-à-vis the refugee camp and the warlord du jour.

"Well, what then?" Jeremy asked.

"Well, we just drove by Fiidka's men on the highway, they all had a breakdown," Thomas began, and thankfully, Jeremy was speechless. "So we're rolling up to his home now. We're going to knock on the door. I don't suspect that there's anybody of consequence home. But maybe some of the children here might belong to some of the mothers there. And if not, well, that might be a good fit anyway. So I could use your truck to come and get them." Thomas asked.

"How many Thomas," Jeremy asked.

"Hold on a second, we'll check," Thomas replied. "Max, if you could please knock on the main door, please. A couple of rounds only please." Thomas asked pointing at the large arched metal doors where the vehicles would go through to Fiidka's walled compound.

Max took his time with the aim and hoped none of the children were playing on the other side, although that seemed unlikely. He crossed his fingers and fired a round at the top of the eighteen-foot high doors at the joint that separated them, fired a second round at the middle where the hinge of the door was connected to the wall of the compound which twisted them further, then a final round at the bottom which took the right side door off its hinges as it fell to the ground.

An armed guard in the open area behind the door was

in plain view as the door fell. He jumped around not knowing what to do but wisely didn't fire. He just stood there dumbfounded. "You and the other men can flee out the back and never come back, or we'll kill you all," Thomas called out with their vehicle's weapons all aimed at him. "And send out the children."

The man held onto his weapon, almost dancing in place absorbing the sudden change of affairs.

"I mean now," Thomas said, hurrying him along.

The man's head then nodded and he ran off. They didn't see any other men, and couldn't tell how many ran out the back, or even if there were any more than the lone gunman.

Nearly a minute later a young dark-haired boy walked into the lot inside, peaking around the corner towards Thomas and the men on the Flyers. "It's alright," Thomas called out, "a truck will come for you and your friends."

The boy shook his head no and took a step back. "It's okay son, the truck will take you home," hoping that the boy understood.

The boy stopped, clearly understanding the word home, but trust was something that would not be given any time soon after what he'd been through. Several other children walked into the lot where Fiidka's vehicles used to be kept to join the boy.

"How many other children are inside," Thomas asked the young boy.

The poor thing put up his hands showing ten fingers, then appeared to struggle with what number came next as the boy looked at his fingers, apparently unable to get the number right himself.

“You still there,” Thomas asked?

“Yeah, I’m still here, what the hell is going on?” Jeremy replied.

“We knocked on the door, the guards are gone, our intel, such as it is, is ten to twenty young children. Maybe more,” as several others came into view, “are here and in need of help. We can’t drive them over to you, and I don’t think they would want to hop in our vehicles anyway.” Thomas replied, turning to look inside at the scared little faces.

“Do you know who they are?” Jeremy asked.

“Just bring a number of the women with you to help bring them back to the camp, you can figure all of that out in due time,” Thomas replied.

“Sure, I guess we’ll be on our way,” Jeremy replied, still overwhelmed from the day’s events.

Thomas looked at his watch, “We’ll secure the place until you arrive, but then we really have to go. So seriously, don’t lose the phone.” Thomas ended the call.

“Max, take the men, clear the compound, grab the stuff,” Thomas ordered. And with the men swept through the compound trying not to scare the children.

# CHAPTER XIX

## *The Payoff*

Jeremy arrived with a truck as Thomas requested, along with three new SUV's courtesy of Fiidka's visit. The vehicles slowed as they approached. Despite seeing Thomas, Jeremy was tentative nonetheless. He was driving up to what was just yesterday thought of as the gates of hell. A shiver went up his spine.

Jeremy stopped the truck just short of where Thomas stood and saw the large metal doors blown open, the one side laying on the ground. "Knocked huh?" he asked.

"It was a hard knock," Thomas replied, now pointing at the children. "I didn't want a firefight through the residence, a stern warning to scare off what few rats were left seemed to be the way to go."

Jeremy saw some of the children; he honestly didn't recognize any of them. He silently hoped that none of these were from his camp. How horrible it would be to have so quickly forgotten their faces, he thought.

Hanna and a few other women exited the SUV's and moved forward slowly towards the children carrying water and what little candy they could find at the camp before departing. Undoubtedly most of the women were mothers from the camp holding out hope as well.

The children, still obviously afraid, not knowing what was going on, at least didn't run. The women's approaching smiles were the first smiles they'd seen for some time. The warming inviting voices, the comforting sounds they thought they'd forgotten were irresistible and one of the younger children ran up to the women with open arms. That broke the dam and the others then approached, if only apparently for the treats, but it was a start.

One of the women from the camp screamed a piercing scream that startled everyone. Thomas looked around to see the woman sprinting towards the compound and scooped up one of the children with both arms spinning around before collapsing onto the ground with the young boy, sobbing. She wasn't going to ever let him go. Never again.

Thomas watched as the other women gathered up the children to help lead them to the truck and the SUVs. None of the other women screamed. They smiled at the children, and teared up when they looked at each other. "At least one," Thomas said. "Maybe you'll get lucky to find their families still at the camp."

"Maybe," Jeremy said. "At least they're safe, we'll take care of them either way, so long as we keep getting donations." Jeremy was grateful for Thomas's actions, he didn't want Fiidka to continue the terror he'd doled out on the people he cared for. Of that, there was no doubt. However, the method never sat right with him. "Thomas, what you did, to Fiidka, I can't complain about that. But that's not going to help feed them, house them, or clothe them. Conflict is what creates more refugees."

Thomas nodded his head in agreement. "Well, there's a number of "damaged" containers of rice onboard our, uh, boat. Some of them are being hauled over to you. The captain on our ship has been ferrying rice to shore since we landed days ago. I believe they were "lost at sea." Plus, we managed to "sell" a lot of the rice to charities at a steep discount so long as it goes through your camp. So those containers will be delivered after the boat docks. There's well over two thousand tons of rice all told, the majority of that will be delivered later still in the containers after the boat docks. Plus, you can use the containers for housing. They may have a few holes that need fixing."

"Hot steel for Somali summer?" Jeremy commented, ignoring the gift of the rice.

"Solid protection, I can't change the temp in Somalia," Thomas joked. "But, for what it's worth, there's another gift that'll be in one of the containers delivered later. There are several high-pressure pumps with hundreds of feet of tubing that could be used for irrigation since you have ample access to pump clean water. Since you have ample water via your desalination system, you'll have enough to use for farming. You're lucky to have arable land. Plus you could run a line over the metal containers to generate hot water and keep the temp down on the containers."

"Might help for a few, but it doesn't solve the problems of so many," Jeremy lamented.

There he is. The man who so desperately wants to help everyone, and it's just never enough. The sad fact was, in Somalia, Jeremy was used to never having enough. There was never a shortage of suffering here.

"There are sprinklers in there too, kids can run through them in the summer. I'm not here to solve everybody's problem, Jeremy, but I hope it helped." Thomas turned to the compound as Max was exiting with a duffle bag full of items taken from the compound.

"So what's all this?" Jeremy asked. "Spoils of war?"

Thomas laughed. "In a way, yes. Laptops, cell phones, records, whatever intel we can scoop up that implicates others for Uncle. Unfortunately Jeremy, just like there's never enough to help everyone, there are always more bad guys."

"So, this was all about *Uncle*?" Jeremy asked. "This was his plan? Figures."

"No Jeremy, this wasn't your *father's* plan, it was all mine," Thomas pointed out. "But as always, he helped out, a lot. None of this would've been possible without him. Or to put it more bluntly, eventually, you'd be dead, and all those you worked so hard trying to save would have been killed along with you. Eventually, that's what bad guys do."

Jeremy shrugged, surrendering. "I'm sorry Thomas. I'm overwhelmed. And I don't just mean I'm overwhelmed with what happened here today, which I totally am by the way. But all that food will mean a world of difference to us. The irrigation system can be used to plant on what good soil we can find. These three vehicles are a huge help. I'm not ungrateful, this..." Jeremy pointed around at the compound, the destroyed large doors to the compound, "...I'm just not good with *this*." Jeremy waved his arms about at the compound of a warlord.

Hanna approached the two. "All the children are on board, we should get them home," she said, smiling a thank you to Thomas.

Thomas nodded a smile to Hanna. "Well we definitely have to go, I still have to pick up two of my men, but you should stick around," pointing at Fiidka's compound. "Speaking of "spoils of war," his men aren't coming back, the place is empty. Max here said there's at least one room with plenty of valuables, artwork, etc. You have a truck and three SUVs with plenty of room."

"No," Jeremy said. "Fiidka's gold is tainted, bought with drug money and the blood of the innocent."

"If Schindler saved a Jew by selling a Nazi flag, is he the good guy, or a bad guy," Thomas asked. "Nothing in life is perfect Jeremy. God knows I'm not. Endure the disgust of selling Fiidka's wealth to help your people, or leave it all for the next bad guy to come this way," as Thomas climbed into the Flyer. "I'd say do what you think is right, but maybe you should just do what you think is best."

Hanna looked over Jeremy raising her eyebrows, saying *we can use the money* with her eyes.

Jeremy relented, smiled at her, "fine."

"Hanna, I hope everything, and I mean everything works out for you," Thomas said, then looking at Jeremy, who understood the inference.

Jeremy stared at Hanna while replying to Thomas, "I'm sure it will."

"Bye, Cousin," Thomas hollered as he leaped into the flyer which moved and sped off as soon as he landed.

Abernathy & Bennett remained on the ridge, albeit now resting in the shade with a view of the smoldering vehicles.

"You know," Abernathy said in a complaining tone. "Thomas could've picked us up first instead of leaving us to wait here baking in the heat."

"You know the Flyers don't have air?" Bennett mused. "We'd be sitting in the open sun, or having to clear a building. Here, we can relax."

"To be honest, I'm conflicted. I'm undecided if the views of the smoldering remains of victory are relaxing," Abernathy laughed.

"You mean you're worried that it is," Bennett asked.

Abernathy nodded, and responded with a firm "Bingo!"

"Plus, if anyone survived and tried to intercept the camp's vehicles, we're here." Bennett reminded him.

"Man, I thought Jeremy was going to drive the truck a mile around Fiidka's guys' remains. It was like he was afraid of ghosts." Abernathy noted. "I liked the silver Range Rover, nice get for refugees."

"Yeah, I think that was the Velar, it was sporty, and I normally don't like cars in silver. They'll probably sell it though, and buy something cheaper." Bennett pointed out as if that was a bad idea for a camp of refugees.

"You could buy one with our bonus?" Abernathy offered.

"Nah, if I'm dropping over $50,000 on a vehicle, it'll be a truck that can do everything, like a Ford Raptor, or an F-150 Texas Edition," Bennett opined.

"If you want a truck that can do everything, why would you want a Ford," Abernathy laughed.

Bennett stood up looking around, "Ah, shut up, I'm not getting into a truck argument with a guy whose favorite vehicle starts with "Mini." Where's fucking Thomas already?" The two Flyers came screaming onto the road from Fiidka's compound as Bennett stood to look.

"Bennett, Abernathy, we're rolling and will meet you on the Northside of the ridge, you copy?" Thomas asked.

"Copy that, we're Oscar Mike," Bennett replied, bending down to grab his gear. "Bout fuckin' time."

"Couldn't just say "on the move" could you?" Abernathy asked.

"Just tryin' to be professional, man," Bennett laughed. "Now let's go see how we made out."

The two walked to the base of the ridge awaiting their ride.

"Miss us?" Thomas asked as the Flyers pulled up. "Any problems?"

"Not a thing," Abernathy said. "There wasn't any movement from Fiidka's men. A bunch of different vehicles drove up, from both directions, saw the mess, turned around, and fled. Apparently, nobody called Somali 911."

"So how'd we make out on the bonus," Bennett asked, cutting to the chase.

"Hop in, we're driving straight to the boat, we'll go over everything there. It's all good," Thomas promised.

"Alright!" Abernathy said, getting into Max's Flyer, "I forgot what day it is, but it sounds like payday."

The two Flyers went back to the main road and straight to the docks. Captain Zhao left information at the gate that two armed vehicles would be arriving and should be allowed to come straight to their ship to provide "security" since they were attacked.

Captain Zhao had contacted Jiang, Mr. Lee's representative regarding the time of their arrival, and to report the "loss" of goods during the pirate attack. A third party adjuster was already waiting for their ship as they docked. Fraud is an issue everywhere in the world, and "losses" aren't always really lost, so companies have reps everywhere to try to prevent false claims.

Captain Zhao looked down at the awaiting suit and smiled. He waved the man aboard. "Come aboard sir, thank God we made it."

The adjuster walked up the stairs looking over the charred boat. While the bodies were thrown overboard, along with any of the spent cartridge casings that weren't melted into the deck, the evidence of the attack remained. The holes the RPG's punched through the shipping containers, the black soot painted almost everything on deck black. The damage was everywhere.

After coming on board, and listening to Zhao's tale about how all the drunken pirates came on board, launching RPG's at the ship, they had no chance. They were shooting up the place as the crew hid in the tower, apparently upset that there was only rice on board. Then the pirates must've tried to torch the ship, and killed many of their own by mistake.

"It was horrifying to watch," Captain Zhao said, feigning concern for their loss.
We were so lucky to have survived."

The insurance representative continued to make notes and take pictures; he asked little. "Were any containers lost at sea?"

Captain Zhao shook his head no, pointing to the damaged containers still on board. "A number of them were heavily damaged, but there was no need to throw them off of the ship. We only tossed the damaged food, the rice that was covered in gasoline, burned, and so forth. The bags were heavily damaged, and as you can still see, rice is everywhere. It's like sand, it gets into everything."

The insurance rep nodded diligently, accepting the story and yet still trying to think it through.

"I didn't want the port authorities to see the rice everywhere, I was worried they'd then deny the rest of the shipment, you know?" Captain Zhao nodded looking for the rep to agree with him. "Did I do wrong?" he asked.

"Your only cargo is rice?" The rep asked to confirm the cargo list.

"Yes, only rice," Captain Zhao assured him, pointing to the bills of lading he'd handed him.

The amount of rice missing was small, given the vast amount on board. The damage to the ship was real, and nobody fires RPGs at their own ship and burns it just to steal that amount of rice. The captain's story was the only one that made sense.

"I'm sorry for your loss Captain, I can just imagine how terrified you and your men were," the insurance rep said with empathy, looking up at the white tower above while imagining what it was like to have looked down on all this fire below.

"I'll forward the information to the carrier along with the pictures, I can't imagine that there will be a problem. I'm sure they may want a statement and may want you to cooperate with local authorities, but," the adjuster couldn't think of one thing that was a problem. "But, I'm sure your coverage limits will cover the loss, so your boss should be happy, or at least he shouldn't want you dead."

"Thank you, thank you so much," Captain Zhao smiled and shook the man's hand with vigor. "After such an experience, thank you so much for your help,"

"Sure, not a problem." the rep said, feeling good for doing his job for once. "Do you have to go back out?"

"Yes, but we have a security team coming, so I'll feel better about it." Zhao nodded.

"Kind of closing the barn doors after the cows got out,"

the insurance rep joked.

"What?" Zhao asked.

"Never mind, it's an old Somali saying. I'll take a few more pictures and be on my way." The insurance rep looked around, marveling that they survived and made it to port. "Remarkable," he exclaimed and waved goodbye to Zhao.

◆ ◆ ◆

The Flyers were living up to the name, they decided not to drive slowly through Mogadishu to the port. Heavily armed men in vehicles looking American aren't necessarily thought of fondly in the region, and they had no interest in engaging anyone else today. They sped to the entrance to the port, and despite how heavily armed they were, they were quickly cleared to enter. They drove the Flyers down to "the boat," their boat. They were given direction, but there was only one boat docked that looked like charred remains.

"Alright, everybody out," Thomas ordered. "Grab your gear. The vehicles will be lifted inside, but if it's not nailed down here, somebody else may lift it." Thomas joked. "Let's walk."

The men gathered their gear as Thomas waited at the base of the long stairway to the deck like a rally point. "Okay, as I'm sure you're all as eager as Bennett to find out the final tally. We sold a little over 2,000 tons of rice to a variety of charitable foundations at a discounted price of $800 per ton, for a total of $1.6 million. Part of that bonus goes to Captain Zhao and his men, but it works out to just over $140,000 bonus per man."

"Wooo!" Atkins exclaimed.

"Sounds like you can now afford that truck," Abernathy laughed.

"Man, that's great Thomas, but I don't get it," Siegfried asked. "Won't Lee, our client, be a little pissed we're selling rice he kinda paid for?"

"You'd think so, but no," Thomas replied. "As it happens, I had a friend in DC who was just dying to broker a deal to get Lee's corporate insurance on their fleet. And, as they *kind* of knew Lee's pirate losses were going to be lower in the future, they could make an extremely competitive bid. Lee didn't mind the "loss" of rice, as he's made whole by his current insurance carrier, who he's leaving and won't pay it back in higher rates."

"Shit this is awesome," Siegfried replied. "I just can't tell you what this'll mean for me and my family. Thank you man," extending his arm to Thomas, who took it gladly.

"Thank *you*. All of you." Thomas said, and bordering on weeping up himself. "I try to be disconnected, it's the only way this works, usually. At least for me. This was different. This was very different for me. I may not have handled it in the best way in the beginning, especially for those closest to me," nodding to Max.

Max nodded back and smiled. "Like I said, hard to stay pissed at the guy who always makes it work out."

"I don't want to be the greedy guy," Bennett interrupted.

Abernathy put his hand to his face, “Oh God, here we go.”

“Just stop, we’re all curious,” Bennett replied. “But what does the second part look like.”

“Does the SAT phone have a speakerphone?” Thomas asked Max.

“Of course, this isn’t 1990,” Max replied.

Thomas took the handset and dialed. “Let’s call Mr. Lee.”

The men had reached the top of the deck, cleared of a number of containers, and looked out on the sea.

Jiang answered the phone.

“Jiang, this is Thomas. Is Mr. Lee available?” Thomas asked.

“One moment while I see if he can come to the phone,” Jiang replied as if it was just another day, just another call.

“Hello Thomas,” Mr. Lee said, overly cheerful without even getting the final report yet. “How are you?”

“We’re well sir. I was calling to report on the outcome,” Thomas began.

“Well, from what I hear from my men at the port, the ship looks like hell on Earth! That, I take it, is nothing but good news.” Lee laughed.

“Right you are sir. I was calling to see how Jiang has made out pitching our story,” Thomas asked.

“Finish the tale for me, my interest has been piqued all

along," Lee begged.

"Well, the pitch is this. What began as a common tale of a meager security team setting sail to scare away rogue pirates quickly escalated into an all-out war sending dozens of small boats filled with pirates to their graves. And when over fifty pirates attacked with larger ships, they were sent to the bottom of the depths as well. Those that weren't faced a far deadlier fate of being engulfed in the fire that ensued onboard. And if that wasn't enough, they then slew dozens more on land and served up a pedophile warlord to the mothers of his victims, and helped free the enslaved children giving them a home." Thomas paused to take a breath. "How does that sell?"

"And we're free to say this is a "True Story," Lee asked.

"We are," Thomas assured him. "First, it is. Second, the International Law of Mercenaries' definition applies to those that undermine legitimate governments. Claiming we undermined the government of Somalia would demand they proved it was "legitimate." But forget parsing words on Somalia's failed government, or even whether the attack on Fiidka's compound applied. Even if the entirety of the story never actually happened, it is the privilege of fiction writers to claim the story to be true. And "Based On A True Story" always sells more."

"Fantastic!" Jiang said aloud on the phone, "I'm sorry sir," he immediately lowered his tone, lowering her enthusiasm.

"I think what Jiang is saying is this is a script that can sell!" Lee added. "And the best part is, the profits can pay for another adventure, which we can then sell as well."

Thomas cringed, as Lee overstepped his bounds. As Thomas reminded him in the beginning, "Mr. Lee, the deal applies to this matter. Perhaps another will arise with your involvement in the future, but for now, let Jiang concentrate on making this one profitable."

"Very well, your rebuff will not phase me. I will not contain my excitement for this venture. It will make us, you, and your men, a great deal I believe. You will be able to do a great many things with your wealth after this Thomas," Lee suggested. "And I will have another trophy on my wall."

"Let me know as things progress, I'll follow up with Jiang. And Mr. Lee?" Thomas asked.

"Yes Thomas. What?"

"With all the profits certain to come your way, I'm going to send you the name of a charity, if you're looking for one," Thomas finished.

"Of course. Hey, we all have to eat." Lee said, a funny line from the capitalist that he most certainly was.

"Yes, yes we do." Thomas then ended the call. "So, look. Like I said before, this idea of a movie is ridiculous. I promoted it to Lee knowing it was something he desperately wanted, it was a button to push. Since we work in the shadows, the idea of a movie makes me cringe, but I integrated the idea of taking advantage of his desire to get the gig. Part of the agreement is that you compose a timeline of your experience, *don't* put your names on any of it! Give it all to Robert, he'll have it put in a report and make sure we're not confessing to any crimes-ish, or providing even metadata information to ID anybody. and he'll send it over to Lee."

"Is that what Lee meant by buying the boat *for future work*?" Max asked.

"Yeah, well, that was the gist. He has a movie set." Thomas replied.

"Needs a big ass paint job," Siefgried joked.

"Again, "in the works" isn't a dollar figure, and I wouldn't hold my breath for a dime from that. If it comes to fruition, then I'll say "I had the utmost faith that it would work." But the rice deal paid off far better than I expected, you guys can thank Robert for all of that work." Thomas stopped to look around the boat, searching for anything he'd forgotten.

"Look," Thomas said seriously. "Enjoy the money, you earned it. Take time off, I'm not certain what's next either. Unwind after the trip on the boat, and stay safe. But whether there's a sequel that Lee wants, there's always a sequel in what we do. This mission was different, a little more involved than some of you may have been accustomed to, but not me. Not to Max here, he knows. There will be a sequel for you all to work with us again if you want it, especially with how well all of you performed. I mean, outside of me taking a ricochet, and Atkins getting shot in the ass," Thomas paused for the inevitable responses.

"God, I knew, I just knew this would never end," Atkins immediately responded as everyone was laughing.

"Seriously. Celebrate Atkins' ass, drink to it. Given the

hell we doled out, I relish these kinds of wins," and with that, he raised an opened bottle of Ben Millam bourbon, took a swig, and passed it around to the men.

"Take your time, finish the bottle, then stow your gear. We're on the boat to the Seychelles, where we'll get off the way we came. The arms will be sent home. I expect the rest of the trip to be uneventful." Thomas raised a hand again in thanks and the men all cheered.

"Max," Thomas nodded to him. "So? We good?" Thomas asked.

"Well, actually, yeah," Max said. "And it's not just that we lived, but everything worked out and you saved children. It's kind of hard to stay mad at you after that, and it paid off handsomely, but it's not just that."

"Well what then," Thomas asked.

Max pointed at him and exclaimed, "You're flawed like the rest of us. Sure, the operation went excellently, but not telling me and Robert. Ha! You handled that terribly, you should be embarrassed. You suck at something!" Max said laughing.

"Great. I dare say I'm glad my failings bring you such joy," Thomas demurred.

"Well, they're few and far between, so I'm happy for what I get," Max smiled. "So what's next?"

"What's next? Just enjoy the slow boat to the Seychelles," Thomas suggested.

Max cringed. He was just too used to Thomas' annoying play on words. "China?"

"Nice pickup. You should try intel work!" Thomas

joked. “It’s all over the place actually. Part of it was a problem Uncle asked me to work on a little while ago,” Thomas said seriously. “It’s gotten bigger. It’s big.”

“So it’s China?” Max asked.

“We have some time to go over it. And I wouldn’t want to deny ourselves a few extra days of Seychelles Rum to go over it thoroughly. I’ll call Robert to let him know,” Thomas replied, thinking through the complexities of the next mission as they spoke.

“Hey, brother,” Max said loudly to get his attention. “The only hard day was yesterday.”

# CHAPTER XX

## *Fin*

With the departure of the insurance representative, the containers destined for Jeremy's camp were cleared to be unloaded from the Fafnir. The two inflatable Ferries that were being stored in one of the damaged empty containers were removed. Mr. Lee was more than happy to send the damaged containers to the camp. As a charitable deduction, it was worth more than salvaging them, and again, the insurance company was going to make him whole with new ones. Given his previous failed attempts to enter the film industry, he was also oh so eager to believe that this time it would be different. Lee valued the idea of some award on his shelf, he could care less about giving junk to Thomas's favorite charity, whatever it was. Sure, he'd donate, but care? Not so much. The real success of the mission was that word spread about what had happened to a warlord of Somalia, and thereafter his ship's main defense was LEE painted in big bold lettering. Knowing he was willing and able to strike on land? It put the fear of Lee into the minds of many other groups. Nobody wanted to be responsible for attracting that kind of retribution ever again. And during negotiations? The simplest inference of how far Mr. Lee was willing to go was worth more than its weight in gold. Mr. Lee reveled in the win but other than that periodic necessary inference, he made no direct mention of it other than desperately trying to promote the film.

Mr. Lee benefited from the broker who managed to persuade an insurance company to give him very favorable rates despite some of the riskier destinations that had previously resulted in sizable losses. This was of course facilitated by Molly, Thomas' girlfriend, who loathed his absence but loved their reunions. He invited her to meet him in the Seychelles, a "vacation" that was happily sanctioned by her firm since she somehow managed to bring in Lee Shipping. That she was able to successfully broker the insurance business was one thing, but then word of a new venture worth millions of dollars with Mr. Lee himself? They'd give the two of them all the time they needed in the tropical paradise.

Of course, it wasn't ever *all* vacation. Robert flew out to meet Thomas and Max to discuss the latest urgent matter. Uncle may have requested Thomas to think about a solution some time ago, but the geopolitical climate of China being a competitor was rapidly changing. The global pandemic exacerbated and accelerated economic differences to the point of not being a competitor, but clearly an adversary. There were multiple forces at play to take advantage of this growing divide, the intent of painting China to be viewed as an enemy, not that they were wrong. As this could spiral out of control, Thomas told Molly that he was thrilled to have her visit the Seychelles, as it may be some time before he'd be back in DC. Max had Ute come to the Seychelles as well to celebrate Oktoberfest; it was July.

After a brief celebration in the Seychelles, Thomas' men all went their separate ways, at least for the time being.

James Abernathy returned to England, he still lived in a small home on his parent's estate. It was a sanctuary for him and he never minded paying a disproportionately high rent to his parents to care for the entirety of the estate. This also meant benefitting several family members he wasn't entirely fond of, but they made his parents happy. He was glad to be home.

Tony Bennett bought a new truck. It wasn't a Ford or a Chevy, so he wouldn't ever have to listen to the never-ending competition of truck enthusiasts. While Jeep didn't have a Texas Edition, which bothered him, the Gladiator had more than enough off-road capabilities for him. Plus, he really liked the name. It was the kind of name that reminded one of hell being unleashed on their enemies.

Kim Nguyen and Francis Marks went to Las Vegas together. While perhaps not the best place to visit after "hitting it big," the two had the time of their lives and lost only enough to have considered the trip a bargain.

Marcus Siegfried went home to his wife and children in New Jersey. They were glad to see him after his long trip abroad. They missed him terribly but understood that the engineering assignments were in remote areas where he had little access to reliable communication. They were always happy to hear about the people he helped. An irrigation system for the hungry, homes for the homeless, and how he even helped a "boat" make it to port after a fire.

Gregory Atkins was not happy to just "sit around." The wound on his left buttocks was still quite sore, but he decided to travel to Japan. He figured that if he had to lay on his stomach, he'd benefit from some of the world's finest hands in the world of massage. Gregory would not be heard from for some time.

Jeremy arrived at the camp with the children. They were all met by hundreds of cheering refugees. One of the children was found to have had a relative at the camp. The others were summarily adopted until an actual parent was found, which was, unfortunately, unlikely. All of the children were welcomed as if they were missing family members nonetheless. The tumult at the camp created a greater interest in helping each other even more. Jeremy promised that they'd never allow guards like the last three, and they all promised to stand against the next Fiidka they'd encounter.

Together.

The containers of rice began to arrive shortly thereafter, and within such a short period of time, their world was changed. While only rice, there was a lot of it. It gave the camp a buffer against shortages and the promise that no one would go hungry, at least not for the foreseeable future.

And while the containers, many of which were damaged, wouldn't all be suitable for living, they were suitable for storage from the elements.

By the time the last container was delivered, it was dusk and the Somali sand was swirling. The earlier cheers of the camp had faded into the contentment often found at twilight. Because there were so many containers delivered, there was little room for the last one to be placed in the back of the camp with the others, so Jeremy instructed them to place it where they were. It was just before the open area where Fiidka and his men were killed not so many hours before.

The container was just dropped off the back of the flatbed truck and allowed to fall to the ground. The noise of the container dropping on the sand was unmistakable, as were the yells that came from within. Ali and Abshir were covered in gas on the boat. Their ships were gone, there was no escape. Whether by luck or fate, the two threw down their weapons and ran away from the gunfire, which led them back to the path Abernathy used in the center of the deck through the containers. The two turned into that path just as the fire had raced to the bow from both sides. Covered in gas, and now unarmed, the two saw the container that was dropped for Abernathy to climb over. They entered the container and closed the door as best they could behind them. They climbed over the rice, concealing themselves in the middle of the container fearing for their lives.

They heard the men working around them on the boat, too afraid to risk being killed by those outside. They heard the container sealed by the workers with them inside. They had no water. The day or so they were inside seemed like an eternity. The two swore that they'd never go back to Fiidka, and talked about how'd they find a way to sail away to anywhere. The heat and despair drove them to the delusion of escaping to a place with unlimited water and endless food with people who wanted nothing of the evil that Fiidka demanded.

Jeremy opened the container only to see Ali and Abshir, exhausted and confused. Two men so weak they could barely raise their hands in surrender.

“Where are we,” Abshir sheepishly asked.

Hanna smiled and took a step forward with her arms out, “you’re home.”

# ACKNOWLEDGEMENT

Edited by Katie Kardelis, a finer savior to my written word there is none.

To my grandfather who served in the Army during WWII (including post-war as a guard at the Nuremberg Trials), my uncle who served in the Marine Corps in Vietnam, my son who served in the Marine Corps during the War on Terror, and so many other family members who've served. That sacrifice is never forgotten to me.

To my mother who raised me well (as far as I'm concerned), my grandmother who was the artist, my daughter, aunt and cousin who served as teachers & counselers. I'm often reminded that service comes in many ways.

To all of those who know me, who've shared in my story, and who've shared so much of their lives and stories that will never make it to print and deserve to be remembered. I'll never forget.

And to Golden Publishing who are committed to the entire Thomas Martin series.

# ABOUT THE AUTHOR

**Edmund T. Calvin**

grew up in a small town in Pennsylvania, started pilot lessons at thirteen, attended Penn State, has traveled including being behind the wall in East Berlin. He has spent his entire career immersed in investigative work. Enjoying life in Texas, with active investigation and security consulting businesses in Texas & Connecticut that have lead to thousands of real stories written for the clients. Now the stories being brought to life in Kill the Grackles, the first in the Thomas Martin series.

A lifetime of real world problem solving experience and creative solutions help to make this work of fiction a very original read.

## Thomas Martin Will Return In

*There's No Stopping Ghosts*

Kill a rogue world leader, stop a corporate manipulator of a pandemic, and be blameless for the wrath that follows. They called Thomas Martin for the solution.

www.ingramcontent.com/pod-product-compliance
Lightning Source LLC
LaVergne TN
LVHW020525100826
845148LV00010B/1344

* 9 7 8 1 7 3 6 3 9 1 5 1 8 *